Int. Congress of Charities

General Exercises

The International Congress of Charities, Correction and Philanthropy, Chicago, June,

1893

Int. Congress of Charities

General Exercises

The International Congress of Charities, Correction and Philanthropy, Chicago, June, 1893

ISBN/EAN: 9783337158736

Printed in Europe, USA, Canada, Australia, Japan

Cover: Foto ©Andreas Hilbeck / pixelio.de

More available books at **www.hansebooks.com**

General Exercises

OF

THE INTERNATIONAL CONGRESS OF
CHARITIES, CORRECTION AND PHILANTHROPY,
CHICAGO, JUNE, 1893

TOGETHER WITH

*LIST OF OFFICERS AND MEMBERS, PROGRAMME
AND RULES*

BALTIMORE
THE JOHNS HOPKINS PRESS
LONDON
THE SCIENTIFIC PRESS, LIMITED
428 Strand, W. C.
1894

TABLE OF CONTENTS.

THE WORLD'S CONGRESS AUXILIARY OF THE WORLD'S COLUMBIAN EXPOSITION.

GENERAL OFFICERS:

President,

CHARLES C. BONNEY.

Vice-President,

THOMAS B. BRYAN.

WOMAN'S BRANCH:

President,

MRS. POTTER PALMER.

Vice-President,

MRS. CHARLES HENROTIN.

DEPARTMENT OF MORAL AND SOCIAL REFORM.

MRS. JAMES M. FLOWER, *Chairman of Joint Committee.*

THE INTERNATIONAL CONGRESS OF CHARITIES, CORRECTION AND PHILANTHROPY.

JUNE 12–18, 1893.

COMMITTEE OF ORGANIZATION.

FREDERICK HOWARD WINES, JOHN G. SHORTALL,

MRS. JAMES M. FLOWER.

Corresponding Secretary and Sec'y to the Committee of Organization,

NATHANIEL S. ROSENAU.

OFFICERS OF THE CONGRESS.

President,

GENERAL RUTHERFORD B. HAYES.*

First Vice-President,

FREDERICK HOWARD WINES, LL.D.

Second Vice-President,

ROBERT TREAT PAINE.

* General Hayes accepted the presidency of the Congress, but died before it met. The vacancy was not filled.

Honorary Vice-Presidents.

England, HENRY C. BURDETT.
France, MARQUIS DE CHASSELOUP LAUBAT.
Austria, DR. ISIDOR SINGER.
Russia, MICHAEL KAZÁRIN.
Italy, MME. F. ZAMPINI SALAZAR.
Switzerland, EDWARD BOOS-JEGLIER.
Belgium, PROSPER VAN GEERT.
Australia, MISS CATHERINE H. SPENCE.

General Secretary,
ALEXANDER JOHNSON.

Secretaries,
JOHN M. GLENN.   JOSEPH P. BYERS.

Executive Committee,
The President, First Vice-President, General Secretary, and the Chairmen of the Eight Sections.

SECTIONS.

I.—The Public Treatment of Pauperism.

Chairman, ANSLEY WILCOX,
Charity Organization Society, Buffalo, New York.

Secretary, JOHN H. FINLEY, Ph. D.,
President of Knox College, Galesburg, Illinois.

II.—The Care of Dependent, Neglected and Wayward Children.

Chairman, REV. ANNA GARLIN SPENCER,
Board of Control of State Home and School for Dependent Children, Providence, Rhode Island.

Secretary, CHARLES W. BIRTWELL,
General Secretary of the Children's Aid Society of Boston, Massachusetts.

III.—Hospital Care of the Sick, the Training of Nurses, Dispensary Work, and First Aid to the Injured.

Chairman, JOHN S. BILLINGS, M. D., LL. D., U. S. A.,
Washington, D. C.

Secretary, HENRY M. HURD, M. D.,
Superintendent of Johns Hopkins Hospital, Baltimore, Maryland.

Subsection on Nursing.

Chairman, MISS ISABEL A. HAMPTON,
Superintendent of Training School for Nurses, Johns Hopkins Hospital, Baltimore, Marylan

Secretary, MISS EMMA CAMERON,
Assistant Superintendent of Illinois Training School for Nurses, Chicago.

IV.—The Commitment, Detention, Care and Treatment of the Insane.

Chairman, G. ALDER BLUMER, M. D.,
Superintendent of State Hospital for Insane, Utica, New York

Secretary, A. B. RICHARDSON, M. D.,
Superintendent of Asylum for Insane, Columbus, Ohio.

V.—The Prevention and Repression of Crime, and the Punishment and Reformation of Criminals.

Chairman, CHARLTON T. LEWIS,
President of New York State Prison Association, New York City.

Secretary, REV. JOHN L. MILLIGAN,
Secretary of National Prison Association, Allegheny, Pennsylvania.

VI.—The Organization and Affiliation of Charities, and Preventive Work among the Poor.

Chairman, DANIEL C. GILMAN, LL. D.,
President of the Charity Organization Society of Baltimore, Maryland.

Secretary, RICHMOND MAYO-SMITH, Ph. D.,
Professor of Political Economy and Social Science, Columbia College, New York City.

VII.—Sociology as a Special Topic in Institutions of Learning.

Chairman, E. BENJAMIN ANDREWS, LL. D.,
President of Brown University, Providence, Rhode Island.

Secretary, AMOS G. WARNER, Ph. D.,
Professor of Social Science in Leland Stanford, Jr., University, Palo Alto, California.

VIII.—The Care and Training of Feeble-minded Children.

Chairman, GEORGE H. KNIGHT, M. D.,
Superintendent of School for Imbeciles, Lakeville, Connecticut.

Secretary, GUSTAVUS A. DOREN, M. D.,
Superintendent of Institution for Feeble-minded Youth, Columbus, Ohio.

PROGRAMME OF SESSIONS AND SUBJECTS.

MONDAY, JUNE 12.

10.00 A. M.—OPENING EXERCISES.
> ADDRESS IN MEMORIAM OF GENERAL RUTHERFORD
> B. HAYES. By Rev. Frederick H. Wines, LL. D.
> ORATION:
>> "*The Problem of Charity.*" By Rev. Francis G.
>> Peabody, D. D.

12.00 M.—LUNCHEON AND CONVERSAZIONE.

2.00 P. M.—SECTION MEETINGS.

8.00 P. M.—GENERAL SESSION.
> "*The Public Treatment of Pauperism.*"

TUESDAY, JUNE 13.

10.00 A. M.—BUSINESS SESSION.

10.30 A. M.—SECTION MEETINGS.

2.00 P. M.—SECTION MEETINGS.

8.00 P. M.—GENERAL SESSION.
> "*The Relation of Public and Private Charity.*"

WEDNESDAY, JUNE 14.

10.00 A. M.—GENERAL SESSION.
> "*Hospital Care of the Sick; the Training of
> Nurses; First Aid to the Injured.*"

2.00 P. M.—SECTION MEETINGS.

8.00 P. M.—GENERAL SESSION.
> "*The Care of Dependent, Neglected and Wayward
> Children.*"

THURSDAY, JUNE 15.

10.00 A. M.—BUSINESS SESSION.

10.30 A. M.—SECTION MEETINGS.

8.00 P. M.—GENERAL SESSION.
> "*The Care and Training of Feeble-minded Chil-
> dren.*"

Friday, June 16.

10.00 A. M.—General Session.
> "*Sociology as a Special Topic in Institutions of Learning.*"

10 30 A. M.—Section Meetings.

2.00 P. M.—Section Meetings.

8.00 P. M.—General Session.
> "*The Uses of Imprisonment*"; "*The Care and Treatment of the Insane.*"

Sunday, June 18.

11.00 A. M.—Religious Service.
> Sermon: "*The Relation of the Church to Charities and Reform.*" By Rev. Anna Garlin Spencer.

8 00 P. M.—General Session.
> "*The Relation of the Kindergarten to Pauperism and Crime.*" By Mrs. Sarah B. Cooper.
> "*American Education from a National Point of View.*" By Dr. Felix Adler.

Closing Exercises.

RULES.

I.—Time, Place of Meeting, Object and Membership.

1. The Congress will meet in the city of Chicago on Monday morning, June 12th, 1893, at 10 o'clock, in a hall of the Art Institute.

2. The object of the International Congress of Charities, Correction and Philanthropy is to bring together in the city of Chicago, during the time of the World's Columbian Exposition, interested persons of all countries, to discuss matters charitable, correctional and philanthropic.

3. The governments of foreign nations, of the United States of America, and of the individual states of the United States, scientific societies, official bodies, and corporations and societies which own or control charitable or penal institutions, or are engaged in any kind

of philanthropic work, are invited to co-operate with the committee of organization and to send representatives to the Congress. Membership in the Congress will be limited to persons bearing credentials from the authorities and organizations herein referred to, and to such private individuals as are interested in charitable and penal work as may be admitted to membership by vote of the executive committee, or who may be specially invited by the committee of organization, or the chairman and secretary of a section.

Delegates must present their credentials before registering as members of the Congress.

From the obvious necessities of the case, no persons other than those herein specified can be permitted to participate in the debates or to vote on questions before the Congress. But a general invitation is extended to all persons who may be interested in the questions discussed to attend the sessions and listen to the debates.

II.—THE WORK OF THE CONGRESS.

4. The work of the Congress will be confined to matters germane to the titles of the various sections into which the Congress is divided. Each section will have devoted to it one general session of the Congress, and will hold, besides, five sectional meetings.

5. An executive committee, composed of the president, first vice-president, general secretary, and the chairmen of the sections, will have charge of the general administration of the Congress from the time of its assembly, under the rules framed by the committee of organization.

6. Copies of all papers presented at sessions of the Congress shall be furnished for publication in its proceedings.

7. In preparing the proceedings for publication, the committee of organization reserves the right to abbreviate papers and the stenographer's report of remarks.

III.—RULES OF ORDER.

8. The Congress will be under the direction of the committee of organization, which will present further rules for the government of its proceedings before its opening.

9. The sessions of the Congress and its sections will be strictly in accordance with the accompanying general programme.

10. English will be the exclusive language of the Congress.

11. Papers may, however, be submitted to the committee of organization, in any language, and the committee will, in its discretion, publish complete translations or English abstracts in the proceedings.

12. No paper will be read at a general session of the Congress unless its author is present, except by decision of the executive committee. When an author is absent, his paper will be read by title and included in the published proceedings, in the discretion of the committee of organization, unless otherwise especially ordered.

13 Not to exceed thirty minutes will be allowed for the presentation of a paper, except by previous arrangement with the committee of organization. In cases where a paper will exceed these limits, and its value will be impaired by condensation, the paper will be received and printed, and the author given time, not exceeding the above limit, in which to present a résumé.

14. Debaters will be limited to five minutes, and no person will be allowed to speak to the same subject more than twice. This rule may be suspended by a special order.

15. It is the duty of the chairman of each section to organize the work of his section, and to prepare programmes for the general session of his section and the five special meetings of his section, which programmes shall be submitted to the committee of organization and the president of the Auxiliary, for approval.

16. It is the duty of the secretary of each section to carry on the correspondence of the section under the direction of its chairman, and especially to secure foreign representation in the work of the section. He shall keep a record of the proceedings of his section, during the time the Congress is in session, and shall transmit the same daily to the general secretary.

LIST OF MEMBERS.*

FOREIGN.

Aderkas, Ottocar d', The Russian Imperial Charitable Institutions of the
Empress Mary, St. Petersburg, Russia.

Austerbridge, Miss I. R., Prince Edward's Island.

Beaton, Miss Annie H., Paisley, Ontario.

Boos-Jeglier, Edward, Director, School of Art and Needlework, Zurich, Switzerland.

Burdett, Henry C., The Lodge, Porchester Square, London, England.

Chasseloup Laubat, Marquis de, 51 Avenue Kleber, Paris, France.

Dupuy, Rev. E. J., Maison Hospitalière, Paris, France.

Haine, Stanislas H., Mont de Piété, Antwerp, Belgium.

Hart, Ernest, Chairman, British National Health Society, 429 Strand, London,
England.

Hughes, Miss Amy, Queen Victoria's Jubilee Institute for Nurses, 23 Blooms-
bury Square, London, England.

Kazárin, Michael, The General Administration of Prisons of Russia, St. Petersburg, Russia.

Lampérière, Mme. Anna Yon, Intérieur Instruction Publique, Commerce et
Industrie, 9 Rue Anice, Leures, France.

Macdowell, Miss F. Louise, Kingston, Canada.

Marshall, Mme. Marie, Oeuvre des Libérées de St. Lazare and Le Foyer Chré-
tien, Paris, France.

Notter, Lieut. Colonel J. Lane, M. D., Surgeon-Major, British Army, Netley,
England.

Salazar, Mme. Fanny Zampini, Rome, Italy.

Singer, Prof. Isidor, Ph. D., University of Vienna, Austria.

Spence, Miss Catherine Helen, Government Commissioner, Charity Organization Society, Adelaide, South Australia.

Van Geert, Prosper, Bureau de Bienfaisance, Antwerp, Belgium.

Van Geert, Mme. Prosper, Antwerp, Belgium.

CALIFORNIA.

Cooper, Miss Harriet, Superintendent, Golden Gate Kindergartens, 1902
Vallejo St., San Francisco.

Cooper, Mrs. Sarah B., President, Golden Gate Kindergartens, 1902 Vallejo
St., San Francisco.

Edholm, Charlton, Florence Crittenton Home, San Francisco, Oakland.

---

*A complete list can not be furnished, owing to the failure of many in actual attendance to
register their names and addresses.

Wallace, Miss Elsie, Superintendent of Nurses, Children's Hospital, San Francisco.
Warner, Prof. Amos G., Ph. D., Leland Stanford, Jr., University, Palo Alto.

COLORADO.

Appel, Mrs. J. M., Ladies' Hebrew Benevolent Society, Denver.
Appel, J. S., State Board of Charities and Corrections, Denver.
Appel, Mrs. J. S., Denver Free Kindergarten Association, Denver.
Brodhead, Rev. Wm. H., Secretary, State Board of Charities and Corrections, Denver.
Gabriel, John H., Young People's Charity Club, Denver.
George, Mrs. Izetta, Charity Organization Society, Denver.
Houser, Mrs. Bella S., Charity Organization Society, Denver.
Mills, J. Warner, State Board of Charities and Corrections, Denver.
Reed, Rev. Myron W., State Board of Charities and Corrections, Denver.
Williams, B. F., Industrial School, Golden.

CONNECTICUT.

Crothers, T. D., M. D., Superintendent, Walnut Lodge Hospital, Hartford.
Knight, Geo. H., M. D., Superintendent, Connecticut School for Imbeciles, Lakeville.
Knight, Mrs. Geo. H., Lakeville.
Stearns, Dr. Henry P., Superintendent, Retreat for the Insane, Hartford.

DELAWARE.

Clark, Mrs. Mary A. T., Superintendent, Associated Charities, Wilmington.
Wright, Mrs. James H., Associated Charities, Wilmington.

DISTRICT OF COLUMBIA.

Billings, John S., M. D., LL. D., Surgeon, United States Army, Washington.
Falls, A. J., Reform School of District of Columbia, Washington.
Gatewood, J. D., M. D., Medical Department U. S. Navy, Navy Department, Washington.
Pope, Georgina F., Superintendent, Columbia Hospital, Washington.
Rogers, Miss M., Children's Hospital, Washington.
Shallenberger, G. A., Reform School of District of Columbia, Washington.

ILLINOIS.

Bagg, Mrs. S. F., Reception Committee, 3764 Lake Avenue, Chicago.
Bartlett, A. C., Home for the Friendless, Chicago.
Bath, Miss Alice K., 901 Jackson Boulevard, Chicago.
Baxter, Mrs. T. W., Newsboys' Home, 343 Dearborn Avenue, Chicago.
Beckwith, Mrs. N. K., Nursery and Half Orphan Asylum, 77 Pine Street, Chicago.
Beebe, Mrs. L. A., Reception Committee, 76 Park Avenue, Chicago.
Bemis, Prof. E. W., Ph. D., University of Chicago, Chicago.
Bonney, Charles C., President, World's Congress Auxiliary, Chicago.

Bowman, Miss Eliza W., Newsboys' Home, 1418 Wabash Avenue, Chicago.

Breeze, Miss Jessie, Illinois Training School for Nurses, 691 Monroe Street, Chicago.

Brown, Mrs. Wm. T., Home for the Friendless, 4637 Greenwood Avenue, Chicago.

Cameron, Miss Emma, Assistant Superintendent, Illinois Training School for Nurses, Chicago.

Cann, Miss Irene, Reception Committee, 3151 Prairie Avenue, Chicago.

Carpenter, Mrs. A. A., Reception Committee, 83 Cass Street, Chicago.

Chafee, Mrs. G. D., Illinois Industrial School for Girls, Shelbyville.

Chamberlin, Mrs. A. S., Reception Committee, 186 31st Street, Chicago.

Clowry, Mrs. R. C., Reception Committee, 524 Dearborn Avenue, Chicago.

Coffin, Chas. F., Chicago.

Corbus, Dr. J. C., Board of State Commissioners of Public Charities, Mendota.

Cushman, B. V., Bethesda Mission, 205 Warren Avenue, Chicago.

Curtiss, Geo. W., Board of State Commissioners of Public Charities, Stockton.

Darrow, Mrs. Geo. W., Chicago Orphan Asylum, Glen Ellyn.

Dewey, Richard, M. D., 1114 Venetian Building, Chicago.

Doering, Mrs. Edmund J., Chicago Orphan Asylum, 2406 Prairie Avenue, Chicago.

Doud, Mrs. L. B., Erring Woman's Refuge, 3257 Michigan Avenue, Chicago.

Draper, Miss Edith, Illinois Training School for Nurses, 304 Honoré Street, Chicago.

Dudley, Mrs. E. C., President, Visiting Nurses' Association, 1619 Indiana Ave., Chicago.

Dudley, Oscar L., Superintendent and General Manager, Illinois School of Agriculture and Manual Training for Boys, 113 Adams Street, Chicago.

Engleman, Miss Emma, Reception Committee, 649 Cleveland Ave., Chicago.

Enrich, Mrs. E. F., Charity Council, Aurora.

Fairbank, Mrs. N. K., St. Luke's Hospital, 1801 Michigan Avenue, Chicago.

Felton, Chas. E., 4206 Lake Avenue, Chicago.

Finley, John H., Ph. D., President, Knox College, Galesburg.

Fitz Simons, Mrs. Chas., Women and Children's Hospital, 161 Ashland Ave., Chicago.

Flower, Mrs. Jas. M., Department of Moral and Social Reform, World's Congress Auxiliary, 361 Superior Street, Chicago.

Follansbee, Mrs. G. A., Old People's Home, 2342 Indiana Avenue, Chicago.

Frake, Mrs. James, Newsboys' and Bootblacks' Home, 625 Fulton Street, Chicago.

Galt, Mrs. Thomas, Aurora.

Galvin, Edw. I., Hyde Park Protective Association, 5725 Madison Street, Chicago.

Gerry, Miss Jennie E., City Missions, Snell Hall, Chicago.

Glenn, Miss Lizzie C., Rockford Hospital, Rockford.

Goodwin, Daniel, Illinois Charitable Eye and Ear Infirmary, 600 North State Street, Chicago.

Gregg, Rev. Frank M., D. D., Children's Home Society, 230 La Salle Street, Chicago.

Groves, Mrs. Denison F., Woman's Board of Waifs' Missions, 3946 Ellis Ave., Chicago.

Hancock, Mrs. Bradford, Department of Moral and Social Reform, World's Congress Auxiliary, 180 N. State Street, Chicago.

Harrison, Mrs. Ursula L., Illinois School of Agriculture and Manual Training for Boys, Glenwood.

Harwood, Mrs. H. W., 5012 Ellis Avenue, Chicago.

Hemingway, A. T., Oak Park.

Henderson, Rev. Chas. R., D. D., Social Science Department, University of Chicago, 6108 Washington Avenue, Chicago.

Henrotin, Mrs. Charles, Vice-President, Woman's Branch, World's Congress Auxiliary, Chicago.

Hill, Mrs. Thomas A., Home for the Friendless, 2924 Michigan Ave., Chicago.

Hobbs, Mrs. J. B., Home for the Friendless, 343 La Salle Avenue, Chicago.

Horton, Miss Sarah M., Chicago Orphan Asylum, 18 Aldine Square, Chicago.

Hotchkin, Mrs. C. M., Chicago Orphan Asylum, 3006 Prairie Avenue, Chicago.

Howe, Mrs. F. J., Half Orphan Asylum, 444 Chestnut Street, Chicago.

Huddleston, Mrs. G. W., Reception Committee, 903 Adams Street, Chicago.

Hutchinson, Miss Florence C., Home for the Friendless, 3145 Indiana Avenue, Chicago.

Jay, Mrs. Milton, Illinois School of Agriculture and Manual Training for Boys, 2510 Indiana Avenue, Chicago.

Judd, Mrs. N. B., Home for the Friendless, 3522 Calumet Avenue, Chicago.

Keep, Mrs. Albert, Home for Incurables, 2010 Michigan Avenue, Chicago.

Kip, Francis E., United Hebrew Charities, 288 Forty-second Street, Chicago.

Kline, Mrs. Matilda E., National Temperance Hospital, 62 E. Forty-third St., Chicago.

Laflin, Mrs. Geo. H., Chicago Home for the Friendless, 1614 Michigan Ave., Chicago.

Lathrop, Miss Julia C., Board of State Commissioners of Public Charities, Rockford; resident of the Hull House, Chicago.

Lett, Miss K. L., St. Luke's Hospital, Chicago.

Lewis, Dr. H. F., Chicago.

McClaughry, Major Robert W., Superintendent, Illinois State Reformatory, Pontiac.

McCullock, Mrs. Catherine, Children's Aid Society, Chicago.

Mack, Julian M., United Hebrew Charities, 4242 Langley Avenue, Chicago.

Maddell, Mrs. Elsie, Temperance Hospital, 3232 Rhodes Avenue, Chicago.

Mangasarian, M., Society for Ethical Culture, Chicago.

Matz, Mrs. Otto H., Chicago Hospital for Women and Children, 431 Oak St., Chicago.

Meech, Miss Marietta, Illinois Training School for Nurses, 242 Winchester Avenue, Chicago.

Millar, Mrs. Allen P., Newsboys' Home, 289 Ontario Street, Chicago.

Moore, D. T., Chicago.
Nichols, Charles K., 608 W. Ohio Street, Chicago.
Nichols, Mrs. Wm. C., Home for the Friendless, 493 Fullerton Ave., Chicago.
Pajeau, Mrs. J., Home for the Friendless, 4345 Grand Boulevard, Chicago.
Palmer, Mrs. Potter, President, Woman's Branch, World's Congress Auxiliary, Chicago.
Ricker, Mrs. Jewett E., Hospital for Women and Children, 401 Superior St., Chicago.
Roler, Mrs. E. C. T., Erring Woman's Refuge, Lexington Hotel, Chicago.
Rosenfeld, Mrs. Maurice, Visiting Nurses, 1620 Michigan Avenue, Chicago.
Ryerson, Arthur, President, St. Luke's Hospital, Chicago.
Shortall, John G., Illinois Humane Society, 1600 Prairie Avenue, Chicago.
Smith, Mrs. Orson, 41 Bellevue Place, Chicago.
Stone, Miss Jessie G., Chicago Hospital for Women and Children, 620 West Monroe Street, Chicago.
Stone, Mrs. Leander, President, Young Women's Christian Association, 3352 Indiana Avenue, Chicago.
Strong, Rev. John M., Children's Aid Society, Waukegan.
Sumption, Miss Martha A., Chicago Hospital for Women and Children, 620 W. Monroe Street, Chicago.
Taylor, Rev. Graham, D. D., Chicago Theological Seminary, Chicago.
Taylor, Miss Winnie Louise, Children's Aid Society, Freeport.
Thatcher, Mrs. Watson, National Temperance Hospital, 787 Walnut Street, Chicago.
Tolman, Mrs. S. A., Old People's Home, 2031 Prairie Avenue, Chicago.
True, Miss M. E., 320 Marshfield Avenue, Chicago.
Trusdell, Rev. C. G., Superintendent, Chicago Relief and Aid Society, 51-53 La Salle Street, Chicago.
Tyrrell, Miss A. M., Illinois Training School for Nurses, 6345 Stewart Avenue, Chicago.
Ullman, Mrs. Frederic, 282 Forty-eighth Street, Chicago.
Vincent, Miss Sarah J., 242 Winchester Avenue, Chicago.
Visher, John, Secretary, Illinois Conference of Charities and Correction, 1037 Mead Street, Chicago.
Walker, Mrs. Edwin, St. Luke's Hospital, 2612 Michigan Avenue, Chicago.
Walker, Mrs. J. M., 1720 Prairie Avenue, Chicago.
Wheeler, Mrs. C. Gilbert, The Lexington, Chicago.
White, Mrs. Wm. R., Presbyterian Hospital, 263 Warren Avenue, Chicago.
Willard, Miss Laura, 5555 Woodlawn Avenue, Chicago.
Wilmarth, Mrs. H. M., Auditorium Hotel, Chicago.
Wines, Rev. Frederick Howard, LL. D., Springfield.

INDIANA.

Bicknell, Ernest P., Secretary elect, Board of State Charities, Indianapolis.
Guild, Mrs. Helen F., President, Fort Wayne Relief Union, Fort Wayne.
Hathaway, Miss Sarah, Children's Aid Society of Indiana, Mishawaka.

Johnson, Alexander, Secretary retiring, Board of State Charities, Indianapolis.
Johnson, Miss Katherine D., Clerk, Board of State Charities, Indianapolis.
Kittring, Mrs. E. G., Children's Aid Society of Indiana, South Bend.
Peele, Mrs. Margaret F., Board of State Charities, South Bend.
Reeve, Chas. H., Plymouth.
Smith, Mrs. C. L., Hope Hospital, Fort Wayne.
Smith, James, General Secretary, Charity Organization Society, Indianapolis.
Snyder, Katherine S., M. D., Southern Hospital for Insane, Evansville.
Wardner, Mrs. Louise Rockwood, Industrial School for Girls, Laporte.

IOWA.

Ayres, Miss J. G., Young Women's Christian Association, Stuart.
Carleton, Mrs. M. J., Charity Organization Society, Burlington.
Gatchel, Theodore, Iowa Humane Society, Des Moines.
Hoover, Rev. Geo. K., Iowa Children's Home Society, Davenport.
Howard, Mrs. Nettie F., Associated Charities, Davenport.
Millard, Mrs. F. A., Assistant Secretary, Charity Organization Society, Burlington.
Powell, F. M., M. D., Superintendent, State Institution for Feeble-minded Children, Glenwood.
Putnam, Mrs. M. L. D., Davenport.
Starr, Miss M. E., Secretary, Charity Organization Society, Burlington.

KANSAS.

Eastman, B. D., M. D., Superintendent, State Insane Asylum, Topeka.
Faulkner, Chas. E., Superintendent, Soldiers and Sailors' Orphans' Home, Atchison.
Hausholder, M. A., State Board of Trustees of Charitable Institutions, Columbus.
Kelly, H. B., State Board of Trustees of Charitable Institutions, Lawrence.
Lease, Mrs. Mary E., President, State Board of Trustees of Charitable Institutions, Wichita.
Martin, Miss Edith M., Ottawa.
Pilcher, F. Hoyt, M. D., School for Feeble-minded, Winfield.
Spencer, Martha S., State Industrial School for Girls, Beloit.
Wait, W. S., State Board of Trustees of Charitable Institutions, Lincoln.
Wentworth, L. F., M. D., Superintendent, State Insane Asylum, Osawatomie.
Yoe, W. T., State Board of Trustees of Charitable Institutions, Independence.

KENTUCKY.

Avery, Mrs. Susan Look, Women's Club, Louisville.
McKechvine, Miss Mary W., Louisville Training School for Nurses, Louisville.
Wilson, Laura A., Children's Free Hospital, 220 E. Chestnut St., Louisville.

LOUISIANA.

Heymann, Michel, Jewish Orphans' Home, New Orleans.

MAINE.

Burrington, Mrs. E. A. D., Belfast.
Stevens, Mrs. L. M. N., Girls' Industrial School, Portland.

MARYLAND.

Boland, Miss Mary A., Johns Hopkins Hospital, Baltimore.
Brackett, Jeffrey R., Ph. D., Charity Organization Society, 210 West Madison Street, Baltimore.
Dock, Miss L. L., Johns Hopkins Hospital, Baltimore.
Glenn, John M., Charity Organization Society, 12 St. Paul Street, Baltimore.
Hall, A. Cleveland, Charity Organization Society, Baltimore, and Bureau of Charities and Correction, World's Columbian Exposition.
Hampton, Miss Isabel A., Superintendent, Johns Hopkins Training School for Nurses, Baltimore.
Hurd, Henry M., M. D., Superintendent, Johns Hopkins Hospital, Baltimore.
Richmond, Miss Mary E., General Secretary, Charity Organization Society, Baltimore.
Stoner, George W., M. D., United States Marine Hospital Service, Baltimore.

MASSACHUSETTS.

Ames, Miss Lucia T., Associated Charities, 28 St. James Ave., Boston.
Balch, Miss Emily Greene, Denison House and Gwynne Temporary House for Children, Jamaica Plain.
Birtwell, Charles W., General Secretary, Children's Aid Society, Boston.
Birtwell, Miss Frances M., Boston Children's Aid Society, Cambridgeport.
Birtwell, Miss Mary L., Associated Charities, Boston.
Bright, Miss Emily H., Boston Associated Charities, Cambridge.
Carolin, Wm. T., M. D., Trustee, State Farm and State Almshouse, Lowell.
Chapin, Miss Mabel H., Brookline.
Crawford, Mrs. Sarah M., M. D., Department of Outdoor Poor of State Board of Lunacy and Charity, Boston.
Curran, Dr. Charles J., State Board of Lunacy and Charity, North Adams.
Dawes, Miss Anna L., Home-Work Association, Pittsfield.
Dow, Miss Helen, Children's Aid Society, Boston.
Durham, Miss Elizabeth P., Children's Aid Society, Boston.
Fernald, Walter E., M. D., Superintendent, State School for Feeble-minded, Waverley.
Fiske, Mrs. Frances, Sloyd Industrial Work, Boston.
Frenyear, Miss Myra G., Associated Charities, Boston.
Hitchcock, Edward, M. D., State Board of Lunacy and Charity, Amherst College.
Jackson, Miss Anna P., Children's Aid Society, Boston.
Johnson, Mrs. Ellen C., Superintendent, Reformatory for Women, South Framingham.
Johnson, Geo. W., Chairman, State Board of Lunacy and Charity, Brookfield.
Lee, Miss Alice, Boston.

Lee, Joseph, Secretary, Massachusetts Committee on Charities and Correction, World's Fair.
Page, Charles W., Danvers Lunatic Hospital, Danvers.
Paine, Robert Treat, President, Associated Charities, Boston.
Parker, Miss Sarah, Roxbury.
Peabody, Rev. Francis G., D.D., Professor of Christian Ethics, Harvard College, Cambridge.
Pickering, Henry G., Children's Aid Society, Boston.
Pratt, Laban, State Board of Lunacy and Charity, Boston.
Prescott, Miss Josephine F., Children's Aid Society, Boston.
Putnam, Miss Elizabeth C., Trustee, State Primary and Reform Schools, 63 Marlborough Street, Boston.
Raymond, Miss Sarah E., Boston Associated Charities, Charlestown.
Richardson, Mrs. Anne B., State Board of Lunacy and Charity, Lowell.
Rogers, Miss Annette P., Overseer of the Poor, Boston.
Rowe, G. H. M., M. D., Superintendent, City Hospital, Boston.
Shurtleff, Hiram S., Superintendent of Outdoor Poor, State Board of Lunacy and Charity, Boston.
Smith, Miss Frances A., Associated Charities, Boston.
Smith, Miss Zilpha D., General Secretary, Associated Charities, Boston.
Somerville, C. E. M., District Nursing Association, Lawrence.
Spinney, Frank C., Boston Associated Charities, Lynn.
Stone, Col. Henry, State Board of Lunacy and Charity, Boston.
Swanton, Mrs. S. B., District Nursing Association, Brookline.
Todd, Miss Hannah M., Probation Officer, Municipal Court, Boston.
Todd, Miss Myra M., Lynn.
Wheaton, Miss Florence, Boston Associated Charities, Roxbury.
Wheeler, Walter A., State Primary School, Palmer.
Wheeler, Mrs. Walter A., State Primary School, Palmer.
Whitman, Mrs. Bernard, Lend-a-Hand Club, Boston.
Woods, Robert A., Andover House, 6 Rollins Street, Boston.

MICHIGAN.

Barbour, Levi L., 661 Woodward Avenue, Detroit.
Bell, Samuel, M. D., State Board of Corrections and Charities, 87 State Street, Detroit.
Crozier, Alfred O., Charity Organization Society, Grand Rapids.
D'Arcambal, Mrs. Agnes L., Superintendent, Home of Industry for Discharged Prisoners, 250 Willis Avenue, Detroit.
Dewing, Mrs. J. A., Dewing's Children's Home, Kalamazoo.
Hinchman, Theo. H., Industrial Home for Girls, Detroit.
Hauber, Carl, Muskegon.
Mott, Mrs. H. C., W. C. T. U. Prison Work, Muskegon Heights.
Randall, C. D., State Public School, Coldwater.
Sickels, Mrs. Lucy M., Industrial Home for Girls, Adrian.
Storrs, Lucius C., Secretary, State Board of Corrections and Charities, Lansing.

MINNESOTA.

Amundson, C., State Board of Corrections and Charities, St. Peter.

Cowie, G. G., Clerk, State Board of Corrections and Charities, St. Paul.

Hart, Rev. Hastings H., Secretary, State Board of Corrections and Charities, St. Paul.

Hart, Mrs. H. H., St. Paul.

Holt, Geo. D., Secretary, Associated Charities, Minneapolis.

Jackson, Jas. F., General Secretary, Associated Charities, 139 E. University Ave., St. Paul.

Merrill, G. A., State Public School for Dependent Children, Owatonna.

Norrish, John F., State Prison, Hastings.

Rogers, A. C., M. D., Superintendent, Minnesota School for Feeble-minded, Faribault.

Wolfer, Henry, Warden, State Prison, Stillwater.

MISSOURI.

Finney, Rev. Thos. M., General Manager, Provident Association, 4028 Morgan Street, St. Louis.

Harrison, Edwin, 3747 Westminster Place, St. Louis.

Harrison, Mrs. Edwin, Episcopal Orphans' Home, 3747 Westminster Place, St. Louis.

Moore, Mrs. Catti, Kansas City.

Rice, Miss Josephine B., St. Louis Protestant Hospital, 1011 N. Eighteenth Street, St. Louis.

Sibley, Miss Elizabeth M., St. Louis Protestant Hospital, 1011 N. Eighteenth Street, St. Louis.

Springer, Mrs. C. R., Women's Charities Association, St. Louis.

NEBRASKA.

Bates, Mrs. Laura A., Soldiers and Sailors' Home, Aurora.

Clark, A. W., Assistant Secretary, Associated Charities, Omaha.

Clark, Mrs. G. W., "Open Door," Omaha.

Laughland, John, Associated Charities, 807 Howard Street, Omaha.

Mallalieu, John T., Superintendent, State Industrial School for Boys, Kearney.

Woods, Albert F., Charity Organization Society, Lincoln.

NEW JERSEY.

Dunlap, Mary J., M. D., State Institute for Feeble-minded Women, Vineland.

Gile, Mrs. F. A., State Institute for Feeble-minded Women, East Orange.

Maddock, Geo. C., Industrial School for Girls, Trenton.

Otterson, Ira, Superintendent, State Reform School, Jamesburg.

Van Meter, Miss Anna H., Charity Organization Society, Salem.

Warman, David, M. D., State Charities Aid Association, Trenton.

Williamson, Mrs. Benjamin, Secretary, State Charities Aid Association, Elizabeth.

NEW YORK.

Adler, Dr. Felix, New York.

Anthony, Miss Susan B., Western New York Industrial School, Rochester.

Betts, Miss Laura A., Homeopathic Hospital, 109 Cumberland St., Brooklyn.

Bliss, Rev. Howard S., Plymouth Church, 51 William Street, Brooklyn.

Blumer, G. Alder, M. D., Superintendent, State Hospital for Insane, Utica.

Bunn, Rev. Albert Carrier, M. D., The Church Charity Foundation of Long Island, 464 Herkimer Street, Brooklyn.

Caldwell, Miss Louise T., Charity Organization Society, New York.

Cary, Mrs. E. M. L., Charity Organization Society, Buffalo.

Cary, Thomas, Charity Organization Society, Buffalo.

Craig, Oscar, President, State Board of Charities, Rochester.

Darche, Miss Louise, Superintendent, New York City Training School for Nurses, Nurses' Home, Blackwell's Island, New York.

Davenport, Mrs. John, State Charities Aid Association, Bath.

DeForest, Robert W., President, Charity Organization Society, 62 William Street, New York.

Dennis, Caroline E., Auburn City Hospital, Auburn.

Folks, Homer, Secretary, State Charities Aid Association, 105 E. 22d St., New York.

Fullerton, Mrs. Marietta, Association for Improving Condition of the Poor, New York.

Gladding, Agnes S., City Hospital, Auburn.

Hepner, Elizabeth R., Charity Organization Society, Lockport.

Iles, George, Secretary, Society of Political Education, New York.

Kellogg, Chas. D., General Secretary, Charity Organization Society, 105 E. 22d Street, New York.

Kellogg, Mrs. Chas. D., New York.

Lathrop, Jas. R., Roosevelt Hospital, 59th St. and 9th Ave., New York.

Lewis, Charlton T., President, New York State Prison Association, 34 Nassau St., New York.

Love, Miss Maria M., Fitch Crêche, Buffalo.

Mayo-Smith, Prof. Richmond, Ph. D., Columbia College, New York.

Merchant, Mrs. G. A., Charity Organization Society, 413 Auburn Avenue, Buffalo.

Moore, Miss Alice, Charity Organization Society, Buffalo.

Moore, Miss Marion J., Assistant Secretary, Charity Organization Society, Buffalo.

Ormsby, Mrs. Mary Frost, St. Michael's Church, 115 W. 96th Street, New York.

Paton, John, President, Association for Improving Condition of the Poor, New York.

Pughe, Rees P., State Hospital for Insane, Utica.

Rosenau, Nathaniel S., Superintendent, Bureau of Charities and Correction, World's Columbian Exposition, Fitch Institute, Buffalo.

Round, W. M. F., Director, Burnham Industrial Farm, 135 E. 15th St., New York.

Savage, Charles C., Roosevelt Hospital, 133 E. 29th St., New York.

Schuyler, Miss Louisa Lee, State Charities Aid Association, 19 W. 31st St.,
New York.
Sutliffe, Miss Irene H., Directress of Nurses, New York Hospital, New York.
Smith, T. Guilford, Charity Organization Society, Buffalo.
Wald, Miss Lillian D., New York Hospital, Rochester.
Wells, Miss Mary E., Homeopathic Training School for Nurses, Brooklyn.
Wilcox, Ansley, Charity Organization Society, White Building, Buffalo.

Ohio.

Ayres, Philip W., General Secretary, Associated Charities, 45 E. Fifth Street,
Cincinnati.
Behrens, Henry, Director, House of Refuge, Cincinnati.
Brinkerhoff, Gen. Roeliff, President, Board of State Charities, Mansfield.
Byers, Joseph P., Secretary, Board of State Charities, Columbus.
. Crouse, Meigs V., Superintendent, Children's Home, Cincinnati.
Crouse, Mrs. M. V., Children's Home, Cincinnati.
Dalton, James, Director, House of Refuge, Cincinnati.
Eyman, H. C., M. D., Superintendent, Cleveland Asylum for Insane, Cleveland.
Follett, M. D., Board of State Charities, Marietta.
Fulton, Levi T., Superintendent, House of Refuge, Cincinnati.
Gano, Mrs. John A., Cincinnati.
Gladden, Rev. Washington, D. D., Columbus.
Greenwood, Miss M. Hamer, Jewish Hospital, Cincinnati.
Hathaway, S. J., Superintendent, Children's Home, Marietta.
Johnston, Miss Sara F., Lawrence County Children's Home, Ironton.
McDougall, A. W., Associated Charities, Cincinnati.
Morse, Miss E. M., Associated Charities, Cincinnati.
Neff, Wm. Howard, Board of State Charities, Cincinnati.
Niesz, Mrs. J. K., Children's Home, Toledo.
Parrott, Charles, Board of State Charities, Columbus.
Peek, Mrs. Sarah O., Superintendent, The Retreat, Cleveland.
Richardson, A. B., M. D., Superintendent, Columbus Asylum for Insane.
Columbus.
Tobey, H. A., M. D., Superintendent, Toledo Asylum for Insane, Toledo.
Waterton, Mrs. R. T., County Visitor, County Jail and Infirmary, South
Newbury.
Webb, John, Jr., Director, House of Refuge, Cincinnati.

Oregon.

Rowland, L. L., M. D., Superintendent, State Hospital for Insane, Salem.
Walpole, William R., Secretary, City Board of Charities, Portland.

Pennsylvania.

Crabtree, Miss Hezzie T., Philadelphia Hospital, Philadelphia.
Davis, Miss E. P., Superintendent of Nurses, University of Pennsylvania
Hospital, Philadelphia.

Donnell, Chas. G., Allegheny County Poorhouse, Pittsburgh.

Milligan, Rev. John L., Secretary, National Prison Association, Allegheny.

Walk, James W., M. D., Department of Charities and Correction; Secretary, Society for Organizing Charity, Philadelphia.

Wilmarth, A. W., M. D., Norristown.

Wright, Edward S., Warden, Western Penitentiary, Allegheny.

RHODE ISLAND.

Andrews, E. Benjamin, LL. D., President, Brown University, Providence.

Nutting, Rev. James H., Board of State Charities and Corrections, Howard.

Spencer, Rev. Anna Garlin, Board of Control of State Home and School for Dependent Children, Providence.

Wilson, Prof. George G., Ph. D., Brown University, Providence.

Woods, J. C. B., Board of State Charities and Corrections, Providence.

TENNESSEE.

Sims, P. D., M. D., State Board of Health, Chattanooga.

TEXAS.

Hayes, Mrs. R. H., Galveston.

UTAH.

Wells, Mrs. Emeline B., National Woman's Relief Society, Salt Lake City.

WASHINGTON.

Bale, Geo. A., Gig Harbor.

WISCONSIN.

Bannister, Miss Lucy A., Wisconsin School for Nurses, Milwaukee.

Chenneworth, Mrs. H. W., Woman's Club of Philanthropy, Madison.

Cleary, J. L., M. D., State Board of Control of Reformatory, Charitable and Penal Institutions, Kenosha.

Graebner, W. H., State Board of Control of Reformatory, Charitable and Penal Institutions, Milwaukee.

Jones, J. E., President, State Board of Control of Reformatory, Charitable and Penal Institutions, Portage.

Lynde, Mrs. Wm. P., Industrial School for Girls, Milwaukee.

Oliver, J. W., State Board of Control of Reformatory, Charitable and Penal Institutions, Waupun.

Parker, C. D., State Board of Control of Reformatory, Charitable and Penal Institutions, River Falls.

Roberts, W. P., American Invalid Aid Society, Evansville.

Snyder, Clarence, State Board of Control of Reformatory, Charitable and Penal Institutions, Ashland.

Wilkins, Frederick, Chairman, Knights of Labor.

Wright, A. O., Wisconsin Veterans' Home, Madison.

PREFACE.

The International Congress of Charities, Correction and Philanthropy, at Chicago, in 1893, was the indirect result of the congress held at Paris in 1889, concerning which a report was made by Miss Elizabeth C. Putnam at Baltimore, in 1890. The Paris congress expressed a desire that the Americans would organize a similar conference of charity workers in connection with the Columbian Exposition. Accordingly, at Baltimore, the Reverend Charles G. Trusdell, secretary of the Chicago Relief and Aid Society and president of the Illinois Board of State Commissioners of Public Charities, extended an invitation to the National Conference of Charities and Correction, on behalf of the state of Illinois and the city of Chicago, to hold its twentieth session in Chicago in 1893. This invitation was accepted. On motion of Dr. Wines, a special committee of fifteen was appointed to lay before the authorities in charge of the Exposition a project for the organization of such a congress, and for an international exhibit of charities and correction in connection with it.* This committee was not called together, but conducted its work by correspondence through its chairman, Mr. Trusdell, who secured from General George R. Davis, director-general of the Exposition, and from Mr. C. C. Bonney, president of the World's Congress Auxiliary, promises of cordial co-operation and aid in the effort to organize both the congress and the exhibit.

At Indianapolis, in 1891, letters of invitation addressed to Rev. Oscar C. McCulloch, president of the Conference, by Messrs. Davis and Bonney, were read and a new committee of nine was appointed,

* The following gentlemen were appointed members of the committee : Rev. C. G. Trusdell, Chicago; George S. Hale, Boston; Oscar Craig, Rochester, N. Y.; James W. Walk, M. D., Philadelphia; John Glenn, Baltimore; Gen. Roeliff Brinkerhoff, Mansfield, Ohio; John R. Elder, Indianapolis; Levi L. Barbour, Detroit; Andrew E. Elmore, Fort Howard, Wisconsin; D. C. Bell, Minneapolis; Rev. Myron W. Reed, Denver; H. O. Nelson, St. Louis; A. S. Colyer, Nashville, Tennessee; Benjamin F. McCulloch, Texas. (See Proceedings 17th National Conference, Baltimore, pp. 360, 432, 450.)

to continue for two years, empowered to arrange for both the congress and the exhibit, and to take any action necessary to that end.* This committee met in Chicago in 1892, and submitted a report to the National Conference at Denver.† The committee elected Mr. Nathaniel S. Rosenau secretary, and secured his appointment by Director-general Davis as superintendent of the bureau of charities and correction, under Dr. S. H. Peabody, chief of the department of liberal arts, to organize the exhibit, and as secretary of the executive committee named, under authority of the World's Congress Auxiliary, to organize the congress.‡

The exhibit was only a partial success. But for any disappointment which may have been felt by any person on this account, it is due to Mr. Rosenau to say that he was not to blame. Many exhibits were promised which were not furnished. The foreign charitable and correctional exhibits were nearly all shown in connection with the general displays made by the nations which sent them to Chicago. The time allowed for preparation was insufficient, and no one was sent to Europe, as had been planned, to make the proper representation as to the importance of this undertaking, which was not fully appreciated by Mr. Rosenau's superior officers. There was also great delay in providing a suitable place (in the Anthropological Building) for the collection. Nevertheless, the showing was, on the whole, and as a beginning—a precedent for future imitation on a larger scale—by no means discreditable, and it attracted a large share of popular attention. Mr. A. Cleveland Hall, of the Johns Hopkins University, ably assisted Mr. Rosenau in explaining it to visitors, many of whom took copious notes. The main exhibits, or many of

---

* This committee was composed as follows : Rev. Frederick H. Wines, LL. D., of Illinois ; Rev. Hastings H. Hart, of Minnesota ; Lucius C. Storrs, of Michigan ; Frank B. Sanborn, of Massachusetts ; Andrew E. Elmore, of Wisconsin ; Gen. Roeliff Brinkerhoff, of Ohio ; Oscar Craig, of New York ; John M. Glenn, of Maryland ; Rev. Oscar C. McCulloch, of Indiana. (See Proceedings 18th Conference, Indianapolis, pp. 349–352.)

† See Proceedings, pp. 367–374.

‡ This executive committee was made up of the chairman of the committee of nine above referred to, Dr. Wines ; the chairman of the men's committee of the World's Congress Auxiliary on Moral and Social Reform Congresses, Mr. John G. Shortall, of Chicago ; and the chairman of the women's committee of the same, Mrs. James M. Flower, also of Chicago. The executive committee had entire and exclusive charge of all arrangements for the congress, subject to the approval of Mr. Bonney.

them, were ultimately given to the Johns Hopkins University, at Baltimore, as the nucleus of a sociological laboratory of practical charities and correction.

The Denver Conference decided not to merge the National Conference into the International Congress, but to hold a separate (historical) session in Chicago during the week preceding that fixed for the congress, of which the Reverend Hastings H. Hart, of St. Paul, secretary of the Minnesota State Board of Corrections and Charities, was president.

The International Congress assembled in the Hall of Columbus, in the Art Institute, under the auspices of the World's Congress Auxiliary, on the morning of Monday, June 12, 1893, and adjourned on the evening of Sunday, June 18. The executive committee arranged the general programme,* and named the chairmen and secretaries of the sections.† The latter had sole control of the work of their respective sections, subject to the approval of the executive committee, including the selection of questions for consideration and of speakers and writers. The actual work of the congress was therefore wholly prepared by them, and they should have the credit which properly belongs to them.

The attendance from abroad was not large, but the papers furnished for publication were numerous and valuable. The number of Americans present was probably about eight hundred. Not all of them were registered. The Art Institute, during the continuance of the congress, presented the appearance of a university, with classes and lecturers scattered all through the building ; and the counter attractions at Jackson Park drew away but few from the serious business on hand. No time was spent in social diversion and festivity, though grateful mention should be made of the receptions by the local committee, composed of the members of the Committees on Moral and Social Reform and representatives of the charitable societies and institutions of Chicago. One of these was held at the Art Institute on Monday ; the other on Thursday afternoon at Mrs. Samuel M. Nickerson's, who kindly tendered her house to the committee for the entertainment of the members of the Congress.

The joy of the occasion was marred by the death of General Rutherford B. Hayes, ex-President of the United States, who had

---

* For a copy of the programme see pages 8 and 9 of the present volume The rules governing the congress are printed on pages 9–11.

† See list on pages 6 and 7.

consented to preside over this congress, but was prevented by death. In his absence, Dr. Wines, the vice-president, took his place.

The publication of the proceedings was entrusted to a committee of two, consisting of Dr. Wines and Mr. John M. Glenn. They have been printed in five volumes, of which this is the first, as follows:

I. *The Public Treatment of Pauperism.*

II. *The Organization of Charities.*

III. *Dependent, Neglected and Wayward Children. Sociology in Institutions of Learning.*

IV. *The Insane. The Feeble-minded. Crime and Criminals.*

V. *Hospitals, Dispensaries and Nursing.*

It is believed that, informal as the organization and proceedings of this congress were, no international congress ever held has covered a wider range of topics nor discussed the questions before it in a more practical and utilitarian spirit.

No attempt was made in the direction of a permanent organization of the movement; but Americans are ready to co-operate with their European collaborators for the establishment of an international society for the free and independent study of all the forms of charitable and correctional work, and of the results attained under each of them, whenever in their judgment the time shall come when such an organization is practicable and can be made effective.

The American plan is not to formulate conclusions, as is customary abroad; but to present the arguments advanced on both sides of every question and leave to individuals the task of passing upon their relative weight and importance. This prevents division and the formation of parties. It leads to a freer discussion. No proposition can fully or fairly state the substance of the debate or the sense of the body; and it is not believed that the dogmatic statement of points upon which there is a more or less general agreement has any special influence upon public opinion, particularly where the propositions put forth are in the nature of a compromise, as is apt to be the case. Such propositions tend to grow into a creed and to exert an influence prejudicial to freedom of thought and breadth of argument. For these reasons the reader who looks for a deliverance on the part of the congress will search for it in vain.

GENERAL EXERCISES.

OPENING SESSION.

Monday, June 12, 1893, 10 a. m.

The World's Auxiliary Congress of the Department of Moral and Social Reform convened at 10 o'clock.

The Rev. Dr. J. G. Johnson invoked the divine blessing.

President C. C. Bonney.—We have assembled to open the fifth series of the World's Congresses of 1893. The truest measure of the progress of the age is the development of what is known as Moral and Social Reform. Antagonizing the fierce strife of selfishness for wealth and power, it offers as a substitute, to enlighten mankind, a generous service of the wants and welfare of others. Moral and social reform follows with the white flag of purity and peace the terrible army of pauperism, insanity and crime, saving and protecting all who come within the reach of its heavenly hand. To charity, using this word in its most comprehensive sense, everything human is sacred, because everything truly human is an offspring of the Divine. Selfishness would let the destitute perish, while charity feeds and clothes and supplies, as far as human power may go, the needs involved in human suffering. Stern justice consigns the offender to prison and to punishment. Charity follows with saintly step the march of justice, seeking to reform, rather than exterminate the offender; seeking to restore him to ways of righteousness and justice and peace. Social order punishes to restrain, while heavenly charity seeks to prevent the first steps to crime and disorder, immorality and vice, and the evils that follow in their train.

Glancing over the splendid programme prepared for this series of congresses, luminous as it is with great subjects and distinguished names, we notice nearly all the American states, England, Scotland, Canada, France, Germany, Austria, Russia, Italy, Belgium, Denmark, Netherlands, Norway, New South Wales—and the list is not complete. Since it was printed other countries have been added to

the catalogue, whose representatives will be named in the announce-
ments as the congresses proceed.

Six congresses are to be held in this series : The Congress led by
the National Prison Association, that by the National Conference of
Charities, Correction and Philanthropy, the General Congress
embracing International Conferences of that name, a Congress of the
King's Daughters and Sons, a Congress of Visiting Nurses' Associations, and a Congress on Preventive Work. There was also
appointed to be held a Congress of the Social Wing of the Salvation
Army, but circumstances have intervened to cause the postponement
of this meeting to a later date.

The first two congresses named have already been held during
the past week, the extent of the several programmes being such that
they could not well be executed in a single week. The General
Congress on Moral and Social Reform is appointed to hold fourteen
sessions. It is also divided into eight separate sections : One on the
Public Treatment of Pauperism, to hold five sessions ; one on the
Care of Neglected and Dependent Children, to hold five sessions ;
one on Hospital Treatment, Dispensaries, Nurses, and First Aid to
the Injured, to hold five sessions ; a section on the Treatment of
the Insane, to hold five sessions ; a section on the Prevention of
Crime, Punishment, and Reformation, with five sessions ; a section
on Charity Organization and Co-operation, with the furnishing of
employment to the poor, to hold four sessions ; a section on Sociology in Education, one of the most important of all, with a similar
number of sessions ; and a section on the Care and Training of the
Feeble-minded, with five sessions. These fourteen general sessions
and these nearly forty sectional sessions outline a scope and thor-
oughness of treatment of all the questions involved which I think it
entirely safe to say has never before been attempted on any occasion
of the kind. The sessions already held indicate the comprehensiveness of treatment which may be expected in those which are to follow,
and in which will be presented the views and methods of proceedings
current, not only in our own country, but in many other lands. Seeing this magnificent array of intellectual and moral treasures, one
might well imagine that unlimited resources had been placed at the
disposal of the committee of organization which has had these congresses in charge ; but it will be one of the wonders of this series of
world's congresses that nearly all this work has been done through
the voluntary efforts of self-denying men and women. Not one dollar

has been provided by the Exposition authorities for the compensation or expenses of attending delegates, and yet there is scarcely any part of the world which has not sent or is not now sending its representatives here to Chicago to participate in the discussion of the most vital problems which affect the human race.

Under these circumstances my first duty is to make a grateful and sincere acknowledgment of the superb ability and devotion to duty which has characterized the committee of organization, whose work centered in the executive committee, of which Mrs. James M. Flower is chairman and Mr. N. S. Rosenau secretary, aided by veterans in the war for moral progress and reform like Dr. F. H. Wines and his eminent corps of coadjutors. It only remains for me now to extend a most hearty and earnest welcome to the World's Congress of Moral and Social Reform of 1893. I give you this welcome, not only in behalf of the World's Congress Auxiliary, but in behalf of the city in which you meet, the state under whose authority you convene, and the government of the United States, which has supported and upheld the World's Congresses of 1893 from their inception. My personal regret is that so many other and pressing duties will prevent my enjoying from session to session the rich feast of intellectual and moral excellencies provided for this occasion.

One thing more remains to be done before the work of the congress proper shall commence. The World's Congress Auxiliary would be but half an organization but for the Woman's Branch, which has had in charge the interests of woman in all the departments of human progress, and has brought them forward for presentation in each of the congresses. That Woman's Branch of the World's Congress Auxiliary has for its chief officer a distinguished leader whose name is known in all countries as one of the foremost champions of woman and her interests, and thus of the welfare of human society, Mrs. POTTER PALMER, who will now address you.

Mrs. POTTER PALMER.—With such a rare and varied programme awaiting, I feel I should not detain you one instant in uttering my word of welcome to the distinguished guests here assembled. My only excuse for doing so is that women have so distinguished themselves in the field of work which you are now to consider and discuss, that some attention should be called to that fact. While governments and the masculine sex have been interested in maintaining and sending their armies out for the defense of the country they loved, they have also uttered the paradox of sending out with the other hand organized armies of women and nurses to heal the wounds which they found it necessary to make. This organization has become so important and so conspicuous all over the world that it forms the greatest and one of the most important factors of modern life. While the government punishes in its prisons and takes care of the injured in its hospitals, it is the women who tend to them and attempt to spread abroad the spirit of benevolence and kindness, the principles of good housekeeping and good order, and the special gift of the temperament of women makes them specially available in work of this field. From the time of Florence Nightingale, who commenced the first earnest work on the field of battle, to the time of our own civil war, when one of the distinguished members of this congress did so much to organize the relief work in this country, and whose name, for that reason, has now become world-wide and known everywhere, the annals of strife are illuminated by the humane record of women. The Sherborne prison at Massachusetts stands foremost among the benevolent institutions of the age ; that is managed and conducted entirely by women.

I am more pleased to welcome you, because we are now entering upon a new era of charitable work. We are now considering the administration of charities in a scientific way. We are not attempting so much to alleviate existing conditions as we are to prevent their existence, and, because of the many distinguished persons who are to address you on these subjects, this congress is one of the most important that will assemble in this city during the coming season. All thinking persons will watch the deliberations with the greatest interest and with a full realization of the significance to the whole world of the words which are uttered here. Our welcome seems faint in comparison to the welcome with which your words will be received everywhere. I have the honor to wish the most successful meeting to this congress.

President BONNEY.—Gen. Rutherford B. Hayes, ex-president of the United States, had accepted the presidency of this Congress of Moral and Social Reform. Before this assembly, as you are all aware, he was called by the Divine Master to that higher realm whence all spirit of charity proceeds. His place in this organization has not been filled. It was deemed a higher and better tribute to his memory that the place assigned to him should remain vacant, and that the duties of the presiding officer should devolve upon the first vice-president, and I have the honor to present to you as your presiding officer Dr. FREDERICK HOWARD WINES.

Dr. WINES.—I congratulate you on the favorable auspices under which this congress has assembled and for the success with which the preliminary arrangements for it have been conducted. We are greatly indebted to Mr. Bonney and to the World's Congress Auxiliary; and we are especially indebted to the Woman's Branch of that organization and to our friends, Mrs. Palmer and her coadjutors. It is true that for success in charitable work we are more indebted to women than to men. I am very sorry that President Hayes could not be here to-day. As he is not here, it has been thought proper that some words should be said by me in the introduction with regard to President Hayes' life and character, which will take the place of the address which he would have made had he been present.*

The following foreign delegates were introduced to the audience by Dr. WINES:

M. OTTOCAR ADERKAS, of Russia.

Mme. MARIE MARSHALL, of France.

Mme. F. ZAMPINI SALAZAR, of Rome, Italy.

M. PROSPER VAN GEERT, of Antwerp, Belgium.

M. EDWARD BOOS-JEGLIER, of Switzerland.

Lieut.-Col. J. LANE NOTTER, M. D., of the British Army.

Miss CATHERINE H. SPENCE, of Australia.

M. MICHAEL KAZÁRIN, of Russia.

M. OTTOCAR ADERKAS.—I have the honor to express to you, in the name of Russia, my native country, and especially in the name of the Russian Imperial Charitable Institution of the Empress Mary, my sincere thanks for the hearty welcome accorded us in this very learned and cosmopolitan assembly. In Russia we are largely interested in all philanthropic and charitable questions, and for that reason we attend this international congress with a feeling of the most profound sympathy. It is on account of the historical and social conditions in Russia and the development of philanthropic questions in Europe that we come here to greet you. For the last twenty-five years we have witnessed a rapid and successful move-

* This address is published in full in the proceedings of the National Prison Association for 1893, and is therefore omitted here. It can be obtained from the Secretary of that Association, Rev. John L. Milligan, Allegheny, Pa.

ment in this direction, and constant efforts are made by the government and by all classes of the Russian people in this direction. Therefore all the questions to be examined here are important and interesting to us, since they bear upon vital conditions of our social life. For instance, the suppression of pauperism, the care of the foundlings of neglected and feeble-minded children, the treatment of the insane, the organizations of charities in large cities and villages, etc. I feel sure that great benefit to the unfortunate of all countries will be derived from your valuable reports and discussions.

It is a well known fact that, for charities and philanthropy, there is no boundary separating countries and peoples. A striking proof thereof was given by the American people last year, when, after the poor harvests in Russia, American ships laden with corn reached the far-away northern shores of the Baltic Sea. As a token of gratitude for such philanthropic assistance, the Russian Imperial Charitable Institution of the Empress Mary sent a complete exhibit to the World's Columbian Exposition, an exhibit of the works of the pupils of various schools, orphans' homes, children's asylums, and homes for the blind and deaf and dumb, including maps, photographs and statistics, and have decided that all these exhibits, after the close of the Exposition, are to be given to the American charitable institutions. Now let me repeat the thanks of Russia and to wish this international congress the fullest success.

Madame MARSHALL.—I shall detain you but a minute, ladies and gentlemen. My voice has gone this morning. I am very happy to bring here my word of thanks in the name of my country, and in the name of the friend whom you have heard before, Madame Bogelot. I hope to have an opportunity to speak about her work and about the work done in France for preventing the young from falling and for rehabilitating those who have fallen.

Madame F. ZAMPINI SALAZAR.—I am thankful to be invited to speak, but I have a paper upon the children in Italy which I shall have the honor to read Wednesday evening. I thank you very much for your kind reception.

M. VAN GEERT.—Being a foreigner, I must first of all apologize for my bad English. The hearty welcome which was wished to us by the President and the Mrs. President is very flattering for me. Coming from Antwerp to your city to attend your International Congress of Charities and Corrections, I did not expect to meet here such distinguished people from all countries of the world. There are so many new ideas to be presented in this congress that I hope and trust there will come some new light for the benefit of humanity.

Lieut.-Col. NOTTER.—I thank you most sincerely, on behalf of the British Army, which I represent, for the honor you confer upon it in the hearty welcome you have accorded me as its representative. Viewing, as I do, this question from a military aspect, I hope it will be followed by discussion to carry out those systems which are in vogue in civil life to lessen to some extent the calamities which are incidental to all, and that the outcome of this congress will be such as to insure a uniform system, alleviating some of the hardships incidental to a soldier's life.

Miss SPENCE.—In speaking to you I do not speak as a foreigner. We are daughters of the same mother nation. The great British Empire is ours, the English language is ours, the English poets have sung to us, the English history is our history, and our lives are lived upon English lines. Nothing thrilled me so much as when in San Francisco I heard the band strike up the hymn of "America," and lo! the air was " God save the Queen."

As an Australian, I shall speak to you at more length upon our methods in Australia at another time.

M. BOOS-JEGLIER and M. KAZÁRIN also made brief responses.

Dr. WINES introduced Dr. FRANCIS G. PEABODY, of Harvard University, who delivered the oration on *The Problem of Charity*, printed elsewhere, in the volume on *Organization of Charities*.

At the close of the morning session the delegates were given a reception in another room in the Art Institute, where a handsome collation was served.

CLOSING SESSIONS.

SUNDAY MORNING, JUNE 18.

Religious services were held in the Hall of Columbus, at 11 A. M., in accordance with the following programme :
ORGAN PRELUDE, Miss HARRIS.
INTRODUCTORY READING.
SONG—"*The Holy City*," *Addam*, Mr. DALE.
SCRIPTURE READING.
PRAYER.

HYMN—*"Life's Service,"* George Herbert.
SERMON—*" The Relation of the Church to Charities and Reform,"*
Rev. ANNA GARLIN SPENCER, Minister of Bell-street Chapel, Prov-
idence, R. I.
HYMN—*" The Law of Love,"* R. C. French.
BENEDICTION.

THE RELATION OF THE CHURCH TO CHARITIES AND REFORM.

REV. ANNA GARLIN SPENCER.

The church, like the state, was born at the fireside, in the home.
The ancient father was both priest and king. The race religions which
developed from this ancient worship of ancestors have each given
some unique and characteristic element in the history of religion;
the universal religion of which these are but a part. Each has given
some note in the symphony of religion without which our present
harmony of worship, of aspiration and of service, would not be so
perfect. Mediæval Christianity, which is our more immediate ancestor
in religion, claimed to be universal, and sought to control and lead all
the higher social, moral and spiritual activities of man. The Protestant
Reformation, so-called, which set our civilization its lesson, broke this
united centralized power of human leadership into many parts. The
state, which had been but a temporal arm of the church, became an
independent power. Education, which had been most jealously
regarded and held as a principal function of the church, became
growingly independent of it, and set up housekeeping in the school
of life on its own account. And charity itself, even now so closely
allied to all church activity, became more and more an object of
secular interest and study, and a function of secular control and leadership. So that to-day, in place of one all-pervading interest in life,
like Latin Christianity, we have, in all our Protestant countries (which
seem to be the leading countries in modern civilization), this variety
of interests, all at work upon the same problem—how to mend the
world and how to grow better men and women.

In this process of differentiation of spiritual forces, many have
seemed to lose sight of the value and worth of the church itself.
Because education and charity, and even government itself, were once
within the power of the church and subject to its leadership, when
those influences are no longer churchly, but have gone out into the

open air, away from the temple and the altar (to the sight of men at least), many fail to see for what the church can now stand and what is its special value. We must, therefore, ask ourselves first of all what the unique and special function of the church is. Is there anything in it which always was its special business, and now remains perhaps its only business, since this change has been brought about. In brief—I must speak, of course, from my own point of view—the church stands with us for religion. And what is religion? Religion is, first, the thought of man about the universe in which he finds himself, his struggle to explain not only the powers which surround him, but himself and his relation to those powers; and, second, religion is the yearning and effort of the human soul to place itself in right relations with this universe in which man finds himself a part so small and yet so great. If that be true, if religion under all its aspects has been the seeking of man's mind to spell out God, the source of all power, as a centralizing influence in this universe; if religion, under all names and in all climes, under all differentiation, has been the effort of man after self-culture toward holy living, the effort of man to place himself at one with the forces drawing the ages on; if this be religion, then is there any other influence in society save the church that stands for it and it alone?

Every charitable agency, every reformatory institution or movement is doing its special work in helping men and women to grow better, and its strength, the strength of individual effort, is its weakness also. Nearly every man and woman to-day is called upon, six-sevenths of his time, to serve as a link only in a great chain of social effort. He is made to feel almost oppressed with the weight of other lives. He sometimes loses himself in his relations; and the danger is quite as great for the special worker in philanthropy or reform as for the man whose business is the promotion of material interests. He who is set a special task, and acquires expert knowledge in order to fulfill that task, is quite as apt to forget that he is simply a part of the great enginery of reform. He is very apt to feel that his cause is the cause of humanity; and so, for the workers in charity and reforms, quite as truly as for the worker in business and for the artisan and for the man or woman set any task in life, it is important that one day in the week he be appealed to as a whole person, as having infinite relation with the eternal, which is here and now.

" We want," says Emerson, " not thinkers, but men thinking." So, in charity and reform, we want not moralists: men at work at this or that specialty in such ways as to lose their personality in their work; but we want men, working morally: those who stand in the beauty of holiness. Let us never lose from our consciousness the derivation of the word holiness—those who stand in the beauty of wholeness, and take hold of their individual tasks, not as specialists, but as whole men and women doing special things. The church stands to me for that altar where man or woman shall find, and where alone they can find, that heavenly manna which feeds the soul day by day, that heavenly manna which comes only day by day, the church of the living God, the living church of the living God, the church of the present revelation of God in human life. It stands with its doors wide open and its windows flooded with the daylight. It stands with its altar facing always north and south and east and west, with its past and its future linked in the present, which includes them both for the soul that struggles and aspires. I see no other institution in society which can thus appeal to the whole man and the whole woman. It is the ideal fulfilment of the command, " Be ye perfect even as your Father in heaven is perfect." Not merely do the thing that thou hast been set to do, and do it well ; but live the life that has been given thee, and live it well. So the church, now that its function has been differentiated and made more exclusive, is more than ever the gift of God in human growth ; it is more than ever the one sacred meeting-place of all souls.

If so, what is its relation to special charities and reforms ? As these children of the old mother of mediæval Christianity—education, philanthropy, reform, government, domestic life—have gone out from the ancient shelter and set up housekeeping on their own account, have they become independent ? so independent, that the church, as mother, has no longer any special relation to them ? If that were true, then the function of the church would be so specialized that it would lose its power. A man or a woman that loses his rooting in the common life is thenceforth impotent. But the church is not set, as a permanent task, the various special works of philanthropy and reform.

Let me explain. Not long ago, an eloquent voice called upon every church in every locality to establish a kindergarten in its vestry. It was a good call to a noble service, but in my opinion not the wisest call. Better than a kindergarten in every church vestry is a city kindergarten, under the public school system, divorced from all sectarian interests, standing upon its own educational feet. Just so,

I heard another eloquent voice call for district nurses to visit the poor to be attached to every church organization. Far better than that is the public dispensary, under charge of the physician, and district nurses going forth with no taint of proselytism, even in the suspicion of those to whom they minister, upon their white garments; going forth as representative of that outside church of humanity that does not even try to spell its creed. And so of all the agencies which make up the great procession of philanthropic effort.

What is the especial effort of the charity organization movement in our time? Is it not to lift the partial and petty charities of individual churches and of little societies, where each person has his pet theory, into the atmosphere of scientific investigation and of universal human brotherhood? That is the distinctive feature in all modern work in charity and reform. As we find our need in the matter and learn our way, we take ourselves out of the narrow path, however dear that path may be, and strike out into the open highway, to the betterment of our own work and to the enlargement of the whole scheme under which we labor.

When our speakers, during this past week, wished to place the highest crown upon their own effort in any line, they all uttered the same sentiment: " We do our work without regard to sectarian interests, without regard to churchly affiliations; we do it on the broadest human ground." The church that would seek to stem that tide, even by its own activity in a special line—the church that should cling, for instance, to its own little kindergarten, instead of putting in its work with the city kindergarten, or to its own little district nursing and its own friendly visiting, instead of going with the crowd, in a large way and on the best lines, is defeating the end for which it stands, the end of uniting the life of man to the life which is its source.

If there can be no such relation between the church and these special philanthropies and reforms, can there be no other? The church is not to be a moral workshop, but it should be a moral exposition. It is not to show the drudgery and the toil of the special worker, still less of special reformers; but the pulpit should exhibit, one after another, the great works of ethical progress and of social reform. For this purpose I believe that lay-workers should receive a fine sympathetic setting of their work in the pulpit. The minister is the only professional person who is bound to be general rather than special in his study. He is the only one who, by virtue of his professional demands, must keep himself open on all sides to truth from all directions. He is the only person who should be what Hartley Coleridge declared Harriet Martineau was, "a monomaniac about everything." But what is the penalty that one pays for knowing a little of a great many things? It is that he shall not know enough about any one. And I believe the pulpit needs strengthening to-day by visits now and then, visits of inspiration, of direction, of instruction, from these laymen and laywomen who minister without the robe and without the laying-on of hands in the great outside church, in humanitarian service. When the minister is recognized to be, what I believe he is, chiefly a teacher, then he will welcome to his teacher's desk every man who can teach some one thing a great deal better than he can teach it; and then we shall see indeed in the church a moral exposition. Then it will be impossible, as I fear now it is alas! possible, for a man or woman to attend church regularly for twenty years, and know almost nothing of what is being done for humanity, almost nothing of the special movements that are lifting people up in social condition. The function of religion is to appeal to the individual where he stands. "Be ye perfect," but what does that mean to the man or the woman, and above all to the little child, who is cradled in degradation, who breathes in pollution with every breath? For such (and they are legion), the outward conditions of life must be made better, in order that the word of religion may be able to reach them.

I do not forget the magnificent efforts of the Salvation Army and others who carry the gospel of Christ, with the old daring of the Master, into the darkest places of earth. I give them my reverence and my honor. But what, my friends, was the most remarkable thing in General Booth's great book, *In Darkest England and the Way Out*? Was it the enthusiasm for humanity? That has been shown by many another. Was it his faith in the power of the human soul to respond to the noble appeal of religion? That is felt by every true minister of religion. The most remarkable thing in that book is that his scheme is a scheme such as the charity organization and every other charitable society is pressing, a scheme to purify conditions, to uplift men by the thousands, by setting them in better surroundings. And that is the testimony, unconscious largely, of a man whose methods in religion are of the older kind. It is the special teaching of the spirit of our age. I cannot give it better than in Herbert Spencer's words: "No man can be fully moral until all are moral; no man can be perfectly happy until all are happy; no man can be perfectly wise until all are wise."

And what does that mean? Precisely the same thing that was meant by Him of old who said, " Ye are members one of another"; only we call it now the solidarity of the human race, and we have learned to translate it in terms of science. It means that every man and woman should every day give thanks, on bended knee, that the justice of God will not let one human being get so far ahead of the rest that he has not to wait for them to catch up. It means that we are all God's children. We tried to believe it in the old days, but we are learning that it is true. The new doctrine of equality of human political rights has forced it upon us. The new method of education by development is teaching it to us in gentler ways. In the administration of charity we see that poverty is an open mouth which never can be filled until we remove the cause. We are learning that nothing is really permanent that does not uplift life. And thanks to God for the lesson, though it comes sometimes in hard ways, and we find ourselves pulled back—and it is God's justice that does it—pulled back and held down by the great mass of creatures not yet emerged from the soil, who, as Emerson says, "are still pawing to get free." We must bring all of music, all of art, all of beauty that we may, to coax the creature out from his bestial surroundings. We must bring as many purified homes, all open air-spaces, all educational appliances, all the tenderness and care, all the wisest direction of which we are capable, to help this creature in his upward striving. For the creature is ourselves. We are one, in a deeper sense than we are separate—we children of a common father. What is it in us that links us to God? Is it the separate self? No, it is a universal self. It is because we, in our souls, are a spark of the divine; and the divine is one. As one of old said : " He who doth not love his brother, whom he hath seen, can not love God, whom he hath not seen."

The relation of the church to charities and reforms is the relation of one uniting aspiration, one altar of worship to all special workers. The church is, as I have said, a moral exposition, where history is shown to be not a collection of dry facts but a series of footprints of divinity, still warm from the holy pressure. It is a place where science is seen to be not merely a studious attempt to master the secrets of the material universe, but a record of the "loitering of the Holy Spirit on its way to the soul of man"; where education is seen to be not self-cultivation chiefly, but the cultivation and development of all; a place where its old appeal to the individual soul to be better here and now just where it stands, has added an atmosphere sympathetic and warm to every movement that seeks to better the conditions in which any and every individual life is placed.

I have a vision of the church that shall be. It will be a place of peace. In it man and woman shall love one another. They shall not quarrel over texts or sects. It will be a place of harmony. It will have its altar reared to the one God of all human souls. It will have a ritual made splendid with the prayers of all the saints of all the ages. It will have a glory and truth which is the shining of the Sun of Righteousness. It shall have a brave word from its pulpit that "nothing human alien deems, nor disesteems man's meanest claim upon it." Into it men shall go, not for rest alone, but for an uplifting of spirit that shall forever put to shame all lowness of aim and all selfishness of purpose. And when the church thus verifies its credentials and magnifies its office, nay, whenever an individual church seeks, however feebly, so to live out its life, there shall be no complaint that men and women do not go to hear its word.

We have lost somewhat, some people tell us, the old faith. It is not true. There never was an age when men so hungered for the revelation of the infinite. There never was an age when men's hearts were so on fire with holy purpose as now. The trouble is, that the church has entangled itself in small ways and in cheap business, when it might be working for the multitudes on the world's great highway.

The true church is in the heart of man. It is not in brick or mortar or marble; it is not in picture or legend or book. The tabernacle of God is with men—with living souls, and the revelation of God is to men—to living souls. "The pure in heart shall see Him as He is, and to him who doth the deed the truth shall be made known."

SUNDAY EVENING.

The following is the programme of the Sunday evening session:

ORGAN PRELUDE, Mrs. PARSONS.

ADDRESS by Mrs. SARAH B. COOPER, President, Golden Gate Kindergarten Association, San Francisco.

Subject: "*The Relation of the Kindergarten to Pauperism and Crime.*"*

VOCAL SOLO—"*Come Unto Me,*" *Cowen*, Miss MARION TREAT.

---

* Published in proceedings of section on Neglected, Abandoned and Wayward Children.

ADDRESS by DR. FELIX ADLER, of New York.*
Subject: *"American Education from a National Point of View."*
Closing exercises of the Congress.
Organ, Mrs. PARSONS.

In closing the Congress, Dr. WINES said: In a few moments this Congress will dissolve without day; but before it separates, I crave permission to say one word in conclusion.

It is customary to pass votes of thanks to those to whom we feel ourselves under obligation. But the cause of humanity and philanthropy is under obligation to nobody. It is rather a privilege to serve it, and for the opportunity to serve it every man and every woman should feel grateful. However, there are certain persons not immediately identified with us in our work whom I wish to mention here. We are grateful to the ladies and gentlemen who have furnished the sweet and inspiring music which we have so thoroughly enjoyed. We have been particularly gratified by the delightful and agreeable services rendered by the young lady ushers who have attended the sessions of the sections of this congress. We shall remember them always with pleasure.

This has been, in spite of great difficulties, a successful congress; successful in the attendance, and especially successful in the character of the papers and discussions. Great permanent results will surely grow out of it. We think that we have placed the work of the trained nurses of this country upon a better and more enduring basis than ever before, and that we have brought philanthropy and learning into closer and more vital contact by forming a connection, which we trust will never be severed, between the institutions of learning in this country and the practical workers in this field of humanitarian effort.

I should feel myself wanting in my duty if I did not say that for whatever success the Congress has had, we are greatly indebted to our friend and co-laborer, Mr. Nathaniel S. Rosenau, who, I think, has done more than any other one person to make it what it has proved to be: an international forum for the philanthropists of the world, and a school of theory and practice for American laborers in the field of correction, prevention and benevolence.

I now declare the Congress adjourned *sine die.*

*Published in proceedings of section on Sociology in Institutions of Learning.

APPENDIX.

WHAT IS THE TRUE WORK OF HUMANITY FOR HUMANITY?*

MRS. ABBY MORTON DIAZ, BELMONT, MASSACHUSETTS.

First, let us make clear to ourselves the purpose of human beings, namely, *to live*. The whole universe is subject everywhere to the same general laws, and the most apparent of these, and including all others, is the Law of Life. Science tells us that, beginning with the most infinitesimal atom and ending with the highest human intelligence, life fills all and is all.

In studying this universal law the world of vegetation serves well as an object-lesson. Here, and co-extensive with life, we find the Law of Individuality. Within a few square yards of ground we find grasses, daisies, mullein, trees, bushes, each form taking heat, light, moisture, air, soil-properties, as its capacities may require. The whole pattern must appear. Complete individual expression, and nothing short of this, means *life*, whether for the blade of grass or for the tree; and just so far as in any case the full pattern is not shown forth, just so far that form of growth fails to live. And note here that in any extent of ground where such failure shows itself in unshapely forms, blight, stunted growths, scanty or imperfect fruit, we see that by this individual failure the grand intent of the whole is interfered with, that the completeness of the whole demands the full development of each.

In nature, so far as appears to us, this law of individual expression acts unintelligently; but to the higher creation, humanity, belongs the power and responsibility of choice. Nevertheless, the Law of Life is inexorable.

Now, this superior order, mankind, has chosen to bring itself under the management of five general systems: the political, the commercial, the religious, the social, the educational. These have wrought

---

* Paper prepared for a meeting on Preventive Work, held in the Art Institute, Chicago, Friday, June 16, and published by request of Committee on Preventive Work.

out for us a wondrous demonstration called civilization. It offers much that is desirable; but as human beings, born to live, we ought to ask if it is carried on in accordance with the Law of Life; is it making the best of each one of us? On the contrary, throughout the whole range we find conditions which absolutely hinder such development, and that our boasted civilization is closely joined with human sacrifice, is based upon loss of life. The term "necessities of life" is made to refer chiefly to the animal necessities—food and bodily protection. The cost of living is calculated on these, whereas all that makes man man lies beyond the animal.

Let us consider our five systems.

First, the political or governmental. Politicians themselves, who surely know, declare this to be utterly corrupt, ruled by bribery and self-interest acting for money-gain. Corruption means a loss of the saving elements of character; means decay, rottenness, destruction. Life cannot come from corruption.

Second, the commercial. This is now largely based on the animal propensities. Its dialect is animalism. These are some of its phrases: "They are at our throats," "Fight 'em off," "Foxy," "Kill 'em out," "They want our blood," "Run 'em off," "Roast 'em out," "Crush 'em out," "Freeze 'em out," "Financial vultures," "Coal cormorants." Success demands "the strong claw," "the quick eye," "the swift wing," "the piercing talon." It is distinctly stated that moral standards are not to be maintained. But when a double standard of morals is recognized as satisfactory it is time to fly the danger-signals. That time is now. In speaking of a deceased millionaire whose unscrupulous "talon" and grasping "claw" had wrought wide-spread ruin and misery, a leading paper makes this significant statement—mark well its import: "He was no worse than thousands of others who stick at nothing short of crime . . . he was not dishonest, judged by the *prevailing rules of commercial morality*." And of a very prominent politician who had made a high governmental position serve greatly his own pecuniary interests it was said: "While a desire for wealth made him unscrupulous, we have looked upon him as neither better nor worse than many of our 'American merchants who have a good standing." But is it not a matter of alarm that the "great mass" of our countrymen acknowledge two standards of action and adopt the lower? Clearly we can look to neither of these two systems as a means of developing in humanity its highest possibilities. Yet they include "the great mass" of our people.

Turning to our third, the religious, we find one of its denominational papers regretting "the connection of professing Christians with stock-gambling, with financial jobbery, and with knavishness in business management"; and a recent article says that "in railroad finance the struggle for life in the savage contests, the slaughter by right of might, the taking from the weak, goes on as if the Christian civilization never existed. Christian gentlemen, good family men, endowers of hospitals and founders of colleges, will follow a financial rival like a sleuth-hound, and slay with the joy of a Comanche cutting throats." In view of all this, and of the general lowering of the moral standard, we may say of our third system that it has by no means established the dominion of the higher human qualities; and it should be added that by its imposition of creeds and doctrines it has hindered the free action of individual mind, and thus antagonized the divine law of individuality as shown throughout creation, the human creation included.

Our fourth, the social system, is rather an outside affair, its social intercourse being conducted chiefly on an upholstery basis and on more or less elaborateness in the preparation of food. This matter of elaborate feeding acts as a perpetual hindrance to a genuine social intercourse and plenty of it. As the chief aims of our social system are wealth and position and the consideration which these bring, it has a tendency to foster pride, vanity, rivalry and unworthy ambition, and it cannot therefore be relied upon as a means of that high and full development which alone is *life*. Moreover, its general law—*follow the leader*—directly hinders individual expression.

Our fifth, the educational system, has been chiefly occupied with instructing rather than in supplying conditions for bringing out the complete life-pattern in each child born. Moreover, it has not yet discovered that the work having the first claim upon it lies in the direction of character. Character rules. Teachers should aim directly, but work indirectly, the purpose not being made apparent. The province of the home? So it is. But beginning at the social top and ending with the abodes of crime and abject poverty, or with the swarming population of the "sweating" dens, we shall find very few homes having the requisites for so difficult a duty—the leisure, the wisdom, the knowledge, and the sense of responsibility. The fact that these cannot be generally found in our homes, even of the better sort, reveals a strange lack in this fifth system of ours; a lack spoken of by Herbert Spencer in his volume on Education. He expresses wonder that while almost everything else is thought worthy of attention, no special preparation is given for the most sacred and important duties of lifetime, those of parents and home-makers.

By introducing into our system a department of parenthood enlightenment, and by giving character work the first rank as an aim of education, it may yet come about that the sound or saving traits, such as truth, love, justice, honor, integrity, shall be put in the ascendant. To make these the absolute controlling power, to sub-stitute their dominion for the dominion of self-seeking and greed and rivalry and money, to do all this would surely prove a true work of humanity for humanity, and it should begin by giving human beings an idea of their own divine possibilities as the temples of the Living God, and of the privileges and the obligations which are theirs by reason of this Divine indwelling.

While waiting for so desirable a state of things, we can lessen the evils of systems one and two by extending our present degree of nationalistic control. This now includes, in greater or less degree, the management of schools, of mail-carrying, of all military affairs, of roads and bridges, of public libraries, of street-lighting and of water privileges. The telegraph and telephone can be added at once and some other things later. Evil conditions are lessened according as the element of self-interest, through money profit, is removed; and the government of any country, especially of a republic, is made less corrupt according as it is freed from the control of corporations and of personal interests generally.

Should it be asserted that these latter will always rule, on account of the badness of poor human nature, let it be counter-asserted that we do not yet know what human nature is, since it has always been under damaging restrictions; also, that as continual progress has been shown on the industrial plane—by application of the more and more immaterial forces—so will it be shown in the higher plane. Moral progress is assured. We are not always to be selfish, any more than we were once always to be cave-dwellers, limited to the industrial use of stone and wood. We must hold fast by this ideal of excellence in order to bring its realization. "The power of a living principle, or a longing, or a hope, or ideal, once planted in society is well-nigh omnipotent."

THE

Public Treatment of Pauperism

BEING A REPORT OF

THE FIRST SECTION OF THE INTERNATIONAL CONGRESS
OF CHARITIES, CORRECTION AND PHILANTHROPY,
CHICAGO, JUNE, 1893

EDITED BY

JOHN H. FINLEY, Ph. D.
President of Knox College

BALTIMORE
THE JOHNS HOPKINS PRESS
LONDON
THE SCIENTIFIC PRESS, LIMITED
428 Strand, W. C.
1894

THE WORLD'S CONGRESS AUXILIARY OF THE WORLD'S COLUMBIAN EXPOSITION.

The International Congress of Charities, Correction and Philanthropy.

PRESIDENT:

RUTHERFORD B. HAYES.

FIRST VICE-PRESIDENT :

FREDERICK H. WINES.

SECOND VICE-PRESIDENT :

ROBERT TREAT PAINE.

GENERAL SECRETARY :

ALEXANDER JOHNSON.

COMMITTEE OF ORGANIZATION :

FREDERICK H. WINES, JOHN G. SHORTALL, Mrs. J. M. FLOWER.
NATHANIEL S. ROSENAU, Secretary.

SECTION I.

The Public Treatment of Pauperism.

CHAIRMAN:

ANSLEY WILCOX,
Charity Organization Society, Buffalo, New York.

SECRETARY :

JOHN H. FINLEY, Ph. D.,
President of Knox College, Galesburg, Illinois.

TABLE OF CONTENTS.

THE INTERNATIONAL TREATMENT OF THE POOR QUESTION.

BARON VON REITZENSTEIN, FREIBURG, BADEN.

Was den grossen Ring bewohnet,
Huldige der Sympathie!

I.

Phases of Development in the International Treatment of the Poor Question.—Present Outlook.

The need of uniting the nations on common lines of action for the solution of the problems connected with the poor question has made itself felt since the middle of the century with ever-increasing force. The constantly growing recognition of this necessity has introduced an element into the development of these questions which has exerted an increasing influence upon their treatment. This element, however, is not entirely new. There have been periods before in which common ideas and a consequent similarity in forms of organization forced the nations to take one and the same course in their methods of caring for the poor. These periods were followed by others in which the effort to emphasize national individuality constituted the prominent characteristic in the development of the question of poor relief. History, then, presents the picture of a rising and falling tide in the influence of unity of ideas upon development—periods in which the prevailing feature was to work on common lines alternating with those in which national individuality was the predominant characteristic of development.

The transition from the Middle Ages to the Renaissance was one of those periods of alternation in which first one and then the other idea had the upper hand. In the Middle Ages poor relief was in the hands of the church and of the institutions which she had founded. It was natural that identity of dogmatic belief and of ecclesiastical organization, extending far beyond the limits of a single nation, should determine the development of the care of the poor in a common direction.   In contrast to this, in the following period, when church separation and the formation of independent states took place, the desire became prominent to find within individual church communities and nations distinct forms corresponding to the conceptions which had there won recognition. In this period of national differentiation, the points of contact between nations resulting from that unity of ideas and organization which had pervaded the life of the Middle Ages as a characteristic feature naturally grew less. The intellectual spirit which was developed by the philosophy of the eighteenth century and by the humanitarian ideas proclaimed by it gave a fresh impulse to fraternity and union ; but this movement also succumbed to a reaction.   The reviving and growing national feeling among civilized nations supplanted these cosmopolitan tendencies and brought again into greater prominence the element of national individuality.   The counter movement, which has been the characteristic feature of the second half of this century, has been essentially influenced by the wider relations brought about through increased facilities of international intercourse, which could not fail in turn to affect the interchange of views in the realms of science. But though those earlier tendencies resulting from a common feeling had later to give way to counter tendencies, they were not entirely without fruit in clearing the way for international co-operation.   As many of the institutions which sprang from the intellectual life of the Middle Ages and which extended beyond the limits of single nations have been preserved, though in altered form, so also we have active among us to-day numerous influences suggested by that period of enlightenment.   Even in the realm of purely national development many an organization has been formed, the importance of which has later been recognized by other nations in the revival of the exchange of ideas.   In spite of these alternating waves, the result has been in general to multiply the points on which the effort to bring about international unity of action rests.   On the whole this development presents itself as an advance towards harmonious action on a larger scale.

What applies to the material results applies still more to the means for bringing about these results.   These too have constantly increased. The realization of the ideas concerning the care of the poor that had become dominant within the church during the Middle Ages rested upon church doctrines and organizations which were in great measure common to all the peoples of Christendom.   Even to-day the common views developed within each individual church community regarding the province and form of poor relief are to a certain extent a happy element in bringing nations to a closer union. In the Illumination Period it was through individual exchange of opinion between leading men and through literary discussion that the mutual clarification of ideas was chiefly accomplished. Even to-day these two methods are those which give the best prospect for progress in the line of greater fraternity. Indeed, ever since de Gerando's great pioneer work first gave us its widely influential example, the collection of materials referring to conditions and institutions among other nations and the comparative treatment of the poor question based upon such information have constantly gained ground in literature. The very use of associations to which we owe in recent times the especially powerful impulse given to this common treatment, had its beginnings in the Illumination Period, and upon these beginnings we are still building. But association life in its development during the second half of the last century remained pre-eminently local. This development first entered on a wider stage through the influence of the recent movement which, favored by the extraordinary growth of facilities of intercourse, has ever striven to extend the organization of associations to the widest circles and over as large a territory as possible. The effort has been not only to concentrate the forces within the limits of a single nation, but to pave the way for united action on the part of different nations. The attempts which have been made in this direction evidence a constantly higher degree of perfection of detail and systematic treatment.

The initiation of these attempts was due to a resolution passed by the *Société d'Économie Charitable*, in Paris, in 1855, on motion of its president, Vicomte de Melun, to embrace the opportunity afforded by the Paris Exhibition to bring about an international conference for the purpose of discussing questions referring to the situation of the poorer classes. This idea met with approbation, and was supported especially by that noble philanthropist, Ducpétiaux, inspector-general of the Belgian prisons. The holding of the International Congress of Charities in Brussels in 1856 was owing to his initiative. This congress was followed by others, in Frankfort-on-the-Main in 1857, and in London in 1862, which latter was held at the World's Fair of the same year. The strained relations which resulted from the wars of 1864-1871 were not propitious to the further progress of this development. The next international congress did not take place until 1880, in Milan. This was followed by the congress held in connection with the World's Fair in Paris in 1889, which was the immediate forerunner of the one about to take place in Chicago. The common aim of all these congresses has been to establish a permanent organization, in order to secure a well-regulated exchange of experiences and views between experts on the pauper question of different nations, not only at the congresses but also during the longer or shorter intervals between them. None of these congresses has had any permanent success in this direction, however. As yet, the maintenance of mutual relations during these intervals rests rather upon the national associations, which have in increasing measure taken cognizance of one another's work and made all the materials pertaining to it accessible to one another. The extraordinary activity shown in the last few decades, in the membership of associations as well as in the establishment of new associations, must be welcomed, therefore, as an advance tending to further the growth of the international idea of the treatment of the poor. The example of Switzerland, whose time-honored "Association for Public Good" (*Gemeinnützige Gesellschaft*) has existed since the year 1810, was first followed by England, through the formation in 1857 of the " National Association for the Promotion of Social Science." Each of these associations, although their programme was much more comprehensive, took special interest in the study of the poor question. The associations which sprang into life at a later period differ from those of earlier date, in that the sphere of their activity is defined by narrower limits, comprising, for the most part, besides the care of the poor, only cognate subjects, such as the care of discharged prisoners. To this class belong the National Conference of Charities and Correction, founded in 1874 in the United States of America, the German Association for Poor Relief and Charity (*Deutsche Verein für Armenpflege und Wohlthätigkeit*) which dates from the year 1881, and the *Société Internationale pour l'Étude des Questions d'Assistance*, in Paris, which owes its origin to the impulse given by the International Congress of 1889, and which has since been in full activity. In Italy, too, national charity conferences have been held, the second of which met in Florence in March of the present year. Although the Paris society calls itself international, it differs very little from the others; not only is it composed almost entirely (its board of directors exclusively) of French members, but it confines its regular work for the most part to questions connected

with the French poor. Other associations, however, interest themselves, when occasion offers, in the work of other countries. The great
majority of the members of all these societies are practical workers
in the care of the poor. The fact that they from time to time inform
themselves as to movements elsewhere has manifestly helped, first,
to give to their discussions a wider scope, and thereby to bring
about a larger participation in these debates, and second, to heighten
the interest in the international treatment of the question within the
circle of experts practically engaged in the care of the poor. Evidently connected with this is the fact that the practical element has
become the greatly preponderating one in the composition of international congresses, and that the theoretical philanthropist has gone
to the rear. The majority of those who participate in these gather-
ings are members of the poor boards and poor relief associations of
the country in which the congress is held. This double change in
the composition of the congresses has necessarily resulted in the
delimitation of the subject-matter of the discussions and in giving to
them a more precise and practical turn.

If we consider the wide range of topics discussed at previous
international congresses, we are especially struck with the increasing
definiteness of the programme. While, in the programme of the
Brussels Congress of 1856, subjects foreign to the practical working
of the poor administration and only indirectly connected with the
care of the poor, as for example the question of the means of subsistence, still occupy a prominent place, the programme of the
London Congress of 1862 shows a far greater specialization of the
subjects considered. Nevertheless, of the two questions there
proposed for discussion, only one, the compulsory education of
neglected children, comes within the province of the care of the
poor, while the other, compulsory elementary education, lies entirely
outside of it. The policy of more narrowly defining the subject was
much more logically carried out in the Milan Congress of 1880. In
framing the programme, the purpose of confining the discussions to
practical questions concerning poor relief proper was kept clearly
in mind. Besides these questions, only special ones referring to
preventive poor relief as well as to the care of discharged prisoners
find a place in these debates. The Paris Congress of 1889 moved in
the same direction. This congress included in its programme the
question of the principle and limits of obligatory poor relief, the
manner of placing children to be supported by public poor relief, the

care of the sick poor in country districts, and the systematic organization of charity. While in this change the increasing influence of the practical element shows itself, this influence is manifested still further in the fact that the treatment itself has become more concrete, and has been brought in closer relations with the peculiar condition of poor relief and the efforts towards reform in the respective countries. This is especially the case in the last two congresses, as in them an unusually large number of the participants belonged to the countries where they were held. The transactions, although in theory intended to be rather of an international character, in practice assumed a decidedly national coloring. This comes out plainly in the resolutions of the Milan Congress, in which we cannot fail to recognize their direct bearing upon the great reform questions then agitating Italy, such as the concentration and modification of endowments, the centralization of administration of institutions engaged in outdoor relief, and the establishment of outdoor sick poor relief in the country districts. The same is true of the Paris Congress. The resolutions adopted concerning the method of caring for children supported by charity, and of establishing outdoor sick poor relief in the country, touch current questions of reform, and reflect in general the conception of the problem in the mind both of French specialists and of the government. Since the trend of reform in France was largely in the direction of the extension of the area of obligatory poor relief, it was in keeping with the local situation to give expression to the recognition of this idea, at least in so far as it referred to those poor who are unable to work. The fourth subject of discussion, the systematic organization of charity, goes, to be sure, much farther. Its discussion assumed a far more international character, and included the details of methods in operation in Germany, England, America, and other countries. No substantial conclusion, however, was arrived at. It was agreed to postpone action until the next congress. The International Congress of Charities, Correction and Philanthropy which will assemble in Chicago on June 12 of this year, under the auspices of the World's Congress Auxiliary, will, therefore, find this question an open one. Of course it will be taken up during the proceedings, or at least touched upon, for it has a place on the programme of two sections of the congress, the first and the sixth. The public treatment of poverty is assigned to the former as the subject of its investigation, and to the latter the organization of the activities concerned with the care of the poor on the part of communes, districts, and the state, and their relations to each other, including also preventive poor relief. The reports to be submitted by the latter section especially concern the demarcation of the province of private charity, the institution of the almoner, and support through work. These preliminaries show plainly that, in so far as it is contemplated again to take up this fourth question, the intention is to enter upon its treatment with a certain amount of reserve. It appears here divided into its several elements, the effort being made first to obtain complete information as to the conditions under which different systems operate.

There are only too good reasons for this reserve. Even if the discussion of this question at the Paris Congress had not suffered from the near approach of the close of the congress, a definite solution would hardly have been reached. In this respect it is unlike other questions treated by the congress. It is easy enough to draw conclusions from a principle which is recognized as valid, or to discover the proper forms of applying the same from the standpoint of general suitability. Thus it is easy to answer affirmatively, in a manner more or less applicable to every kind of condition, the question whether the organization of public sick poor relief is a necessity in country districts. In the same way we can say that, as a rule, the boarding-out system is preferable, where the question relates to the mode of caring for children maintained at public expense. Where, on the other hand, the general organization of a charitable system is under consideration, inasmuch as the system has grown out of the previous historic development of the nation and is in harmony with the national character expressed in the constitution, laws and policy of the government, the solution of this question can for the most part be only relative, that is, it can be said to be valid only where certain preliminary conditions exist. This is the case, to a certain degree, with the question of the limits within which the principle of obligatory poor relief is applicable, limits differently defined according to the manner in which public poor relief is administered, the measure of forces at the disposal of the administration, and the views prevalent as to public poor relief and its relation to private charity. Still more, however, is this true of the question of the practical organization of poor relief. The answer depends essentially on the extent to which this organization, according to existing concrete conditions, belongs to the province of public or private charity, and, where the former is the case, on the character of the unions upon which the duty of relief devolves. Here also are to be further considered both the quantity and the quality of the means at disposal for carrying out the plans of organization. If a solution of the problem is to be attained, the forms and operation of each of the systems prevailing in different countries, as well as the preliminary conditions upon which their existence depends, must first be definitely settled. The question of the universal adaptability of arrangements and of their availability for introduction among other nations is by no means left out of view here, but merely takes a second place in our deliberations. Only after we have learned to understand the conditions under which the separate systems of poor relief in different countries operate, can we proceed to the examination of this question.

If, then, the international congress about to convene in Chicago, as we may expect from what has already been intimated, wisely intends to confine itself to the study of these opposite systems and the preliminary conditions of their operation, and, upon the foundation of the agreement as to these questions that may be reached through its discussions, to shape its further deliberations in regard to the absolute value and adaptability of the systems, it will have made an important step forward in the treatment of the subject. We shall thus enter upon a path more extended, it is true, but at the same time a safe one; a path on which the steps once made need not be retraced. At any rate such a treatment may lead to results which, upon every future reconsideration of the subject, will be looked upon as useful and welcome points on which we can rely.

II.

Points of Comparison between the Charitable Systems of Different Nations.

In the discussions to date as to the most practical method of poor relief, the English-American and the German systems have been contrasted; in other words, the Elberfeld principle with that which lies at the foundation of the charity organization societies. First of all, therefore, a precise statement of the resemblances and differences between these two systems is demanded. The greater our success in this, the clearer the ground for an exhaustive treatment of the question, and for a judgment as to how far either of them meets the requirements met by the other.

Both movements are animated by a common purpose, namely, the
desire to secure greater individualization in the administration of
charity. But while one of them seeks to accomplish this end entirely
through the medium of private organization, the other depends for
its accomplishment almost wholly upon the organization of public
poor relief. Both are agreed that, in order to secure greater indi-
vidualism, the active participation of a larger proportion of the
citizen element is necessary in practical charity work. Finally, both
may be viewed in contrast with the system now in operation in
France and Italy, where such development in this direction as it has
been possible to attain has been of inconsiderable importance. The
existing conditions are there unfavorable to such development.
Wherever the funds for the support both of public and private
charities are derived chiefly from endowments, it is for the most
part impossible to draw a strict line of demarcation between the two.
Besides, the will of the testator fetters the action of the trustees to
such a degree as to be inconducive to any extensive enlistment of the
citizen element in this service.

France.—In France, under the ancient *régime*, attempts were
made to organize the systematic care of the poor by the commune.
But these efforts remained without lasting result, because in their
prosecution the needed persistency was lacking; and because, from
and after the seventeenth century, the government interested itself
exclusively in the creation of new hospitals,* and in the enlargement
of those already in existence. Since that date, the state charitable
system has had these institutions for its centre. This policy, after
suffering a temporary interruption during the Revolution, received
a fresh sanction in the reconstructive legislation of the year V. It is
upon the hospitals that the care of the poor chiefly devolves. They
are supplemented by the " bureaus of charity " (*bureaux de bienfaisance*), which, as organs of outdoor relief, stand at their side. The
efficiency of both is limited by their financial resources, which, particularly in case of the hospitals, consist mainly of the income derived
from endowments, any deficiency in which must be supplied by voluntary contributions on the part of the separate communities. On
account of the magnitude of the interests comprised in the care of
poor children and of the insane, and the imperative necessity of syste-

---

* The word " hospital " is here used in the Continental, not in the English
sense, and is very nearly equivalent to our English " home " or " asylum."—
Translator.

matic care for these classes of dependents, the primary responsibility for such care has been laid upon the departments. A recent bill proposes in addition to compel each separate community to provide relief for the sick poor, the cost of which is to be assessed jointly upon the departments, and the national treasury, according to a fixed scale. Nevertheless, individuals in need of help have no other ultimate dependence than the hospitals and the charity bureaus, whose assistance is optional, or rather is measured by the means at their disposal. Scarcely more than two-fifths of the communities have charity bureaus; and hospitals are usually found only in cities, often only in the larger cities.

Italy.—In Italy the situation is similar; though here greater progress has recently been made in the application of the principle of obligatory poor relief. Special attention may be called by way of illustration, to the sanitary law of December 22, 1888, which requires the communities to furnish medical aid to the poor; and to the law of June 30, 1889, on public safety, which makes provision for paupers unable to work. Here, as in France, the care of foundlings and of the insane devolves wholly or chiefly upon the provinces. But the way was not effectually cleared for a reform in the character and for the centralized control of endowed institutions and other charitable establishments, until the passage of the act of August 3, 1862, and especially the act of June 17, 1890. In Italy also, the extent of relief granted, in many departments of charity, is proportionate to the resources of the institutions. The first result of this situation is, as has been intimated, the absence of any distinct boundary line separating public from private charity. Institutions which are richly endowed often encroach upon the customary domain of private initiative; if their resources are restricted, they are frequently not in a position to meet the most scanty requirements. Since the bulk of their income is derived from interest on endowments and from voluntary contributions, it is impossible to prevent them from doing their work in a manner characteristic of private charity. For this precise reason it is difficult to assign to any larger organization, based upon the systematic utilization of voluntary workers, any clearly defined sphere of duty, in relation to either public or private charity. But this assignment is one of the first preliminary conditions for the success of such an organization. The difficulty growing out of the restrictions laid upon the greater part of the work of institutions, in consequence of the obligations and limitations imposed upon them as endowed institutions, is even more insuperable. The citizen element is unsuited to cope with these hindrances, for the superiority of this element in charitable work depends upon absolute freedom of judgment and of action. These difficulties are further enhanced by the fact that the charitable institutions, in the discharge of their functions, are controlled by the religious orders, especially by the sisterhoods, or employ them to do their work. These are the causes which have prevented the systematic organization of charity, except within narrow limits, in France and Italy.

The efficiency of the form of organization which has been given to public outdoor relief in Paris, and its administration, under the control of the *direction de l'assistance publique*, by the bureaus of charity, aided by agents of both sexes (*commissaires* and *dames de bienfaisance*), has not been fully demonstrated, as appears from a bill lately framed for the reorganization of the system. In the domain of private charity it is for the most part only the *œuvres du travail*, working, as they do, in restricted areas of activity, in which the need for a better organization of volunteer workers has found emphatic expression.

The situation just described differs from that in England and America, on the one hand, and in Germany, Austria and the German cantons of Switzerland, on the other, in the following respect. In all these countries the principles of public relief are substantially the same. The granting of aid is confided to public *unions*, whose legal obligation is theoretically absolute; that is to say, it is not limited by the amount of the resources in their possession. The service is not conditional upon the procuring of the necessary funds, but the procuring of the means required is conditioned upon the demands of the service. In this fundamental principle of relief the two groups are in accord, but they differ widely in their methods of carrying it out. This difference is the governing factor in the aforesaid contrast between English, American and German modes of application of the forces of private initiative in the administration of poor relief.

England.—The most salient feature of the English poor law system is its characterization by a fundamentally broad conception of the task in hand, as opposed to an administrative machinery inadequate to meet fully the demands of individualization. This wide conception of the task finds clear expression as early as 1601, in the act of Elizabeth, which forms the point of departure of pauper relief in England. That act expressly extends the obligation of relief to the able-bodied, who are to receive it in exchange for labor. An obligation so far-reaching naturally demanded for its discharge the most careful specialization on the part of the officers entrusted with its fulfilment ; an individualization the more difficult in proportion to the loss of stability in the condition of the poor, due to the growth of industries. But the unions upon which the administration of the law devolved were unequal to this demand. These unions were the parishes ; unions of dissimilar capabilities, which, the more they assumed the form of special organizations intended for carrying out the aims of poor relief, the more they lacked intercommunal life. A lax and routine performance of the duties pertaining to them in this regard, by the administrative organs of the parishes, was almost universal in the eighteenth and in the earlier decades of the nineteenth century. Moreover, the attempts made to remedy this defect by a larger utilization of the justices of the peace were unproductive of any lasting result. The latter officials were devoid of special qualifications for the undertaking and felt no lively interest in it. The want of administrative capacity in the communal organization was the cause of evils which found expression in the enormous increase of the poor rates and led to the great reform of 1834. The process of disintegration of the communal organization, occasioned by the formation of other districts for various administrative purposes, was the negation of reform of that organization in the direction of a better individualization of the poor. The definite abandonment of the search for a remedy in this direction, therefore, is a characteristic feature of the amended act, which substitutes for individual inquiry into the circumstances of applicants for relief, the deterrent influence of the workhouse. Since the maintenance of workhouses necessitated larger unions, they were created by uniting parishes. The perfunctory, mechanical character naturally inherent in the administration of such unions, and their peculiar lack of living relations to their inhabitants, resulted in devolving the duty of outdoor relief upon salaried under-officials (relieving officers). These relieving officers are unsatisfactory to an extraordinary degree. The efficient administration of out-relief depends not so much upon mechanical training as upon knowledge of local conditions on the part of the officials entrusted with it, their being in touch with the applicants and beneficiaries, their independent judgment, and the degree of their interest in the success of the administration—prerequisites more often found in unsalaried officers taken from the body

of the people than in paid subordinates. The abundant funds with
which the unions are supplied intensifies the character of mechanical
uniformity which thus attaches to the work of poor relief in England.
The county governments have little share in this work, outside of
the care of the insane. The development of their participation in it
is still in its infancy.

The United States.—The influence of the example of England in
the form given to American institutions explains the English stamp
upon the pauper legislation of the United States. Nevertheless, we
meet with important differences. For instance, the workhouse
principle is by no means so general or prominent here as in England.
The dominant tendency is to make local communities chargeable
with the care of their poor, instead of forming unions for that
purpose; and more is done by the states than by the English
government. But here, as in England, public relief is principally
given in institutions. What out-relief is granted is here also
distributed by paid under-officials. The perception of the evils
arising from out-relief thus administered, evils considerably enhanced
by haphazard private benevolence, has produced that new movement (which continually gains ground in England and has been
transplanted to American soil) whose double aim is, by voluntary
organization, to secure individualization in outdoor relief and to
restrict public relief, as far as possible, to institutions. This movement has found its characteristic expression in the charity organization societies. The chief aims of these societies are to secure
co-operation between all local private charities, central supervision of
their operations, investigation into the circumstances of each applicant, and careful consideration of the appropriate means to be
employed in each case; finally, when aid is deemed requisite and
proper, to act as intermediary in procuring the same and if necessary—
at least this is the case with the societies in England—to grant it
themselves. In these societies there is large scope for the utilization .
of the citizen. The machinery of public poor relief has, it is true,
here also exercised such an influence in the way of example, that
many of these societies employ paid agents as visitors to the poor,
side by side with voluntary workers selected from among their
members; and sometimes the visiting is left entirely to these agents.
This occurs very frequently in the English societies, while in
America the practice is to make larger use of friendly visitors chosen
from the members of the society. It is needless to add that women,

especially in America, form a large contingent among the forces taken from the circle of private life for the service of poor-relief.

Germany.—According to what has been said, the reaction against the evils which have sprung up in connection with the public care of the poor in England and America takes the form of organized private charity. In Germany, on the contrary, the effort has been chiefly to bring about the needed improvement through reforms in the machinery of public poor relief. Above all, the endeavor has been to give to the pauper administration such an organization as would render it capable of a higher degree of discrimination between individuals. Outdoor relief has thus succeeded in maintaining for itself, in the domain of public care of the poor, not only an important, but even a largely predominating position. This development was favored by the fact that in Germany, in contrast with England, not only was the task a more limited one, but the government had at its disposal an administrative apparatus better fitted for the accomplishment of this special purpose.

Although by law the duty of caring for the poor in Germany includes the able-bodied, public relief is in fact almost everywhere bestowed only upon those who are entirely or partially incapable of work. In so far as granting aid to the able-bodied poor has been a necessity, such aid, as a rule, has been afforded by means lying outside of the province of poor relief proper. By the imperial law of June 6, 1870, and the Bavarian law of April 29, 1869, the duty of caring for the poor, thus limited in fact, devolves now in principle upon the local communities in all Germany, except Alsace-Lorraine. Unequal as these local communities are, both in their administrative and financial capabilities, they have this in common, that their sphere of activity includes in itself the various tendencies of local, communal life; also that the management of their administration is in great part in the hands of citizens elected by the community. Almost without exception this is especially the case in small, rural communities. To the elasticity thus secured in the administrative life of the community is due the adaptability of the community for individual treatment in the bestowal of public poor relief. The powers incident to this branch of administration are, in the rural communities, mostly vested in the local municipal authority (*Ortsvorstand*) chosen by the community. As a rule, there is no need of any mediate agency between it and the inhabitants, since in these smaller communities every man's condition is more or less well known, and the local authority is thus in position to act from personal knowledge of the situation and the individual. At any rate the restrictive idea in the treatment of applications for relief by the local authority reaches its full development, and the danger of supplying relief beyond the need, or even lavishly, is almost wholly prevented. We find, therefore, in the rural communities in general no such increase of the burden of pauperism through laxity of management as was the case in the English parishes before the amendment of the poor law. In the towns the contrary is true, especially in the middle-sized and larger ones. Here, by reason of a larger area and a denser population, the details of individual cases escape, as a rule, the immediate knowledge of the chief authority, so that special intermediate agents are required, in order to obtain the necessary information. But they, too, in the performance of this part of their task, have not infrequently difficulties to contend with. In fact, instances have not been wanting in which the burden of pauperism reached disproportionate dimensions, on account of the inadequate investigation of individual cases. For these evils, however, the municipal organization itself presented the remedy. It is a leading feature of these organizations, that while salaried officials, trained for their vocation, have a large and often preponderating share in their direction, on the other hand, private citizens are designated to perform the executive and controlling functions of the administration in the separate city districts, who must attend to these duties, and who hold offices of honor only, therefore without salaries, by virtue of a general political obligation.

We owe to the Prussian Municipal Law of November 14, 1808, the great work of the never-to-be-forgotten Minister von Stein, the first impulse in this direction and its application also in the domain of poor law administration. According to the requirements of that act, the direction of poor relief in every town is in the hands of a so-called bureau of charities, (*Armendircktion*), a body composed of the burgomaster and other members of the magistracy, town councilmen, citizens, and in certain cases also of clergymen and physicians. The act provides that

"Under this directing body the relief of the poor must be attended to solely by committees of citizens, and the town for this purpose must be divided into suitable poor districts"; "it is the duty of the town councilmen and citizens elected on the committee to look up the poor in their districts, and to investigate their condition : but it devolves upon them as a whole to care for the maintenance, medical care, employment, education and instruction of all the poor in the town ; the entire care of the poor is, therefore, entrusted to the citizens, their public spirit, and the benevolence of the inhabitants."

The substance of these provisions afterwards found its way into the town constitutions of other German countries also. It forms the basis of that organization which, first called into existence in the city of Elberfeld in the year 1852, afterward obtained celebrity under the name of the Elberfeld System.

The cause of this movement was here too the increase of the burden of pauperism through defective investigation. Its leading feature was the endeavor to insure such an examination and control of each case as to render it possible to refuse aid to those not in need, and at the same time to grant to the needy adequate and suitable assistance. The essential element in this reform consists chiefly in the multiplication of the citizen force working in the administration of poor relief; the number of persons entrusted with the investigation of individual cases—almoners (*Pfleger*)—is increased to such an extent that only a comparatively small number of the poor is assigned to each visitor, who is thus placed in position to give to each case individual treatment. As a precaution against attaching too great weight to the personal opinions of individual almoners, aid is granted, as a rule, subject to certain exceptions, only upon the decision of the district board (*Bezirkskommission*), a body in which the almoners of the district meet under the chairmanship of the district-superintendent (*Bezirksvorsteher*). For the regulation of the relations between these district boards and the superior city board, the principle has been formulated that the local boards should be given the largest possible independence of action, but uniformity in principles and methods should be maintained. The highly favorable results attained by this system have smoothed the way for its introduction into the great majority of the medium-sized and larger towns of Germany. It follows, as a matter of course, that there is considerable variation in detail, corresponding to the varying conditions in the different towns. This so-called system only indicates a principle, which is capable of being more or less fully carried out according to the degree of interest taken in the work by the unpaid visitors, and which will produce the best results only where the office of almoner is regarded as a dignified and responsible one. On the other hand, the value of this system has been diminished in exceptional cases, fortunately rare hitherto, in which communes have subjected the citizen-workers holding these offices to the control of paid under-officials, partly with reference to the communal treasury, partly through distrust of the element of self-government, or through tender consideration for the convenience of the inhabitants. Whatever progress has been attained in the management of poor relief in the larger cities is principally due to the application and development of this principle. By means of it a large body of citizens and a wealth of useful forces have been drawn into the domain of poor administration and led to take part in it; and the poor administration has been to them a school of public spirit and of the faithful discharge of public functions. So much the more has this been so, since the care of the poor is precisely one of the branches of administration thus far least influenced by political currents of opinion, and in which the habit of a purely business management has been preserved in an especially high degree. This training of forces for service in the municipal administration has in many ways inured to the benefit of these municipalities as a whole.

The prospects for a flourishing future development of the care of the poor in German towns, therefore, must essentially depend upon the universal application of the Elberfeld system, if possible; upon its further improvement in accordance with a variety of conditions; and upon its adapting itself to the changing needs of the pauper administration. That in the accomplishment of this there will be many difficulties to be overcome is a foregone conclusion. Such a one, for example, is presented by the mode of growth of many large cities. In these, following the example of England and America, a greater tendency is continually manifest to assign different districts to the different classes of the population or to the different trades. Commerce and industry, labor and luxury, dwell in separate quarters. By this separation, much to be deplored from a politico-social standpoint, the relations between the wealthier and the poorer classes, which depend upon personal acquaintance and direct intercourse, are weakened. The exercise of the duties of the office is also rendered much more difficult on account of the distances between their dwellings. We must regard as a difficulty not less formidable the probable modification in the scope and character of relief due to the impending change in the condition of the laboring class. On the one hand, we may anticipate a diminution in the demand for relief in consequence of the increased amount of life insurance by workingmen, though it is impossible to arrive at even an approximate estimate of its extent, and although we must utter a warning against the over-appreciation of this tendency. It may already be regarded as certain that that portion of the laboring class reached by insurance is to a great extent raised above the level of pauperism. But on the other hand, the burden of relief is increasing through the growing influx into the larger towns of the indigent classes of the population, and through the more and more unreliable and irregular character of production in consequence of the rapid changes in methods of manufacture and in the condition of the market. This change is the cause of temporary want of work, which ever assumes a more important rank among the causes of poverty. While, as before mentioned, the operation of the machinery of municipal relief is rendered easier, because its function is so often limited to the care of the poor who are unable to work, this favorable condition will in the future be much less frequently met with. The task therefore remains, to adapt the system in a practical way to the care of those temporarily out of work, regarding whom no fixed rules have yet been agreed upon in Germany. Consequently, the problem of relief of the able-bodied poor, with which the English system has busied itself from the very beginning, must be classed in Germany with questions which have not yet found a definite and fundamental answer. The somewhat unsystematic and isolated efforts made by public administrative boards and by associations more and more clearly prove the necessity which exists for its solution.

There is a broad field, therefore, for reform in the care of the poor, even in the towns. Still more is this the case in the country. In the towns, through the application of the Elberfeld system, a sufficiently intense charitable activity has been in many instances insured, together with a thorough inquiry into individual cases of distress and the rejection of unfounded claims. It is otherwise in the country, where the aid granted is only too often inadequate and far below the actual need, on account of the deficient resources of many communities, which makes it the policy of the local bureaus of charity to restrict the giving of relief within the narrowest possible limits. Here a remedy has been sought mainly in the direction of imposing upon the larger unions a greater relative share of the expense, partly by assigning to them particular branches of poor relief, partly by assessing them for the expense of the local care of the poor; and in numerous instances service of this kind has been voluntarily rendered by them. The attempts of which we are speaking lie entirely within the discretion of the local legislatures of the several provinces or in the region of the autonomy of the unions concerned. In this single fact we may see why these attempts are so widely divergent in respect of the application both of principles and methods. Here, too, greater clearness in the development of principles is needed. The complete transfer of the care of the poor in rural districts to larger poor unions, each to be formed out of a number of communes and manors, though advocated by many, meets with some obstacles arising from the peculiarities of the German communal system, and it would in any event be disadvantageous, in so far as it would tend to detach the relief of poverty from its hitherto close relations with the other branches of local administration, and to disrupt the central bond of union between the various administrative functions. It is doubtful whether, in poor unions of this kind, an organization modeled after the Elberfeld system could be successfully introduced, since one of the essential preliminary conditions of that system, namely, the effective control of the individual almoner by the joint action of other almoners equally familiar with all the circumstances, would be impossible to establish in unions composed of a number of communes.

Austria and Switzerland.—The condition of Austria and German-Switzerland, though not exactly the same as in Germany, is yet similar. In both countries, individual treatment in public poor relief, according to the Elberfeld system, is less general, even in the larger towns, than in Germany; for not until recently has a beginning worthy of attention been made in this direction. In Switzerland it was principally the reorganization of the local government of Zurich, brought about by the consolidation of the suburbs with the city, which was the occasion of a movement in this direction, merely tentative as yet. The difficulties with which poor relief has to contend in the rural districts are in Austria still greater than in Germany, especially since the co-operation of the larger unions is less developed there than in Germany. In a bill lately proposed by the government and passed by the legislature of Lower Austria, an attempt was made to transfer the care of the poor to larger unions and to organize it upon the Elberfeld system; this measure, however, failed to receive the sanction of the Crown. In Switzerland, on the contrary, the cantons usually do more in the way of sharing the burden of local poor relief than do the larger unions in Germany. But the peculiarity of the situation is that in the majority of the cantons the obligation to relieve ordinarily devolves upon the home commune as distinct from the local commune. But there is an apparently growing movement in opposition to this relic of communal development belonging to a historical epoch long since obsolete.

Adaptability of the Elberfeld System.

Among those organizations, then, which are the result of the development of poor relief in Germany, and which have at present reached a certain completion, the one known as the Elberfeld system is plainly that which, originally limited in its application to the larger and medium-sized towns, has received proportionately the greatest measure of recognition and has the best prospect of extension of its sphere of operation. Of late much study has been given to the question of transplanting it to other countries, to England and America in particular. The expediency of such a transfer is not negatived by the growth of charity organization. Although both systems rest upon the same principle, in so far as charity organization also aims as far as possible to secure individualization in charity by attracting to it the personal force which resides in voluntary service, yet the significance of such an enlistment of forces is less in the domain of private than in that of public charity. In the first place, the realization of this idea, if confined within the limits of private charity, must always fluctuate more or less in accordance with the views of the persons who direct it and with the temporary mood of influential circles of the population. But in the domain of public charity it rests upon the communal organization, so that a more durable foundation can be laid for it in the legal obligation of citizens to respond to the demands of the service in question, and upon this foundation a more enduring structure can be erected. A second essential difference results from the fact that the development of private charity must lead to a delimitation of the sphere of operation of public poor relief, which will therefore be more extended in the country than in towns; for in the country, organizations for private relief will not spring up in equal number, nor will they be so strong. If, therefore, the existence of such organizations in towns makes it possible to entrust to private initiative that part of the care of the poor in which individual treatment is most necessary, in other words, outdoor relief, the same cannot be the case in the country. This difference in the demarcation of the sphere of activity of public poor relief must prove an obstacle to its further development not to be lightly estimated. The Elberfeld system, therefore, has this argument in its favor, that it secures individualization within the domain of public poor relief itself. Corresponding organizations of private charity in connection with this will not be by any means superfluous.

To the establishment of organizations of this·sort within the province of public poor relief, so far as England is in question, an obstacle will exist, so long as the duty of relieving distress devolves upon special unions created exclusively for that purpose. In these there will never be begotten the lively communal public spirit demanded in order to give the requisite moral impulse to the work of almoners selected from among the citizens. There seems, however, no prospect of a reform in the constitution of the English commune looking to the inclusion of the care of the poor, together with the other functions of local governments, within the working sphere of an undivided local commune.

In this respect, the situation in America is more favorable. Here, at least, where the township system prevails, the communes and the pauper districts have the same geographical boundaries. But a difficulty of another sort here grows out of the wide-spread practice of regarding public office, even in local administration, as a spoil of party politics and a means of perpetuating party control. This is obviously incompatible with the proper administration of charity, particularly of municipal outdoor relief. This conviction is a principal reason why American authorities on the problems of poverty regard the furnishing of relief by municipalities, outside of institutions, as dangerous, and recommend that this form of relief be left to private benevolence. Especially in the National Conference of Charities and Correction in 1891, this view received distinct expression, though not without encountering a no less decided opposition. Others, on the contrary, point out the necessity of emancipating municipal government, in the interest of honest and economical administration, from the influence of party rule, and of resting it, as in Germany, upon the basis of a participation in it by the citizens of universal obligation, entirely free from any admixture of political considerations. In keeping with this opinion, and as a feature of municipal reform, the organization of relief in cities upon the basis of the Elberfeld principle is advocated. This is the point of view lately presented with such ability by Professor F. G. Peabody. His eloquent exposition of his theory could not fail to meet a hearty response and approval in Germany.

The charity organization movement might be made a valuable first step in the direction of the adoption of the Elberfeld system. The enlistment of individual workers by these societies for service, although at first only in the voluntary care of the poor, will nevertheless accustom them to a businesslike and cautious treatment of cases needing relief. Through the training thus given these forces become available, also, for the purposes of public poor relief.

But it would be a one-sided view to consider that movement from this standpoint alone. For us also it is more than merely a transition stage. This co-ordination of efforts and forces in private charity, forming as it does the fundamental trait of the movement, has a value of its own, independent of any relation to the future reform of public poor relief. Organizations working for this end are a need also with us, which heretofore has been felt in a less degree only because we were able to remedy a portion of the evils in the domain of public poor relief, and because reform in that domain was for us the primary necessity. We, too, feel more and more keenly the importance of securing a systematic interlocking of the activities of private charity now working so far apart; and, indeed, beginnings worthy of notice have been recently made in this direction. In the effort to perfect our organizations in this respect, we can make use of the experiences of the charity organization movement of England and America as valuable guides.

Thus, upon another field we receive back again that which we were able to give, by setting up a model for the organization of public poor relief; we take part in a competitive contest and commerce, in which the noblest conquests of the mind become objects of reward and exchange. The differences that exist between these methods are not comparable with what they possess in common. Each desires to interest workers who will busy themselves with the condition of their suffering fellow-citizens ; and in caring for the same we may discern in both actively at work the teachings of Him who has in the command to love our neighbors as ourselves laid down a rule of conduct and given a watchword for all social development, which shall one day unite all the world in the bond of brotherhood. The words of the great poet which I have placed at the head of my paper are penetrated through and through by this spirit of brotherhood. They are an admonition from the past to the present century to press forward to the ideal of peaceful agreement and hearty co-operation between nations in the great questions of civilization, as we have received this ideal from the intellectual movement of those times. And they are also a greeting from the Old World to the New, from Germany to America, an expression of the warm interest with which we are following the great movement now in progress on the other side of the sea, a stimulus to earnest, united effort for the elevation of humanity, which is the solution of the questions which agitate mankind. May the hopes which we, too, cherish for success in this undertaking be richly fulfilled!

PAUPERISM IN GREAT CITIES: ITS FOUR CHIEF CAUSES.

ROBERT TREAT PAINE, PRESIDENT OF THE ASSOCIATED CHARITIES OF BOSTON.

The problem of poor relief in great cities requires to be re-stated in ampler terms. The diseases of society are more aggravated, the dangers are graver, the need of radical remedies is more absolute, than the new charity has yet fully and fairly faced.

This last quarter of a century has witnessed a noble outburst of the energies of good men to help suffering brethren.

"Science and sympathy" have been moved to do their utmost, under such fiery inspiration as that of Phillips Brooks when he threw the whole power of his support into the movement to create the Associated Charities of Boston. [Speech of March 12, 1879.]

The world is brighter and better for the devotion of the great galaxy of noble men and women all through the civilized world, who, seeing how the problem needs wisdom, bring to it deep and faithful study, and how it needs their sympathy and aid, bring to it loving devotion.

These are the men and women who are making this world fit to live in and this life worth living.

When the poor sink below their poverty into pauperism, and pauperism becomes hopeless and degraded and brutal; when powerful and prolific causes are at work to swell the rising tide; the day has gone when it is enough to go on dealing with details.

Society must study till it knows the whole measure of the problem, seek whatever heroic measures can remedy the evils, and especially can cut off the supply, and invoke all the powers in our modern life of wisdom, energy and love, under the guidance and inspiration, and with firm faith in the aid, of God.

Conditions of Life in Large Cities.

The conditions of life in our great cities excite deep concern. Pass them in brief review. The growth of city population, rapid and irresistible, compels the prophetic imagination to ask, but in vain, what is to be the limit of the number of souls in London and Paris, New York, Chicago and Philadelphia, and even in Baltimore and Boston.

With population, rents rise so that the average man, that is the masses of the people, are forced to live in utterly unfit homes, fearfully overcrowded; hence low vitality of body and soul, diseased morals and diseased bodies.

The extremes of society grow more pronounced, so that from the increasing numbers of the very poor, a larger residuum, Charles Booth's Submerged Tenth, Charles Loring Brace's Dangerous Classes, reach such proportions that they can no longer be dealt with in detail and hopefully as individuals, but fill up whole areas like that great ward in Liverpool, crowded with the dock laborers, where the level of life is at such uniform dead low tide, that to uplift a part is impossible without uplifting the general level of all, and the idea of uplifting the whole suggests attacking the Atlantic; to me the saddest spectacle of hopeless despair I have ever anywhere beheld, Liverpool's Dead Sea.

Society by its loving energies can deal with evils in detail, but who can find the remedy when evils of all kinds are aggregated into a vast mass at a uniform low level of degradation, destitution and despair?

Strong drink is almost the sole solace of their dull routine. Saturday night and Sunday find so many, that it seems a large proportion, sodden with drink, the aged as well as those in youth, even babies at the breast. Nay, let me recall the words of the chief of police as he took me through these sights of sadness, children begotten by drunken parents, born of drunken mothers, nursed by drinking mothers, and thus saturated with liquor from the start.

Crimes of violence, crimes of lust, crimes against property, not only prevail, but cease to shock, where the general level of life has lapsed into a new phase of barbarism.

What hope for boys and girls growing up in such atmosphere of sin, in overcrowded cities from which playgrounds have been excluded by rising rents; playgrounds for the innocent outpouring of the boys' animal spirits which will have some vent, if not in hockey and football, then in breaking into empty buildings, stealing lead pipes, and stoning dispensary doctors or police with even-handed delight.

Yet critics say " The Bitter Cry of Outcast London " is a bit overdrawn.

"We have opened but a little way the door that leads into this plague-house of sin and misery and corruption, where men and women and little children starve and suffer and perish, body and soul. We shall not wonder if some, shuddering at the revolting spectacle, try to persuade themselves that such things cannot be in Christian England, and that what they have looked upon is some dark vision conjured up by a morbid pity and a desponding faith. To such we can only say, Will you venture to come with us and see for yourselves the ghastly reality?" [Page 20.]

What is my conclusion? Shall I not say that in the largest cities where conditions are worse, and the evils of pauperism, grown chronic and contagious, are blended with habits of drunkenness and other vice, breaking out into crimes against the law, pauperism cannot be wisely considered alone, but the problem of how to uplift the general level of life must be studied *as one whole problem*, especially as to the causes of the evils?

Boston can speak words of encouragement. Boston is of just the size for the best study of the data, as well as a successful combination of forces for a thorough, encouraging and permanent success. I rejoice to be able to say that in Boston the conditions of life among working people, counting all, even those on the lowest levels, are on the whole visibly improving.

Does not this same encouraging condition prevail amongst most of the smaller cities of the United States? Have not the various agencies, working together for good in the social awakening and religious life of our times, attained such vigor that they are waging winning war against the forces which drag life down? On the whole, are not things mending rather than growing worse?

What more can I hope to achieve on this point, than to fasten the acute observations of leaders in each city on this exact question, whether the *standard of life of working people* is rising or falling?

In New York and London, no doubt in Paris and Berlin, the data are largely different. I hope I am wrong when I express the fear that in these cities the general tide is still falling, in marked contrast to its rise in almost all other cities of less size.

But what hope is there for these four greatest cities—may I add Chicago—unless they are stirred to superhuman efforts, in part at least by candid and friendly criticism?

Pauperism Assuming a Worse Type in Large Cities.

One main purpose of my paper is now to draw attention to this tremendous fact, that pauperism is assuming a new and more terrible type in the largest cities, where paupers have lived so long in this condition that they know nothing better;—

Where pauperism is hereditary and paupers are born into a condition not unlike the castes of India, whence there is no hope; and they are content with their lot, which varies with the seasons, tramping on lovely country roads in summer, robbing hen-roosts or houses, perhaps from hunger or partly from delight in pleasurable excitement, increased by the risk of an encounter, or of a month or two in a spacious building with all reasonable comfort, so much better than they get outside;—

Where out-relief, or private charity, or loose alms guarantee against serious suffering:—

And where, as in London and New York, their numbers are so large that, first, the evil influences they receive from each other far exceed any good influences which Christian society has yet learned to apply; second, their treatment in casual wards, almshouses, jails, reformatories or prisons, by police or officials, is—I had almost said of necessity—almost always mechanical, and too often hard and brutalizing, as for instance in the casual wards* of London with cold

---

* The Wayfarers' Lodge in Boston seems to unite such decent treatment of inmates with clean bed in ample rooms, fairly good food, with enforced bath and a stent of about three hours' labor in sawing wood in the morning, as to meet the present conditions of pauperism in a city like Boston. The system is not so harsh that humane citizens refuse to send casuals to the Lodge, nor so attractive as to promote vagrancy.

Wayfarers' Lodges have been established in Philadelphia and are proposed in New York, similar to that in Boston.

stone walls, in prison-like cells—a stent of stone to be broken and thrown out through the meshes of the net, before they are free, after a confinement of a day and a half at the least, so that the great facts stand out for all students of city life to see.

Brutality and Sullen Defiance.

Brutality and sullen defiance are added to and engrafted on the pauper character. With the sullen endurance of the North American Indian they meet their fate; gentler treatment not repelling, and harsh treatment only embittering and degrading.

When the pauperism of a vast city is sunk in sullen despair and degraded life is no longer abhorrent to its victims, and brutality sinks men into savages, so that despair, degradation and brutality become the dominant traits of character of a great pauper mass, then, in the name of God, society has got to put forth mightier energies in more judicious array than heretofore, or fail in its attempt.

I declare before this great audience representing the best civilization of many countries, that the methods of dealing with pauperism hitherto applied are impotent against this swelling tide of brutal, degraded pauperism.

England's great poor law reform of 1834 is always cited first. The fundamental principle of this reform was "THAT THE SITUATION OF THE PERSON RECEIVING RELIEF SHOULD NOT ON THE WHOLE BE MADE REALLY OR APPARENTLY SO ELIGIBLE AS THE SITUATION OF THE INDEPENDENT LABORER OF THE LOWEST CLASS." (Nicholl's History of English Poor Law, Vol. 2, p. 257.)

This principle has been everywhere accepted.

Seth Low cites it in his famous attack on the evils of "outdoor relief" (1879, p. 3) as an accepted principle.

The charity organization societies of London and of all other cities concur.

The earlier system which prevailed, of sending to police stations casuals who asked bed or food, has been generally condemned.

Shall we not agree that every city should have a lodge for wayfarers, combining humane treatment, enough though very simple food, clean bed, with insistence on a just return in labor from every able-bodied man, and a full measure of genuine sympathy for those seeking work, nay for all, and especially with best possible counsel where to seek employment? Boston has its great Labor Bureau in an adjoining building.

In fact, the soundness of this principle is unquestioned. The lot of the pauper must not be made too attractive. Yet I am led to ask whether Repression has not been guilty of a fatal error. Has not the system been left to such mere officialism as to be hard and depressing and at last brutalizing?

And this in two directions. First, to the worthy poor, so that all England is now vibrating in recoil from the sad lot of the old and worthy and suffering poor. Second, to the idle, the dissolute, the loafer and the tramp—the unworthy poor.

Do not present conditions in London and New York force us to face a new and graver problem? Yes, and the conditions in cities of the second rank also.

They will not live by Labor.

Do not the new race of brutally degraded paupers laugh to scorn the principle of the English Reform of 1834, that their lot shall not be made too attractive? Do they not defy differences of detail of poor law administration? Must we not reckon with the fact that they have resolved only upon one sure and certain thing, that they will not live by labor?

For proof I cite that malignant talisman, the story of the Jukes. If any have not read Dugdale's story, let them straightway do so, and see how the mere principle of repression, as society has applied it, in almshouse or jail or by denial of out-relief, failed to prevent a numerous and degraded offspring through many generations enjoying life in every imaginable form of degradation.

Or who can forget that similar story of horrors, "The Social Degradation of the Tribe of Ishmael" by Oscar C. McCulloch, five years ago, which will long endure as a powerful argument for speedy and radical reform, to which he gave the wisdom and enthusiasm and organizing energy of his noble life?

If you love statistics, count the number of applicants for relief in the great cities of this land or of England or Germany. Count the convicts annually sent to jail. How many are old repeaters? Can many cities surpass Boston in its list of offenders sent down to the House of Industry two or three or four or five score of times, till the leader of the throng is found perhaps boasting of his one hundred and forty sentences?

What a parody on punishment when the drunken ruffian whom I knew in the South Cove comes home from jail so reckless that he takes from Johnnie's feet the new boots his wife has bought, and the calico gown off his little daughter, to sell for rum, and so degraded that he likes the " Island" as well as his home.*

No wonder Governor Altgeld of Illinois, in his welcome through a friend to the Prison Commission last week, said arrests were too many, 70,000 a year in Chicago. Expand this mere statistic to its full meaning. The length and breadth of its lessons are too tremendous.

Has not the principle of repression miserably failed, when its effort to make the lot of the pauper not over eligible hardens tramps into such brutal degradation that in their game with society they seem just now to hold in their hands the winning cards, and yet on the other hand the worthy poor of England are in such straits that a great pension scheme throws its baleful shadow across the land? No doubt the conditions of labor there are less favorable than in the United States, wages lower and demand for labor slack, the army of Londoners unemployed increasing, and the lot of worthy poor in their old age appealing to every sympathy.

Do not misunderstand me. I do not object to repression, but to its failure. Why has it failed? Partly no doubt because the whole system of punishment by fine and by brief terms of confinement has failed to be deterrent. Sentimentality has also refused to permit punishment to be reasonably severe.

But the chief reason is that officialism has lacked the humane element absolutely necessary to save its influence from being mechanical and degrading.

Officialism without humanity can punish, but it only sinks the sufferer into worse debasement.

* "There are soft-hearted persons who would cry out in the name of philanthropy against indeterminate and cumulative sentences, and still more against the incarceration for life of vagabonds who have never done anything worse than go on in beggary, dirt, and drunkenness, and beget children doomed by their birth to idiocy, profligacy, or crime. Yet the sterilization of the unfit by life-long segregation is demanded in the interests of every hope of social morality, and it is a blot upon our civilization that men and women should be sent to the Island or the Bridewell, a dozen times a year for ten days or two weeks at a time, year in, year out, from their first commitment for drunkenness at eighteen or nineteen years of age, till they stumble at last into a pauper's grave. What a senseless mockery of corrective discipline to suppose that a drunkard of forty years' standing is going to be reformed by giving him ten days at the Island for the hundredth time !"—Father J. O. S. Huntington, in *Social Progress*, p. 186.

When also punishment ceases to prevent crimes, the problem assumes the most terrible aspect.

How such pauper criminals and criminal paupers can be restored to manhood, is so hard a question that theology sometimes fears it may be beyond the power of God.

No wonder that it is a supreme task for man. Yet this is the exact task which scientific charity now has got to accept—to deal fittingly with degraded need. Sympathy loves to aid the tender and attractive child. It hastens to the side of a widow in her woe. It cares for the sick or the suffering, for victims of fire, flood or other casualty, but it has not yet begun to do its duty to the pauper, and too often recoils with horror from that compound of pauperism and vice which is the worst phase of great city life.

Repression alone is a Failure.

Charitable work has two sides, the positive and constructive, and the negative or repressive.

The last is content to prevent overlapping, stop begging, discover imposture, cut off needless alms and reduce excessive outdoor relief.

The first aims at improving the condition of a family in any possible wise way, health, home, skill, work, trade, temperance, thrift, cheer, by personal influence, by organizations like stamp savings, or the Bedford Industrial Building, or by whatever other wise ways ingenuity can discover. This charity I will call constructive, and the other repressive. Who will not agree with me that repressive charity alone is hard, and that negative measures alone will fail? Only as charity learns to diagnose and discriminate, and then brings ingenuity to the various problems, with deep and genuine sympathy, boldly summoning to this imperative duty the social and christian powers of all good men and women in personal service, only so can charity succeed.

The height of this ideal for great cities, I know too well to seek to belittle. Only by stating it in its utmost demands can the mighty powers, as yet dormant or little aroused, of great cities be stirred to their tremendous task. Little cities delight in this duty, and can do it with a measure of success full of inspiration for us all.

Newport offers a picture of beautiful and devoted work, which I have always delighted to honor and to cite as encouraging proof of what will follow from thorough, patient, persistent, personal work, wisely guided and well done, in a small community, where the right influences may be applied in each different case.

Their C. O. S. report in 1880 shows the exact change and improvement in the condition of 220 families classified at the beginning and at the end of their first year's work.*

Success in Newport has continued. It is largely due to the devotion and wisdom of a few leaders who threw themselves into the new work, and to faithful friendly visiting.

Cities of the first size, like London, New York, Chicago and Philadelphia, differ in no more important respect from smaller cities than in their apparent inability to create and maintain " friendly visiting," on any large scale.†

This great topic will be worthily treated to-morrow. Enough here to say that this spirit underlies the best efforts to improve the conditions of the poor, whether *en masse*, or more especially in their individual needs, in many other cities from Brooklyn and Boston, down.

With absolute candor I must say, that in my judgment where cities are too large for personal relations of friendly sympathy and help—where distances are too great or absorption in the whirl of other cares is too intense, the chasm between the happy and the

---

* "The amount of outdoor relief given by the city for the year 1879-80 was about $2500 less than the previous year. This was partly due to the fact that the winter was an open one, and outdoor work was carried on to an unusual extent. For the current year, 1880-81, the appropriation for the Poor Department has been reduced by $2000. Up to December first there have been less than one-third as many applicants for relief as there were up to the same date in 1879.

"Last year we dealt chiefly on the necessity for the work, the need of investigation, the duty of withholding indiscriminate alms; this year we show you as the result of those principles, put in practice through some difficulties, that the worthy poor are well cared for, that homes have been bettered, characters improved, the unworthy and disabling spirit of pauperism checked, and above all, that *thrift*, one of the first duties of a citizen, is being taught, if slowly, yet surely."

†"What," says Miss Hill, speaking of the Charity Organization Society, " is its living call to us all? To come ourselves and help. In every Metropolitan district is its group of workers, men and women of every kind united in but one thought—how to help in wisest and most patient ways every case of want and suffering. Its remedy is the eternal remedy of patient care and thought and wisdom, brought to bear on men and women and children in their own homes by their neighbors. Money, yes, certainly, and *plenty* of it; but abiding and large gifts as citizens for fellow-citizens, sown like separate seeds with care, watched and watched over and given with ourselves to the real service of those we know and love."

wretched must go on growing more deep and terrible, till the condition of the pauper criminal mass becomes intolerable.

Chicago in this season of her glory, can she pardon critics who suggest that the star of friendly visiting is needed to make her diadem complete?

Philadelphia began with a goodly corps of friendly visitors, but has failed to maintain their efficiency or numbers.

New York has not yet conceived it possible to obtain friendly visitors in large numbers.

Read in Hon. A. S. Hewitt's admirable address at the opening of the United Charities Building in New York these words of the Charity Organization Society: "Its mission is by investigation and registration to guard the public against the abuse of benevolence and to devise and institute measures of prevention, in which reside the only solid hope of a permanent moral improvement."

Whereby it appears that gathering and using a large number of friendly visitors is not alluded to as any part of the New York conception of organized charity.

From London we read in the Charity Organization Review (July, 1893, p. 46), in an article perhaps written by Mr. Loch, entitled "American View of Charity Organization Society work":

"The second institution to which we should like to refer, as evidently held in high estimation by many leading Charity Organization Society thinkers, is that of friendly visitors.

"How, in America, they manage to obtain qualified friendly visitors on a large scale, we do not know.

"The World's Fair at Chicago will give any who wish the opportunity of noting the enthusiasm and hopefulness of the American societies at first hand."

Boston is perhaps the city where friendly visiting first became an essential part of the new charity. It formed no part of the original movement in London in 1869. It had been done in Boston on a small scale in ward seven, by the co-operative society of visitors before the organization of the Associated Charities; but that body first made formal and definite announcement that friendly visiting would be seriously undertaken in a large way.*

"The great work for friendly visitors" was here explained and

* See inaugural address of Robert Treat Paine, March 12, 1879, when chosen president of the Associated Charities of Boston, "Charity Organization," No. 6, Publications of Boston Associated Charities.

developed substantially upon the same lines that it has followed to the present time.

The principle was thus stated in my address at the Social Science Conference, at Saratoga, in September, 1880 ("Not Alms, but a Friend." No. 17):

" Whenever any family has fallen so low as to need relief, send to them at least one friend—a patient, true, sympathizing, firm friend—. to do for them all that a friend can do to discover and remove the causes of their dependence, and to help them up into independent self-support and self-respect."

Let me call attention to one fact. The original draft of the Boston society authorized giving relief, if it could be procured from no other source. But this clause was stricken out, owing to the opposition of relief societies, and, as it seems to me, by the finger of God. Visitors were compelled to devote their thought and sympathy in other directions, so admirably described by Miss Octavia Hill, with whatever measure of success has been attained.

Fourteen years' experience justifies more strongly with each new year's results the encouraging claim that, in almost every case, a friendly visitor can learn how to help, and can often succeed in helping into independence, a family in distress, if he (or usually she) goes into their home and learns the truth, going there not to give alms, but prohibited usually from giving alms, and therefore forced to study how to aid the family in permanent ways.

Statistics year after year show in how many varied ways real help has been given.

Brooklyn is the largest city which has successfully developed and maintained efficiently the work of friendly visiting. See report of Brooklyn Bureau of Charities for 1892, p. 16, for an interesting organization of their visitors for study as a class, and an admirable statement of the

Duties of Friendly Visitors.*

" It shall be the duty of a friendly visitor to visit the poor and distressed as a friend ; to examine, in the spirit of kindness, the causes of their trouble ; to do what can be done to remove those causes ; to become acquainted with the ability which each may have, and to aid in developing it and in finding ways in which it may be employed in self-help ; through friendly intercourse, sympathy and direction, to encourage self-dependence, industry and thrift ; to recommend whatever may be possible and wise to alleviate the sufferings of those

*Art. 9, Sec. 2 of By-laws.

whose infirmities cannot be cured or removed ; if material aid be necessary, to obtain it from existing organizations as far as possible ; and in every case to promote in all practical ways the physical and moral improvement of the families in the visitor's charge."

Mr. Alfred T. White, president of the Brooklyn Bureau of Charities, has recently described the excellent work done in that great city. ("The Friendly Visitor's Opportunity," Charities Review, April, 1893, p. 329.)

"It may appear," he says, "a slow process to eliminate poverty piece by piece from our great cities, and it is natural to long for some quicker way, but *there is no way which does not reach to and touch the character of the individual poor. . . .* Surely there never was a time when so many were interested in the elevation of those less favored than themselves."

"Where is the call so clear to us in city life as this need of our neighbors for our personal consideration and service ?—a need doubly commanding since the organization of charity has so greatly increased the possibilities of successful interest and effort" (p. 331).

Here in Mr. White's words is the supreme aim and need of friendly visiting : to "touch the character of the individual poor."

Radical Remedies.

What reply has scientific charity to the question whether the grand aggregate of degraded pauperism in great cities is to increase or decrease, when the forces that work for evil are all weighed :—

The unemployed, an army in London, numerous in New York, not many usually in smaller cities ;

The inefficient, always in all cities a great number vibrating between work and idleness ;

Paupers resolved only on one thing, that they hate work ;

The terrible element of vice, and the great army of criminals, who war upon society, not deterred by present penalties ;

Then add the causes of sickness and low vitality ;

In some cities all these evils aggregated into great masses.

Simply and surely this first, that merely to deal, no matter how wisely, with single cases of distress or crime as they arise, is infinitely insufficient.

Nay, worse, Prof. W. G. Tucker in his Phi Beta Oration at Harvard, last June, compels us to seek more radical cure, by more radical measures, when he says: " THE PHILANTHROPY WHICH IS

CONTENT TO RELIEVE THE SUFFERER FROM WRONG SOCIAL CON-
DITIONS, POSTPONES THE PHILANTHROPY WHICH IS DETERMINED,
AT ANY COST, TO RIGHT THOSE CONDITIONS."

"Who does not know," says Professor H. C. Adams, "that much of our so-called philanthropy *tends to perpetuate those conditions* which seem to make philanthropy necessary? Father Huntington has rendered a marked service in the strong protest which he urges against the charities of our day. He shows to the discerning mind that a philanthropy which is satisfied when the cry of the sufferer is hushed has no place among the permanent forces of social progress." (Social Progress, p. x.)

This brings me to the main purpose of my paper. Has not the new charity organization movement too long been content to aim at a system to relieve or even uplift judiciously single cases without asking if there are not prolific causes permanently at work to create want, vice, crime, disease and death; and whether these causes may not be wholly or in large degree eradicated?

If such causes of pauperism exist, how vain to waste our energies on single cases of relief, when society should rather aim at removing the prolific sources of all the woe.

THE FOUR GREAT CAUSES OF PAUPERISM AND OF DEGRADED CITY LIFE HAVE LONG SEEMED TO ME TO BE THESE:
1. FOUL HOMES.
2. INTOXICATING DRINK.
3. NEGLECT OF CHILD LIFE.
4. INDISCRIMINATE ALMSGIVING.

Who can closely study the conditions of life among the poor of cities without seeing these malignant forces working day and night to create all forms of degraded life?

Who then will not agree with me that resolute and heroic measures must be taken in all large cities, before conditions become hopeless?

What happier augury can come from this conference than the conviction that all the forces of scientific and christian charity must combine to extirpate these outrages upon the virtue, health and happiness of the masses of the people?

Charles Booth* counts up twenty-three principal causes of pauperism:

* "Pauperism and the Endowment of Old Age," p. 9.

Crime, vice, drink, laziness, pauper association, heredity, mental disease, temper, incapacity, early marriage, large family, extravagance, lack of work, trade misfortune, restlessness, no relations, death of husband, desertion, death of father or mother, sickness, accident, ill luck, old age.

But may not all these twenty-three causes, except old age, accident and death, come from wretched life in a foul home, or drunkenness, or neglect when the victim was a child, or indiscriminate giving of alms?

Yes, these four causes are the primary, potent and prolific sources of the degraded life in cities. All of them are remediable in different ways and to different degrees.

How long will it be possible for the public to witness these outrages against itself and against the welfare and the rights of our poorer citizens, without such indignant wrath as to cleanse them away from city life?

Foul Homes.

Which of the two causes dragging down the conditions of life among the.masses, foul homes or intoxicating drink, is more potent, I do not know. Each leads surely to the other.

Everywhere the conviction gains ground that it is impossible to elevate the conditions of the lower class of working people above the condition of their homes. If they are left in foul and overcrowded slums or damp basements or dilapidated barracks, it is too much to expect them to be virtuous or self-respecting or independent. These rotten slums are hotbeds which propagate low life, shattering the health of occupants and so promoting pauperism, loosening the morals and so promoting vice and crime; and perhaps worst of all in their poisonous influence on the children who grow up in them too often without virtue, self-respect, health or hope.

We all rejoice to see that the increasing interest of society in the homes of the people is taking shape in many efficient ways.

What I believe to be of great importance to this cause, is that its close relations to the whole pauper problem of great cities should be recognized; so that all observers may see and know that the two causes are only one cause; and the friends of each may see the larger relations of their work and gain power and motive from this consciousness that they are not merely dealing with details, but rather are shaping the conditions of the present and future welfare of the people.

A Higher Standard of Habitability.

If the aim of all charitable work among the poor is a general improvement of their condition, so the aim of all who are interested in their homes must be to establish a higher standard of habitability.

Grand impulse has been given to this movement in England by four persons, Lord Shaftesbury, Octavia Hill, Sir Sydney Waterlow and George Peabody.

Lord Shaftesbury began the movement to improve the homes of working people in 1842, of which time he says: "So little were people acquainted with the state of the houses in which laboring people dwelt, that we treated the question as an entirely new one. Many persons then thought that we were undertaking a quixotic work, and that there was really very little that required amendment. But I am happy to say that the improvement of the condition of the working classes in a domiciliary aspect is now almost a trite subject."

He was the first witness before the Royal Commission of 1884, and his words describing the horrors of the abodes of the poor shocked all England. When he died in 1886, full of honors and beloved of all, he had no juster claim to honor and love than his life-long services for the homes of plain people.

Octavia Hill came next in order of time, but she stands supreme thus far in the world's history among and above all others who have thought, labored and lived for and among the poor, to improve their homes.

Octavia Hill and Sir Sydney Waterlow are entitled to rank among the great discoverers of this world, now that sociology takes its due rank, above all natural sciences, next only to the knowledge of God.

Miss Hill discovered and has taught the world the true relations of landlord and tenant. She has created a normal school in this art. Men and women from this country as well as England try to learn the sweet and beautiful and wonderfully potent, uplifting influence which she and her band of rent collectors have been exerting for years among the very humblest classes of tenants in some of the gloomiest courts of London. Let sociologists watch the spread of this new power through the world, and teach it to every school.

Sir Sydney Waterlow's discovery ranks next in value to working-men. Risking first his own means alone, he learned and proved that even in a great city like London, where land values are high, model tenement-houses, built with all reasonable conveniences and comforts, can be made a commercial success. This discovery introduces into modern civilization a potent force to improve the homes of the people. Its effect has been so powerful as to have changed the face of London. Capital has been attracted by the millions of pounds sterling; one company alone of which Sir Sydney is president, " The Improved Industrial Dwellings Company," has built thirty blocks in different parts of London at a cost of $5,000,000, and offers to some 30,000 souls homes not devoid of æsthetic charm, at moderate rents, which yield five per cent. on the capital.

Alfred T. White has achieved a like success with model blocks in Brooklyn, on a large scale.*

The Boston Coöperative Building Company has in 22 years provided 76 houses, with 962 rooms, for 325 families, at a cost of $400,000 in Boston. These tenements are eagerly sought by intelligent tenants, and the investment has been most successful in all respects.

Three Agencies.

Three agencies directly deal with the task of fitly housing the people:

1. Philanthropic agencies, which aim to improve the condition both of tenants and of the tenements they occupy.

2. Economic agencies providing decent homes, often in model buildings.

3. Municipal agencies aiming to abolish the worst evils and to destroy foul homes.

High above each and all of these three agencies in its influence and promise of grand results, I place the rising ambition of workingmen themselves to own their own homes.†

If this laudable ambition is lacking among the lowest class, so also do both of the powerful agencies at work to provide model homes, whether by philanthropic or invested capital of which I have just spoken, shoot over their heads.

---

* Described in his "Improved Dwellings for the Laboring Classes," 1879, and "Better Homes for Workingmen," 1885, Conference of Charities.

† H. M. Hyndman, of the Social Democratic Federation, addressing the Labor Commission in England, objects to thrift in workingmen, because it only makes them small capitalists, buttressing the class they should supplant and intensifying the competition from which they suffer!—[Econ. Journal, March, 1893, p. 169.]

The agency which must be invoked to rescue the very poor, whether virtuous and struggling, or degraded and indifferent, is *the municipal power to destroy utterly unfit abodes of habitations.*

Sad, indeed, is the fact that when charity aids some wretched family to move out of a vile basement or dark and nasty slum, presently some other like family moves in.

The growth of public sentiment towards practical unanimity in this decision has been marked by important measures in London, Glasgow and other cities of Great Britain.

The London Charity Organization Society reports on the dwellings of the poor record this progress.   (1873 and 1881.)

I will only quote here the judgment of one man, which has aided in this enlightened movement.

Dr. Gairdner, Medical Officer of Health for Glasgow, wrote:

"I believe that nuisance removal, epidemic inspection, cleansing, ventilating, and suppression of overcrowding, are all good up to a certain point . . . *But in relation to the persistent and slowly accumulating evils of our great towns, the social rottenness, so to speak, that is in them all, these are mere surface-measures. . . . I am putting it roundly, perhaps you will even say paradoxically, but I am stating the result of a deep conviction, when I say that the destructive part of the duty of the authorities is of more importance, if possible, than the constructive ; that the first and more essential step is to get rid of the existing haunts of moral and physical degradation.*"*

This movement to destroy the slums is under powerful headway.

Rome, Paris, London, Glasgow, New York and Boston, and so on in different degree, have all set to work to exterminate those rotten spots or foul abodes which tainted human life.

I place this movement at the head as the most powerful force conducing to improve the condition of the abject poor.

How it can be made more thoroughly effective is the most important question I may send home with each of my hearers.

Pass in review our co-workers, and then let us see how they can be strengthened.

The medical profession to a man, economists, ministers and churches, philanthropists and workers among the poor, novelists and the press, and last and most efficacious, boards of health.

New York gave a powerful impulse by the investigation and report of the board of health in 1887.

* Report of the Dwellings Committee of the Charity Organization Society, 1873, p. 9.

Boston did the same by the report of Professor Dwight Porter in 1889, and Gen. F. A. Walker, whose judgment carries weight not surpassed in the United States, at the meeting where this report was presented, stated:

"I believe that a true view of the economy of state action may not infrequently disclose the occasion for saving a great deal of interference and a great deal of state action, in subsequent stages, by putting the firm hand of government upon the very sources of evil, and applying the powers of the state to crush out social mischief in its inception. I confess that it has for some time seemed to me increasingly probable that the social philosophy of the age would soon come to recognize the housing of the very poor as *the* point at which the remedial action of the government may be applied, not only with the highest effect upon the happiness and health of the community, but actually with large resulting reductions from the sum of state action and governmental authority.

"It would be an act, either of monstrous ignorance or of monstrous impudence on the part of any man, contemplating the changes of public sentiment which have taken place on this subject within the last fifteen, ten, and five years, to put his foot down and say, 'Thus far and no farther will I go towards enlarging the functions of the state.' In view of the great developments of the immediate past, the most likely thing in regard to each one of us by turns, is that, in five, ten, or fifteen years from now, he will be occupying a position on this subject very different from that he now anticipates. Yet I confess I have of late been coming rapidly to the conviction that ere long there will be a general consent of conservative citizens, in every enlightened state, to regard as thoroughly good politics all interference by law which may be necessary to prevent any portion of the people from living in houses which are unfit for human habitation, residence in which is incompatible with health, or with social or personal decency.

"I expect soon to see the time come when the commonwealth of Massachusetts shall declare that no one of its citizens, under whatever plea of poverty, shall have his home where he has not a sufficient access of fresh air and of God's sunlight, and where the conditions as to drainage and the disposal of refuse are not such as to afford reasonable security for the health of the individual, and to protect society against communicable disease. I believe that not only will the law of the commonwealth say this, which, indeed, is little more than it now says, but that the public sentiment of the community will have been so educated on this subject as to support the officers of the law in whatever rigorous and painful measures may be required for the thorough, systematic and unrelenting enforcement of the most advanced sanitary requirements."

Destroy the Slums.

No movement can be inaugurated in any city, more potent to improve the conditions of the most wretched poor and to cut off the supply of degraded pauperism, than the movement to destroy the slums.

Probably no city has been wholly inactive. But I am sure no large city in this country has begun to act up to the standard required for the health or morals of the poor, or by economy to the public, or by principles of justice and right.

Boards of health have power probably in all cities to vacate dwellings unfit for human habitation. All that is needed is *aroused public interest* to learn the unspeakable horrors of the homes of the wretched poor to-day, and then to insist on a *higher standard of habitability*.

Boards of health will follow the public command and the public conscience.

Boston is taking active steps in this direction. A number of public-spirited men and women have organized a " Better Dwellings Society," which has directed attention to many intolerable rotten spots. The board of health is acting with judicious firmness in vacating unfit homes below an accepted standard, which has been steadily rising for a score of years in compliance with enlightened public judgment.

Yet Boston has many terrible abodes of vice and wretchedness still left where all circumstances concur for evil life.

It is a cause of surprise and regret to find in the reports of charity organization or relieving societies of different cities so little attention paid to this supreme yet eradicable cause of pauperism and crime.*

New York finds this problem of housing the poor more difficult than any other city of the world. The report of " The Association for Improving the Condition of the Poor " (1892, p. 60), describes their action as to homes of the poor, viz.:

516 inspections,
251 reports to the board of health,
760 causes for complaints, and of these
    76 were for filthy premises,
    54 were for dirty yards,
    27 were for wet cellars.

Yet the surprising thing is that only thirty complaints seem to point at radical evils, " Buildings generally dilapidated." Even here action hardly seems to be aimed at, of *wholly vacating* the buildings as fatally and hopelessly unfit.

* Nor any allusion to it in that superb history by Mr. Kellogg last evening of all the C. O. S. work for these twenty years.

The Pittsburg report of "The Association for Improving the Condition of the Poor" (1892, p. 8) states that visitors made 20,915 visits to the poor, visiting "homes in basements that are *unhealthy through dampness and no sunshine*, and to people who live in old boats." Yet no fierce protests of righteous indignation are made to boards of health.

Chicago will, I hope, permit a few frank words about this terrible source of pauperism.

The report for 1892 of the "Chicago Relief Society" states:

"The general circumstances and conditions of the poor in Chicago are much more favorable than in most large cities in this or any other country. The proportion of paupers is much less. Most of the working class in Chicago live in their little cottages, in many cases owned by their occupants, or in comfortable rooms in houses usually occupied by two or three families and seldom by more than four or five, at rents from five dollars to seven dollars monthly."

Yet on the other hand, the last report I have seen of the "United Hebrew Relief Society" of Chicago states, (1885–86) under the heading of "Tenement Houses for the Poor":

"Sickness has been deplorably prevalent. The evil may be traced to the unwholesome habitations in which the poor generally reside. These dwellings not only destroy physical vigor, but they stifle the mind and blunt the morals. They are inimical to the cause of education as they are dangerous to bodily health."*

As you ride out to the World's Fair to see the latest triumph of architecture and art in these days, look down from the South Side Elevated Railroad (the Alley road, so-called) near the 21st street station on the west, or again at 26th street, at the wretched slums below you. The protracted picture of conditions of intolerable life points my argument that the problem of poor relief in great cities knows no possible solution till these hotbeds which propagate degraded pauper life are absolutely abolished.

---

* On June 8, 1893, I visited some of the wretched abodes of the very poor in Chicago with an officer kindly detailed by Chief of Police Mr. McClaughry. The sights were too sad for words. One cellar was so poisoned with sewer gas and the effluvia of leaking water-closets that the tenant said, in not wholly crushed despair, "I have lost one child here and don't propose to lose another," (No. 359 Clark Street). Another utterly dilapidated barrack, (543 Clark Street) about 30 × 90 feet, swarming with Italian children from eight to ten families, has long been utterly unfit for human beings to live in.

Would to God my words could strengthen the conviction of every delegate to this Congress, as he goes home to his own city, that slums must be abolished.

So might public interest be more keenly aroused and the good cause gain momentum, as one city after another joined in judicious and resolute action.

Intoxicating Drink.

Intoxicating drink is the second great cause of pauperism, crime and many other wretched conditions of degraded life.

The temperance reform makes perceptible headway, although the most powerful passions of mankind oppose its progress. In the last ten years England has seen a great improvement in the conditions of the working people in this respect.

In the United States prohibition or high license or restricted license, or the Gothenburg system, or that new state system in South Carolina, or local option which secures no license in many cities and towns, all these movements mark a great popular awakening to the terrible influence of drunkenness upon the welfare of the people.

Their improved conditions where temperance prevails are so evident, that for instance in Massachusetts the smaller cities are making steady progress in the direction of voting for no license in the annual struggle. The contest in such states as Iowa and Kansas marks the growing popular condemnation of the evil. In spite of all this progress, more or less visible throughout the civilized world, the gigantic power of the rum-shop to drag its victims down rages through the world with insolent defiance of the sympathy and intelligence of good citizens to discover and execute any efficient method of suppression.

My object here is to propose and stimulate an alliance of these two forces, the friends of temperance and all the other forces working to improve the conditions of the poor. Such an alliance will strengthen both and lead each party to see the broader scope of their task.

Neglect of Children.

The third prolific cause of pauperism is found in the conditions of neglect or maltreatment of child-life in great cities.*

* Hon. A. S. Hewitt, in his address at the opening of the United Charities Building of New York (*Charities Review*, April, 1893, p. 304), says : " In this

Two specifications of the boy's indictment against society have been mentioned. Absence of playgrounds almost compels him to choose, in a great city, between stupidity and crime. Absence of manual training forces him to live by his wits or by commonest forms of labor.* But I wish especially to draw attention to the need of a great development of charity in the treatment of widows with young children.

Large cities are disputing about the comparative merits of systems, all of which are so unworthy of our age, and so cruel to the mother and dangerous to the welfare of the child that the time has come for worthier treatment by the best method science and sympathy can devise.

No one will deny the influence growing out of different systems of dealing with this class of children. The systems in England, New York, and Massachusetts are radically different. No one of them can escape condemnation.

England very largely refuses out-relief to the widow with children, breaks up the family, and sends one or more of the children into the district school or into that department of the almshouse called the industrial school, usually a vast institution where children are gathered by hundreds. The mother is left with only one or two children whom she may be able to support.

Am I wrong in ranking the English system as least favorable for the happiness of the home or the future welfare of the child, unjust

---

city a large number of children of both sexes live in an atmosphere of poverty and vice, and even crime, which educates them to be paupers and criminals instead of training them to become honest workmen and good citizens. And for this result, which is generally no fault of their own, they are punished, and, along with them, the industrious class of the community is also punished by taxation for the support of poorhouses, hospitals and criminals. Gangs of young men not yet twenty-one years of age are to be found in many parts of the city, who, not having been permitted to learn trades, or having been denied the opportunity to follow some useful occupation, have grown up in idleness, and expend their animal energies in excesses which make them a terror to the neighborhood and a trial to the police, the only barrier between them and crime. In time most of them necessarily become criminals and they are very sure to breed criminals. The public is not dealing with this great menace to society either with sense or firmness."

* Which alcoves in all the vast and varied World's Fair are richer in promise for the welfare of the coming generation of men than the alcoves full of the results of manual training in many cities?

to both mother and child, and not worthy of the Christian philanthropy of the age? *

The New York system has no provision of outdoor relief for such a family of children, and resembles the English method in that the family must be broken up, but the children instead of being sent to great public institutions, are distributed among private institutions which receive a per capita allowance from the State ; tempting them to promote this destruction of family life.

This method seems to me next to merit condemnation because it allows money consideration to break up families, even where a worthy mother is struggling to preserve her child and her home, and because secondly these children are condemned to institution life, and as yet, as Mrs. Lowell of New York says,† "It is to be remembered that the poorest home, unless it be a degraded one, is better than any institution."

Mrs. Lowell brings this further charge:

"That unfortunately in New York city at least, the custom has grown up of requiring that judges shall commit children to private institutions, as a necessary condition of obtaining payment from the city for their support This undoubtedly is a dangerous proceeding, since the familiarization with a court of law tends to destroy the dread of arrest, which should be fostered as one of the strongest deterrent influences against crime. To bring a child before a judge in a criminal court in order to secure his entrance into an institution of charity is a most unwise measure."

The dependent child problem has attained great proportions in New York city where 15,697 boys and girls are supported at an

---

* Quest. 5838.— What system would you like to see substituted ?

Mrs. Charles.—"I should like to see boarding-out as far as possible, and the plan of taking children from their mothers and sending them to a district school, by way of giving them poor relief, I think is a mistake. It would be far better, in my opinion, I having had very considerable experience, to give the poor widows a little outdoor relief, and allow them to keep their children at home. It acts in this way also upon the mothers. They find that they can part with their children and throw off their responsibilities; and it is not right for any one to be allowed to throw off the responsibility she has voluntarily incurred. That is another evil of the district school system, that poor law guardians will give widows relief in the shape of sending their children to these schools; then the widows are free, and I am sorry to say I have known many instances where the widows have not conducted themselves as well as they would have done if they had had the responsibility of their children at home."—Report House of Lords Com., Poor Law Relief, Aug. '88, p. 641.

† Public Relief and Private Charity, p. 74.

annual charge of $1,500,000 out of a population of 1,600,000 in 1889, or a proportion of 1 to 100. While Massachusetts had 1951 dependent children out of 2,000,000 souls, or 1 to 1025, Pennsylvania had 10,000 dependent children, 1 to 450, while Michigan had only 200 dependent children, or 1 to 10,000.*

The Massachusetts system aims to keep families together where there is a not totally unfit home, and if relief is not obtained from some other source, the overseers of the poor give, and continue, needed relief to a widow until the children grow to an age when their labor added to their mother's earnings can support the home.†

Many competent judges cannot believe that the Massachusetts system works well for the child, though it is certainly more humane for the mother than the system either in England or New York.

The poisonous influence of our outdoor pauper relief must be felt upon the child's character in many cases, yet the family is kept together, and the children are brought up under the loving care and influence of their mother, free from the injurious influence of any institution, and especially escaping the almshouse brand.

Critics who urge the total abolition of outdoor relief may claim that this system works badly even in this class of cases, and sometimes with justice when pauper relief leaves upon the child a pauper taint.

Do you ask whether in Massachusetts we think our system the best and are resolved to maintain it? I answer frankly, *No.*

Here is a better method which I believe to be the best. Aid the mother to maintain her home, provide adequate relief, but free from any pauper poison. Let it go from her church, from some private society, from some benevolent individual. Let it go as from the hand of a friend, as the circumstances of each special case may suggest to be best to the friendly visitor who undertakes the continuous task. Shame on the charity of any city which shrinks from this duty.

This is the reform which in the judgment of many of us in Massachusetts, should be engrafted upon our public relief system.

* Report State Board of Char. of N. Y., 1890, p. 33.

† Prof. Francis Wayland in his paper on outdoor relief [1877] gives the weight of his judgment in favor of outdoor relief, especially in " cases where the head of the family is removed by death or prostrated by sickness, and where there is reasonable prospect of the mother being able to keep her family together and ultimately maintain them " (page 9).

This is the class of cases which has always been used most effectively by our overseers of the poor in advocating the necessity of outdoor relief. Taking from the overseers this class of cases would greatly facilitate its total abolition, or great reduction. This is the special reform which I strenuously advocated in the report of the Associated Charities of Boston in 1882, basing my argument upon the analysis of 938 families in the care of one conference, of whom only 370 received aid in 1884–5 or 1885–6. Only 119 of those were aided in the last year by the overseers of the poor, and of these only 20 received over $20 each, of whom four were aided because there were children, receiving in all $159.50.*

The result of this analysis was that a few thousand dollars of benevolent funds would replace out-relief to this class of widows and orphans, and provide for them in the best possible way, by judicious aid from a friendly hand, usually not known either to child or neighbor. How long will it be before charity fully assumes this loving but imperative duty to the widow with her children?

I have not yet exhausted the list of wrongs which boys and girls suffer at the hands of society, often thereby started on a wrong road through life.

Enough if I can show that neglect and maltreatment of the "child problem in great cities" is one of the prolific causes of pauperism and crime which must be remedied if society is in earnest to improve the conditions of the poor.†

Indiscriminate Almsgiving.

Indiscriminate almsgiving is the fourth and a most potent cause of pauperism. It has been considered in these conferences from the start. Yet we have much to learn. Charles Lamb is its only defender, who says "Give, asking no questions." Fowle states the

---

* Boston is in recent years devoting more thought and care to the child problem and with excellent results. See reports of *Children's Aid Society*, *North Bennet Street Home*, and *Boys' Institute of Industry*.

† In "*Poverty and its Relief in the U. S.*," p. 14, Dr. Aschrott says : "The societies for organizing charities took up this movement, and to their inspiration it is due that the number of charitable societies which care for poor, deserted, neglected and exposed children, has increased in a very rapid manner. All America is now covered with a network of so-called children's aid societies. There is scarcely a state in the Union in which there is not at least one such society to be found."

rule to be "that the amount of pauperism is in proportion to the amount of relief."

Let me avoid the vexed question whether total abolition of public outdoor relief is judicious, in order to fasten attention on the principle universally accepted by experts, that as lax relief has created pauperism, so adherence by private as well as public relief, especially by the charitable public, to rigid rules, excluding all but those whose need is well founded, has greatly lessened both the number of paupers as well as the cost of relief.*

Brooklyn, with its dramatic and wonderful reform, little Brookline† also, and several great English unions, all teach the same . lesson.

---

*The Boston Commission of 1878 on the treatment of the poor, declared (page 5) :

"Experience shows that a steady persistence in limiting relief to support in some public institution, where labor is required under reasonable restraint, diminishes the amount of outdoor relief without any proportional increase of indoor relief. The applicant supports himself, or is provided for by his friends."

But the committee are not ready to recommend the abolition of outdoor relief, but only that rules for its sharp limitation should be rigidly adhered to, and they say (page 8) that the "rules may be relaxed for recent widows with young children."

† The experience of Brookline shows how effectively an improved system may reduce pauperism.

Mrs. James M. Codman states that outdoor relief had amounted to $9,000 for a population of 6,000, and that after careful investigation had somewhat reduced the numbers, there were still 355 persons on the list of paupers. After strong opposition, it was decided to build an almshouse, and "notice was then given that in future no rent would be paid for any one, no fuel allowed, no able-bodied man would be helped in any way, and outdoor relief would be given only in very exceptional cases."

"Now for the results. Within a year the number of persons relieved fell to 53, no able-bodied man has ever even applied for help, the number at the almshouse has never exceeded seven, and this number was only at the time when the experiment was tried of caring for some of the harmless insane there, an experiment speedily abandoned. While the population of the town has doubled, the amount expended for the relief of the poor is now $6,000, of which $2,500 goes to pay the board of our largely increased number of insane in the state institutions, leaving $3,500 the amount actually expended for the poor; $1,500 for the almshouse, and the balance for outdoor relief in our own town, and largely for temporary relief of our poor in other towns and cities. With all this there has been no suffering."— *Conference of Charities and Correction*, 1891, page 47.

Yet the recent facts must give us pause.   Rev. S. A. Barnett, of St. Jude's, Whitechapel, the head of Toynbee Hall, states that the effort to provide pensions by private charity for the aged worthy poor must be counted a failure; since it is with great difficulty that 100 pensioners in the three East End missions of London, where out-relief is given up, are provided by appeals through the whole of London.

Again, the conviction that the lot of the poor in England is too hard and their treatment under the poor law too severe has caused such reaction that a pension scheme of $85,000,000 a year hangs in the air, and a Royal Commission has been created to consider the condition of the poor.

Of course the lot of the laborer in England cannot be compared with that in this country.   Still let us beware of any extreme attack upon outdoor relief which shall result in violent reaction.

Three reforms of the abuses of outdoor relief should receive universal sanction, and will effect in very large measure the end which all parties desire: dealing with the unworthy, those out of work and the inefficient.

First. To the unworthy, rigid prohibition of all relief, public or private, so that, abandoning all hope of it, they shall seek their own support.   This includes the lazy, idle, shiftless, extravagant or vicious paupers, as also in most cases those with relatives or friends.

Second. The provision for men or women out of work demands most serious study of ablest economists and statesmen.   The magnitude of the problem in London, present and prospective, affrights the imagination.   One road leads to danger; permanent municipal industries which would attract the shiftless into larger masses, whereas the only safety lies in scattering them through the community.*

Not of course that they should starve.   They must be dealt with as individuals.   How great cities like London, Chicago and New York escape the dilemma of cruelty or of indiscriminate almsgiving, without friendly visitors in goodly number, we in Boston do not know.

The third and grand reform aims to recreate the inefficient, always in great cities a numerous class, into self-support by skill and cheer,

---

* Beware, however, of aiding by alms able-bodied men or women.

and to save them from gratuitous relief as deadly poison.*   I cannot learn what New York, Chicago or London do with this class except to leave them to struggle with the law that the unfit must perish.

Charles Booth in his brilliant chapter on " The Unemployed," expresses regret that the problems of the working class are often confounded with the problems of the inefficient.

To confound these two problems is to render the solution of both impossible.†

The problem of poor relief in cities has no department where results are more largely dependent on the most judicious treatment of both science and sympathy.

To the inefficient, when out of work and in need, nothing can be worse than alms and doles, dragging them down into paupers. Nothing can be better than cheer, counsel and assistance to gain needed skill and courage.

Professor Franklin H. Giddings, in his essay on the Ethics of Social Progress, develops a new law of the evolution of society, or rather of a new possible slavery, with startling power :

" Neither oppression nor greed has been at any time the first cause of legal bondage or of economic dependence.   Both are secondary causes, induced by experiences with a slavery already existent.

" Modern civilization does not require, it does not even need, the drudgery of needle-women or the crushing toil of men in a score of life-destroying occupations.   If these wretched beings should drop out of existence and no others stood ready to fill their places, the economic activities of the world would not greatly suffer.   A thousand devices latent in inventive brains would quickly make good any momentary loss.   The true view of the facts is that these people continue to exist after the kinds of work that they know how to perform have ceased to be of any considerable value to society.   Society continues to employ them for a remuneration not exceeding the cost of getting the work done in some other and perhaps better way.

" The economic law here referred to is one that has been too much neglected in scientific discussions.   It ought to be repeated and illustrated at every opportunity, for at present it stands in direct contradiction to current prepossessions.   We are told incessantly that unskilled labor creates the wealth of the world.

" It would be nearer the truth to say that large classes of unskilled labor hardly create their own subsistence.   The laborers that have no adaptiveness,

---

* " I consider it the greatest problem in philanthropy to make human beings who are capable of work out of individuals who otherwise must become paupers, and in this way to create useful members of society."—*My Views on Philanthropy, by Baron de Hirsch*, p. 1, North American Review, July, 1891.

† Miss Jane Addams, in Social Progress, page 55.

that bring no new ideas to their work, that have no suspicion of the next best thing to turn to in an emergency, might be much better identified with the dependent classes than with the wealth-creators. Precisely the same economic law offers the true interpretation of ancient slavery. In strictness civilization did not rest on slavery. It was not in any true sense maintained by slavery. The conditions that created the civilization created economic dependence, and they are working in the same way, with similar results, to-day.

"Ancient civilization accepted the dependence, and utilized it in the crude form of slavery. Modern civilization accepts and utilizes it in the slightly more refined form of the wages system. Certain great social tasks of creative organization have always confronted our race. The enforced effort to achieve them has been history's great competitive examination. The slaves and serfs have been those who have failed. The first great necessity was social unity, the power to act together in a disciplined way, and the first slaves were those who could not create a sufficiently coherent social organization to sustain a growing civilization. They had to make way before others who were equal to that great achievement, and they became slaves not solely nor chiefly because of a conqueror's tyranny, but primarily because slavery or serfdom was practically the only economic disposition that could be made of them. To-day social unity has been in good measure established and the world has entered on yet larger undertakings. The condition and assurance of freedom to-day is the ability to devise new things, to create new opportunities, to make not only two blades of grass grow where one grew before, but to make a hundred kinds of grass grow where before grew only one kind.

"Accordingly, the practically unfree task-workers of this present time are those who, unaided, can accomplish none of these new things. They are those who might do well in old familiar ways, but who have nothing to turn to when their ways cease to be of value to the world. To live they must force depreciated services upon society on any terms that society can continue to pay. They are unfree task-workers not because society chooses to oppress them, but because society has not yet devised or stumbled upon any other disposition to make of them. Civilization, therefore, is not cruel. It is ever supporting and trying in many ways to utilize the wrecks and failures of its own imperfect past."

What can withstand this new inroad of slavery, this sinking of the unskilled into social bondage, but a thorough system of teaching skill to the inefficient, supplemented by almost infinite social sympathy for those who fail?

One of the best standards to-day to test the progress of constructive Christian charity of the various towns and cities of our own or any country, is to see what practical measures have been devised to convert the inefficient into an efficient worker.

Charity sewing-schools were rather a poor start. Laundries followed, and promise well.

In Boston, Trinity Church has for a dozen years carried on Trinity Laundry to teach skill and provide work, employing about a hundred different women annually, and paying out in wages about $3,500 each year.

Several other agencies are at work also expressly aiming to teach skill in some handiwork to adults who desire this aid, some of whom should rank as inefficient, while others may have used well all their opportunities, but are ambitious of further progress.

Then the Wells Memorial Workingmen's Institute has for years offered free evening instruction to journeymen seeking knowledge in their own trades. The class on the steam engine attracts mechanics to the weekly lecture from towns within a radius of twenty miles, while that on electricity given by Prof. Puffer to over a hundred of the journeymen working in all departments of that difficult art, is perhaps the most interesting attempt to aid workingmen to increased skill.

The Cooper Institute in New York, and the Pratt Institute in Brooklyn, train young men before they begin work. So also do Col. Auchmuty's admirable trade schools in New York. The mechanic art schools of Philadelphia, Baltimore, Boston, St. Louis and Chicago, are full of promise for the increased skill and larger earnings and brighter future of the youth of our land.

Has all of this nothing to do with my subject? Everything to do with it. I will be silent in despair, unless we who want to solve the problem of our cities' poverty can hope to see our whole land tingle with the fixed and intelligent resolve that the boys and the girls as they grow up, shall have, besides such training of the brain in books as they can get and hold, such training also of all the rest of the body, the various senses, especially the eye and the finger, as will fill the land with artistic and skilled mechanics, and so increase the earning powers of labor and open a brighter future for workingmen.

Here then is one great remedy for the evil conditions which create need. The whole standard of manual skill and of cultivated taste must be raised and widely disseminated, so that the children of the working classes shall have a fair chance in the race of life, and not start under such heavy handicap that they soon fail and despair.

What city will, however, dare to appeal from my decision that for thorough system for training the inefficient into skill, and inspiring them with new courage for the struggle of life, Brooklyn is entitled to the palm?

*The Bedford Industrial Building** just completed at Brooklyn
under the guiding inspiration of Mr. G. B. Buzelle, who has just

* "The work of our Bureau of Charities in Brooklyn has been in part the
evolution of our surroundings in Brooklyn, part Mr. Buzelle's ten years
devoted service, and part and most largely the experience of some of our most
capable friendly visitors, committeemen or trustees, in which together with
many others I have had a certain part. Actually the woodyards, laundries
and work-rooms in turn were embodiments of suggestions and requests
coming back to the board from our visitors, and not provided in advance of
such.

" We have been occupying for five years, as tenants, a building which we
fitted up in very much the same way as the new Bedford Building is fitted up,
and in which our central offices, central laundry, workrooms, etc., are now
located under a twenty years' lease. In the Bedford Building, which we own,
we were not able to make a great many changes that seemed to us improvements. The changes we did make are really of minor importance. That tells
you better than anything else how satisfied we have been with the plans
evolved five years ago. Besides the building which we lease, and the Bedford
Building which we own, we need one more building, but shall have to wait
some years for it. The three buildings together would give us a triangle with
about two miles distance on each side, three centres of work from which we
think we could take care of our work in good shape for a good many years to
come. We should not change the scheme or plan of the buildings in any way
that I can now think of.

"As to the general interest in Brooklyn in the Bureau of Charities, I should
say it is steadily increasing and in a wholesome fashion, but our supporters
are more among the middle and less wealthy classes than among those of the
largest means. This is wholesome for the future, while it drops the financial
burden on a few for the present."—*Copy of Letter of Alfred T. White to R. T.
Paine, May 27, 1893.*

" Day after day and week after week," writes Alfred T. White, "our friendly
visitors came back to us saying, 'This man or this woman says he cannot get
work, but would take it if he could. What shall we do?' To-day we answer
the question in two well-equipped laundries, two large workrooms for
unskilled and unrecommended women, and two woodyards for able-bodied
men, all under the control of the Brooklyn Bureau of Charities. There the
visitor quickly learns whether the applicant really wishes work, and whether
he will stick to work if found ; and if this be proved, effort is made to secure
for him more permanent and remunerative employment. *Some of our visitors
are wise enough to recognize that the moment a woman enters the workroom
marks a crisis in the life of many an applicant for aid, and as the chemist stands
by his crucible and watches for the time when the pure metal may be detached
from its impurities, so the friend who stands by in such a crisis of life sees the
elements of character slowly separating, and may eliminate some of the baser stuff
before this supreme opportunity is lost. Such work-rooms without the friendly*

closed a life of exquisite devotion, and of Mr. A. T. White, and by gifts incited by their aid, at a cost of about $40,000, seems to me on the whole the best building ever yet built as a workshop of human character, to lift on to their feet the poor who largely for lack of skill are discouraged and down, and to enable them to stand and walk.

The Bedford Industrial Building seems to me to serve such a useful function in the supremely interesting problem of how to deal with the inefficient, broken-down, depressed poor of our great cities, not properly equipped for the struggle of life, that I try thus to attract the utmost attention to its methods and aims.

What city has got its one or more Bedford Industrial Buildings? What city is there which can do without?

Let me magnify my office for a good purpose, and declare that no city is adequately equipped which has not one or more Industrial Training Buildings to provide training for the inefficient, and while this process is going on, also powerful personal encouragement and cheer from loving friends.

Conclusions.

These are the conclusions drawn from a study of the sadder side of life in great cities.

The separate problem of poor relief is insoluble.

Pauperism, vice and crime are common factors of the inseparable and tremendous problem of how to uplift the general conditions of life among the poor.

First. The difficulties increase in more than geometrical ratio with the masses of congestion no longer of pauperism alone, but of vice and crime and broken health commingled into base and often brutal degradation.

Second. Negative treatment, the mere principle of repression, while just as needed to-day and always, as when declared in the reform of 1834, not only fails to repel paupers in their lowest estate, but tends to degrade them into that reckless or brutal indifference, so much sadder for them as well as more hopeless for society, while also it is open to such charge of harshness to the worthy aged poor, more numerous in England than here, that English philanthropy

---

visitor would be worthless; they would be solely so many shops; but the friendly visitor's work gives them a character and influence which can hardly be over-estimated."—On the Friendly Visitor's Opportunity. Charities Review for April, 1893, p. 328.

wavers towards a vast scheme of pensioning all the aged, good and bad, rich and poor alike, a burden I fear too tremendous to be borne.

This principle of repression sinks the humane Wayfarers' Lodge of Boston, or Philadelphia, or as proposed in New York, into the prison cell of London's casual ward.

Repression alone makes guardians or overseers of the poor, and all relieving agents, managers of almshouses, jails and prisons, and especially the police* who guard the city's peace, hard, cold and unsympathetic, so that the sad multitude who pass under their influence grow more brutally defiant.

In short, mere repression is a cruel and unchristian failure.

Third.   Therefore, all work among the poor and wretched, whether done by official agents, or police, or friendly visitors, whose name should be legion, all efforts to keep families unbroken and children near to the love of a widowed mother, all efforts to train and cheer the inefficient must be permeated, energized, ennobled by the mighty force of love;—

Love, which Drummond shows to be the greatest thing in the world, in that burst of inspiration which every one should read;—

Love, described by St. Paul in one of the three noblest chapters of all human literature;—

Love, which so moved the soul of God, that He sent His Son to our rescue;—

Love, not in weak sentiment, but strengthened by all the vigorous firmness of strong men, so that repression may be resolute; yet conscious love shall permeate every fibre of the force which would hope to deal successfully with the pauper, the criminal or the brute.

Love is the motive to summon hundreds of friendly visitors from their sunny homes, to go down into the wretched abodes of gloom, where the battle of civilization is to be lost or won, ready to act up to their motto of "Not alms but a friend,"† and seeking a fuller

* "Moreover, there are few persons in the community more deserving of the sympathy and support of good people than an honest policeman located in a bad city quarter.   He has to stem the tide of the city's moral defilement, as no other person is called upon to do; and he is almost wholly deprived of the uplift, which nearly every social worker now feels, that comes from knowing of a great body of true men and women who are glad of the work he is doing."

† First used by Robert Treat Paine in his address to the Baptist Union on Dec. 29, 1879

measure of ingenuity, discrimination and patience than Boston has learned, guided by the lesson of encouraging success described by Alfred T. White, in Brooklyn, inspired by the life work and words of wisdom of Octavia Hill in London, till this spirit shall recreate the relations of the wretched and the happy ; and the superb energies of philanthropy in New York shall not rest content even with such noble gifts as John M. Kennedy's offering of a United Charities Building at a cost of $600,000, as a headquarters for organized charity, but all shall rather see in it a proclamation of hope for every sufferer, and of summons to every child of God to give personal service in adequate measure till the sunlight of heaven shall dispel miasma from every home of woe.

So that before long personal service, easily equal to the task in every other American city, shall not fail in Chicago, nor even in New York, whose congested population gathers into crowded limits the various forms of degraded life from many foreign lands, and across the ocean shall find some remedy for that Dead Sea of Liverpool, and rise to the supreme task for charity which earth now offers in the countless multitude of London.

Love is the motive which builds into beauty and power Toynbee Hall and Oxford House, Neighborhood Guilds, Andover House and Denison, and, not surpassed by any, Hull House here at Chicago; all these college settlements, the latest and loveliest manifestation of the fierce grip which suffering and sin fasten on the sympathies of noble culture.

Love is the force which impels Brooklyn to build its Bedford Industrial Buildings and to fill them with a spirit of wisdom and sympathy which alone can save the army of inefficient from their impending slavery.

Love is the force which summons all whose lot is sunny to join workingmen in their strenuous demand for justice.

Love is the force to ennoble the career of the policeman into dignity, prompting him to save by friendly counsel the wild lads before their wildness issues in such crime that he must strike it down.

Love is the motive and personal service is the method by which tens of thousands of Christian churches are to go out in their ministry, not only by their thousands of priests ordained by the hand of man, but more effectively by their hundreds of thousands of men and women, consecrated by the spirit of God, into every haunt of wretched life.

Repression guided by love, love reinforced by repression, must unite to deal with every one of the various phases of the pauper problem.

Wisdom too must stand at the helm as pilot. No cause for fear when among the leaders of the social reform are the wise and strong men who are at the head of the great universities of learning. President Daniel C. Gilman, of Johns Hopkins, Seth Low, of Columbia, William J. Tucker, of Dartmouth, Charles W. Eliot, of Harvard, John H. Finley, of Knox, and your own Frederick Harper, at Chicago and Francis A. Walker of the Boston Institute of Technology bring to any cause they support strength and wisdom. Sociology takes rank in the colleges as a worthy study for men who propose to rule or aid their fellowmen. The rise of this study has been so rapid that only a few years ago it was introduced at Harvard as a half course, and a bit later the printer's devil would have had Professor Peabody say that it was "raised from a half curse to a whole curse." Now no college is equipped without a competent professor of sociology.*

Public sentiment in the community must also be aroused to take interest in all judicious movements, for instance, to support overseers of the poor in enforcing strict rules against lax relief, police in preventing children from begging, boards of health in preventing "any portion of the people from living in houses which are unfit for human habitation."

We rejoice to count as sure allies, literature and the power of the press. If "Uncle Tom" abolished slavery, so has the "Bitter Cry" been heard round the world; "Prisoners of Poverty" must go free; "All Sorts and Conditions of Men" have their Palace of Industry. The author's pen dipped in the blood of those who suffer, writes with power.

Nothing is more wonderful than the speed of modern events, the rapidity with which an avalanche of reform overwhelms all opposition after it has begun to move.

This International Congress of Charities meets to-day for the first time on the soil of America. It is honored by the counsel of illustrious men and women distinguished for philanthropic devotion from many lands.

---

* It was my hope to promote this study at Harvard as well as to strengthen this movement by the aid of thoroughly trained experts, by founding a fellowship for sociology.

What result laden with larger measure of blessing for the humbler ranks of men can issue from this Congress, than a deep conviction upon all minds that the great preventible causes of human degradation can be and must be abolished?

AMERICAN ADMINISTRATION OF CHARITY IN PUBLIC INSTITUTIONS.

OSCAR CRAIG, LATE PRESIDENT OF STATE BOARD OF CHARITIES OF NEW YORK.

My invitation to present a paper on topics relating to "The American Poorhouse, its Past, Present and Future," conveys from the secretary of the section, the following suggestions, viz. :

"A discussion of this subject would probably show, as well as that of any other, the character of our public relief system, for the poorhouse may fairly be called, I presume, the corner-stone of this system. The committee would suggest that perhaps your paper might show, among other things, the growing specialization of relief, and so might properly speak of the provision that has been made on the part of the state and municipalities, for classes once housed in the poorhouses and almshouses."

It will, however, within the allotted compass, be impossible to take in the points thus indicated in the circumference of each of the forty-four states. Selection is therefore made, not by eliminating any of the sections indicated, but by confining their consideration mainly to one of these nearly half-hundred circles of statehood. For, while each is a sovereignty in respect of the subjects here considered, all are akin in language, literature and institutions. The Empire State excelling in population and wealth, and not surpassed in moral enterprise and intelligence, is therefore chosen as the proper theatre for treatment of the themes presented by the secretary.

In passing to our topics we note by the way that general descriptions of the poorhouse systems and the poor laws of various states may be found in the published proceedings of the National Conference of Charities and Correction, at its annual sessions, including reports from states and also articles by specialists, among which particular mention is made of the paper given at the eleventh session by Mr. Frank B. Sanborn, of Massachusetts, on the Management of Almshouses in New England.

The political unit in New York being the county, unlike that in Massachusetts, which is the town, the administration of its poorhouse system is vested by the Revised Statutes (p. 620, §24) in the county, and the existence of town poorhouses is by sufferance of the county. The second annual report of the State Board of Charities, in the year 1869, refers to out-relief as the chief form of dispensation to the indigent in Hamilton and Schuyler counties, and to several town poorhouses in Suffolk and Queens counties on Long Island. There are now four town poorhouses, two in Schuyler county and two in Queens county, and there is no county house in either Hamilton or Schuyler county.

Including the almshouse of the city and county of New York, with its various departments, and the almshouse of the county of Kings, which embraces the city of Brooklyn, there are now fifty-eight county poorhouses, besides five city almshouses proper, situate respectively at Kingston, Newburgh, Oswego, Poughkeepsie and Utica. In the larger towns of Buffalo, Rochester, Albany, Troy and Syracuse the city poor are cared for in the poorhouses of their respective counties. On these and related points there have been few changes during the last twenty-five years.

But the quarter-century presents remarkable variances from beginning to end in many respects. The average population of the county houses has increased from 7,760 to 20,918 ; and their total census in the first year, 21,529, was, in the last year, raised to 83,667. The ratio is more nearly in geometrical than in arithmetical progression, and is out of all correspondence with the growth of population in the state, which, by the federal census of 1870, was 4,382,759, by the federal census of 1890 was 5,981,834, and by the state enumeration of 1892 was 6,513,343. Thus while the period shows that the number of the inhabitants of the state increased about fifty per cent., it discovers an increase in the average number of inmates of these county houses almost three hundred per cent., and in their total number annually received nearly four hundred per cent. In brief, the dependents domiciled in the poorhouses multiplied six to eight times faster than the inhabitants of the state.

Though relief outside of institutions comes within the scope of this paper only in its relation to indoor relief, it is, for such relativity of knowledge, proper to observe that the number receiving out-relief at the beginning of the quarter-century was 50,983, and at the end was 131,439, showing increase at less rapid rate than indoor relief. It is the tendency of counties and cities to lessen the public administration of out-relief, and to favor the substitution of its private dispensation, and to refer its problems to charity organizations and other voluntary instrumentalities. This trend is in accordance with the views of the State Board of Charities, which regards governmental agency in out-relief as open to the objections against municipal politics in charity administration, the influence of which is apt to be in the promotion rather than the prevention of pauperism, together with the neglect of the modest and honest poor, whose votes are not purchasable, and whose wants and griefs are not paraded in the market-places.

It is of practical as well as curious interest to note that the ratio between native and foreign born paupers, at the beginning of the era, was about three of natives to six of foreigners; while at the end it is about three of natives to five of foreigners. This decrease in the proportion of alien paupers, though apparently small in effect, is relatively of large moment in comparison with the increase during the same period in volume of immigration, including defective, degenerate, delinquent and otherwise dangerous and dependent classes.

These considerations lead to inquiries respecting the evils of illicit immigration, and the remedies which have mitigated if they have not completely corrected them.

There can be no doubt that municipal governments, charitable societies, families and individuals, in Great Britain and various countries in Europe, have promoted the emigration of criminals, lunatics, outcasts and paupers, directed or destined to the United States, principally through the port of New York. The late Martin B. Anderson, LL. D., president of the Rochester University and member of the State Board of Charities for the Seventh Judicial District, submitted to the board a paper, dated January 12, 1875, which cites admissions made by publicists and other authorities abroad, showing this fact. And it has been confirmed by proofs annually gathered since the year 1873 by the observations and examinations of Dr. Charles S. Hoyt, secretary of the State Board of Charities, and by the correspondence of Hon. John H. Van Antwerp, its vice-president, and by the findings of the board made in its annual reports to the Legislature.

The state of New York has sought relief in various enactments. Chapter 277 of the laws of 1831, and chapter 230 of the laws of 1833, were practically inoperative, on account of the difficulty of proving the intent or knowledge of the master of the vessel or other person introducing the convict or the pauper into the state. The act passed May 15, 1847, entitled "An act concerning passengers in vessels coming to the United States," and the amendatory and supplementary acts created commissioners of emigration, and among other things made the consignees, masters, agents and owners of vessels liable for the support of immigrants who were "lunatic, idiot, deaf, dumb, blind, infirm, maimed, over sixty years old, widows having families, or for any cause unable to support themselves," provided that such liability might be discharged by paying a commutation tax of two dollars and fifty cents *per capita* on all immigrants, within twenty-four hours after leaving the vessel. The result, of course, was that the commutation money was always assessed on the emigrant at his place of departure. The law directed the commissioners to pay from such money the cost of maintaining such immigrants as became a public charge within the state, but not beyond a period of five years from landing. This statutory indemnity was inadequate, on account of the short term of maintenance and of the small sum of "head money"; by reason of which the commissioners, though restricted by the five years' clause, incurred debts which their resources would not cancel. While about nine thousand foreigners were thus maintained from such commutation money between the years 1868 and 1873 inclusive—a period just prior to the first subsequent legislation hereafter mentioned— there were foreign-born inmates of county poorhouses and city almshouses in the state during the same six years to an annual average of thirty-five thousand to forty thousand, being about two-thirds of the total population of these houses, though foreign-born persons were only about one-third of the total census of the state. Another inevitable limitation in the law was that it could cover only the ports of entry within its jurisdiction, while the classes of defective and dependent persons provided against were in large numbers shipped to Canadian ports, and thence forwarded over the border, with their destinations practically fixed, as if ticketed, to the poorhouses and almshouses of the counties and cities of the state.

This statute provoked comments from jurists on the question of its validity. Finally, the Supreme Court of the United States, in the case of Henderson *et al. v.* Mayor of New York *et al.*, decided in

October, 1875,* declared that the provisions in the law for levying the tax on immigrants, and the penalties leading to it, were in regulation of commerce, and therefore in violation of the federal constitution.

After this decision, cutting off the inflow of the "head money," the unnaturalized paupers, who had floated on the currents of immigration and had become moored by our charity cables and the five years' clause, were supported by the commissioner of emigration on Ward's Island, from appropriations by the legislature of the state, in the years 1876 to 1883, amounting to $1,140,500; and on credit in county poorhouses, city almshouses, incorporated hospitals, orphan asylums and other charitable institutions, in the further amount of $105,008.96, which is a debt against the state to be paid from the proceeds of the sale of its property on Ward's Island; and also from a loan of $200,000 made in 1875 by the Emigrants' Industrial Savings Bank of New York, secured by a mortgage on the Ward's Island property, which mortgage was, in 1882, assigned to the comptroller of the state as an investment for the United States Deposit Fund, thus making the funny combination of a mortgage held by the state on its own property and as security for trust-funds.

But these various sums represent only a small part of the deficiency of the "head moneys," as already shown by reference to the ordinary statistics of alien pauperism, which was a public charge not on the state at large, but on counties and cities. The proofs demonstrate that the Supreme Court, in cutting off the commutation contracts, released the people of New York state from a most destructive and deplorable policy of inviting foreign convicts, lunatics and paupers to come under an implied covenant of maintenance for five years and probably for life.

At the time of this decision (1875) there was no national statute on the subject. Subsequently federal legislation was repeatedly invoked by the State Board of Charities of New York, in correspondence with the State Department and senators and representatives at Washington, and with the National Conference of Charities and Correction, and the boards and authorities of other states. The result of the agitation was the act of Congress to regulate immigration, passed in 1882, by which it was provided, among other things, that if there shall be found among emigrants on vessels, "any convict, lunatic, idiot, or any person unable to take care of himself or herself without becom-

----

* 92 U. S. Reports, 259.

ing a public charge, . . . such person shall not be permitted to land." This law was, in pursuance of its provisions, at first executed by state authorities, but subsequently by virtue of further enactments was enforced by federal officers, under regulations of the Secretary of the Treasury of the United States. Assuming, for argument's sake, that its administration has been reasonably diligent, the fact remains that great numbers of alien paupers have annually eluded the federal examinations and obtained a footing on our shores, perhaps the majority of whom infest the city and the state of New York.

The legislature of the state has provided for the return of such foreign and unnaturalized paupers as are assisted by cities, charitable societies and other agencies to emigrate, after the expiration of one year from their immigration (which is the period limiting such action by officers under the federal statute). Under the alien pauper law of New York, enacted in 1880, and enforced by the chief secretary of its State Board of Charities, eighteen hundred and seventy-nine of these assisted immigrants, most of them being remnants of the imperfect execution of the law of Congress, have been sent to their homes or places of settlement, by through tickets to those places in foreign countries. Such returns have been accomplished in humane ways, at an expense of less than twenty-one dollars *per capita*, or about one-fifth of the cost of maintenance for one year, computed at two dollars per week, and about one seventy-fifth of their support for life, on an estimate of expectation of fifteen years, which is verified by experience. Thus at a total expenditure of $40,916.40, the expulsion of these organized invaders of the soil of New York has saved to the taxpayers of the state over $2,890,000.

These general statistics are taken in substance from the annual reports of the State Board of Charities to the legislature of New York, from the last of which the following data are copied, to wit:

"During the fiscal year ending September 30, 1892, the Board removed 150 alien paupers from the poorhouses, almshouses, hospitals, asylums and other charitable institutions of this state, and sent them to their homes in different countries of Europe, pursuant to chapter 549 of the laws of 1880, as follows: To England 16; to Ireland 11; to Scotland 9; to Germany 34; to Austria-Hungary 14; to Russia 11; to Italy 39; to Switzerland 8; to France 4, and to Sweden and Denmark each 2; total 150.

"The examinations showed that these persons were deported to this country from their several European homes by the following agencies, viz.: By cities, towns and other municipalities, 13; by various benevolent, charitable and immigration associations and societies, 38; by relatives, guardians and friends, 77; by individuals and companies under agreement to labor, 22; total, 150.

"According to the statements of these persons, they were landed in this country as follows: In New York, 125; at other United States ports, 17; at various Canadian ports, 8; total, 150.

"Their condition at the time of landing, as developed by the examinations, was as follows: Lunatic, 9; imbecile, 6; epileptic, 3; paralytic, 5; vagrant and diseased, 27; old and decrepit, 22; blind, 2; crippled, 7; deformed, 4; feeble-minded, 26; otherwise diseased, 39; total, 150."

Preceding the alien pauper law was the state pauper law, enacted June 7, 1873, and amended in 1874 and 1875, which is still in full force and effect. Under its provisions, the secretary of the State Board of Charities returns to their homes or friends in other states of the Union and other countries, state paupers, that is to say, dependent persons having no legal settlement by sixty days' residence in any of the counties of the state, and found by the secretary in the state almshouses, which are certain county poorhouses selected and designated by the state board as receptacles of these classes.

The report of the State Board of Charities, transmitted to the legislature for the fiscal year 1892, shows that the whole number of persons committed as state paupers under this act since it went into effect, October 22, 1873, has been 25,520, viz: males, 19,908; females, 5,612. Of these 15,980 have been furnished transportation to their homes or places of legal settlement in other states and countries, and this state thus released of the burden and expense of their support and care through life. To have maintained these paupers in the poorhouses and almshouses of the state, at the low rate of $100 each per annum, would have involved an annual outlay of $1,507,100; and, calculating the average duration of their lives at fifteen years, they would, in the end, have entailed the enormous expenditure of $24,928,800, by the various cities and counties of the state. The average annual expense since the law went into effect, for maintenance, supervision and care, and for the removal of 15,980 helpless paupers to their homes or places of legal settlement, has been less than $40,000, or about $25 per person.

Every invasion of the delinquent, diseased and destitute classes which is finally turned back by the state government, if not at first repelled by the federal authorities, deters unnumbered irruptions of similar sorts; by making such experiments of vagrant mendicants through interstate migration uncertain, or rather rendering it almost certain that their ventures will prove unprofitable and unpleasant to themselves; and by discouraging benevolent societies, municipalities and government agencies in Europe, from their bolder attempts to organize such immoral incursions into our territory. Thus the state pauper law and the alien pauper law have not only immediately effected an actual saving of over $25,000,000 as already computed, but on a fair estimate of probabilities have resulted in sparing the resources of the state the useless expenditure of still larger sums of money.

These results are due to the conservative but effective execution of these laws by the secretary of the state board, Dr. Charles S. Hoyt, whose wise exercise of discretion has prevented occasion for any well-grounded complaint during the whole period of his administration.

The residue of alien and other unsettled paupers not returned to their homes are maintained by the state in certain county poorhouses selected by the State Board of Charities and designated State Almshouses. At the beginning of this fiscal year there were thus maintained in the various state almshouses, 159; at the several state hospitals for the insane 53, and at an orphan asylum 1, making altogether 213 state paupers.

Comparisons with other states show that this special work in New York has been accompanied with similar labors and results in Massachusetts and Pennsylvania on the seaboard; and, as to interstate migration, in other commonwealths of the Union; and that regarding state almshouses, the West has generally followed not the law of Massachusetts for their separate establishment, but the law for their selection from county houses which obtains in New York.

While these improved methods for reducing the number of alien and unsettled paupers have been followed, improved measures have been adopted for the dispensation of indoor relief to the diseased, defective and dependent inhabitants of the state. The organization of such relief has been developed by differentiating the beneficiaries, first, on lines of classification under the poorhouse roof; and second, on lines of separation and segregation in institutions respectively adapted to various sorts of special needs.

The classification of the inmates of the poorhouses has not been carried far beyond the distinction of sex. But this distinction has come to be well observed in most of the poorhouses and almshouses, both day and night. The contrast in this respect between the present time and the beginning of the quarter-century of the State Board of Charities is marked.

The second report of the state board represents the conditions at the beginning of the quarter-century, from which the following is an excerpt:

" But few of the poorhouses of the state, owing to their arrangement, admit of a proper classification of their inmates. The authorities, in most of them, aim to keep the sexes separated at night, but this is only partially accomplished. During the day there is an indiscriminate and unrestricted association of all classes, including the aged and respectable, children, insane, idiotic and blind; together with the middle-aged, able-bodied, slothful, debased and profane of both sexes. In most cases they partake of a common fare at a common table, and not infrequently share with one another a common dormitory. The effects of such an association can be better conceived than described. Its fruits will be reaped in a large increase of pauperism and crime, coupled with grievous and burdensome taxation. During the year 304 children were born in these establishments, a large proportion of whom were illegitimate; and 799 of their inmates absconded, many of them to become, quite probably, a public charge, as vagrants or criminals."

Other features of this picture of 1868 are as follows:

"An examination of the foregoing table shows that, at the time of visitation of the several poorhouses of the state, there were found present 7,019 persons of all classes. Included among the number were 1,222 children under sixteen years of age; 1,528 insane; 314 idiotic; 87 blind, and 44 deaf and dumb; all others, 3,825. Full one-fourth of the latter were middle-aged, and apparently without infirmity or disease. There were also a considerable number of sick and crippled, many of whom, it was stated by those in charge, had been inmates for a long time. A few were observed presenting appearances of intelligence and respectability, but these were mainly among the aged and children.

" Nearly all the poorhouses throughout the state are old, and most of them are out of repair. With but few exceptions they are badly constructed, ill arranged, and are without proper ventilation or suitable appliances for bathing. In a large proportion of them the rooms are small and the ceilings low. At the time of inspection, in many of them the air was hot, foul and oppressive, and to the casual visitor hardly endurable. The rooms are often crowded, especially in winter, and much of the sickness and wretchedness of their inmates doubtless results therefrom.

" In the absence of proper hospital accommodation, the sick in most of the poorhouses are treated and cared for in the ordinary rooms associated with others ; and in several instances, owing to the lack of suitable buildings for the isolation and treatment of contagious diseases, the infection has spread among all the inmates, resulting in great mortality. During the past year 841 deaths occurred in these institutions, in an average population of a little over 7,000 persons. Such a large ratio of mortality would seem to indicate inexcusable negligence of the sick, and it should attract public attention and the attention of the authorities responsible for their treatment and care. . . .

"In nearly all of the counties of the state the authorities have provided separate buildings for the insane. These are generally small and ill arranged, and, with but few exceptions, wholly unsuited for the purposes to which they are applied. None of them are constructed so as to admit classification of the insane, with reference to the various forms and stages of the disease—the acute and chronic, the maniacal and quiet occupying the same floor, and not unfrequently share with one another the same cell. The sexes generally are kept separated at night, but in most cases they hold unrestricted intercourse during the day, nor are the insane protected from the intrusions of the ordinary paupers. Instances frequently occur where insane women become mothers in the poorhouses, and two such cases have fallen under observation, at the time of inspection, during the present year.

"But few of the county institutions contain the appliances necessary for the treatment of the insane, yet recent cases are being constantly received and held in these institutions, without effort on the part of the authorities to secure them admission to the state asylum. Several such cases were found at the time of inspection. When excited they are locked up in cells or chained ; when quiet they are allowed their liberty, and escapes often occur. Two hundred and thirteen were found thus restrained at the time of inspection, many of whom, it was represented, had been confined for years, and several of them were nearly, and two entirely nude. . . .

"The condition of the insane, idiotic, blind and others, unavoidably compelled to accept a home in the county poorhouses, is truly deplorable, allusions to which will be fully made in the detailed accounts of the inspection of these institutions in the after pages of this report. The poorhouses of the state, to a considerable extent, have become the abodes of the vagrant and idle, and if by chance respectable citizens, in consequence of poverty, infirmity, disease or misfortune of any kind, are compelled to accept a home in them, they necessarily become their associates. Vice and poverty assemble under the same roof, and this association in a great measure defeats the objects for which the institutions were established. The citizens generally manifest but little interest in their condition, and really know but little of their true character. They are usually visited annually by the board of supervisors ; but are seldom inspected, except upon the occasion of such visits."

But over these chaotic conditions there hovered the brooding spirit of humanity, evoking order and reforms and remedies for almost all the evils here depicted. The exception is in the failure properly to classify the inmates under the poorhouse roof, save as has been already stated on the distinguishing line of sex, where classification is now well observed and maintained as a rule ; and save also on the line of plain demarcation between the merely infirm, who at present comprise the great majority of inmates, and the very sick, who now are usually cared for in hospital buildings or rooms set apart. With these two saving clauses there is no proper classification.

The separation of the sexes, which has been effected in the county houses, will, it is believed, be followed by better classification of the inmates. The obstacles now in the way are not so frequently the results of mal-administration as they are the necessary effects of bad construction of old buildings. But all obstructions must give way to the obligation of respecting the worthy poor, who have become dependent through losses of friends or health or property, and of separating them from vagrant or vicious paupers. Such classification for indoor relief, with private charity properly organized outside, will remove the last excuse for the public dispensation of out-relief. The consummation will afford another illustration of the harmony between humanity as a social and political duty and public policy.

This imperfect distribution and administration by classes is, in large measure, due to defective construction of buildings. To secure relief, much attention has been given by the State Board of Charities to "poorhouse construction," chiefly through Mr. Letchworth, one of its members, whose paper on this subject, appended to the report of the board to the Legislature in 1879, and his subsequent article read before the state convention of county superintendents in 1891, are authorities. Among the exhibits furnished by the state board, and now in the Columbian Exposition, is the model of a poorhouse in a rural county.

But while complete classification within the walls of the poorhouse for the protection of the cleanly against the filthy, of the morally clean against the defiled and the corrupting, and of the refined against the vulgar and the brutal, has not been secured; the segregation in separate institutions of the blind, the deaf, the insane and the feeble-minded, as well as of children, has progressed to present certainty and promised completeness of development. The domiciling of these classes in their respective schools, hospitals and asylums clearly indicates the humanitarian spirit of the last quarter-century.

It was even earlier that asylums or schools for the blind and the deaf were inaugurated.

By chapter 325, of laws of 1863, as amended by chapter 180 of laws of 1870, chapter 548 of laws of 1871, and chapter 213 of laws of 1875, deaf children of indigent parents are provided for as follows:

"§1. Whenever a deaf-mute child, under the age of twelve years, shall become a charge for its maintenance on any of the towns or counties of this state, or shall be liable to become such charge, it shall be the duty of the overseers of the poor of the town, or of the supervisors of such county, to place such child in the New York Institution for the Deaf and Dumb, or in the Institution for the Improved Instruction of Deaf-Mutes, or in the Le Couteulx St. Mary's Institution for the Improved Instruction of Deaf-Mutes, in the city of Buffalo, or in the Central New York Institution for Deaf-Mutes, in the city of Rome, or in any institution of the state for the education of deaf-mutes.

"§2. Any parent, guardian or friend of a deaf-mute child within this state, over the age of six years and under the age of twelve years, may make application to the overseers of the poor of any town, or to any supervisor of the county where said child may be, showing by satisfactory affidavit, or other proof, that the health, morals or comfort of such child may be endangered or not properly cared for, and thereupon it shall be the duty of such overseer or supervisor to place such child in the New York Institution for the Deaf and Dumb, or in the Institution for the Improved Instruction of Deaf-Mutes, in the city of Buffalo, or in the Central New York Institution for Deaf-Mutes, in the city of Rome, or in any institution in the state for the education of deaf-mutes.

"§3. The children placed in said institutions in pursuance of the foregoing sections, shall be maintained therein at the expense of the county from whence they came, provided that such expense shall not exceed three hundred dollars per year, until they attain the age of twelve years, unless the directors of the institution to which a child has been sent shall find that such child is not a proper subject to remain in said institution."

Besides such provisions for county pupils, there are provisions for the education, care and maintenance of state pupils between the ages of twelve and twenty-five years, being deaf, which further provisions are incorporated in the statutes relating to public instruction, being laws of 1886, chapter 615, §1, and laws of 1875, chapter 213.

In addition to the institutions named in the foregoing acts, there have been several new ones since established with provisions of law bringing them within the same terms respecting county and state pupils. All of these schools, eight in number, are private corporations receiving public aid, of which the following is a complete list, with census, October 1, 1892, to wit:

	Males.	Females.	Total.
New York Institution for the Deaf and Dumb, New York	208	88	296
Institution for the Improved Instruction of Deaf-Mutes, New York	97	93	190
Central New York Institution for Deaf-Mutes, Rome....	66	67	133
Le Couteulx St. Mary's Deaf and Dumb Asylum, Buffalo	70	60	130
St. Joseph's Institution for the Improved Instruction of Deaf-Mutes, Fordham	141	158	299
Western New York Institution for Deaf-Mutes, Rochester	87	56	153
Northern New York Institution for Deaf-Mutes, Malone .	51	33	84
Albany Home School for the Oral Instruction of the Deaf	7	5	12
Total	727	570	1297

The aggregate number of pupils in these schools has been stationary during the last decade.

The average per capita cost for each pupil, for the last fiscal year, was a little less than $300; but the aggregate cost was more than the public appropriations.

The said schools being close corporations, there are, in the proper sense, no state institutions for the deaf.

Hon. William Rhinelander Stewart of the State Board of Charities has made careful inspections and examinations of the methods obtaining in these schools during past years, and his reports have won recognition throughout the United States.

"An act to authorize the establishment of the New York State Institution for the Blind," passed April 27, 1865, with "An act to define the objects" of the same, passed April 24, 1867, has resulted in a flourishing school for the blind at Batavia, the end and scope of which are ordained as follows:

"§4. The primary object of the institution shall be, to furnish to the blind children of the state the best known facilities for acquiring a thorough education, and train them in some useful profession or manual art, by means of which they may be enabled to contribute to their own support after leaving the institution; but it may likewise, through its industrial department, provide such of them with appropriate employment and boarding accommodations as find themselves unable, after completing their course of instruction and training, to procure these elsewhere for themselves. It shall, however, be in no sense an asylum for those who are helpless from age, infirmity or otherwise, or a hospital for the treatment of blindness."

Besides this one state school for the blind there is a private institution for the same class, incorporated under an act passed April 21, 1831, which was continued in force under chapter 333 of the laws of 1852, which was amended by chapter 166 of the laws of 1870. Section 1 of the act of 1870 is as follows :

"§1. The managers of the New York Institution for the Blind are hereby authorized to receive, upon the appointment of the superintendent of public instruction, made for a term of not exceeding five years, all blind persons, residents of the counties of New York and Kings, between eight and twenty-five years of age, who, in the judgment of the board of managers of said institution, shall be of suitable character and capacity for instruction, and shall have charge of their maintenance, education and support, and shall receive compensation therefor from the state in the same manner as is now provided by law. The term of such appointments may be extended, from time to time, by the superintendent of public instruction, on the recommendation of the board of managers of the said New York Institution for the Blind, for such further period as they may deem advantageous in each individual case."

The census and the cost for each pupil in the respective schools for the blind, the State Institution at Batavia, and the corporate body in New York, both of which have their current expenses met by the state, are as follows :

State Institution.		Corporate Institution.	
Average population,	130	Average population,	202
Per capita cost per year,	$250.64	Per capita cost per year,	$286.52

The aggregate number in public schools for the blind, 332, contrasts strongly with the aggregate number in public schools for the deaf, 1,297. But during the same period there were in the almshouses of Kings and New York counties, and in city almshouses, 212 blind persons, besides 67 in the Home for the Blind, New York, making a total of 705 blind persons, indigent and dependent for maintenance or education, upon public provision. This total it seems is about one-half the total of indigent deaf persons similarly dependent. The tables published by the State Board of Charities in 1891 show that in the county poorhouses and city almshouses there were for the preceding fiscal year, 299 blind persons and 54 deaf persons.

"An act to establish an asylum for idiots," passed July 10, 1851, is the first enactment for such a state institution in New York. Under acts amendatory and supplementary the asylum has developed into a school for the education and training of teachable idiots. Chapter 220 of the laws of 1862, as amended in 1867 and 1878, provides among other things for the selection, admission, removal and support of pupils as follows :

"§20. There shall be received and supported gratuitously in the asylum one hundred and twenty pupils, to be selected in equal numbers, as near as may be, from each judicial district, from those whose parents or guardians are unable to provide for their support therein, to be designated as state pupils; and such additional number of idiots as can be conveniently accommodated may be received into the asylum by the trustees, on such terms as may be just. But no idiot shall be received into the asylum without there shall have been first lodged with the superintendent thereof a request to that effect, under the hand of the person by whose direction he is sent, stating the age and place of nativity, if known, of the idiot, his christian and surname, the town and city or county in which they severally reside; the ability or otherwise of the idiot, his parents or guardians, to provide for his support in whole or in part, and if in part only, then what part; and the degree of relationship or other circumstance of connection between him and the person requesting his admission; which statement shall be verified in writing, by the oath of two disinterested persons, residents of the same county with the idiot, acquainted with the facts and circumstances so stated, and certified to be credible by the county judge of the same county. And no idiot shall be received into said asylum unless the county judge of the county liable for his support, shall certify that such idiot is an eligible and proper candidate for admission to said asylum as aforesaid; provided, however, that idiots may be received into said asylum upon the application therefor signed officially by any county superintendent of the poor or by the commissioners of charity of any of the cities of this state, where such commissioners exist."

An offshoot, under the patronage of the State Board of Charities, was planted at Newark for the "enforced custody and protection, during the child-bearing age of feeble-minded young women of proper physical development to become mothers." Chapter 281 of the laws of 1885 enacted, among other things, as follows: "The asylum established by the State Board of Charities at Newark, Wayne county, for feeble-minded women is hereby continued"; and provided for the government thereof by trustees to be appointed by the Governor by and with the consent of the senate.

Besides these two state institutions there is an idiot asylum department in the almshouse of the city and county of New York, which is educational as well as custodial. The following table shows the population of idiots and feeble-minded women at the beginning of the last fiscal year in public institutions of the State of New York, to wit:

State institution at Syracuse	510
State institution at Newark	345
Idiot asylum, city of New York	386
Kings county almshouse	39
Other county poorhouses	251
City almshouses	12
Total	1,543

the care of whom is educational as well as custodial in all but 302 cases.

The weekly average expenditure per capita in the two state institutions for idiots and feebled-minded women, for the last fiscal year, was as follows: in the institution for idiots, $3.12; in the institution for feeble-minded women, $2.32.

There is no public institution in the state of New York, save poorhouses and almshouses, for epileptics. The Legislature of 1892 passed and the Governor signed a bill charging the State Board of Charities, which is an unpaid body, with the duty of selecting a site and obtaining an option for land, not less than one thousand acres, and reporting an organization for an epileptic colony. At great expense of time and labor the State Board reported to the legislature of 1893 a site and an organization for such a colony, which both the senate and the assembly passed unanimously, but the Governor vetoed on alleged grounds of economy.

There are now in the poorhouses of the state about five hundred epileptics, and in very poor families many more, most of whom are incumbrances upon the productive labor of the people, while in such a colony they would become self-supporting by their labor expended for their physical and mental benefit under medical direction.

At the beginning of the quarter-century there was the New York State Lunatic Asylum at Utica for the acute insane, and there were in process of construction two other state institutions, viz: the Hudson River State Hospital for the insane at Poughkeepsie, which was also designed for acute cases, and the Willard Asylum for the chronic insane on Seneca Lake. The Willard Asylum was the first state provision for the chronic insane, the only public accommodations for whom, by previous law, had been the poorhouses and almshouses. The statute establishing this asylum made it incumbent on the counties to be designated by its trustees to send to it all their pauper and indigent insane who were proper subjects of public care, and not proper candidates for either of the two state hospitals; and in pursuance of its authority the trustees of the asylum designated all the counties of the state as properly under its supervision except New York, Kings, Monroe, Albany and Jefferson. Subsequently it was found that the capacity of the asylum was not one-fourth the demand; and a new statute entrusted to the State Board of Charities power to exempt counties from the operation of the Willard Asylum act. During nineteen years this board exempted nineteen counties, acting on the rule of the choice of the less of two evils, and preferring the exempted county asylum, though a mere department of the poorhouse placed under license and regulation, to the poorhouse unlicensed and unregulated. At length, however, and in the fall of 1888 the standing committee on the insane appointed by the State Board reported to it facts concerning these exempted asylums showing great evils and abuses, and conclusions, from which, as the writer was chairman of the committee, excerpts are made as follows, to wit:

" Your committee are united in the conviction that a revised lunacy code should enact one of two alternatives, viz : either, first to abolish county care ; or second, to restrict and regulate it. . . . Your committee are of the opinion that county care can be made what it should be, if at all, only under some such system as will take it entirely out of political control, and subject it to some such authority as that now committed to the state board, with the more flexible and elastic powers to be conferred by some new provisions as proposed. . . .

" In conclusion, your committee cannot refrain from referring to misapprehensions and misconceptions which sometimes prevent and arrest reforms and remedies in lunacy legislation and administration. Some of these mistakes, with their corrections, may be stated as follows:

" 1. A misapprehension that lunatics and voluntary paupers are generally the products of the same causes operating in similar ways is often expressed, when, in fact, the contrary is the case, as shown by the opinions of alienists as well as by statistics.

" 2. A misconception that the right of the county, as the unit in political organization, is to dictate the treatment and care of its indigent insane, is sometimes represented ; while on the contrary, lunatics are, as infants are, but as paupers are not, the special wards of the Supreme Court, which has control over their persons and estates, in chancery and by common law, as well as by statute, thus exercising a special jurisdiction, which is not of the county, but of the entire people of the state.

" 3. A misunderstanding of Darwin's law of natural selection, or of Spencer's law of the survival of the fittest, provokes criticism of attempted reforms in lunacy matters, as designed unnaturally to prolong the lives of the useless and wretched ; the case being in truth that such endeavors are intended primarily to increase the cures of acute, and as may be done, even cures among chronic classes, and to render the incurables more useful and less wretched ; while their secondary purpose of lengthening the existence of these unfortunates is also required by these very laws of nature acting in the realms of sociology and morality, for society has no more right negatively to leave its infirm to die or suffer than it has affirmatively to inflict on them suffering or death, either of which is in opposition to altruism, the last outcome of evolution, and in violation of nature, which executing the divine decree selects those civilized peoples as the fittest to survive who obey among them-selves the Christian law of kindness."

These conclusions, among others, were adopted by the State Board of Charities and transmitted with its annual report to the legislature in 1889.

As a sequel, the bill which the State Charities Aid Association of New York city had introduced into the legislature for the state care of the insane, having been argued and urged by representatives of the association and by the committee of the state board, while opposed by the superintendents of the poor, passed the senate and nearly passed the assembly in the same year. Meanwhile, a bill for the creation of a commission in lunacy, superseding the old commissioner in lunacy, was drawn by Dr. Stephen Smith, a distinguished medical authority of New York city, who was then the commissioner in lunacy, and who had been and is now again a member of the State Board of Charities. This bill was promoted by the committee of the state board, and was enacted, being now chapter 283 of the laws of 1889, with statutes amendatory and supplementary. In the following year the bill for exclusive state care of the insane became a law, being chapter 126 of the laws of 1890, with acts amendatory and supplementary.

"The New York Law for the State Care of the Insane," is the title of a paper prepared by the writer for the eighteenth annual session of the National Conference of Charities and Correction, and published in its proceedings for 1891 (pp. 92–94), from which extracts are made as follows:

"The new system makes state care coterminous with public care, with the exception of New York, Kings and Monroe counties, which were independent of the Willard Asylum act; but with the option in each of these three excepted counties to come under the law. Monroe county has already elected to take its benefits and bear its burdens.

"The new statute puts the state institutions, including the four hospitals for the acute insane, with the new St. Lawrence hospital, and the two asylums for the chronic insane, upon the same basis. These seven institutions are now hospitals for all the dependent insane. This feature of mixed hospitals or asylums for acute cases and all chronic classes of the insane was severely criticised by the former president of the state board, Mr. Letchworth, than whom, perhaps, no alienist or specialist was better qualified to speak, from study and travel among institutions in this country and abroad. His opposition to this part of the new system did not, however, lead him to oppose the system as a whole. His noble nature overruled his special objection, for the sake of the general movement of progress towards state care. . . .

"There is no actor in the movement, now happily consummated, who is authorized to give a compendium of all the grounds on which all the movers were actuated in urging the enactment of the measure. But it is believed that such a synopsis would include the following summary of reasons, namely :

"*First.*—The medical supervision of the state hospital, with its semi-daily inspection of all its patients by competent and trustworthy physicians, and the absence of anything like it in the average county poorhouse or asylum, are reasons enough for exclusive state care.

"*Second.*—The more beautiful environment of the state institution, with its adaptation and facilities for graduations and variations and successions of scene for different patients or phases of the same patient, tending to excite more healthy correspondence in their nervous organisms, and playing often the chief part in recovery, is sufficient to justify our contention in favor of state care.

"*Third.*—The county institution with four wards, being two for each sex, has most inadequate means for classification, in that seldom will the cleanly and quiet cases be simply equal in number to the filthy and disturbed classes, so that almost always will such wards, which the casual or superficial observer might call homelike in the daytime, become in the night season, without night service, filled with disgusting and repulsive horrors for the better class of patients.

"*Fourth.*—Inasmuch as one hundred patients need as many classifications as do one thousand, but with wards containing twenty-five inmates each, the former population would fill only four, while the latter population would fill forty wards, it is manifest that the state institution, with the larger census, has the advantage over the county institution, with the smaller census.

"*Fifth.*—Moreover, the state institution alone is likely to have the means for changes of classification to meet the demands of changes of cases, and, above all, changes in the same case.

"*Sixth.*—The labor of the state patient is for his own benefit under medical supervision, while the labor of the county patient is for his own support without medical supervision.

"*Seventh.*—In fine, the state institution always, and the county institution almost never, treats its patients as sick persons, as in fact they are, whether suffering from acute attacks or succumbing as chronic invalids.

"*Eighth.*—The pauper associations of county care, caused by putting the indigent insane in the poorhouse, or in a building adjoining or adjacent or on the poorhouse farm, or under poorhouse officials, are degrading to the indigent or dependent insane, who, as has been shown, are seldom paupers.

"*Ninth.*—Individual care is practicable to a greater extent in a state institution, though larger, because its medical and personal treatment, its more extensive, varied and inspiring environment, and its means for more correct and complete classification, differentiate the treatment in accordance with the differing cases and the changes of the same case.

"*Tenth.*—Though the mixed system is not essential to exclusive state care, it has one important advantage in the opportunity which it gives for transfers back and forth between the hospital and custodial or domiciliary treatment and care, following successive changes in the same case as well as changes of cases.

"*Eleventh.*—While constant watch and ward by a central commission or board is impossible, it is the part of wisdom to provide a smaller number of larger institutions under the immediate control of medical superintendents of high honor, in order that the continuing influence of the supervising body may be kept alive in the intervals between its visits of inspection. Another and a similar advantage of such superior institutions is that they may be held to a reasonable standard without reducing them to a dead level of uniformity, but with the liberty which, within proper limits, leads to the differentiation which is the law of development.

" *Twelfth.*—Though state care is based on humanity, and not on economy, it is, as has been shown, no less economical, while it is more humane.

" *Thirteenth.*—The system of exclusive state care is more practical as well as philosophical in its simplicity, as compared with the former exemption system of New York, or the present Wisconsin system, which introduces state administration to correct the evils of county administration, and which, so far as it insures good results, is in reality qualified state care, encumbered with useless machinery engendering unnecessary friction and producing wasteful loss of power as evidenced in limited results.

"*Fourteenth.*—New York's new law is a development from the first principle of state care in the Willard Asylum act ; it is an evolution or growth, and not a special contrivance or creation.

"*Fifteenth.*—While the county is for practical purposes the political unit, it is as such only a small and subordinate part of the whole, which is the state paramount and sovereign. The criminal law recognizes this principle in determining not only the nature and penalty of felonies and other offenses, but their place as well as mode of punishment. Lunacy legislation even more legitimately proceeds upon the same basis ; for its subjects, the insane, both by statute and common law, and in respect of person as well as property, are the wards of the state."

The board for establishing the hospital districts of the state, composed of the commission in lunacy, the president of the State Board of Charities and the comptroller, was charged by the statute with the duty of providing, upon the grounds of existing institutions, cottages for the classes of the insane who are chronic in a medical sense, the legal definition of chronicity by the term of two years having been abolished. The state institutions are now all hospitals for the cure of the insane, with provisions for the proper care of such as may prove to be incurable. On the first day of October next, all the indigent and dependent insane except those of New York and Kings counties, will be domiciled in these hospitals, the new cottages of which, including the necessary equipments for heating, lighting, ventilation, fixtures and furniture, have been built at a cost not exceeding $550 per capita. The appropriation of last winter for the maintenance of the patients in these state institutions is less per capita than the former cost to the counties of the state. This result is in part due to the contribution of New York and Kings counties by taxation. But should these two counties share in the benefits as well as the burdens of state care, it is believed that the cost would be less than under the old system, taking into consideration that the expenditures of the counties cannot be taken at their own estimate, for the reason that but one of the counties exempted by the state board kept its accounts or finances for the insane separate from those for its paupers, while Monroe county, which had an independent asylum created by statute, gave less accommodations at greater expense than Willard Asylum for the Chronic Insane.

Statistics compiled by the state board from returns by the state hospitals and county asylums for the insane, have been reported by the board to the legislature for the last fiscal year, including the following:

" The daily average number of insane in the various state hospitals during the year ending September 30, 1892, was 7,173, and the number in their custody and care, October 1, 1892, 7,484. The average number in these institutions during the year ending September 30, 1891, was 6,508, and the number in their custody and care, October 1, 1891, was 6,961. The increase in the daily average during the year ending September 30, 1892, it thus appears, was 665, and the increase in the number under care, October 1, 1892, was 523. . . . The number of insane in the several state hospitals, October 1, 1891, was 6,961. The admissions during the year ending September 30, 1892, were 2,474, making a total of 9,435 under care during the year, as against 8,777 the preceding year. The following changes occurred in these institutions during the year, viz.: discharged recovered, 561 ; not recovered, 362 ; improved, 135 ; unimproved, 200 ; not insane, 21 ; died, 672 ; thus leaving 7,484 under care, October 1, 1892, of whom 3,653 were men and 3,831 women. . . . The number of insane in the asylums of New York city, October 1, 1892, was 5,767, as against 5,390, October 1, 1891, of whom 2,638 were men and 3,129 were women, the increase for the year being 377, as against 343, the increase the preceding year. The admissions during the year 1892 were 1,592, as against 1,401, the admissions for the year 1891, an increase of 191 during the year. The discharges in the course of the year were as follows : cured, 166 ; not cured, 457 ; not insane, 3 ; died, 589, thus leaving 5,767 under care, October 1, 1892, distributed as follows : on Blackwell's Island, 1,918 women ; on Ward's Island, 2,168 men and 90 women ; on Hart's Island, 78 men and 1,081 women ; at Central Islip, 392 men and 40 women. . . . The number of insane in the care of the institutions of Kings county, October 1, 1892, was 2,120, as against 1,997, October 1, 1891. The whole number under treatment during the year was 2,496, as against 2,461 the preceding year. The distribution of those under care, October 1, 1892, was as follows: in the buildings at Flatbush, 518 men and 881 women; total, 1,399; in the buildings at King's Park, 376 men and 345 women; total, 721; aggregate 2,120, of whom 894 were men and 1,226 were women.

The capacity of the buildings for the insane of this county is for 1,680 patients, viz: at Flatbush for 1,000 patients; at King's Park for 680 patients. The daily average number of patients during the year has been 2,051, or an excess of 371 patients beyond the capacity of the buildings, and the excess, October 1, 1892, was 440 patients, the greatest crowding being at Flatbush."

Homes for the friendless, being private institutions in the state of New York, contain 2,403 men and 5,633 women, making 8,036 adult inmates.

The first orphan asylum in the city of New York was established in 1806.

Numerous acts, notably those of 1855, 1857, 1869, 1870, 1875 and 1878, provided for the support and care of poor children, until they were consolidated in chapter 438 of the laws of 1884, entitled "An act to revise and consolidate the statutes of the state relating to the custody and care of indigent and pauper children by orphan asylums and other charitable institutions." Among other provisions of this law are the following:

"§1. The guardianship of the person and the custody of any indigent child may be committed to any incorporated orphan asylum, or any institution incorporated for the care of orphan, friendless or destitute children, by an instrument in writing signed by the parents of such child, if both parents shall then be living, or by the surviving parent if either parent of such child be dead, or if either one of such parents have, for the period of six months then next preceding, abandoned such child, by the other such parent, or if the father of such child shall have neglected to provide for his family during the six months then next preceding, or if such child be a bastard, by the mother of such child; or if both parents of such child shall then be dead, by the guardian of the person of such child, legally appointed, by the approval of the court or officer which appointed such guardian to be entered of record; or if both parents of such child shall then be dead and no legal guardian of the person of such child shall have been appointed and no guardian of such child shall have been appointed by the last will and testament or by a deed by either parent thereof, or if the parents of such child shall have abandoned such child for the period of six months then next preceding, by the mayor of the city or by the county judge of the county in which such asylum or other institution shall be located, upon such terms, for such time, and subject to such conditions, as may be agreed upon by the parties to such written instrument. And such written instrument may provide for the absolute surrender of such child to such corporation. But no such corporation shall draw or receive money from public funds for the support of any such child committed under the provisions of this section, unless it shall have been determined by a court of competent jurisdiction that such child has no relatives, parent or guardian living, or that such relative, parent or guardian, if living, is destitute, and actually unable to contribute to the support of such child.

"§2. It shall not be lawful for any county superintendent or overseer of the poor, board of charity or other officer, to send any child between the ages of two and sixteen years, as a pauper, to any county poorhouse or almshouse for support and care, or to detain any child between the ages of two and sixteen years in such poorhouse or almshouse; but such county superintendents, overseers of the poor, boards of charities or other officers shall provide for such child or children, in families, orphan asylums, hospitals or other appropriate institutions, as provided by law. The boards of supervisors of the several counties of the state are hereby directed to take such action in the matter as may be necessary to carry out the provisions of this section. When any such child shall be so provided for or placed in any orphan asylum or such other institution, such child shall, when practicable, be so provided for or placed in such asylum or other such institution as shall be controlled by persons of the same religious faith as the parents of such child."

This act was secured by the State Board of Charities, with the co-operation of the county superintendents of the poor. The article which was destined to mark the beginning of this bright epoch of reform and beneficence in child-saving, came from Hon. William P. Letchworth, a member of this board, and was with its annual report in 1875, transmitted to the legislature; which thereupon enacted the law, forbidding the subjection of children to the evils and perils of poorhouses, and providing the proper administration of relief to them, between the ages of sixteen and three years, which minimum age was afterwards reduced to two years.

In the following year, 1876, Mr. Letchworth visited all the orphan asylums in the state, then 136 in number, and reported on them through the board to the legislature. Thus in two successive years the conscience of the people and their representatives was informed of the evils and abuses respecting children in the poorhouses and almshouses, and of the remedies and means of relief and conditions in the orphan asylums.

Mr. F. B. Sanborn of Massachusetts stated in the fourteenth session of the National Conference of Charities and Correction, "that at the time when the state boards were first established, poor children in most of the states were associated in asylums and poorhouses and other public establishments with the adult poor, often insane, incurably diseased or vicious in life." That this state of things no longer existed he ascribed to the early and persistent efforts of these boards, selecting as an example that of New York, and emphasizing the work of Mr. Letchworth.

These orphan asylums shelter 15,027 boys and 12,580 girls, besides their wards already placed in families, being an increase of 441 inmates during the last fiscal year.

There is reason to believe that the tendency in these institutions has been to enlargement and aggrandizement, by omitting to place their children in families, and thus assuming to be permanent domiciles rather than transitional places in the transfer of their wards to family homes. If so, the remedial legislation, while succeeding in moving its wards from the poorhouses to the orphan asylums, has failed to secure its ultimate intention of removing them from asylum to family life. This may be due in part to the fact that these institutions are close corporations, while maintained in large part by municipal contributions. That there is a growing danger in this direction is shown by statistics gathered by the State Board of Charities. The following figures are approximate, as they relate only to the institutions that reported these special data in 1891, which, however, are a majority of the whole number.

Of 18,556 orphan and destitute children in such asylums, October 1, 1891, there were 3,671 orphans, 10,356 half-orphans, 4,065 who had both parents living, and 465 whose social condition was not given; while there were supported by cities, counties and towns, 11,061 ; by parents and friends, 1,717 ; by the institutions, 2,430; and not stated, 3,348; and there were committed, by magistrates and courts, 8,130; by commissioners of charities, 1,005 ; by superintendents of the poor, 1,823; by overseers of the poor, 938 ; by parents and friends, 4,422 ; and not stated, 2,238; and the duration of institution life had been 5,763 for less than one year; 5,757 for one year and less than three ; 3,051 for three years and less than five ; 2,782 for over five years ; and not stated, 303—though the total number of sick, infirm, crippled, deformed or disabled was only about three per cent., and of feeble-minded only one and two-tenths per cent., with thirteen cases of idiocy.

A high authority on these questions, Mrs. Charles Russell Lowell, in her report to the State Board of Charities, transmitted with its annual report to the legislature in 1890, has given proofs of the evils in the present system or want of system, and proposed remedies. The report shows about $1,500,000 expended for the care and maintenance of about an average of 14,000 children for the preceding fiscal year in the city of New York, with other facts, from which the inference is plain that many parents with their offspring are pauperized by removing them from the natural relations of life, with unwise kindness, if not inhumanity, to them, as well as injustice to the taxpayers.

In the State Charities Record for December, 1891, published by the State Charities Aid Association, the leading article, by Mrs. Anna T. Wilson, formerly of Philadelphia, now of the State Charities Aid Association of New York, contrasts the care of dependent children in the two cities, and it is stated that, in the year 1890, the city of New York, with a population of 1,500,000, appropriated $1,647,295.10 for the support of 15,449 children in its private institutions, and $192,997.74 for the support of 909 children on Randall's Island, making $1,840,292.84 for an average of not less than 15,000 children; while the city of Philadelphia, with a population of 1,000,000, appropriated $28,724.82 for the support of an average of less than 250 children in institutions. The system of boarding-out children until they can be permanently placed by adoption in families is in Philadelphia made the substitute for the system of asylums in New York; and from all accounts it appears to be working well, as may also be said of the new extension of the plan from dependent to destitute children, including those convicted of felonies, of which Homer Folks writes hopefully in the *Record* for last November. It should, however, be borne in mind that the results have been partly due to fortunate combinations of circumstances, including the assistance of the Children's Aid Society of Pennsylvania; and that data from large fields in other states and countries show that the boarding-out system has not always proved humane, even for dependent adults.

For juvenile dependents the system is reported from England as unsatisfactory (p. 171, appendix to the last edition of the "Poor Law" of England, by T. W. Fowle: Macmillan & Co.). The extended and successive reports of Hon. William P. Letchworth, member of the State Board of Charities, on the asylums for orphan and destitute children in the state, are of high authority and value, and give cogent reasons for preferring the asylum system of New York, with its incidental evils, to the boarding-out system of Massachusetts and Pennsylvania. Among the papers of Mr. Letchworth here alluded to is that on pauper and destitute children, transmitted by the State Board of Charities, with its annual report, to the legislature in 1875; another in the symposium by various members of the committee on preventive work among children, in the proceedings of the National Conference of Charities and Correction, in 1886; and his article on the New York state system for the care and training of dependent children, prepared on invitation for the International Congress, held at Paris, June, 1889.

The remedy for the incidental evils of orphan asylums, as well as for the essential evils which obtain in the absence of such institutions, is in the placing of children as inmates in families, but not as boarders, unless with the most protective safeguards, limiting such measure as a merely provisional expedient. The interstate agency best known and appreciated is the Children's Aid Society of New York city, the methods of which, in selecting its fields and transplanting its cases in western states, have been sometimes criticised, but are generally justified, as conditionally approved in the eleventh session of the National Conference of Charities and Correction, by Rev. Hastings H. Hart of Minnesota, the last president of the Conference.

In the incorporated hospitals of New York there were at the beginning of the present fiscal year, 5,312 patients; of whom a large number were non-paying, and in part provided for by municipalities. Such indigent patients, however, are dependent upon private charity, inasmuch as the public allowance granted seldom defrays the whole or even the greater part of the cost of their maintenance, care and treatment.

In the New York State Soldiers and Sailors' Home, the daily average for the last fiscal year was 864, being 139 less than the preceding year; the greatest number was 1,012, and the least number 723 present during the year.

There is no public institution for inebriates, the former state asylum for this class having been converted into the Binghamton Hospital for the Insane.

The State Asylum for Insane Criminals and the Criminal Insane, at Matteawan, and the adult and juvenile reformatories are not specifically mentioned, inasmuch as in their absence their inmates would be in jails, penitentiaries and prisons, rather than in poorhouses. But there is a class of intermediate institutions intended for juvenile delinquents who are not felons or hardened offenders, which come between the reformatories and the orphan asylums.

Among such intervening corporations are the Catholic Protectory, with a census of over two thousand, and the Juvenile Asylum of New York city, and the Burnham Industrial Farm near Albany.

None of the private institutions for the insane or other classes of afflicted persons, who do not belong to the indigent and dependent classes, and which do not receive public aid, are described, for the reason that their inmates would not in any event be residents or contingents of the poorhouse or almshouse.

Including orphan asylums and private hospitals receiving municipal aid, and therefore treated as semi-public institutions, and already described, there are about 500 charitable corporations in the state of New York, which are generally exempt from state, county and city taxes, but not from special assessments for local improvements to real estate.

These corporate charities, with state and municipal institutions, are subject to the authority of the State Board of Charities, which includes powers of inspection and of examination under oath, and other supervisory functions, but none executive or administrative, save those relating to the alien and state pauper laws already described, and those respecting the incorporation of orphan asylums and other institutions having to do with children, concerning which, the certified consent of the state board is made a condition precedent.

An impression of the expenditures by public and private institutions for the destitute and dependent classes in the state of New York may be obtained from the tables published by the State Board of Charities in 1891, and from their returns to this board for the last fiscal year, some of the conclusions from which are here epitomized.

The census of state and private institutions receiving public aid for the deaf, the blind, the idiots and feeble-minded, the insane and other special classes, having been given already, the population of the same classes, in the county and city institutions, namely, the poorhouses and almshouses, is here presented approximately and in round numbers, as follows:

Idiots.	Epileptics.	Blind.	Deaf.	Children under 2 years of age.	Children between 2 and 16 yrs of age.
600.	500.	200.	50.	150.	600.

Of the number of children between two and sixteen years of age, five hundred and forty were in the almshouse of the city and county of New York, but classified in special departments, though not separated as they should be from the almshouse system.

The amount expended in relief, through county and city officers for the fiscal year, was in round numbers as follows:

In Poorhouses and Almshouses.	In Out Relief.	Total.
$2,700,000	$570,000	$3,300,000

The value of the establishments of the counties and cities for the poor is in round numbers $7,800,000, and the value of the labor of the inmates for the fiscal year was $75,000.

The small income from employment of the paupers may be explained in part by their general condition, which is infirm, as shown not only by returns, but also by the observation of visitors at these poorhouses and almshouses, which in fact at the present time are, more nearly than many persons believe, in the nature of municipal infirmaries. But medical direction of the energies of these sufferers in channels of proper work would doubtless yield the greatest benefit to them in improving their physical, mental and moral condition and character, as well as lessen financial burdens in justice to the taxpayers.

Returning now to private institutions of special sorts, we find that the estimated value of the property owned by the orphan asylums and homes for the friendless, October 1, 1891, was in real estate $20,193,722.27, and in personal property $5,765,717.47, making a total valuation of $25,959,439.74; that their receipts for the prior year were $7,464,439.77, and their expenditures for the same period were $6,776,265.43; that the incorporated hospitals for the same year returned receipts, in the aggregate, $3,477,942.61, and expenditures, in the aggregate, $3,338,097.31; and that the free dispensaries, for the same period, show receipts $346,689.86, and expenditures $292,942.63.

The total expenditures for the indigent and dependent classes, including paupers, for the year ending 1891, were $17,605,660.58.

Our review of laws and agencies relating to humanity and social economy in the state of New York, has not lost sight of the vital relation between the primary work of protecting the producers in society from lapsing into indigence, and the secondary work of preventing the poor from falling into pauperism. But the means of performing the paramount duty of protection to the workers come directly within the purview of this article upon the care and cure of pauperism only in the matter of the cost of private and public charity and relief. From the tables of statistics collected and compiled by the State Board of Charities, and appended as schedules in its annual reports to the legislature, the following comparative statement has been made, showing expenditures for charitable and reformatory purposes between the years 1880 and 1891, both inclusive, to wit:

Year.	Amount expended.	Year.	Amount expended.
1880	$ 8,482,648 71	1881	$ 9,260,147 77
1882	9,320,142 60	1883	9,938,037 05
1884	10,642,763 86	1885	11,538,739 86
1886	12,027,990 01	1887	12,574,074 67
1888	13,315,698 97	1889	14,868,733 77
1890	16,349,842 43	1891	17,605,660 58

It thus appears that in this period of twelve years the expenditures have increased a little more than one hundred per cent. Though the population of the state increased only about nineteen per cent., as is shown on the basis of the federal census, it also appears from the reports of the comptroller of the state that its wealth has increased about fifty per cent. during the same period. Of this increase in expenditures—$9,123,011.87—the sum of $1,222,282.61 relates to institutions managed by the state; and the State Reformatory at Elmira, and the Soldiers and Sailors' Home at Bath, two of the state institutions existing prior to 1880, did not appear in the statistics at the beginning of this period of twelve years. Again, of this increase the sum of $1,171,053.58 relates to institutions owned and controlled by counties and cities, leaving $6,729,675.68 increase in the institutions under the direction and control of incorporated benevolent associations. Thus it will be seen that more than two-thirds of the increase of the cost of public and private relief and charity is due to private charity, with public aid administered through private corporations; and that the fraction of less than one-sixth of such increase chargeable to the state institutions is further reduced on account of two of them existing, but not reporting to the board in 1880.

There is no reason·to disbelieve or doubt that—excepting perhaps the Soldiers and Sailors' Home, the existence of which is justified by patriotic sentiment—each and all the state institutions for relief or reform, including the eight state hospitals for the insane, the State Institution for Feeble-minded Children at Syracuse, the Custodial Asylum for Feeble-minded Women at Newark, the reformatories and the asylums for the blind and the deaf, do save to the people more than their cost in preventing pauperism, and therefore in protecting both the industrial and the indigent classes.

But when all thus accomplished for the harmony of humanity and economy, and in the reconciliation of kindness to the afflicted with prudence for the taxpayers and bread-winners and burden-bearers of society, is considered with reference to the remaining evils resulting from the vicious habits of a large residue of the dependent classes, the problems of pauperism seem to be insoluble. The cure of the evils must be found, if at all, in radically new remedies.

The paupers go by families. Hence the Code of Criminal Procedure produces no appreciable effect by providing that "the father, mother, and children of sufficient ability, of a poor person who is insane, blind, old, lame, impotent or decrepit, so as to be unable by work to maintain himself, must at their own charge, relieve and maintain him in a manner to be approved by the overseer of the town where he is, or in the city of New York by the commissioners of charities and correction."

While the able-bodied pauper practically has been excluded from the poorhouse, his relative, the impotent, who is "unable by work to maintain himself," but who is improvident, intemperate and incontinent, is supported in seasons and periods of his own election, in order, as if by express design, to prepare him to procreate a progeny of paupers. Thus the humane expedient of the revised statutes injures both the subject and society, in providing without restriction or condition that "every poor person who is blind, lame, old, sick, impotent or decrepit, or in any other way disabled, or enfeebled, so as to be unable by his work to maintain himself, shall be maintained by the county or town in which he may be."

Relief is impracticable and impossible under existing laws. The remedy, if any, may be found in classifying vicious and infirm, as well as vagrant and able-bodied paupers, with the criminal classes, and subjecting them to indefinite confinement. The indeterminate sentence is the proper and potent corrective. Already approaches to its principle have been made in cases of recidivous criminals, by legislation in several states relating to felons, and in Ohio respecting mere misdemeanants. But the despairing thought in criminal anthropology is, that criminal characters are being recruited from pauperdom faster than they can be reduced by counteracting processes.

Radical and reformatory legislation is required to protect the state from crime as well as pauperism, by sequestering from society the habitual and hardened pauper, as well as the recidivous criminal, until he reforms or dies.

Questions of civil or moral right are not here involved, as if the relief proposed was by the sacrifice of life or mutilation of the body. The alteration of the physical organism so as to prevent the propagation of the kind is not necessary, and therefore is not justifiable. Indeed it is inadequate and inexpedient, inasmuch as the data of experiments in child-saving, as well as theories of natural selection, show that the vicious and criminal classes are transmitted by succession with more facility and potency through their creation of environments and external influences, thus producing correspondence in their offspring, than through heredity.

The principle of indeterminate sentences for vicious paupers being not for retribution, but for restraint and reform, is just and merciful; and its application for the protection of the people has nothing to overcome except the inertia of society.

The foregoing review of the New York system of indoor relief for her infirm and indigent people, who may be characterized as her worthy poor, as well as for her worthless paupers, is representative of similar systems of sister states. Though the progress of the Empire State is greater than the average of the advances of her sister commonwealths, there is one prevailing trend among them all tending toward general unity of design, if not uniformity in execution. The concrete presentation confined to the one may therefore be taken as a suggestion of the many better than would be their separate consideration in the abstract.

The New York dispensation through the poorhouse, with its development into distinct and distributive relief to children, and to the deaf, the blind, the feeble-minded, and the insane, in their respective schools, hospitals, and homes, state, municipal and corporate, is therefore taken, in its imperfection, as typical of American administration of charity in public institutions.

The evolution of this system is less advanced on lines of classification and administration under the roof of the poorhouse proper, than on lines of segregation and organization within other walls. While the sexes are separated, and to some extent the very sick are retired from the merely infirm, there is no distinction observed between the virtuous and the vicious poor.

What of the future? Does the progress in the last quarter-century forecast the next? Yes and No.

Yes, as the segregation in separate institutions has been the proof and the fruit of development, and so will be continued until provision shall be made for all the worthy poor in separate homes.

No, in that the proper discipline and detention of paupers who are unworthy and unsafe, must be provided not by an evolution of the poorhouse system, but by its conversion into a place of continued security for the protection of society.

PUBLIC RELIEF AND PRIVATE CHARITY.

PROFESSOR CHARLES R. HENDERSON, UNIVERSITY OF CHICAGO.

The purpose of this paper is to present in outline some of the more important relations of state and voluntary charity. The ultimate social ideal of modern philanthropy does not contemplate almsgiving and almstaking, but rather fellowship in opportunity and justice. We are not here to patch up a decaying caste-wall which divides mankind into lofty patrons and cringing, begging clients. Perhaps there is no form of social organization which excites more distrust and hatred among wage-earners than conventional benevolent societies. No doubt this is largely due to the ordinary misunderstanding of their motives and aims. Often do we hear the bitter reproach of those whose earnings are scant, that philanthropy is dealing with symptoms and not with causes; that charity in the sense of relief is mockery. A brief review of the recent literature of charity will show that this reproach is not altogether deserved. Those who have undertaken to cut off this devil's grass have most of all men found the strength and length of its roots. Look at the programme of this very Congress and you will see that serious study is being given by administrators of charity to the economic, domestic, educational, and political defects which cause or aggravate the evils of pauperism and crime. It may honestly be said that one of the chief incentives to sociological investigation is the desire to go below the mere machinery of administering relief funds to the complex origins of social miseries. No one entitled to consideration regards social pathology as more than a temporary phase of social organization and development, and all feel that to heal social diseases and to promote health all the factors of social energy must be called into play.

The first duty of charity is to secure higher wages, shorter hours, better physical and moral conditions of labor. It was once thought by some persons that orthodox political economy must question or deny·the possibility of making any change in these factors by any voluntary human effort. Now it seems to be more generally believed that wages, hours and conditions are not altogether fixed by fate and fore-ordination, but partly also by free will. The blind drivings of natural selection are helped out by social selection after a conscious design. Philanthropy, law, coöperation, united demands, may secure substantial, though not unlimited, improvement in industrial conditions. The first-rate economists of England have very frequently been misread or carelessly interpreted. Perhaps the name of Ricardo is most of all connected with the awful "iron law," that wages tend of necessity to fall to the minimum where the laborer must be in constant peril of becoming a dependent; but many forget that it was Ricardo who taught these memorable words :

" The friend of humanity cannot but wish that in all countries the laboring classes should have a taste for comforts and enjoyments, and that they should be stimulated by all legal means in their exertions to procure them. . . In those countries where the laboring classes have the fewest wants and are contented with the cheapest food, the people are exposed to the greatest vicissitudes and miseries."

Economics teaches us that hope may take the place of dull despair. Starvation rates of wages are not part of the order of eternal justice or of omnipotent and relentless destiny. The starvation of one willing to work, in sight of palaces, green fields and bursting granaries, is to our minds intolerable. The word " overproduction " of coats, where there are a million bare backs, signifies social wrong and stupidity, a cover for inaccurate thinking and unjust doing. It is as intolerable to see any class of persons partly supported at public expense as parasites, who should be wholly supported by the trade which makes their employers rich. If these employers declare that they see no way of raising wages, and plead the " wickedly overworked " law of supply and demand, we accept their confession of ignorance and incapacity as "captains of industry," but we do not accept their conclusion. For the history of industrial agitation during this century has taught us something. It has not taught anarchy, hate, rebellion, but kindness, patience and strong hope. It has not taught us to curse the rich nor to despise and slander the trades-unions. It has shown the possibility of a slow but steady gain in the material conditions out of which domestic and civil progress can grow. English factory legislation has proved, what the iron and cotton kings once denied, that money can be made in face of the competition of the world without working naked women in the mines, and babies at the loom, and grown men beyond the average power of endurance. The "captains of industry" are now as sure of that as Shaftesbury and Oastler were when they formed the forlorn advance which made the fight. The trades-unions of England, with all their faults, have proved that it is safe to trust political power to workingmen, that responsibility sobers men, and that a savings-bank account or huge strike fund makes them conservative. We admit that loveless and ugly deeds deform noble aspirations; and yet we can see that Britain has not erred in giving to unions of workingmen recognition and respect.

While multitudes are being paid a rate below the life-line, charity as a substitute for justice is cruelty. All the charity in the world can never sweep back this ocean-tide of misery caused by an unjust rate of pay and hours of toil prolonged till they kill. The average rate of life for toilers must be brought up nearer to that of the well-fed, well-clothed, well-taught people who live on rents and interest, even if thereby the rate of interest and rent falls a point or two. Worse things are happening than passing a dividend on copper stocks or distillery investments. Slavery was not indispensable to the South, and sweating-dens may be omitted without injury to the progress of the North. To assure yourself that this is the right place for scientific charity to begin, go with a volunteer friendly visitor in a city where they believe in friendly visiting. Many such have gone out with pockets full of pennies for poor children, and buoyant with expectation, only to discover that pennies thrown about do no good, and that pity is not such a crying need as justice. Not more alms, but more wages, should be the aim of our charity. The "higher classes" are the persons to lead in this crusade. The best proof that one belongs to the really superior people is that he has the will and inclination and ability to help emancipate multitudes from the most degrading form of slavery, living upon public alms. Culture has no higher task. Universities may perform no worthier work than showing how a better economical basis can be laid for the future intellectual and social deliverance of the masses of mankind. It is a great achievement to describe and account for the actual systems of finance, transportation, communication, banking, tariff, and to show

how wealth is produced and exchanged. But it will be an immensely greater achievement, intellectually and morally, for our great economists to show how this wealth can be more equitably distributed. Who can doubt, when he surveys the vast strides of science and goodness in our age, that such economists and merchant princes will be found?

But economists and captains of industry must have the aid of others. They must have the co-operation of "laboring men." They must even have the consent of drunkards, sots, idlers, vagabonds, tramps. All the world cannot make drunkards well-to-do. The gold of California would slip through a tramp's fingers and leave him poor. So all teachers, parents, editors, preachers, missionaries, women with varied gifts, godly demagogues, ambitious attorneys, agitators, reformers, retired merchants with time heavy on their hands—philanthropy needs them all. Before all free soup-houses, lodging inns, charity balls, gambling raffles for widows' benefit, subscriptions for orphanages, we must have diffused knowledge, means for social recreation, night schools, all preventive agencies which stand against pauperism as with sword of flame. Administrators of charity know best of all that what they do is a makeshift. They know that almstaking cannot be made harmless to recipients. No one has invented a way of living at the expense of others or by the permission of others without degradation. There is boundless room for widening justice, for the fellowship of social equals, for reciprocity in services, but there is no place for almsgiving as an excuse for neglecting fair dealing. There is no territory on God's earth for a class of idle and dependent rich or idle and dependent poor.

Comparative and Historical.

While all social agencies are busy dealing with causes of pauperism, that malady itself confronts us as a tremendous social fact. It cannot scare us nor force bounty by display of numbers. We are not generous upon compulsion. It would be possible for the capable majority to exterminate the incompetent members. But this method, which was precisely that employed by our barbarian ancestors, who kept family clubs to kill off feeble grandsires, is not to be thought of in our age. We cannot endure the sight of pain. Sympathy is organized to relieve distress. Social remorse torments us in the enjoyment of unshared luxuries. Sensitiveness of nerves and conscience establishes relief.

In the modes of relief administration we discover great diversity, due to peculiarities of situation, history, temper, habits, sentiments, laws and governments of various peoples. Turning to Germany, we see that since the sixteenth century the state has recognized as its duty the public care of the poor. First, it enforces the obligation of those immediately bound to care for dependent persons, as relatives and neighboring communities. But even when a legal obligation does not exist, the public care of the poor will not forbid the free benevolence of individuals, societies, and the church. Public care of the poor must merely complete private care and enter when this is inadequate. Both pursue a common end, and they should work in harmony. More than in any other departments, those of charity are decentralized. The burden is laid on local political organizations, as parishes and poor unions, since the necessities are best known in the neighborhood, the best administrators can be chosen, and the burden of taxation is less likely to be excessive. Private persons are selected for this purpose, those who have knowledge of the conditions, a sound understanding of human nature, and devotion to the common weal. The number is so large that it is impossible to pay salaries; . the almoners work for honor and from sympathy. In Elberfeld and in the cities which have imitated its example, the public districts include all who apply for aid and show the need of it; but the officers appointed by the authorities work in harmony with private and church charities, so that none are neglected; voluntary charity has ample scope, and abuses are swiftly corrected. The local political unit should bear the expense of those who belong to it and have a residence. If a case does not properly belong to a parish or union it is cared for by the state, and questions of responsibility are determined by a state tribunal. The aid is regarded as a loan, and the relatives are expected to reimburse the parish if the indigent person cannot do so. The sources of funds are endowments, collections, gifts or legacies, fines, taxes and imposts.

In France, the principles are stated by M. Chevalier as follows:

"The *commune* will limit the circle of its action, will encourage and stimulate the development of private beneficence, in which it ought always to see a valuable auxiliary and not a rival. It will come to its aid and will obtain for its assistance the influence necessary to have its useful counsels accepted, and to co-ordinate without confusing aid coming from both sources. Charitable legislation in France is actually dominated by this principle, that if society has the moral duty never to leave any real suffering without solace, yet assistance can never be demanded by the indigent as a right. The greatest liberty is left to works of private charity. When these works reach the dignity of institutions they obtain the privileges of civil life by means of conditions easy to fulfil. Public charity has no monopoly in France, not even of solicitations and public subscriptions. Charity is administered by the state, by departments and by *communes*. The *commune* is the unit of organization of charity, and it is there that it becomes personal and direct."

In the same article occurs this criticism, which shows how we are regarded by a high authority over sea :

" In certain states of the Union politics plays a rôle in public relief, and it is believed that for some politicians the functions of overseer of the poor are his part of the victors' spoils. And of what he receives for the office a part goes to the future voters for the same politician."

That seems hard for a European to understand. It is only too easy for us.

In the United States we have as many different systems as there are states ; and in each state as many plans as there are counties ; and in each township as many devices as there are trustees, and some of these devices are not exactly heavenly in origin and character. Out of so many competing experiments we ought to reap some results, for the process of vivisection without anæsthetics is costly enough to raise expectations. Yet it should be said that the state laws, originally derived from the English sources, give a degree of uniformity to administration. Speaking of the rule, the state cares for all defective and dependent persons who are homeless and helpless in its institutions. The local officers give a certain amount of aid to the friendless and helpless in their homes. In addition to this, churches and benevolent societies, lodges and individuals, give aid to many who have not been entirely cut off from personal connections with some social group. The charitable efforts of European countries are studied, and the inventiveness of our inventive people is taxed to find new and hopeful methods of relieving distress. State supervision of private charities is much needed and hardly exists, while private charities are administered as a rule without mutual understanding and co-operation.

In England, to take another example, the establishment of a government board has helped to unify the aid given by local authorities, but, save where the organized charities are well established, there is no mode of intelligent co-operation between public and private modes of help. Indoor relief is used as a check upon outdoor relief.

Points of General Agreement.

The Christian nations of our age generally agree that all dependents, defectives and delinquents are wards of society. The state, as the only organ of the collective will, must see to it that no citizen perishes, physically or morally, without care. Of course the forebodings of Mr. Spencer may prove to be wise warnings, and the most sympathetic administrator of charity will admit the peril of the position. But, for good or ill, the modern nations have launched upon this troubled sea of experiment. No man is to be driven from door to door until with curses on his lips he freeze or starve. Whatever the state permits, authorizes or encourages, it is never free from the moral duty, in the last resort, to see that relief is given. It must then be the duty of the state to see that general society is not profoundly harmed by the vicious working of a local and limited association.

It is generally agreed that personal and private charity surpasses official charity in spontaneity, versatility, adaptability, idealism, religious fervor. It is thought that official charity surpasses private charity in completeness, adequacy, equality of burdens, and in the control of criminal tendencies often mixed up with pauperism. Thus it is agreed that it is wise to combine the working of public and private charity as far as possible.

Some system is needed to secure harmony and unity between public and private beneficence. In Germany the famous Elberfeld system seems to be the one best adapted to the conditions of the country. In America, at present, that system would be impracticable. Our citizens have not been taught by custom to accept such tasks from the state. We are, therefore, looking to the voluntary and paid services of officers and visitors of the associations of charities. In these associations visitors are secured by appeals to goodwill and civic virtue. In no city have we secured an adequate supply of competent visitors, but steady advance has been made. A still further step of progress will be made when public administrators learn the value of full co-operation with these associations. The inspectors of public charity are usually shrewd detectives of fraud, but that very quality unfits them for the personal influence which a friendly visitor can wield. The salaried officers are too few to do such work as the Elberfeld visitors, even if they were inclined to do it.

It seems certain that the state should never subsidize denominational charities, but, if compelled to employ them, should simply pay for services actually rendered. But there is no objection to encouraging the most cordial co-operation in the work of charity and reform.

Changing the point of view, we may consider the *private initiation of charity*. And first, of the individual benefactor. The personal element is the most vital, direct, and human, especially if it is not official. It is an acknowledged social and legal principle that the relatives, associates, neighbors and co-religionists are first of all bound to assist an indigent person. It is only after all these sources have failed that the state consents to open its hand. But individual beneficence should not be insulated. The right can never be conceded to a man so to do as he will with his own as to work harm to society. Kindness may find ways of usefulness with organized charities, even when money is not in possession. The busy rich, able and willing to give large sums, can do most good in experimental, preventive and educational charity.

The relation of church to public charity is delicate and vital. The church is no longer the chief almoner of charity. The poor apply to public authorities when they come to want. The members of our churches who are indigent are relatively few. It is the habit of church members to refer needy persons to the public authorities in most places. If public outdoor relief were abolished, the church would again come to care for the helpless. But the necessity of civic co-operation would then be as great as ever, for ecclesiastical charities have been as much abused as state relief. Churches need to cultivate a sense of social unity. Benevolence that is insulated from a general system corrupts recipients.

All religious services in public prisons and hospitals should be given by churches and the expense should never be met from the common treasury. Those who believe in religion should not ask unbelievers to help sustain religion by enforced taxation. I honor all good chaplains in army and prisons, and I know that they are rendering faithful and holy service. It would be cruel injustice not to have such men where they are, and the state should not forbid their access to those who wish their presence. But they should be paid by an alliance of churches, not by a tax. I say this just because I believe in Christianity and dislike to see it go begging to the state for appropriations.

Good people should also support societies to aid discharged prisoners. Lady Meath, of England, has shown to Christian women a way of lightening up the cloudy, dreary days of their sisters in the county poorhouses all over the land. Public as well as private hospitals can be made more cheerful and successful in their divine work of healing by the ministry of flowers, fruits, songs and kindly looks of the King's Daughters.

Thus we see a growing integration and unification of charity work. The university sends to London's East End students to ponder misery at its source. Church and state join hands. Private and public agencies seek an understanding. The Prince of love and peace is drawing all men to Himself, and hence closer to each other.

TRAMPS.

PROFESSOR JOHN J. McCOOK, TRINITY COLLEGE, HARTFORD, CONNECTICUT.

Aimless wandering, no visible means of support, capacity to labor along with fixed aversion to labor, begging from door to door, camping on property of others without their consent—no one of these by itself, but all of them together, make up the legal picture of that species of vagabond whom we have come lately to call the Tramp. In the days of Richard II, five hundred years ago, he used to be called "sturdy vagabond, valiant beggar," and was so objectionable then and later that the whipping-post, ear-slitting and hanging were his legal portion, and a fine was the reward of the man who harbored or helped him.

In those days, and for centuries, the average pauper clung to his parish because, within orderly limitations, an existence was assured him there. The sturdy vagabond must therefore have been a person to whom orderly life was intolerable, mere existence insufficient, fixed conditions of any kind unendurable, and who broke away from the inglorious hum-drum of the birth-spot and ventured out into the life and stir of the wide world. That is to say, he was built on the general lines of our nineteenth-century tramp ; and mere convenience and brevity seem to be the only justification for the invention of a new name for him.

Whether the name tramp originated in England or America I cannot be sure. It has no place, so far as I have been able to find, in the statutes of Great Britain or Canada, while many of our states have adopted it into their legal phraseology. New Jersey began in 1876; and up to 1892, when I made an examination of the statute-books of all the states, eighteen others had followed; while a nineteenth and twentieth use the word in the index or in defining Vagrant. The word is now freely used in England in every-day life, and in the literature of pauperism and vagrancy.

For whatever reason, it is not in general favor among tramps themselves in this country. I have talked with a considerable number of them on a footing of friendliness and apparent confidence, and find that "bum" is the generic term used by them. They carefully distinguish, however, between class and class, and there is manifestly an aristocracy among them, and a middle and lower order; although, as might, perhaps, be expected, absolute agreement has not been reached as to which is upper and which lower crust. A few weeks ago I had a long talk with one of the "saltigrades"—if my spider friends will permit me to borrow one of their names—one of the order of jumpers, that is, train-jumpers. He put his family first, and spoke with undisguised contempt of the "pike bum" who "hasn't the nerve to jump a train,"—even rising and imitating the pike bum's long, awkward gait. He was still more disdainful in his description of the "city" or "shovel bum" and the "mission" or "religious bum." And he almost lacked vocabulary to express his feelings towards the "gay cat," an inferior order of beings who begs of and otherwise preys upon the bum—as it were a jackal following up the king of beasts.

He called the nobility of the order "hobos." It was thus he spelled it. He had often asked old hobos—for he was but twenty-six—how it ought to be spelled and what it meant. They did not know. It is, however, now unquestionably the generally accepted title for the railroad tramp, in America; and I may venture to say here, though I should not care to say it to one of the nobility for fear of unduly exciting him, it is even appropriated at times by "pike bums" and by "shovel bums." I am in almost daily correspondence by letter with one of the former class who not only uses it but spells it in the most approved French fashion—"haut-beaux!"

My saltigrade friend above referred to as priding himself upon belonging to the nobility of the order, gave me many incidents concerning his own career which are curious. They may not all be true. In fact, I doubt not he told me more than one lie. Still men are not apt to invent things to their own discredit, and the following was not given in a spontaneous or boastful manner, but in answer to very direct and leading questions. He had "done" thirty days each in Erie county, New York; White Plains, New York; Brooklyn, Connecticut; thirteen days in San Francisco, California; twenty days in Savannah, Georgia; ten days in Chicago; five days in the Tombs, New York City, and had been arrested in Syracuse, New York, and Richmond, Virginia.

He had passed part of one winter in an almshouse—"to get a new suit of clothes"; had been nine days in Charity Hospital, Blackwell's Island, for a finger bruise got in jumping a train; six weeks in a Philadelphia hospital for a secret disease:—they have no aversion to such a disease when winter is coming on, he told me in passing, and several eminent medical specialists confirm his story; a whole winter in a poorhouse hospital in the interior of New York for a toe lost while jumping a train; five months in a Boston hospital for an abscess on his neck, caused, as the doctors thought, by the jar of riding on trucks—he had only been six months on the road at that time, he explained apologetically! And he had also been to dispensaries now and then for medicine required by some trifling cold, though he generally carried stuff with him for this.

Apart from the above he had "never had a day's sickness in his life," he said, and spoke with much enthusiasm of the vigor and physical strength of the fairly initiated hobo.

It would be a pity to overlook one other item in the self-confessed activities of this gentleman. He had voted eight times on one single election day in New York city, receiving therefor a total of sixteen dollars. The manner in which the thing was accomplished was described by him in such fashion as to convince me that he was telling the truth —and I am not naturally credulous, nor yet void of knowledge of the ways in which this branch of practical politics is cultivated in New York and elsewhere. I should, however, perhaps add that I have been assured by a New York city detective and by another tramp that this was undoubtedly a lie. The detective's confidence was based on the record of prosecutions, "showing how careful they had been!"—the tramp's, on the high price obtained. He had never got anything like that money himself! Which reminds me that nearly half of the dozen or so of tramps whom I have recently picked up on the street here, and with whom I have had opportunity for free conversation on this and other points, have admitted that they have received compensation direct or indirect for their vote, mentioning the four states of New York, New Jersey, Connecticut and California as the places where they had done business. One, who belonged rather to the order of " city bums," at first resented the mere suggestion that he could ever have voted for money. Presently I returned abruptly to the subject with the question, " Do you mean to say then that your own side gave you nothing for turning out?" Whereupon he lifted his head and with dignity replied, " What me own side give me for voting 's nobody's business but me own." Beyond this I could not go, and he would not.

I have spoken of tramp laws in the various states. Here is a list of the states which one tramp tells me he has been in (I select the first on my note-book; I have talked with several whose record is similar) Maine, New Hampshire, Vermont, Massachusetts, Rhode Island, Connecticut, New York, New Jersey, Pennsylvania, Delaware, Maryland, North Carolina, South Carolina, Georgia, Florida, Louisiana, Texas, California (twice), New Mexico (three or four times), Arizona, Montana, Colorado, Indian Territory, Missouri, Kansas, Nebraska, Illinois, Indiana, Kentucky, North Dakota, Wisconsin, Minnesota, Utah, Arkansas, Michigan, Oregon, Nevada. He had been in Washington, D. C., of course, and had passed through Tennessee, though he had not stopped there. He had been through a great part of Canada, and had visited England in a cattle steamer, landing at Liverpool and tramping thence to Manchester. He had spent the night in a casual ward, and did not like oakum-picking, since it made the fingers sore. He thought England not comparable with America—people would not give as freely there. He got back, he said, through the offices of the American consul, and gave details concerning the return passage which may have been wholly false, but which needed only to be half true to be painfully suggestive of the extent to which the brute survives in the human animal.

This particular man had a rather gay, light-hearted way of talking. His face was not bad, though his eye was hardly true. He was decently dressed; but he wore no collar, and had other earmarks which, combined, had emboldened me to accost him upon the street. He looked temperate and had not even the odor of liquor about him. He was, however, no total abstainer, and described with much glee what he thought a remarkably good plan for getting a drink—a plan almost too ingenious to be either true or false.   But there is no question of these three things ; that the average vagabond is no total abstainer, that he always manages in some fashion to get drink when he particularly wants it, and that he is enough of a " rectifier," albeit holding no license from the United States government, to know that the real thing in drink is alcohol, and that water is the cheapest and best adulterant.   In this as in some other things he is a close observer and an astute philosopher.   I shall presently have something to say of this in a statistical way.

Both this man and three others whose faces I now recall, reeled off the names of the states they had visited, giving the railroads patronized from point to point, with a facility and a rapidity that made one's head swim.   I confess it was all beyond me, though I have traveled somewhat.   And yet localities and lines of communication were occasionally identified in such fashion as to give me general confidence in the genuineness of the itinerary.   In one instance I mentioned a number of places familiar to myself, but by no means prominent for size or otherwise, and purposely put them in wrong states.   In every case I was arrested with, " Did you say Steubenville?   Yes, I've been in Steubenville—on the Panhandle road.   But see here, sonny, Steubenville ain't in Pennsylvania ; it's in Ohio "—and so on.   This man professed to be from Rhode Island.

Such knowledge, it is true, could be obtained by a railroad brakeman of sufficiently wide experience.   And indeed I am more and more inclined to think that many of our jumper-tramps have been brakemen, and the reverse.   I have talked with several enginedrivers and firemen who are of this opinion, and in four instances tramps have personally informed me that they had been brakemen. There can be no question that many a brakeman has a very tender spot in his heart for a tramp, and that he finds ways of helping him along in spite of the universal reprobation of the management.   He fails to discover him in box car, or open car, or on the bunters, or the trucks.   He puts him off when he must, and is more than half pleased when he finds at the next stop that he has stowed himself away again.   He rescues him from starvation, as in one instance related to me, when he finds him only too successfully concealed for a long transcontinental stretch.   Engineers, firemen and conductors are far more stern.   But they too are not insensible to the pathos of " the poor devils trudging along by the rails."

This interchange explains the wonderful skill of the tramp in jumping and riding trains. One of them told me he had dived from the platform into an open car—a "gondola" as they call it—while the train was passing at full speed. It tore every button from his clothes, but didn't hurt him. I thought this a lie until an officer employed in a freight station mentioned incidentally that he had seen that sort of thing himself. And I hear from all sides among railroad men of their remarkable expertness in the ordinary ways of catching on.

The brakeman is the land sailor. An instance came to me lately of a man who had gone to sea once or twice, against the wishes of his family. He compromised eventually on railroading, and had crept up from brakeman to conductor. And I know a man of excellent family and education, who has left a good farm in eastern Connecticut, first for braking, and then for firing on a train. In the old days he would have gone to sea. Our tramps have the instinct of the brakemen, but without the industry and laboriousness of the better part of them.

However, this easy transition from the one to the other suggests the propriety of railroad managers having a more careful eye than they seem always to have had to the record and the habits of their candidates for the responsible office of brakeman.

The number of female tramps of whatever kind is not large. There is, however, a limited number of them. I have heard them called magpies, petticoat bums, and bags. They mate with a male, often arranging the alliance during a winter in an almshouse, leaving the institution at different dates to avoid suspicion, meeting at an agreed-upon spot, and sharing thereafter bed and board. The man has the lion's share of this co-partnership. The woman begs, occasionally raises money by solicitation at extremely low rates—from 10 to 50 cents—cooks, washes, and serves her lord as his will and her devotion may suggest. They camp out, occupy vacant houses, stop with farmers, or even in taverns. With the winter the partnership expires by limitation. I have been told of one instance in which such a female served, in every way, a camp of sixteen or eighteen tramps—to such a degree of baseness can the sex relation be lowered. I have read of similar arrangements in the vagabond life of Germany, but these have been actually told me here.

But I must give over this gossiping for a more severe view of the field. My observations above given have followed, not preceded, an attempt at statistical investigation. And first, the number of tramps in America. Massachusetts is the only state which, so far as I know, attempts to collect the facts necessary for a calculation. In 1891, the average daily number lodged in police stations or public lodging-houses for wanderers was 427.3. In answer to the question "Where do you usually sleep?" on the blank from which I received 1,349 replies in the winter of 1891-2, 377 gave police station or other public lodging-house. Assuming this proportion of 377 to 1,349 to be approximately representative of the ratio between the number frequenting such places at night and the total, we shall conclude that the Massachusetts total contingent to the tramp army was 1,529.7. And, assuming that the Massachusetts contingent bears the same relation to the entire army that the population of Massachusetts bears to that of the United States— 29.97—the total for this country will be 45,845. I suspect this is not far from correct, though it is partly built upon assumptions. It is from five to fifteen thousand below the current guess estimates, which fact is slightly confirmatory; since estimates of crowds are almost invariably over the truth.

I have spoken of blanks with 1,349 replies. These came from fourteen different places to which blanks had been sent. The answers were taken down generally by police officers, a separate blank being used for each case. There were twenty-four questions and eight sub-questions, with a space for remarks.

Besides the large amount of material thus secured, Mr. W. Vallance, clerk of the Board of Guardians for Whitechapel, London, secured for me tabulated replies to similar questions from 841 of his casual lodgers, October, 1891. The basis for careful conclusions was therefore far broader than anything ever before attempted, so far as I am aware. These results have been compared with the analysis of the 52,335 cases which have come under the observation of the German *Arbeiter Colonien* since their establishment, so far as the much more meagre statistical scope of these would allow.

A brief account of the more important results of my inquiry may be of use here:

Fifty-seven per cent. of our American tramps have trades or professions; forty-one per cent. are unskilled laborers. Ninety-eight trades were represented by the 1,349 individuals—and nearly half of the persons belonging to these were attached to employments which require constant locomotion, as sailors, firemen, teamsters and brakemen, or are associated with these occupations—such as shoemakers, curriers, hostlers, blacksmiths and horseshoers. Three and six-tenths per cent. more are in a trade which is drawn upon for some of the most striking figures illustrative of the unrest and transitoriness of human existence—the weavers.

One tramp in twenty is under 20 years of age; three out of five under 35; seventy-five out of one hundred under 40, and only one in one hundred and eleven over 70. Ours are much younger than the English and considerably younger than the German, though they too are in the prime of life.

This was the winter when the *grippe* was raging, and yet only 8.5 per cent. of them claimed to be suffering from bad health, and 83.5 per cent. declared specifically that their health was good. In England 91 per cent. admitted that their health was good. The German colonies gave no statistics under this item.

What makes people tramps? The question designed to throw light on this was "Why did you take to the road?" And, of course, most of them attributed it to their being "out of work"—82.8 per cent. in fact. A few were "tired of work," or "wanted to take life easy"; still more "wanted to see the country"; more still charged it to "drink," a few to "roving disposition" and a very few to "won't work." 55 per cent. of them, however, admitted that they had not tried to get work the day they were questioned, which is suggestive; and 18 per cent. of them "didn't know" when they were going to work again, while 2 per cent. more frankly replied "never," to the question, "When are you going to work again?"—which is still more suggestive. And most suggestive of all will be thought, perhaps, the reply made later on, which showed that 63 per cent. of them are confessedly intemperate.

If ever accurate statistics are collected, I think it will be found that this is almost exactly the percentage of cases of pauperism in general due to intemperance. I believe industrial causes have but little to do with pauperism in general, or vagabondage in particular.

Fifty-six per cent. of our tramps are of American nativity. Next follow Ireland, England, Germany, Canada, Norway and Sweden, and Scotland. There were only two Italians. A considerable num-ber, possibly a majority of the American section, are of foreign, chiefly Irish parentage. I have no statistical basis for this statement, but think it to be probably correct. England has almost no foreign element to deal with among her tramps, and Germany practically none at all.

More than nine-tenths of them are unmarried, and a like proportion can read and write. This is not far from the proportion of adult white literates according to the 1880 census. In intelligence and education it is my impression that the average tramp is not appreciably different from the general population. He is certainly not inferior, I think.

"How they are housed and fed" is an important question. In pleasant weather they live out of doors. Eleven per cent. admitted having been at some time inmates of almshouses. I suspect this to be below the truth. But in any event the close quarters presently become insufferable, and by April the captives are off. Some of them go south for the winter, living thus in perpetual summer. A friend tells me that while running an engine on the Baltimore and Ohio railroad he always passed a troop of them with faces turned south in October, and another troop with faces turned north in April.

Thirty-two per cent. of them admitted having been in hospital, many of them more than once. And I have it from hospital surgeons and from the lips of members of the fraternity, that a hospital is considered a good place for the winter, and that certain diseases commonly regarded formidable are rather welcomed by them late in the fall, as promising indefinite asylum in this comfortable and healthful resort. Only one-sixth of them claimed to have been in hospital at their own charges; the rest were paupers of some kind. And such slight work as is done in almshouses is done in summer, when they are away. So that the hospital and almshouse fraction may be set down as a public burden pure and simple.

While outside institutional walls they are variously housed in boxcars, police stations, wayfarer's rests, cheap lodging-houses, hotels, wagons, water-closets, churches and school-houses; and the balance accept lodging at "Mother Green's," to use the German tramp's phrase for camping out.

"How do they generally secure their food?" Twenty per cent. say they beg; nine per cent. more "beg and work"; over two per cent. more "beg and steal." Three per cent. live off their "friends." Twenty-seven per cent. "work" or "work and want." Thirty-eight per cent. say they "pay for it." How for the most part this is done is left to the imagination. I am convinced that the life of a fraction, possibly the greater part of this company consists in alternations of work and travel or debauchery. The work is suspended as soon as the means for the last named have been secured, and the "sobering up" is commonly at public expense.

Counting their house-room at nothing, I am convinced that $240 a year would be a moderate, and $200 a year a very conservative estimate for the actual cost per head of our army of tramps. This would amount to about $10,000,000 annually. This has to be paid for, of course, by somebody. And that somebody is the taxpayer.

Only six per cent. admitted having been convicted of crime. Manifestly they thought drunkenness no crime, for thirty-nine per cent. admitted conviction for drunkenness. I suspect that these figures give a fairly correct impression of the real state of the case. Things to eat and things to wear are probably looked upon by the vagabond as common property. That view of things is apt to come to the front as soon as men get away from the restraints of orderly life; of which the history of war gives ample evidence, and that of picnicking and summering is not lacking in it. But felony is, I believe, confined to the few. Criminal assault is possibly the commonest form of felony known among them. I doubt if weapons are often carried by them.

One of their number who has been on the move for thirty years, in writing to me complains bitterly of the lawless minority who are "mean enough for anything," and who by their evil deeds bring the quieter majority into disrepute. Since I have spoken of the contempt in which the "jumper" holds the "pike bum" and other "bums," it is only fair to add that this informant lays the burden of crime upon that same proud and haughty aristocracy of jumpers.

In answer to a circular containing various questions, I received replies from thirty-five chiefs of police and a number of other persons of supposed wisdom and knowledge. Of the chiefs of police twenty-one stated that no conditions of person—as cleanliness, etc.— were insisted upon in their cities for public lodging, and twenty-two that no conditions of work were imposed.

Sixteen stated that the same persons returned frequently, three occasionally, two periodically; ten that the same persons did not return frequently.

Twenty-seven stated that applicants were always received; four that they were not; six that they were liable to be arrested; two, imprisoned as tramps or vagrants, if they returned often.

Twenty-two put the able-bodied at from ninety to one hundred per cent. Only three fixed it as low as fifty.

Sixteen thought it on the whole advantageous to offer lodging at public expense; eighteen were of the opposite opinion. Of the sixteen, four favored it on grounds of general humanity, two out of regard to the possible deserving minority among the tramps. Nine favored it on grounds of public policy, of which six for protection of property, one for protection of person.

Eleven thought compulsory work was the best solution of the tramp question; two confinement; two corporal punishment, of which one the shot-gun; one severer laws; two enforcement of present laws; one furnishing employment; three believed in the workhouse; one thought encouragement ought to be refused; and one thought the repeal of the McKinley bill would do it!

Not a single one advocated moral measures. I am sure this is not because our police authorities attach no importance to such instrumentalities. I fear it is because they think the tramp is impermeable to them. I should be sorry to declare myself wholly of this opinion. On the other hand, moral measures when tried have generally been unsuccessful. Two habits have chiefly to do with the conditions of vagabond existence—the habit of idleness and the habit of intemperance: to which perhaps a third might be added—the habit of physical uncleanness. Now moral means are very powerful as preventives of these habits, and are invaluable allies in overcoming them. But the first thing, I suspect, must be forcible restraint from all these habits, and forcible inculcation of their opposites.

And from this it will be plain that I should recommend uniform laws in all the states committing drunkards and vagrants to places of detention where they must abstain from drink, must work, must keep clean, must avoid licentiousness—and that for an indefinite period. They might be made to nearly or quite support themselves in such establishments. And in that event we should save $10,000,000 or so a year. And then there would be the chance of reforming some of them, of which there is now almost none whatever.

But as long as they are left to roam at will, restrained only by an occasional spasm of enforcement of the vagrant laws, it would be an immense gain if soft-hearted people would stop giving them money. Be sure it goes almost without an exception for drink or worse. The person who will give any beggar a coin just because it seems too hard to refuse him, ought on similar grounds to give razors and guns to madmen and children.

VAGRANCY.

A. O. WRIGHT, MADISON, WISCONSIN.

Vagrancy is an offense not confined to our own country or our own time. It has been known in all lands and all ages. Perhaps the largest amount of vagrancy ever known was a little before and after the Middle Ages, in Europe, when the breaking up of the feudal state of society and the false ideas of charity inculcated by mediæval Christianity created a large amount of vagrancy and begging. The mendicant monks had consecrated one form of vagrancy to the service of the church. The universities sent out swarms of beggar students. The artisans, after having served their seven years of apprenticeship, were then expected to spend an indefinite number of years as *Wander-burschen*, traveling from place to place in search of work, and often eventually became tramps in our own sense of the word. There was no system of public poor relief, but charity was supplied either by loose and unsystematic individual benevolence or by the doles of nobles or of monasteries, both of which encouraged vagrancy. In England, in the time of Elizabeth and James, the great increase of vagrancy was attributed at the time to the changed conditions of agriculture, which threw large numbers of farm laborers out of employment. All sorts of remedies were tried for the great evil. At one time "sturdy beggars" were hung by the hundred. Whipping was the common method of punishment. The authorities of each parish whipped vagrants at the cart's tail from their own parish to the next. In more recent times there are still large numbers of able-bodied beggars tramping through "merry England," although an effective poor law system has provided amply for all the disabled poor, so amply that one-half of the laboring population of England to-day, if they live more than fifty years, will die in the workhouse.

In this country there is very little begging by persons who are actually maimed or disabled, or who pretend to be so. Our systems of poor relief provide bountifully for all cases of real need, and in all ordinary times there is work enough for every one to do in this paradise of the poor man; and yet we find a large number of able-bodied men tramping around the country and living upon the public in one form or another. These constitute the tramp problem. The tramp is an anomaly in this country. Where the demand for labor is so great, and the pay is comparatively so high, it is a surprising thing that we have a large number of able-bodied men tramping around the country, apparently looking for work. I remember very well, about twenty years ago, in the city of Austin, Minnesota, hearing the farmers in harvest-time offer on the streets four dollars a day for men to work binding wheat, and at the very time I saw dozens of able-bodied men standing on the streets and refusing to accept those wages. The city marshal at that time told me that, along with the annual migration of harvest hands following the northward ripening of the grain, there came also a large number of tramps, who refused to labor at any price. The harvest was merely their excuse for tramping.

The characteristic of the genuine tramp is that he will not work if he can help it. I saw a tramp, some years ago, in the Waukesha county poorhouse, who had been kept in a cell on bread and water for six months, every day being offered his choice of good food and liberty if he would work, and every day refusing to work on any terms. I suppose he got some other food besides bread occasion-ally smuggled into his cell by other inmates of the poorhouse, as he could not live for six months on bread and water alone. But he was a prisoner, and he had been a prisoner for six months on very limited rations, rather than degrade himself by working. He was a martyr to his principles. About three years ago, while inspecting jails and poorhouses, I fell in with the state high-school inspector. As we were both approaching one of the principal cities of our state on a railway train, I invited him to spend the evening with me in visiting the jail and seeing and studying the tramps, whom I well knew I could find there in abundance; and I noted the effect of a crowd of tramps upon a thoughtful and sensitive man, accustomed to meet persons ambitious and industrious, mentally and physically. He saw in the jail some sixty able-bodied men contented to merely exist, having the form of humanity but having little of the spirit of it. It was a question which he tried to solve for several days after he had left that school of crime and vice, but which he confessed to me finally he could not solve.

There is a regular organization of tramps in this country as in England, and I suppose elsewhere. Like other savage societies they have certain recognized leaders. Like most secret societies they have signs of recognition and passwords, and they also have certain marks by which they indicate the reception given them in the houses which they have visited, so that other tramps who follow them may profit by their experience.   They also leave their cards in the police stations and railway depots on their regular routes of travel, something like this: " Chicago Kid, Nov. 30, '92. Going east," " Jersey Bill, March 3. Pointed for St. Paul." I have seen hundreds of these cards on the walls of a single police station, accumulated in one season, before the annual house-cleaning had erased them.   A few years ago they were organized in bands of a hundred or more, who captured freight trains and terrorized villages.   At one time the militia in Wisconsin were called out and did picket duty on the border of the state at Beloit, while the hostile camp-fires of hundreds of tramps reddened the evening air of Illinois.   At another time the militia of Madison were called out to receive a freight train when it arrived, and captured the tramps who had captured the train, and the jail was filled as it never was filled before. The vigorous action of the sheriff at the time in compelling the tramps to work gave such a hard name to Madison in the tramp circles that for years it was shunned by the fraternity. The severe laws against these organized mobs of tramps, and their enforcement by the authorities, broke up all the large gangs in Wisconsin about the year 1880.

After having seen many thousand tramps in jails and poorhouses and houses of correction, after having interviewed hundreds of them, after having talked for many hours with officers who have had them under their charge, I am satisfied that the mass of the tramps consists of men who are trying to find out where work is so as to avoid making its acquaintance.   There are a few criminals among the tramps, either hiding there purposely as the best way to avoid arrest, or having been reduced from regular burglars or pickpockets to tramps by drink or by too inquisitive police officers.   There are also among the tramps quite a few drunkards, who have become so broken down by drink that they cannot be trusted with work of any value. But, as a rule, criminals are not tramps ; and, as a rule, drunkards are not tramps.   The mass of the tramps are simply lazy loafers who hate work and cleanliness.   They are savages in the midst of civilization. At best they are persons who love to wander from a restless disposition or a desire of novelty.   At the worst they are enemies of society, ready for any crime that may come handy, but restrained largely by cowardice from anything but minor depredations.

There are certain classes of persons who are on the border-line of vagrancy and yet are not genuine tramps in the strict definition of that word.

No one considers as tramps the Winnebago Indians, who still haunt the four lakes around Madison, as their ancestors did, even if they do add to their ancestral diet of fish and muskrats occasional cold victuals begged from the white man's table, and if they do wander from one place to another.

Nor are the gypsies, whom Borrow, Leland and others have glorified, real tramps, although they lead a vagrant life. The gypsies are a curious survival, in the midst of our high civilization, of the lower civilization of a wandering Hindoo tribe.

There are many sailors and lumbermen and other laboring men who have no settled home or are far away from home, who work when they can, who usually spend their money freely (when they get it) for liquor and other vices, and who are then often reduced to all kinds of shifts to live till they can get work again. I have heard of one thrifty fellow who regularly deposited his wages in a savings bank, and, as soon as navigation closed, had himself sentenced for the winter to the House of Correction, thus compelling Milwaukee county to furnish him good food and clean quarters in return for light work.

It is scarcely fair to put this class of laboring men with the real tramps, because they merely beg at private houses and because they are willing to work. Still, any measures of treatment of tramps, whether by public or private authority, will be sure to get some of this class, and in all our plans for dealing with them we must not forget that the apparent tramps include many laboring men who are not real tramps.

Tramps are rarely country-bred boys; they are mostly the young hoodlums of the great cities. A few years ago I found sixty-eight tramps one day in a certain jail, herded together in idleness and what a tramp would consider comfort. Over sixty of them appeared to be between fifteen and twenty-five years old. I questioned each one where he came from, and about fifty claimed to be from Chicago. I judged that most of them told the truth.

Tramps live by begging and stealing. Although charitable individuals in the last few years have largely learned to refuse money or food to able-bodied beggars, there are still enough people willing to give at least food to make it easy for tramps to live by begging. In the summer there are many tramp resorts hidden in the woods here and there, to which the plunder of the hen-roost and garden are brought, as well as the proceeds of begging and an occasional bottle of whiskey for a grand picnic reunion. Within recent years it is noticeable that the tramps are fairly well clothed, instead of going in rags, as they are still depicted in the comic papers, which are always behind the times in their jokes. This is due to the fact that the cheap clothing-houses have pushed their goods into the country stores, which are not well guarded at night. Thus the ready-made clothing suit which began in a sweating-shop in the city sometimes ends by clothing a tramp in the country.

Tramps love to wander. In the summer, tramps follow the fashion and take long tours of the country. In winter, they partly go south with other northern tourists, partly they crowd into the great cities, and partly they find refuge in jails and poorhouses all over the country. In traveling, the tramps almost invariably follow the main lines of railroads. In the winter, those tramps who remain north are driven for shelter to various public institutions. They apply in large numbers for admittance to the police stations of the cities, where they stay night after night in places provided for them especially, until warned to move on, when they try some other police station in the same city, unless committed to the House of Correction ; in which case the comfortable quarters and good food reconcile them in a measure to the very moderate amount of work required of them. In the country they pass from one county-seat or city to another, applying for admittance, and being received in this or that jail or police station very much according to the discretion of the local magistrates and officers.

The fact that the tramps have become the occasion of a species of official plunder, under which the people are quite restive, has kept this question before the public mind, and is probably the occasion of this topic being selected for discussion here and now. The waste of public money in this way by the counties and cities of Wisconsin runs from $50,000 to $100,000 a year. It is less now than it was, because public opinion has really had some effect upon the officers, and because several of the counties which were most burdened have salaried their sheriffs.

The root of the whole difficulty is in the foolish system of paying fees instead of salaries. The tramp problem as a serious burden upon the taxes would disappear at once if sheriffs and justices of the peace were paid no fees.

It can scarcely be expected of a sheriff, who is elected for two years and is then ineligible for re-election, and who is paid by fees, that he should refuse to arrest tramps when they ask to be arrested, or when citizens ask their arrest to get rid of the danger of having tramps around. It can easily be seen that some sheriffs and justices of the peace would be tempted to form a virtual conspiracy to rob the public by sentencing tramps for one day each, and by making it so pleasant for the tramps that they will pass the word around to their fellows to call that way. It could hardly be expected that an average officer would take vigorous measures to drive away such profitable guests. And the few sheriffs who have worked efficiently for the interests of their constituents at the expense of their own pockets deserve high commendation. As a rule, however, the fee system demoralizes all concerned. If the sheriff wishes to drive away tramps, he cannot oppose too strenuously the justices of the peace and the various village marshals, who all get a little of the plunder. And many of the members of the county board hope to be themselves elected sheriff some time, and therefore do not object too loudly to the bills that are presented, especially as they are all strictly legal bills. The justices of the peace and the marshals also are apt to remember a sheriff or a member of the county board who is too particular, and when he comes up for some office they will " knife him." All which shows that the fee system cannot be cut off by inches but must be destroyed as a whole.

Many counties in Wisconsin have attempted to discourage tramps by providing work for them in connection with the jail. The idea of labor for tramps is correct, but the execution of it by sheriffs and their deputies is ineffective. A sheriff who is paid by fees is not likely to discourage tramps. He may not take any pains to encourage them; indeed, I think few sheriffs nowadays do so. But it is too much to expect of human nature that a sheriff shall take special pains to work directly against his own interests. In several cases the county board has employed a guard over the tramps while at work, but the guard has usually discovered very soon that he had better be on good terms with the sheriff than with the county board. And in fact the foolish economy of county boards usually leads to the employment of such cheap help for this work as to defeat its own object, by making the guard as ridiculous to the tramps themselves as is a country scarecrow to a flock of blackbirds.

Another ineffective remedy which has been tried is the reduction of the fees in all tramp cases from about five dollars to one dollar. When that bill was before the legislature I warned the committee

that it would be ineffective and showed them why. The result
has verified my predictions. The returns show that fewer tramps
have been committed to jail as such, but that there has been an
alarming increase of drunkenness and other petty crimes. One
sheriff reported to me in one year 72 persons sentenced to jail for
"indecent exposure of the person." A tramp is very accommodating to an officer who is accommodating to him. He will plead
guilty to any charge the sheriff brings against him, so that he can
get into jail, but he is very careful not to plead guilty to a state prison
charge. I was told that, after a revolution in one of our counties,
so that tramps were no longer encouraged at the jail, a fellow coolly
took a coat from the display in front of a clothing-store and walked
along to the next corner, where he stopped and, with a disappointed
look, hailed the first-comer with the remark, "Say, stranger, hain't
you got no police in this town?" All of which shows that tramping
may be abolished in official reports and still exist in full vigor in
reality.

Amid a collection of unsuccessful experiments at suppressing
vagrancy, of which I have given only Wisconsin cases, there have
been a few successful efforts, which I will name. A little over a
hundred years ago, Benjamin Thompson, a native of Massachusetts,
became Count Rumford and prime minister of the King of Bavaria.
Being given absolute power over this subject, he provided factories
and workhouses, and on a given day arrested every beggar and
vagrant in the kingdom and put them at work at such things as they
were capable of doing. He paid them according to the value of their
work, encouraging them in every way not only to earn something
by honest labor, but also to learn how to perform skilled labor at a
higher rate of pay. By using force on the one hand and inspiring
hope on the other, he converted the swarms of vagrants and beggars,
with which the kingdom had been infested, into industrious and self-
supporting citizens. At the present time the kingdom of Prussia has
settled a large number of vagrants upon the waste lands of Westpha-
lia. They are held under commitment for a time, but are encouraged
to self-support, and given freedom as soon as they can be trusted.
The scheme which Booth, the head of the Salvation Army, proposed.
in his book, "In Darkest England," although it has had only a year's
trial, is already working very successfully, and a large number of
vagrants and drunkards and other broken-down wrecks of humanity
have already been rescued from the slums of London and are earn-

ing an honest living and are nearly if not quite self-supporting. In the United States, the state of Connecticut, although close by the great city of New York, which sends out its swarms of tramps every summer, has for many years prevented the tramps from coming near its border by sentence to a state workhouse. The superintendent of the Industrial School for Girls told me with great delight how the father of one of his charges, who was a tramp, when he came to visit his daughter, was obliged to disguise himself as an honest man in order to avoid arrest and imprisonment. In Indianapolis and other cities the provident wood-yard, by offering meals and lodging for a certain definite amount of labor, has sifted out all the vagrants who were at all willing to work, and left those who were either persistently lazy or vicious to be sentenced to the House of Correction.

These examples in actual experience show that the tramp problem is not insoluble. Any agency, public or private, which will offer decent board and lodging in return for a fair amount of work is a true charity for the homeless but industrious poor. The labor test will sift out the genuine tramps from the destitute workers. Along with the labor test necessarily goes the test of cleanliness. No institution but a jail or police station can afford to keep such dirty lodgers as many tramps are, without using a bathroom and a room in which clothing is steamed. Any agency, public or private, which will furnish food, shelter and cleanliness in return for unskilled labor will relieve the public of the need of giving food, clothes or money to tramps. But to reach the cases of the genuine tramps, legal measures only will suffice, because the genuine tramp will not work unless compelled to do so.

One plan which has been proposed for Wisconsin is that of a state workhouse. Under proper conditions, this plan can be made effective, as the experience of Connecticut shows. But the experience of Massachusetts also shows that, where the length of sentences and the election between the state workhouse and a local prison is left optional with the local magistrates, it will work about like all other kinds of local option. In some towns in Massachusetts the magistrates sentence tramps for ninety days to the state workhouse, and the tramps of course shun those towns; in other towns the magistrates are more lenient to the tramps, or more anxious for fees for themselves, and the tramps patronize those towns.

I have already spoken of our experience with tramps appearing on the records charged with drunkenness, with petty larceny, with

assault and battery, or with indecent exposure of the person. This
shows how easy it is to evade the law providing a state workhouse,
if that workhouse is for tramps only. The way to avoid this is to
have all sentences for misdemeanors executed in the state workhouse
and to abolish the foolish system of sentencing for very short terms.
There are excellent reasons for establishing a state workhouse for
misdemeanants, entirely aside from the tramp question. In Michigan
the state workhouse has been tried for misdemeanants with good success. It is nearly self-supporting, without convict labor, and it is not
a school of vice and crime, as other jails are, to which misdemeanants
are sentenced. Such a state workhouse ought to have its prisoners
sentenced for one or two years, unless sooner discharged, with the
understanding that all first offenders shall be discharged in about
three months, but that old hands shall be kept longer. The Bertillon
system of identification of criminals will detect professional criminals
and habitual tramps, who should be kept much longer, to protect
society and to weary them of Wisconsin justice, so that when
discharged they shall seek " fresh fields and pastures new."

But I am convinced that a yet greater good can be done if we are
only willing to undertake it. The best jail I ever visited (not in the
architecture, but in its management) is the jail at Media, Delaware
county, Pennsylvania. The Quakers are the original prison reformers,
and the Quaker end of Pennsylvania has the best managed state
prison and the best managed county jails in the United States. The
Delaware county jail is not controlled by the sheriff, but by a jailor
who is appointed by a board of directors, and who is paid a salary
and no fees. The jail is managed on the public account plan. Every
prisoner labors in his own cell, and may earn something by a proper
amount of work. As no tobacco is furnished free, all the prisoners,
whether required by law or not, willingly labor in order to earn their
tobacco. There being no fees, the jail is managed in the interests of
the people. Tramps shun this jail, although near a large city. All
the jails in Canada are governed by jailors appointed by the provincial governments, and are paid salaries, and tramps are not
numerous in Canada.

My remedy for the tramp problem would be to adopt the Quaker
idea of jail management. This will also be a remedy for all the
various difficulties now surrounding the jails, the most absurdly
managed and most dangerous part of our whole prison system.

This plan is not an ideally perfect plan, but it is one which could
be carried out practically. An ideally perfect system could only be

attained by destroying our local self-government, which would be too high a price to pay for even an ideal prison system. The evils of centralization might prove in the end to be greater than the evils of local self-government.

The tramp is one portion of the débris of our civilization. All the various forms of crime and pauperism link in with the tramp question. Whatever is done wisely in one line will irresistibly aid everything else. Getting rid of tramps from one state will tone up the administration of justice in petty cases; it will prevent our jails being polluted and overcrowded by the presence of large numbers of uncleanly vagrants; it will relieve our poorhouses and our insane asylums of many undesirable inmates; it will reduce the criminal expenses of many counties; it will relieve railroad employees of much trouble and some risk; it will banish the annoyance and fear which tramps have brought to many homes in the country; it will save the people from the demoralizing spectacle of idle loafers in the midst of an industrial civilization, and of lawless vagrants in the midst of a law-abiding population. Tramps may be driven away, which is a gain to ourselves, or they may be reformed, which is a gain to humanity. But to do either, we must reorganize in a large measure our defective machinery for the treatment of criminals, which is a gain both to ourselves and to humanity.

MUNICIPAL PROVISION FOR SHELTER OF HOMELESS POOR IN BOSTON—TEMPORARY HOME FOR WOMEN AND CHILDREN—WAYFARERS' LODGE AND WOODYARD FOR MEN.

THOMAS F. RING, BOSTON.

My theme is the municipal provision made by Boston for the temporary relief of the immediate needs of the transient and casual poor, who, penniless, friendless and homeless, ask for a meal or a night's lodging; it does not extend to the poor admitted to the almshouses or hospitals.

Adjacent to the Charity Building in Boston, where nearly all the public and private relief agencies and societies have their offices, is a large brick building known as the Temporary Home for Women and Children, owned and maintained by the city of Boston and under the charge of the overseers of the poor.

Here, women and children, meaning little children, if of the male sex, are provided with beds, good food and shelter for a longer or shorter time, according to their needs. In actual experience the term has been from part of a day to even six weeks. A nursery department is provided for babies and for mothers with babies. The whole number of admissions for the year 1892 is stated as 3,564 (2,703 women and 861 children), but the number of different individuals who entered was only 2,023 (1,283 women and 740 children), some of course entering more than once during the period. Women may have meals and lodging at the home while searching for employment, but are required to do some house-work during their stay. Meals are given gratis to women who apply for them.

The average daily population of the home is 30; some infants are born in the house (17 last year), but the rule is to obtain accommodations elsewhere for lying-in cases when it is practicable to do so. Lost children are kept until claimed by relatives or friends. 370 children came with their mothers to this house in 1893; 127 were stated to be illegitimate.

What can be said of the Lives of the Women who ask for Shelter?

One-half are known to be of the class that spend much of their time in the almshouses, much of their time in the penal institutions, with a brief freedom among dissipated companions while in the city.

It is purely a matter of accident with them where they go next; it may be to the Island for a term of imprisonment, it may be to the almshouse, where they may stay practically as long or as short a time as they wish, being discharged on their own application, unless the medical officer at the almshouse objects in the interest of public health.

A second class is made up from women-servants who have too strong a liking for liquor, who cannot or do not remain long in a situation, and have no place to go while out of employment.

Female paupers waiting investigation of their legal standing or other circumstances are lodged here, pending definite action of the city or state relief officers.

Sometimes a poor, unfortunate girl, thrust into the street in the hour of her trial, asks for a bed and is tenderly carried through her confinement.

Of the rest, little is known ; they come for a meal or a lodging and on the morrow " move on," God knows where; they are not residents of the city, they have no acquaintances among us, and are going somewhere in search of employment or of friends.

In this charity, Boston expended in 1892, $7,369.63, and it was for the protection of homeless women and little children that Boston's first shelter was provided.

Wayfarers' Lodge and Woodyard for Men.

When it became known that women were given meals free at the Temporary Home, numbers of men out of employment applied daily for meals also ; they were served, upon condition that they first made compensation by sawing or splitting wood, of which a large quantity thoughtfully provided was conspicuously heaped in the yard of the house.

This was the beginning of the kindling wood business, afterwards transferred to and still carried on by the Wayfarers' Lodge and Woodyard owned by the city. The money to pay for the relatively small stock of wood and saws for the experimental yard at the Temporary Home was furnished by public-spirited overseers from their own pockets, since the city solicitor ruled that money for a speculative enterprise could not be drawn from the city treasury. The Lodge since that time has paid into the city treasury $21,cco from the profits of the business ; the payment, doubtless, is a legal transaction, for no objection has been made so far by the law officers of the city.

The tramp, as a species, first became known in this country in the decade following the close of the Civil War. No marauding invaders were more feared in the thinly settled country places than were the tramps.

In the cities they were rather a nuisance than a danger, for police control awed them into a sneaking obscurity. They congregated at nightfall about the police stations, and were admitted to the hospitality of the cells, which they shared with the drunken men arrested on the street.

One can judge of the number of such idlers when he reads that in 1877, the year before the Lodge was opened, the police stations of Boston furnished 55.973 lodgings to men and 6.746 to women. No decent provision could be made for the miserable wretches, they were not given food nor a chance to wash, but at daybreak turned into the street to beg or steal a breakfast somewhere. The police stations were not designed for such a swarm of human beings, and the atmosphere was next to poison for officers or inmates.

Acting under the provisions of a law passed by the Massachusetts Legislature of 1875, the overseers of the poor of Boston in 1877 applied to the city for the use of a schoolhouse on Hawkins street, then badly damaged by fire and unoccupied, that they might carry out the provisions of the law enabling overseers of the poor to require some labor from persons applying for food or shelter. The city council promptly voted to supply a house and other means, and I had the honor, as a member of the board, to be one of the committee to organize and manage the new Lodge and Woodyard, and was a member of the same committee for nine years, until I declined a fourth term on the board.

Our committee studied the situation carefully, took advice from the police, read what they could find printed on the subject, and opened the Wayfarers' Lodge (a name suggested by Mr. T. C. Amory, the chairman of the committee) in 1878.

A leading purpose was to get rid of many of the tramps infesting the city, by closing the police stations against lodgers, compelling all applicants for lodgings to call at the police stations for cards on the Lodge, and retaining the applicant at the station if he were noisy or intoxicated, giving cards only to men who appeared to be sober.

On arriving at the Lodge, the applicant presents his card of admission, is asked his name, age, occupation, birthplace, and whether married or single. A striking proof of the wisdom of the institution of matrimony is found in the fact that very seldom is a married man a tramp; the tramp has only himself to care for, and he seems to take very poor care of that. With us he is becoming more of a rarity; speed the day when he shall be extinct, and the last specimen of the race, after repenting of his sins and making an edifying death, may atone for all his offenses in a dry purgatory in a glass case in the ethnological department of the Museum at Harvard University.

Our applicant, after registry is completed, is given a ticket bearing a number, which is his number while in the house. He descends to the basement, where he completely disrobes; I have seen one tramp take off four pairs of trousers, peeling like an onion. The clothes are tied up in a bundle and placed for an hour or so subject to the action of dry steam, thoroughly disinfecting them and destroying all germs of vermin or perhaps disease. About ten thousand suits of clothes are so treated annually, certainly a great sanitary advantage to the general public. The clothes shaken out of the bundle are hung on a hook numbered the same as the man's ticket, and dry in a few minutes, with no apparent damage to the garments. The lodger in the meantime has been through a warm bath, his hair drenched with a special preparation, he has taken a clean night shirt, and gone up to the dormitory, where he has a neat cot bed to himself. There are three rooms with fifty cots in each, and some smaller rooms with more cots ready for use. From forty to one hundred and seventy men sleep here every night in the year. Gas burns low in the rooms; closets are on each floor for use of the men; there is always peace in the house. The men, after the unaccustomed luxury of a warm bath and a fresh, clean night robe, sleep soundly until called at six in the morning, when they go down and dress, then pass into the yard covered by a roof, where each man finds a foot of wood and a saw waiting for him. When he has finished the task he gets a ticket admitting him to breakfast. Some men can do the work in three-quarters of an hour, some take two hours; but unless a man is sick he must do the work before he can have any breakfast. By nine o'clock most of the men are gone, and the yard is empty until the men come in to work an hour for their dinner.

The cost of the Lodge in 1892 was $9,436.68 (no rent for the use of the building is charged by the city), 32,611 lodgings were furnished, and 71,549 meals given. The cost of the materials used for the table makes the meals average six cents each man. Here is the *ménu:* Soup (quart bowl), stewed beef, bread, potatoes, Boston baked beans on Sundays, fish chowder on Fridays, tea, milk and sugar at all the suppers. A man may suit himself as to the quantity he wishes to eat. No one watches him. He can take his time and eat what he wishes. Counting the cost of the Lodge last year at $9,400 and the lodgings at 32,000, the daily cost of a lodging is thirty cents, including meals. Each lodger could, if space were available (and not half the needed space is provided), saw and split a foot of wood, advancing the commercial value of the same twenty-five cents, and thus almost cover the whole cost of his keeping for the day.

But for want of space the men are not fully employed at productive labor, some are piling wood or doing something to keep them moving, so that the result is that the labor of all the men produces about one-third of the cost of the Lodge.   That, placed on the basis of one day, means that it costs the city thirty cents a day, and the lodger returns ten cents a day by his labor.

On the wharf, however, the men who come during the day for meals are employed, being given a meal ticket on the completion of their task.   About one-third of all the wood prepared is sawed and split on the wharf by the dinner men, as they are called, to distinguish them from the lodgers.

An attempt was made some time ago to try a plan that had worked well in Providence, namely, to employ all comers who wanted money at the rate of fifty cents a day in cash and their meals while at work, but it was found the men so employed mixed themselves with the tramps and did no more work than they could avoid doing; the results, as far as they could be traced, were of no tangible value, and the experiment under the conditions was deemed a failure and was discontinued.

A wharf is hired for the receipt of cargoes of wood from vessels, and if the place were owned by the city and the men were lodged there, a much larger return would be secured from the labor than is possible now.   The experiment was tried of marching lodgers from the Wayfarers' Lodge to the wharf, to do their work there before breakfast, but the men scattered in all directions on coming out from the yard.   True, it is possible to have police escort, but a four dollar policeman to a ten-cent tramp would not be a profitable outlay for the overseers.

Seven years ago I prepared a paper on this Wayfarers' Lodge, and since beginning the present sketch I have read over my notes and I am struck with the great changes noticeable in the classes that now come to the Lodge compared with the men as a whole who lodged in the house when it was first opened in 1878.

The worst class, the stowaways from the foreign steamers, do not come at all.   A law passed or enforced since forbids the landing of stowaways.

Men claiming to be strikers or traveling in search of work do not apply so often; either they have money and go elsewhere, or there are fewer looking in this way for employment.

The tramp avoids the Lodge; only dire necessity compels him to ask a shelter or a meal that must be paid for in labor.   The cheap lodging-houses, of which Boston has far too many for its peace, are the places where he can find congenial company and an occasional, but welcome drink. As long as he can steal, or rob a drunken passer on the street, he will not face the Lodge. These men spend their winters in ease at the almshouse, from which they are discharged on their own application in the spring; then they manage to go to some penal institution for awhile; when cold weather approaches they are snug in the almshouse again.

As a means of securing conviction of some of the idle vagrants, the Lodge has failed completely to meet the expectation of the first committee. The discouragement thrown by a judge on the first good case presented made the superintendent feel that it was wasting time to do anything further; he simply refuses to let the vagrant in if he recognizes him as one who has made trouble, and so dismisses the matter.

The largest of any distinct class now at the Lodge are railroad laborers, employed most of the year at construction works. When the winter stops operations they spend carelessly what they have saved, and those who have no acquaintances or friends come to the Lodge for a few days (three days is the limit). Ask any one of them why he came to the Lodge and he will tell you that he was foolish with his money when he had it, but hopes soon to be at work again.

Summing it all up: the Wayfarers' Lodge is useful to the city of Boston. It is not claimed that all the men out of work can find employment here, or that all without means to pay for a lodging can be provided for, but it does this much, it contributes largely towards the health and safety of the lodgers under its roof. It offers a fair test of the sincerity and capacity of the man who says he is willing to work, for many good places for laborers have been found by the Lodge.

It takes no payment in money from a lodger, it supposes the applicant to be without money. All who come are humanely treated, and when they leave they feel that they have earned the cost of their food and shelter and are in debt to no one, except so far as to thank the Christian instinct ingrained in our national life, which has provided a means by which a poor man may without shame eat the bread set before him, for he has already done all that was asked from him in return for it.

FREE PUBLIC EMPLOYMENT OFFICES IN OHIO. AN EXPERIMENT IN SOCIALISTIC·LEGISLATION.

P. W. AYRES, GENERAL SECRETARY OF ASSOCIATED CHARITIES, CINCINNATI, OHIO.

Free public employment offices, established by the state of Ohio in five of its largest cities, are certainly a unique experiment. The legislation establishing these offices was new and bold. It has aroused peculiar interest, because it undertakes to deal in some measure with the relation of the state to industrial action, and at the same time is a step toward government control, the end of which was not easily seen when the bill passed.

The offices have been in operation a little less than three years. It is, therefore, too soon to estimate their final value.

The following sketch will endeavor to show to what extent the offices have proved useful to laborers, notwithstanding the political changes in management, and to what extent they have failed to carry out the original ideals of those who framed the bill.

The Municipal Labor Congress of Cincinnati, an organization composed of all the trade and labor unions in that city, started the agitation in favor of free public employment offices to be established by the state government. The bill, as introduced into the state legislature during the winter of 1889–90, made the employment offices a branch of the State Bureau of Labor Statistics, fixed the salaries of superintendents and clerks, and placed the expense upon the state. Senator M. T. Corcoran of Cincinnati, who introduced the bill, fought hard to have it passed in its original form. The shrewd farmer legislator, however, proved too much in this case for the city representative of labor, and refused to pay from the state treasury the salaries of officials, the benefit of whose work would accrue largely to the local cities in which they were employed. It resulted, therefore, that the city governments should pay the salaries which constituted the greater portion of the expense connected with the offices, while the state government should pay the rent of offices.

The Plan as proposed.

The original intentions of the framers of the bill were:
First, that the local offices collect statistical data relating to the

industrial interests of the state, supplementing the statistics of the State Labor Bureau.

Second, that they exchange industrial information between the various cities of the state, so that scarcity of a given class of laborers in one city could be supplied from the excess of such laborers in another city.

Third, that they assist employers to secure employees.

Fourth, that they furnish working men and women out of employment free and reliable information as to the kind and character of employment to be had. It was the intention of the framers of this law that the free employment offices should be entirely devoid of partisan politics, that labor leaders should be appointed to the superintendencies, and that the collection of statistics should be more complete than had hitherto been made in the state. These intentions of the framers have not all been carried out. Legislation proposes ; the spoils system, like the voice of God, disposes.

Prior to the establishment of the free employment offices there were "employment agencies," which were run for private profit. Some of them were leeches engaged in sucking the life-blood from the poor. It is stated that these private agencies charged men and women anywhere from one to fifteen dollars for securing them employment, and that they obtained their victims chiefly from the rural districts and neighboring towns, often bound them by contract, and left them in worse condition than before. One of the chief benefits of the free offices in Ohio has been to prevent the evils arising from extortionate private agencies, although some continue to do a nefarious business, sending laborers to unsatisfactory places in Dakota, Tennessee, West Virginia, etc. Private agencies in several cities still do business limited by competition with the state office.

The Bill analyzed. (Revised Statutes of Ohio, Section 308.)[*]

The bill passed the Ohio legislature, April 28, 1890. It provides that the state labor commissioner shall have an office in the state house which shall be a bureau of statistics of labor. It authorizes the commissioner to establish in the five largest cities of Ohio free public employment offices, with a superintendent and suitable clerical help. "No compensation or fee shall directly or indirectly be

---

[*] The bill is printed in Fourteenth Annual Report of the Ohio Bureau of Labor Statistics (for the year 1890).

charged to or received from any person or persons seeking employment, or any person or persons desiring to employ labor through any of said offices." The superintendent is directed to make a weekly report, on Thursday of each week, to the state commissioner, of the persons desiring to employ labor, and of the persons applying for employment, and of the character of employment in each case. This weekly list from each office in the state is printed and posted in each of the other offices in the other cities. It is provided that each superintendent shall receive a salary fixed by the council of the city in which he is employed. The salary of the clerical assistants is limited to fifty dollars per month, though a less sum may be paid by the local city council.

Under this act, the five offices were at once organized in the summer of 1890; Toledo paying a salary of $1000 per year, without an assistant; Dayton paying $1000 per year, with an assistant at $600 per year; Cleveland, Cincinnati and Columbus paying $1200 per year each, with an assistant at $600 per year each.

The report of the state labor commissioner for that year makes this criticism upon the law: "A bad feature of the law is that it leaves it optional to councils of the different cities to make and unmake salaries. This position endangers the existence of the offices, and has a tendency to bring the superintendents and clerks into collusion with members of the city government as against the commissioner."

Relation to Politics.

The offices have not been kept free from political interference. When the offices were first opened the state had a Democratic governor. The state commissioner of labor appointed by him was a fair-minded man, who put into the five free public employment offices three Democrats favorable to the labor party and two representatives of the People's party. These gentlemen had no sooner become familiar with the office, having held it about one year, just time enough to learn the field and to begin a systematic collection of statistics, when the state changed its political head for one of the Republican party. The newly-appointed state commissioner of labor was a Republican. All of the original superintendents with their assistants were requested to resign, and new appointments were made from the Republican ranks, with more or less regard to the labor interests. Thus there are nine more offices than formerly that belong to the spoils of state.

State politics, however, are better than municipal politics, and the offices have not been interfered with by the local city councils, nor have there been places where local jobs have been given away for votes. Fortunately, the appointments have been in the hands of the state commissioner of labor, and not in the hands of the local ward politician. The political interference, therefore, has not been of that despicable variety which would change the office from free state employment to local ward boss employment. The offices have fortunately escaped the exceeding fine grinding of the local political machines.

In the second place, the collection of statistics has not been so complete as was hoped for. The failure in this direction probably results from the failure to keep the system free from politics. The superintendents in the different cities have not been in office long enough to develop a uniform system of collecting statistics, while changes in office tend to cultivate disrespect on the part of large employers. In Dayton, for instance, the employers objected to giving the statistics asked for, on the plea that the state had no right to collect statistics from the internal secrets of business men, to be pried into by designing politicians and business competitors. Six firms absolutely refused to comply with the requests, preferring the risks of litigation, until events should prove the law a good one or a bad one, and either sustain it for its good qualities or repeal it for its alleged corrupt and unjust features. It was found also that the state commissioner of labor was obliged to withdraw the blanks sent out by the local superintendents, to prevent confusion in the work of the special agents sent out from the state office. In one instance the special agent found that the blanks from the local superintendent did not command respect, they had not been sent out with tact. The agent refused to work until these local blanks had been withdrawn.

The Work of a Labor Exchange.

Still further, the free employment offices have not been the means of exchanging knowledge of the industrial situation between different cities to the extent that was hoped for. The reports made on Thursday are sent to Columbus and printed, and returned on Monday or Tuesday, so that it is fully a week before the notices are posted in each office as to the condition of labor in other cities. When this is coupled with the fact that a large proportion of the applicants are unskilled laborers, it will readily appear that the posted notices are not much considered.

Nor have the free public employment offices rendered large assistance to employers in securing employees. As one employer said, "So far as the mechanic or skilled laborer is concerned, manufacturers are overrun with applicants at the shop. Therefore they have no practical need of the services of the office." The number of skilled artisans who have received employment from the Public Agencies have been few. The vacancies, or the possibility of vacancies, have become known and the position applied for before the manufacturer or contractor has had an opportunity of seeking help through the free office. The superintendent in Cincinnati reports a favorable growth in this direction, and seeks to make his office a local labor exchange.

Furthermore, the work of different offices in the state has been very uneven. In the report for the year 1891 the positions secured in the Cleveland, Columbus and Dayton offices have been very largely for females in the line of domestic help, while many of the men who have secured employment have been coachmen, hostlers, cooks, butlers, etc., all in the line of household service. Take for instance the report of the Cleveland office for the week ending April 14th, 1893:

> Positions secured for men......... 38
> Positions secured for women and girls, 55

Of the thirty-eight positions for men, eleven were for servants and work about the house or barn; of the fifty-five places for women and girls, thirty-nine were for servants. Of the remaining sixteen women for other than domestic work, the positions were as follows: Wet-nurse, 1; light work, 3; day's work, 6; house-cleaning, 4; laundry work, 2. For that week, therefore, all of the women and one-third of the men were sent to household work in some of its branches. It would appear that the state of Ohio has gone into the domestic servant business! This unfavorable balance of female domestic labor does not appear in some of the other offices, though it forms a considerable portion elsewhere.

The following table shows the kind of labor secured in each city and the number of male and female laborers employed through the five offices, for the week ending April 21, 1893:

MALES.	Columbus.	Cleveland.	Toledo.	Dayton.	Cincinnati.	Total.
Laborers	22	3	19	6	14	64
Carpenters	3	..	8	4	1	16
Painters	2	..	1	..	..	3
Marble workers	..	2	..	..	..	2
Moulders	..	..	..	2	..	2
Upholsterer	1	..	..	..	..	1
Plasterer	..	..	..	1	..	1
Core-maker	..	..	..	1	..	1
Shoemaker	..	..	..	1	..	1
Varnish rubber	..	..	..	1	..	1
Shop works	..	..	..	5	.	5
Blacksmiths	..	..	..	4	..	4
General work	5	1	..	2	2	10
Clerks	1	1	..	..	..	2
Canvassers	..	..	..	1	2	3
Farm hands	..	4	1	..	5	10
Gardeners	..	..	..	..	3	3
To private families	1	1	..	5	..	7
Dish-washers	1	..	..	1	..	2
Waiters	1	3	..	1	..	5
Porters	..	2	..	1	1	3
Hostlers	..	..	..	..	3	3
Drivers	..	1	..	4	2	7
Scrubbers	..	..	..	..	2	2
Boys for work	2	4	..	1	8	15
Total	39	22	29	41	43	173

FEMALES.	Columbus.	Cleveland.	Toledo.	Dayton.	Cincinnati.	Total.
General housework	10	15	15	10	23	73
Chambermaids	3	2	1	..	3	9
Dining-room girls	2	3	1	..	..	6
Upstairs work	1	5	5	2	8	21
Cooks	1	3	3	2	12	21
Day work	1	6	1	..	..	8
Nurse girls	1	..	..	..	3	4
Dish-washers	..	..	..	..	4	4
Seamstresses	2	..	..	2	..	4
Hotel work	..	2	4	2	..	8
Laundresses	..	1	..	2	6	9
Solicitor	..	..	..	1	..	1
Factory work	..	..	..	2	..	2
Total	21	37	30	23	59	170

```
Males...................................173
Females.................................170

                          243 for one week.
```

	Situations Wanted.		Help Wanted.		Positions Secured.	
	Males.	Females.	Males.	Females.	Males.	Females.
Columbus	3,128	1,739	1,534	2,268	915	1,481
Cleveland	6,308	3,830	925	3,471	886	2,508
Toledo....................	3,859	1,799	2,481	2,479	2,064	1,391
Dayton	3,351	2,118	1,386	2,004	790	1,119
Cincinnati	4,811	3,428	3,369	3,291	2,312	2,129
Total................	21,457	12,914	9,695	13,513	6,967	8,628

Situations secured, males and females, 15,595.
The amount of help wanted was 67.52 per cent. of situations wanted.
Positions secured was 66.9 per cent. of help wanted.
"   "   "   45.2   "   situations wanted.

The total number of persons who secured employment through
the offices in one year was 15,525. Of this number, 6,967 were
males, 8,558 were females. While it appears from the tables given
that most of the persons benefited by the offices are of the lowest
industrial grade, few of the men or women being skilled laborers,
yet it must not be supposed that the work which is accomplished is
of little value. The five state offices cost the state about $10,000 per
year. If each of these 15,525 persons had to pay one dollar or more
for his position, the sum would have been at least $15,525, all of
which has been saved to the people who need it most and at the
time when they need it most. The offices are a boon to the unskilled
laborers, and for their sakes should be continued.

The offices have not been used by the large employers nor by
skilled artisans, but they have done a work for the unskilled laborers,
preventing extortion by private agencies, and directing them to
places where help is wanted, to which they never would have drifted
of their own accord. The chief work, therefore, of the free offices
has not been to influence the labor question materially. They have
done very little to change the attitude of employers and employees
toward each other. They have done comparatively little for regular
employees, who, of course, seldom need the services of the offices;

but they have caught the driftwood of the labor market and have directed it into useful channels. They have assisted these out-of-works to $15,000 in cash which they otherwise must have spent, in addition to the service of information rendered, and thus act as preventives of pauperism in a very true sense, without in anywise being helpful in the creation of new paupers.

PAUPERISM AND CRIME.

JOHN B. WEBER.

The ordinary definition of a pauper is one who has become a charge upon the public; but, as applied to a foreigner, there is a disposition, widely extended and firmly lodged in the minds of many of our people, to have it embrace arriving immigrants who have little means, notwithstanding they may possess in a marked degree the physical capacity and apparent willingness to gain a livelihood by labor.

Mr. Gladstone, in a speech delivered in the House of Commons on the 11th day of February last, in speaking to the amendment relating to destitute aliens, among other things said:

"Now the first thing we have to consider is what is meant by the words 'destitute aliens.' What aliens are destitute? . . . . How can we make good that definition of a destitute alien, a man who is supporting himself by wages which he earns, which his employer is willing to give him, and with which he is contented? In what sense is he destitute? He is destitute in this sense, that if he had not got employment, and wages as a result of such employment, then he would be destitute. Yes, sir, but that is the definition of the condition of the entire laboring population. They are not destitute, but they would be, if they did not get the wages which they earn in their trades."

Upon this point Commissioners Kempster and Weber, who as representatives of the government visited Europe in the summer of 1891 to investigate and report upon the subject of immigration to this country, used this language:

" In investigating your proposition with reference to pauperism, the question was raised as to the definition of the word 'pauper' within the meaning of existing law. We did not regard a person as a pauper who presented every appearance of industry, willingness and physical capacity to labor, even if his means on landing were limited, nor yet if he was assisted by friends, relatives or philanthropic persons, unless such assistance implied a leaning upon others for support. The greatest number of those arriving within the last year, who, because of special conditions surrounding their cases, received assistance *en route*, were Jews, yet they very rarely became a charge upon the public. Indeed, no race or nationality presents so clean a record in such respect as they. A person who by reason of unexpected misfortunes or persecutions is deprived of his accumulations, who has been subjected to pillage and plunder while fleeing from the burdens which have become unbearable, if capable of supporting himself and family—if he has one—with a reasonable certainty after obtaining a foothold, and if that foothold is guaranteed by friends or relatives upon landing or strong probable surrounding circumstances, is not, according to our definition, a pauper. The history of this country is full of instances of men from all countries who have reached great prominence in our commercial, financial, professional and legislative bodies both in state and nation, who would have been returned as paupers if the standard of pauperism was based upon money possessions when landing."

It is true that foreigners contribute an undue quota of paupers and criminals in proportion to their numbers, but they are burdened with excessive conditions from which the natives are free, and in weighing the value of immigrants there should be taken into the account the vast net benefits which we derive from the influx as a whole. They come into a strange country where new customs and methods confront them, many of them unfamiliar with our language, and to this extent start handicapped in the competition for a livelihood. We should rather wonder at the small number who become discouraged and yield to the temptation of crime or, heartsick and despondent, apply for relief to the poor authorities.

Viewing the subject simply from the standpoint of dollars and cents, which is perhaps a very low but a very practical one, the incoming of foreigners has been, now is, and I believe for a long time to come will be, the best investment this nation has yet made. Charge against them all the cost of crime and pauperism—going back a generation or two, if necessary—charge against them all the real and alleged evils of their influence in the administration of the municipal affairs of our cities where foreigners or those of immediate foreign extraction predominate, and the net advantage remaining is still colossal. Formerly it was estimated that every able-bodied arrival added a thousand dollars to the wealth of the country, and if this is correct, it is not a difficult calculation to measure the gain to the state of New York for the year 1892, during which period about 40,000 families settled therein. Assuming that only the heads of those families were able-bodied producers—and this is a liberal assumption on the opposite side of my contention—it meant an increase of $40,000,000 to the resources of the state. The cost of the alien criminals and paupers who cannot under any system of inspection or plan, other than total prohibition of immigration, be entirely eliminated, is absolutely insignificant in comparison. Nor is there any convincing evidence that the value of the immigrant has diminished. The fact that he comes indicates that the conditions here require him. The movement is not a haphazard one, nor is it based on whim or caprice; except as to Russia, it is in obedience to the law of attraction, not repulsion. It is founded on the law of supply and demand. Place the figures of arrivals alongside of your years of panic or industrial distress and you have a plain revelation.

The arrivals of 79,000 in the panic year of 1837 were cut down to 38,000 in 1838. In 1857 the arrivals were 246,000, falling to 119,000 the following year. The next panic year of 1873 showed 450,000, dropping to 313,000 in 1874, 227,000 in 1875, 169,000 in 1876, 141,-000 in 1877, 138,000 in 1878, rising to 177,000 in 1879, and regaining its normal volume of 457,000 in 1880.

Immigration statistics have proven an unfailing barometer indicating industrial conditions; and in tracing immigrants to final destination in this country, it will be found that the movement is most sluggish where development is least active; or in other words, where the immigrant is a novelty, the sheriff is a necessity.

Of course it is not contended that we should let in every applicant, simply because there is, and will continue to be, a large balance on the credit side of the account; but I regard it as an unwise policy to close the gates, wholly or in great part, whether in express terms of law or indirectly by alleged improvement in the method of inspection. I am in favor of any plan practicable in its enforcement and honest in striking at real evils, having for its object the exclusion of those who are physically and mentally weak, vicious, diseased, dangerously ignorant, or whose labor is contracted for abroad to the detriment of the better paid and higher grade labor of this country.

The statistics, however, should not be twisted to strengthen demagoguery or foster narrow-minded prejudice. If the census returns are made so as to show that about 15 per cent. of our population is made up of persons of foreign birth, the tables of crime and pauperism chargeable to aliens need not be swelled in their totals by adding to the foreign-born those who were born here of mixed or foreign parentage. The figures, in respect of crime at least, do not exhibit marked improvement of foreign stock by contact with our civilization. On the contrary, one nationality, according to the census returns, shows the following, viz.:

> Foreign-born parents of foreign-born criminals............11,118
> Foreign-born parents of native-born criminals............16,695

The pauper statistics of the same nationality make a more gratifying exhibit, showing a reverse result, but of increased emphasis, viz.:

> Foreign-born parents of foreign-born paupers number.....28,256
> Foreign-born parents of native-born paupers number...... 3,758

These figures seem to indicate that the Americanized generation improves as to pauperism, but retrogrades as to crime.

In analyzing the census statistics of criminals and paupers of foreign extraction there were developed some interesting, and to me surprising exhibits, differing so materially from popular belief that I append a table extracted from the returns and arranged in groups for purposes of ready comparison.

FIGURES FROM THE UNITED STATES CENSUS OF 1890.

WHITE CRIMINALS AND PAUPERS.

Color and Nativity.	Criminals.		Paupers.	
	Number.	Per cent.	Number.	Per cent.
Total white........................	57,310	100.00	66,578	100.00
Native, white.......................	40,471	70.62	36,656	55.06
Foreign, white.......................	15,932	27.80	27,648	41.53
Birthplace unknown..................	907	1.58	2,274	3.41
Both parents native or foreign	36,969	100.00	49,167	100.00
Natives born of native parents..........	21,037	56.90	21,519	43.77
Foreigners born of foreign parents......	15,932	43.10	27,648	56.23

IMMIGRATION AND PARENTAGE.

Nationality.	Immigrants 1886–1890.	Parents of Native Criminals and Paupers.			Total foreign parents.
		One parent foreign.	Both parents foreign.		
			Same nationality.	Different nationalities.	
CRIMINALS.					
English speaking	673,158	2,229	9,104	1,941	41,584
England	330,719	449	590	514	5,997
Scotland	85,619	191	240	355	1,996
Wales	6,332	35	46	36	343
Ireland.................	250,448	1,276	7,935	825	29,184
Canada	(a)	278	293	211	4,064
Non-English speaking .	457,765	9	69	16	2,192
Italy..................	197,805	5	33	4	1,209
Poland, }	183,445	1	19	..	339
Russia, }		3	16	2	382
Hungary..............	76,505	..	1	..	262
PAUPERS.					
English speaking	673,158	702	2,231	363	41,103
England	330,719	174	240	99	4,688
Scotland................	85,619	75	47	64	1,392
Wales	6,332	8	30	8	590
Ireland.................	250,448	345	1,806	146	32,421
Canada	(a)	100	108	46	2,012
Non-English speaking .	457,765	5	32	10	1,037
Italy..................	197,805	3	9	5	317
Poland, }	183,445	1	18	..	476
Russia, }		1	2	2	136
Hungary............ ..:.	76,505	..	3	3	108

(a) No statistics of immigrants from the British North American Possessions since 1885.

NOTE BY THE EDITOR.—This table has been recast and corrected to conform to Census Bulletin 352, "Nativity and Parentage of Prisoners and Paupers." Mr. Weber's argument has been rather strengthened than otherwise by the slight alterations in his figures.

The following figures, also from the Census of 1890, but as yet unpublished, may be added to those which he has given.

The fairest possible comparison is that between the total population of any given nationality and the group of the same nationality which is the subject of

study. The total number of English in the United States, June 1, 1890, was
907,259; Scotch, 242,197; Welch, 100,065; Irish, 1,871,339; Canadians, 973,-
488; total, 4,094,618. These figures may be taken as divisors. There are two
distinct sets of dividends, of which the first is composed of foreign-born
prisoners and paupers; the second, of the foreign-born parents of prisoners
and paupers. By adding six ciphers to the latter we obtain the ratios to
1,000,000 of the same element of the total population. The adoption of this
process gives the following result:

RATIOS FOR PRISONERS AND PAUPERS.

ELEMENTS.	Population.	Prisoners.		Paupers.	
		Number.	Ratio.	Number.	Ratio.
Total white	54,983,890	57,310	1,042	66,578	1,211
Native	45,862,023	41,378	902	38,930	849
Parents native	34,358,348	25,690	748	34,219	996
Parents foreign	11,503,675	15,688	1,364	4,711	410
Foreign-born.................	9,121,867	15,932	1,747	27,648	3,031
SELECTED NATIONALITIES.					
English speaking...........	4,094,618	9,628	2,351	17,846	4,358
England....................	907,529	1,918	2,115	1,962	2,162
Scotland	242,197	479	1,977	575	2,375
Wales.....................	100,065	89	889	256	2,559
Ireland....................	1,871,339	5,559	2,970	14,128	7,550
Canada.	973,488	1,583	1,626	925	950
Non-English speaking......	574,781	1,050	1,826	524	912
Italy	182,342	562	3,115	149	817
Poland.....................	147,416	149	1,011	219	1,485
Russia.....................	182,614	209	1,144	107	586
Hungary...................	62,409	130	2,083	49	785

RATIOS FOR PARENTS OF PRISONERS AND PAUPERS.

SELECTED NATIONALITIES.					
English speaking...........	4,094,618.	41,914	10,236	41,350	10,099
England....................	907,529	5,997	6,608	4,688	5,166
Scotland...................	242,197	1,996	8,241	1,392	5,747
Wales.....................	100,065	343	3,428	590	5,896
Ireland....................	1,871,339	29,184	15,328	32,419	17,324
Canada....................	973,488	4,394	4,514	2,261	2,323
Non-English speaking......	574,781	2,192	3,814	1,037	1,804
Italy	182,342	1,209	6,630	317	1,739
Poland	147,416	339	2,300	476	3,229
Russia	182,614	382	2,092	136	745
Hungary...................	62,409	262	4,198	108	1,731

As the objections usually heard against particular classes of immigrants are leveled at the Italians, Poles, Russians and Hungarians, I have grouped the criminals and paupers of these four countries on the one hand, and those from English-speaking countries on the other. I select the latter to compare with the first named for the reason that so much has been said of the easy assimilation with us of our British cousins, because they speak the same language, spring from the same stock, and will sooner become "Americanized" than the others, that by comparing the best and the worst (according to popular estimate) an interesting and perhaps instructive exhibit may be furnished. In order that the comparison may be fairly based, I give the number of arrivals in each group for the five years preceding and including the census year in which criminal and pauper statistics were taken ; the totals showing that those in the group of what may be termed Southern Europeans are nearly two-thirds as large as those from Great Britain, and therefore the totals of undesirables should bear the same proportions, to place them on a level. The figures in every column show the English-speaking people so far in the lead, both in respect of criminals and paupers, that it almost staggers belief. Thus in the class of criminals confined in our prisons in 1890, the number of natives with one foreign parent from Great Britain or Canada are 2229 and only 9 from Southern Europe; of both parents foreign there were 9104 English-speaking and but 69 from Southern Europe ; of both parents foreign, but of different nationalities, 1941 of the assimilable class, and but 6 of the others; while the nationality of foreign parents of criminals born abroad and here, there were 41,584 of English-speaking people as against 2192 of those who are not readily assimilated because they do not speak our language. The same results substantially are found in the pauper classes, except that in the last column we find 41,103 English-speaking parents as against 1037 Southern Europeans. These figures demonstrate that those who more readily assimilate with us furnish the greatest number of criminals and paupers.

But after all, the question is, Are we making gains and improvements in keeping out bad elements? and we must solve the problem, How can the weeding process be still more improved?

That there has been decided improvement in the matter of inspection by the immigration authorities at New York since the federal government superseded that of the state officials, the figures amply demonstrate ; that the laws can be amended so as to produce still better results, I confidently believe. The policy of the United States officials at the chief immigration station from the beginning has been to strengthen the medical and other inspection force at the threshold, and thus reduce the number to be cared for after landing. This necessarily increased the expense at the starting point, but materially reduced it at our hospitals, making the total expense less. Not only did it save to the government in the matter of caring for those who fell into distress within the year from landing, as evidenced by ascertainable figures, but it must have saved largely in the classes not separated or distinguished, who, after the year, fall as burdens upon local communities. For instance, the federal authorities at New York turned back to Europe, in the first two years and seven months of their administration, twice as many as the state officials did in the five years preceding federal control. Under the state authorities the daily average attendance of those who were cared for within the year of landing at the expense of the "immigrant fund" reached 266, while under the federal authorities it fell to 73½ in 1891, and 81 and a fraction in 1892, with increased immigration during the latter years. The number of insane immigrants (the most serious burden), under federal officials, never reached 25 per cent. of those turned over to them by the state board, after disposing of the subjects so transferred by recovery, death or removal to local institutions at the end of the year. There is other corroborative evidence of improvement in the sifting process.

The number of steamship tickets for immigrants returning to Europe, based upon reduced or charity rates, issued by the companies to persons having some means, but who failed in successfully competing here for a livelihood, show a decreasing tendency ; the figures from several of the more important lines marking in 1892 a decline of 25 per cent. over those of 1889.

The number of immigrants returned to Europe at government expense was reduced from 109 for 1891 to 11 for 1892. The old law prevailed for the first three months of 1891, during which 36 of the 109 were returned, but the same law governed for the rest of the stated time, and material improvement is shown in these reduced figures.

I believe, however, that further practical improvement in the sifting process is possible and available. While every plan must in the nature of things be in a sense experimental, and none can be expected to yield absolutely perfect results, I still adhere to suggestions heretofore made on various occasions, and conclude this paper by quoting, as pertinent to this point, from an address on the subject of immigration delivered by me at Cooper Union, New York, in January, 1893.

"Plan recommended. Sub-agents' Certification. Inspection Here and Compulsory Return after Landing.

" The plan that I would suggest is that laid down in Dr. Kempster's and my report referred to, from which I have seen no reason to deviate in its general features, except to add a clause vesting in the President the power to suspend immigration temporarily in the case of threatened pestilence, and possibly an educational qualification ; the report having been written before the outbreak of the typhus and cholera of last year, and before illiteracy statistics were kept at the Immigration Bureau. I would hold the sub-agents of steamship companies, of whom there are many thousands scattered over Europe, responsible for the sale of a ticket to a prohibited person, reaching them not directly by our law, for that is impossible, but striking at their pockets through the steamship agencies or companies in this country ; compelling them to pay the return passage of a defective immigrant and levying a fine in each instance in addition, if necessary; or in other words, imposing a penalty, which in a single case would wipe out the commissions received in a great many. The sub-agent, in almost all cases, knows the applicant personally; lives in the village with him ; is familiar with his family history; knows his conduct and deportment, and his mental and physical defects, better than any one who comes in contact with him after he leaves his home. No other person who can be reached knows so well. As one of the details of this plan, I would have each intending emigrant, when he applies for a ticket, sign and swear to a duplicate statement covering all necessary points, one copy to be sent through the S. S. Agents to the Inspection Bureau in the United States, retaining the other for personal presentation by the immigrant upon arrival, which would answer as a descriptive list showing precisely what he had sworn to upon purchasing his ticket. I would continue a rigid inspection here, and besides hold every alien immigrant after landing subject to compulsory deportation, in the discretion of the courts, whenever he develops into pauperism or criminality, and until he has assumed the burdens and acquired the privileges of citizenship; or, in other words, I would have him passing through the Immigration Bureau continuously until he became a citizen. Every country in Europe deports alien paupers and criminals to their homes except Great Britain, and there is no sentiment or reason which we would violate if we adopted the same plan. This would rid us of paupers when they reach that stage, of criminals after serving their sentence, and they would properly become a burden upon the community from whence they sprang, or upon the governments to which they still owe allegiance. I regard this feature as practical and important. In a minor degree we now have this power, and it works very well. We are now authorized to return to Europe within twelve months after landing, a person who has come here in violation of the immigration laws, or who becomes a public charge from causes existing prior to landing; and under this limited power we have returned over five hundred persons during the last year, who could not be detected by any process of inspection, here or abroad, and nearly all of whom would have become a permanent burden upon some of our communities. Wipe out this year limit, extend it to cover the period to citizenship, and eliminate that requirement that we must show that the cause existed prior to landing, so as to take in one who becomes a pauper or a criminal here, and we solve the problem of how to get rid of the undesirable element coming to us from abroad. Then guard better your avenues to citizenship, and a great many of your immigration evils will disappear.

"One Feature of Naturalization.

"As one of the details of naturalization, I would have permanent records kept at the Immigration Bureau of the names of arriving immigrants, alphabetically arranged and indexed, and would furnish to each a certificate setting forth a brief description, with name, steamer and date of arrival, which should be required by courts of naturalization as evidence of time of residence in this country. These papers could be recorded or filed in the various clerks' offices to guard against loss, certified copies made in case of change of residence, while the record at the immigration station would be available for verification in case of necessity."

THE PROBLEM OF INEBRIATE PAUPERISM.

T. D. CROTHERS, M. D., SUPERINTENDENT OF WALNUT LODGE HOSPITAL, HARTFORD, CONNECTICUT.

Some conception of this problem may be obtained from the fact that in 1891 over eight hundred thousand persons were arrested in this country charged with being intoxicated and committing petty crimes. It may be fairly presumed that at least half as many more who used spirits to excess did not come under legal notice. If to these are added those who used opium, chloral and other drug narcotics, the number reaches enormous proportions.

Practically this vast army of inebriates represents all classes and conditions, and its members are literally withdrawn from the ranks of active workers and producers, and become obstacles and burdens to sanitary life. They are centres of pauperism and progressive degeneration and of the most unsanitary physiological and psychological conditions. This army literally follows a continuous line of retrogression, which antagonizes all evolution, growth and development, and seems to be governed by a uniform law of cause and effect, marked by a beginning, development, decline and extinction, the mystery of which makes it the most absorbing scientific problem of the age.

To-day over a million workers are waging a great moral crusade to break up this evil. Politics, religion, education, the pulpit and press are combined in a struggle with this problem, approaching it exclusively from the moral side. Medieval superstition and moral theories are urged, through the pledge, prayer, persecution and punishment, to explain and check this evil. Above all this moral agitation and effort the voice of science appeals to physicians for help. This army of inebriates is increasing, and with it losses and degeneration both of individuals and the race. While inebriates are a part of the great army of the "unfit" who are "mustered out" and crowded out in the race march, there is yet unmistakable evidence that some can be halted, headed off, and returned to health.

Already science has pointed out possibilities of cure and prevention, which give promise of practically stamping out this evil in the near future. Some of the outline facts from the sanitary side will show the extent of the evil, and the possibilities of cure from a larger and more accurate study of the subject. The great sanitary problem of to-day is the knowledge and removal of the causes of disease, and the placing of the victim under the best conditions for a return to health. To remove the conditions which favor and encourage disease, and break up the breeding-places of crime, pauperism and allied forms of degeneration, is one of the future certainties of science. There are to-day over a million unrecognized inebriates who are the most defective, dangerous and degenerate of all classes. They are centres of pauperism and sanitary evils, which pass on into the next generation, entailing misery and loss beyond estimate.

The superstition of personal freedom with free will permits this army of inebriates to go on year after year destroying themselves, increasing the burden of their families, and building up veritable centres of physical and mental degeneration. Nothing can be more disastrous from a sanitary and scientific standpoint than the indifference which permits men and women to use alcohol and other drugs, not only destroying themselves, but entailing all degrees of degeneration on their descendants.

Sanitary science teaches that no one has a right to destroy himself and peril the health and comfort of others. The moderate and periodic drinkers are always sources of danger to themselves and others. To wait until they become chronic and degenerate into law-breakers is to apply the remedy when it is too late. Public sentiment should not permit one to become an inebriate, nor tolerate him after he has reached such a stage. He should be prevented and forced to undergo treatment, and should be regarded as dangerous to the safety and welfare of the community, and isolated until fully restored.

In the near future science will demand that every inebriate have legal guardianship and restriction of personal freedom until he recovers. When these cases realize that such restrictions will be enforced they will seek treatment in the early stages of their disease. The teaching of science demands that both the pauper and millionaire be seized at the very onset and forced into conditions of health and sobriety; and saved from becoming burdens on the community and centres of ruin and misery.

The saloon, with free sale of spirits, is, from a sanitary point of view, a source of extreme danger. Its influence in any community is bad. It brings sanitary perils by destroying the physical and mental stability of its patrons, and both directly and indirectly favors the worst conditions of life. The saloon has no claim for recognition as a business. It is simply a parasite thriving on the decay and degeneration of the community. It is only tolerated by the dense ignorance and selfishness of its defenders. It should be classed with foul sewers, dangerous waters and unsanitary, death-dealing forces. Persecution of it as a moral evil keeps it alive, but examination from the standpoint of science would be fatal to its perpetuity. The drink problem would be largely solved could the favoring conditions of saloons be changed.

Unregulated marriage, now a mere matter of accident and impulse, is another source of danger perpetuating the drink-curse. Inebriates, insane, and neurotics of all degrees are permitted to propagate and transmit their defects to succeeding generations. The result is a race of neurotics, who develop inebriety and all forms of insanity and idiocy, together with all associated conditions. The army of neurotics beyond all question reappears in succeeding generations with similar or interchangeable diseases. The inebriates of this generation who marry and raise up children are creating paupers, criminals and insane for the next. They are wrecking their descendants by crippling and incapacitating them to live healthy lives. Every community illustrates this fact, and the drink problem is more complex and difficult of solution on this account. We need scientific study and instruction on this point, and a public sentiment that will make marriage a question of sanitary science. Then we shall have the means for practical prevention and cure of many present evils.

The drink problem has another sanitary side in defective nutrition, bad ventilation and other conditions of an unhealthy character. Build up the physique, relieve the condition of starvation, remove the defects of unhealthy living, and in many cases the tendency of the drink craze is thwarted. Mental change, unrest and sudden change involving a strain on the organism to adapt itself to the new conditions for which it is unfit, overwork, underwork and diseased conditions, defective and retarded growths, and nearly every kind and degree of mental and physical defect, enter into the drink problem and must be recognized and studied.

The present methods of dealing with this problem are followed by startling results. Of the 800,000 persons who were arrested last year for inebriety not one per cent. were benefited. Over 99 per cent. were made worse and confirmed in their habits. The station-house and jail are active recruiting places, and the hosts of inebriates who are forced into them are transformed into legions of incurables who never desert or leave the ranks. Physically the short imprisonment of the inebriate simply removes him from spirits and leaves him less capable of leading a temperate life. Mentally he has lost a certain self-respect and pride of character essential to recovery.

The first legal punishment of inebriates is followed by a species of fatality, seen in a constant repetition of the same or allied offenses. This fact is so apparent that these cases are called "repeaters" in the courts, and the number of sentences of the same person often extends to hundreds. In one thousand cases confined at Blackwell's Island, New York, 935 had been sentenced for the same offense, drunkenness, from 1 to 28 times. The first sentence was a regular switch-point from which the victim was precipitated to a constantly descending grade, becoming more and more incapacitated for temperate living.

The system of fines is equally ruinous, because it falls most heavily on the families, making it more difficult to support themselves, thereby increasing the perils of pauperism, both to the victim and those who depend on him for support.

It may be said, and the statement is sustained by many facts, that the legal treatment by the lower courts of cases of inebriety is fully as fatal as the saloons themselves where spirits are sold. The saloon and police court are literally the school and college for the training and graduation of classes of incurable inebriates, who endanger every sanitary interest in the country. The fault is not in the courts and their administration of the law, but in the laws themselves, and in that state of public opinion which urges that all inebriates should be treated as wilful criminals and arrested and punished as such.

Thus, year after year this terrible farce of prevention of inebriety by fines and short imprisonments goes on and the incurability of the poor victims increases. Crime is increased, pauperism is increased, the most dangerous sanitary conditions are fostered, and the burdens of taxpayers and producers are increased. The inebriate is always debilitated, and suffers from impaired brain and nerve force; alcohol has broken up all healthy action of the body. In prison both the quality and quantity of food are ill adapted to restore or build up the weakened organism. The hygienic influences of jails and prisons are defective in every respect, and adverse to any healthy growth of body or mind. The psychological influences also are of the worst possible character. The surrounding and the associates precipitate the victim into conditions of mental despair from which recovery is difficult, if not impossible. The only compensation to the inebriate is the removal of alcohol, and in this deprivation the state most terribly unfits him and makes him more and more helpless for the future.

Thus, while civilization is one of the sources from which inebriety is produced, the blundering effort to remove it by penal punishment is an actual factor in increasing and intensifying the disorder. The treatment of inebriety from a scientific standpoint has passed the stage of experiment and is supported by a great variety of experience and collateral evidence that cannot be disputed.

Probably the largest class of inebriates in this country are without means of support and may be termed the indigent and pauper class. This class, non-self-supporting and burdensome, should be recognized by law and committed to workhouse hospitals built for this purpose, preferably in the country upon large farms and amid the most favorable environment. These hospitals should be training schools in which medical care, occupation, physical and mental training could be applied for years, or until the inmates had so far recovered as to be able to become good citizens. Such hospitals should be built from moneys received from a tax imposed on liquor dealers or a license fund, and support themselves in part from the labor of their inmates, and be independent of the taxpayer or of state support. These places would receive the classes who are now sent to jail, and that other class whose numbers are neglected until they have passed into the chronic stage and have become inmates of prisons and insane asylums.

A very large proportion of these several classes could be made self-supporting while under treatment, and in many cases be an actual source of revenue. The hospitals would naturally be divided into two classes. The first would receive the better, or less chronic, cases; the second would have the incurables, and those whose recovery was deemed more or less doubtful. In the one case the surroundings and discipline would be more adapted for the special inmates than in the other, but the same general restraint would be followed in each. In both, recoveries would follow. A large class would be restored to society and become producers. In the second, cases would be housed and made to take care of themselves, which would be an immense gain to society in economy and safety.

Private enterprise should be encouraged by legislation to provide smaller hospitals for the better class, and for those who would be unwilling, or whom it would be undesirable to compel to enter public asylums. Here the commitments should be both forced and voluntary, and the restraint combined with the fullest and latest appliances of science for the end to be accomplished, blending seclusion and good surroundings to build up and make recovery possible.

The first step is to recognize the fact that the inebriate, whether continuous or periodic, has to a greater or less degree forfeited his personal liberty and become a public nuisance and an obstacle to social progress and civilization. Second, that he is suffering from a disease which affects society and every member of the community in which he lives, and from which he cannot recover without aid from other sources, making it absolutely necessary that he should be forced into quarantine on the same principle as the smallpox or yellow-fever patient. This is simply carrying out the primitive law of self-preservation. Naturally the money to accomplish this should come from the license revenue, on the principle that every business should provide for the accidents and injuries which follow from it. Railroad companies and other corporations are required to pay damages for the accidents which follow their business, and this is conceded to be justice. But to-day the tax on the liquor traffic is used to support courts and jails where the inebriate, by fines and imprisonment, is only made worse or more incurable. Thus, literally, the business of selling spirits is increased by the almost barbaric efforts of courts and jails, and every person so punished is made a permanent patron of that business. Against this all the teachings of science and all practical study utter loud protest.

The practical success of workhouse hospitals for inebriates is demonstrated in every self-supporting jail and state's prison in the country, where the obtacles are greater and the possibilities of accomplishing this end more remote. This can also be seen in asylums for both insane and inebriates, in the various sanitaria and hospitals through the country, where the capacity for self-support and the curability of these cases are established facts. More than that, these hospitals would relieve society of great burdens of loss and suffering; the diminution of the number of inebriates would become a practical certainty to an extent of which we can have no conception at present.

It is impossible at the present time to estimate the beneficial results that would follow such a systematized plan of housing and treating the inebriate, but there are positive indications that its effect would be felt in all circles. One of the great fountain-heads of insanity, criminality and pauperism would be closed, and a new era would dawn in the evolution of science.

CAUSES OF PAUPERISM AND THE RELATION OF THE STATE TO IT.

A. O. WRIGHT, LATE SECRETARY OF THE STATE BOARD OF CHARITIES AND REFORM OF THE STATE OF WISCONSIN.

Pauperism is not poverty, which is generally self-supporting. But it is dependence upon alms in some form or other. Pauperism is therefore an outgrowth of charity, paradoxical as that statement may seem. In times and countries where no alms are given there may be starvation, but there is no pauperism. If we imagine an ideal state of society from which all want is banished, there would of course be no pauperism, for there would be no needy to relieve. If we imagine another state of society, one of absolute selfishness, where no one ever aided another in whatever distress he might be, then again there would be no pauperism, because there would be no relief for the needy. But given such a society as we really have, one with many needy persons, and one with much helpfulness for the needy, and a dependent class comes into existence at once. In this sense pauperism is an outgrowth of charity, but in another sense pauperism is actually created by the charity intended to destroy it, because when people find they can get poor relief, they are inclined to depend upon the relief instead of upon their own exertions. Pauperism is therefore the product of two sets of forces—the needs of extreme poverty on the one hand, and the aid offered by public or private charity on the other hand. These forces act and react on one another, and their result is pauperism as it exists. To study the causes of pauperism we must study both the causes that produce actual need and the causes that foster factitious, if not fictitious need.

Pauperism is brought about by something that prevents productive labor in those who have no capital laid up. The following classes of persons include nearly all who call for poor relief:

1. Children deprived of their natural protectors by death, desertion or neglect.

2. Old people past work, who either have no children, or whose children are not able or willing to support them.

3. Persons sick or crippled, or broken down before old age.

4. Mothers with young children, and women about to become mothers, who are widowed or deserted by their husbands, or who were never married.

5. Persons willing and able to work who cannot find work to do.

6. Persons able to work, but idle, and willing to be supported by others.

Of these classes it would seem at first that only the last class is unworthy—those able but not willing to work.

But a little investigation shows further facts like these. Many of those who profess to be willing to work are not willing to do anything that may come to hand, but would pick their work. Many persons now disabled from work were disabled by their own vices, especially by drunkenness. Many women with illegitimate children are not innocent victims, but have children again and again, only to give them away to infant asylums or to public officers. Many mothers with families, deserted by husbands, have made home so uncomfortable as to drive them away ; or on the other hand, the father is a drunkard or a criminal, and hence leaves his family to charity. Many old people make life so unpleasant in their children's homes that they are sent to the poorhouses in self-defense. If to these we add the idleness and improvidence of many people, which finally drifts into pauperism under the appearance of misfortune, we have discovered that a very large part of pauperism is due to the vice, the shiftlessness, or the crankiness of the paupers or their relatives. Whether we call these avoidable causes or not depends upon our view of human nature.

But now comes in the fact that giving alms very frequently creates pauperism. It took the Christian world many centuries to realize that almsgiving might easily be no charity at all, where it made people depend upon it for a living and created a breed of beggars. The waste of money in lavish almsgiving is the least of its evils, the waste of manhood being a far greater wrong. The evil is essentially the same whether the giver of alms is the public or a society or an individual. Public poor relief, especially outdoor relief, however, is subject to the danger that it will be used for political effect. By this is meant that the local officers will gain votes for themselves by giving poor relief liberally.

Over two-thirds of the outdoor relief given in this country, and possibly as much as one-third of the poorhouse relief and one-third of the private charity are absolutely wasted on persons who could support themselves if they knew that they had to do it. This class is not confined to the cities. In many places in the country lavish poor relief is given from a mistaken idea of charity and from the petty political ambition of local officers.

So much for the immediate causes of pauperism. Back of these lie the more remote causes which exist in society itself. The ignorance, the shiftlessness, the lack of self-respect, the vicious habits which are found even in America among many of the poor, being both the cause and the effects of their poverty, tend directly toward pauperism. Then the badly adjusted relations of laborers to their employers produce strikes and lockouts, mobs and riots, with all their attendant miseries, out of which some persons drop into pauperism. .Worst of all, there are families and groups of persons who are hereditary paupers and criminals, who live a parasitical life on society in some form or another, and who hand down a degenerate condition to succeeding generations of defectives.

It is very difficult for public authorities or for such semi-public authorities as administer large private charities to do much in the way of preventing pauperism. They can, indeed, refuse to relieve those who do not need poor relief; but what this amounts to is to prevent their own machinery from creating pauperism by lavish pcor relief. It is not in any other sense an attack on the abuses of pauperism. But so greatly is poor relief abused, that cutting off unnecessary relief is a great gain. When we can say that several large cities have cut off all public outdoor relief without any increase in the demands on other private or public charities, and without any apparent suffering by the poor, it is obvious that poor relief has been greatly abused and that this particular cause of pauperism ought to be cut off by those who have created it.

Similar abuses are those of keeping in poorhouses able-bodied persons who ought not to be there. of bringing up children in poorhouses, of allowing association of the sexes in poorhouses so as to breed pauper children. These are ways in which the unwisdom of public officers tends to create pauperism. Of course these causes should be removed ; but removing them is not preventing pauperism, except as it prevents public poor relief from itself creating pauperism.

When we come to the causes of pauperism which are not the results of unwise relief, the case is quite different.

The part which public authorities can take in the administration of poor relief is not exactly the same as that which private individuals or societies can take, even when they cover precisely the same ground. Public authorities are administering funds which are taken from everybody by the compulsory processes of taxation, so that while such charity is voluntary so far as the community as a whole is concerned, this charity is involuntary and grudging on the part of a large number of individuals. The minority has some rights, even in a government where King Majority rules supreme, and their right to criticize does prevent the public undertaking many forms of charity. And then there is the tendency to reduce things to an average, to treat large classes of cases as classes instead of as individuals, to work by easy mechanical methods which do not require much care or thought. These tendencies are found not only in public officers, but also in the officers of large private societies. Such wholesale methods are not favorable to the nicer and more discriminating kinds of charity. Again, the public authorities, and also the almoners of large private charities, are apt to regard themselves, and are very sure to be regarded by the recipients of relief, as simply givers of inexhaustible funds which cost them nothing. It is difficult for them to get out of the rôle of almsgivers, in cases where something else than alms is best, and it is not easy to convince the professional recipient of such alms that he has not a vested right to help, and that in the form of alms.

Most cases of pauperism, when we go back to their real origin, are either the result of defects in society or of defects in the pauper.

To what extent society itself should be reformed to abolish pauperism is beyond our present purpose and is very difficult to answer in a practical way.

But to a certain extent reformatory methods can and should be used by the public to decrease pauperism. For instance, vagrancy and tramping ought to be treated by providing work for all who are willing and able to work, and sending all persistent vagrants to reformatory workhouses. So all mothers of illegitimate children who apply for poor relief ought to be compelled to work out the cost of their care before being discharged and should not be allowed to give away their children without good reasons. So also the necessary regulations of a well-managed poorhouse, such as careful separation of the sexes, compulsory abstinence from intoxicating liquor, requirement of light labor from all not absolutely disabled, and other similar regulations, make a properly managed poorhouse a reformatory institution. Unfortunately, a very large number of poorhouses are not well managed institutions, and therefore tend to increase pauperism rather than to discourage it. In such ways as these public authorities can reduce the tendencies to pauperism. But in general we may say that what public authorities do in the way of reducing or preventing pauperism is to simply prevent their own machinery from creating it.

The real work of abolishing pauperism must be done by private effort, and mostly in the general line indicated by the friendly visitors of the charity organization societies. What the poor need who are on the verge of pauperism, and in danger of being drawn into that slough of despond, is " not alms, but a friend." This is work which, from the nature of the case, cannot be effectually done to any extent either by public authorities or by the managers of large semi-public charitable societies or institutions. Personal work is the only effective agency to abolish pauperism—personal work done from philanthropic motives, but guided by the wisdom of experience, and felt by the recipients to be an aid to them in keeping their places as self-supporting members of society, not as a substitute for their own industry and prudence.

THE ENGLISH POOR LAW: ITS INTENTION AND RESULTS.

MRS. MAY M'CALLUM.

It may seem, at first sight, useless to inquire at all minutely into the details of bygone enactments which have been modified or superseded in consequence of changed conditions and habits, but something is to be gained by such a retrospect if it enables us to distinguish between those social difficulties which are transitional, and those eternal problems which perplexed our ancestors and are present with ourselves, problems which have their roots in human character and exemplify the action of natural laws.

A French author has well said that "There is no nation, whatever may be its rank, which may not serve as a lesson or an example. Who can doubt," M. Faucher continues, "that the peoples may gain as much by interchange of their experience and their ideas as by that of their products, but such an interchange must take place with perfect freedom on both sides, and without any attempt to control or to misrepresent the characteristics of the national spirit."* These conferences are a concrete expression of a similar opinion, and I esteem it an honor to be permitted to lay before an American audience a brief review of the English poor laws, which chronicle the struggle of centuries with perennial evils.

From the earliest times, four fundamental ideas may be continuously traced in the history of our system of public relief. These are, first, that the nation must not allow any of its members to perish; secondly, that each locality should care for its own poor, and that therefore destitute persons should be compulsorily removed to the place of their birth; thirdly, that vagabondage and idleness should be checked and punished; and, fourthly, that charity should be largely exercised in mitigation of the hardships of life.

---

* *Études sur l'Angleterre.* Quoted by Dr. Aschrott in "*The English Poor Law System.*"

It is beyond the scope of this brief paper to examine the growth of these opinions; but among their proximate causes were the petty struggles of an unsettled time, the abolition of villeinage in the fourteenth century, and the ceaseless efforts of a warlike nobility to control the labor and the movements of a peasantry in whom the desire for freedom was deep and undying. But in legislation as in life it is the unexpected that happens, and while on the one hand our statute books from before the fourteenth century teem with repressive measures of a stern and even barbarous description, and while on the other hand the mistaken generosity of the monasteries weakened personal responsibility, the evils that law and kindness alike sought to repress grew and spread like noxious weeds.

Already in the reign of Richard II, who died in 1399, it is directed that "beggars impotent to serve" shall abide where the proclamation finds them, but if the townspeople cannot or will not provide for them, they "must draw them to other towns within the wapentake," or to "towns where they were born, and there continually abide."

In 1530 the justices are to give begging licenses to the impotent, and are to punish "persons whole and mighty in body and able to labour," who are vagrants and cannot explain how they live. By-and-by sheriffs and local authorities are to "charitably receive" the poor sent back to their district, and on Sundays and holidays the churchwardens and others are "in good and discreet ways" to collect alms in boxes, and to distribute them "without fraud or affection," so that "none diseased or sick who cannot work shall openly beg," while "the lusty shall be kept in continual labour."

Wealthy parishes are to help the poorer, a proposal that is carried out in London to-day. Again, to quote the quaint old phrases, "curates are to exhort to alms with such talent as God has given them," and when it is found that they "gently ask and demand" in vain, the spiritual power over froward persons is supported by temporal threats of imprisonment, and finally a tax or poor-rate is levied and collected.

Curiously enough, more than one law was passed for the purpose of punishing any one who gave alms to vagrants, and though these statutes were naturally inoperative, they arouse a lurking sympathy in the minds of those who watch the manufacture of vagabonds by needless charity to-day.

In 1601 was passed a famous act know as the Forty-third of Elizabeth, which consolidated and to some extent improved previous legislation. Both praise and blame have been freely lavished on this act, but it makes little change in that fatal system of interference with labor and with wages under which the English nation continuously suffered. At this distance of time we cannot judge whether its promoters were actuated chiefly by motives of humanity or by the promptings of class interest, but two of its clauses are of high importance; by the one, the duty of the family towards its aged and less fortunate members was legally recognized, and by the other relief was restricted, in the case of the able-bodied, to persons "without means." The existence of this ancient and most wise limitation proved of great service to the reformers of 1834.

In the year 1722 the overseers of a parish were empowered to purchase or hire a house in which to maintain paupers, who were not to receive relief in any other form. This is the well-known workhouse test, which at first was productive of excellent results, but speedily failed of its purpose, owing to the scandalous lack of regulation in the workhouses themselves. Such institutions may either be refuges in which a decent amount of comfort is combined with deterrent discipline, or they may become the habitual resort of the idler and the ruffian, who are there supported at the expense of the rates.

The eighteenth century increased the current confusion of ideas with respect to the meaning of the word *poor*. Instead of being used to describe a small minority, who through infirmity, accident or misconduct have ceased to be self-supporting members of society, it was placed more and more in simple opposition to the word rich, and the belief spread that the state could and ought to provide for all such poor, including finally all wage-earning laborers. In 1795 the Berkshire magistrates actually "settled the incomes of the industrious poor," by fixing a scale of relief, in pursuance of the instructions in a statute known as Gilbert's Act, which introduced some improvements, but more than counterbalanced them by reversing the policy of Elizabeth and creating a rate in aid of wages for the able-bodied. The workhouse test was abolished, and the country was launched on a career of degradation which perhaps has no parallel. Relief was bestowed recklessly and in various ways, sometimes at the price of a few hours confinement in some enclosure, or of attendance at repeated roll-calls; allowances were freely given, so that wages were kept down to starvation point; sometimes "head-money" was granted for each child, and immorality was soon a recognized source of profit; farmers were forced to employ pauper labor, often in excess of their requirements; and to sum up, the man who would not work at all received from the parish as much as the honest laborer who toiled his day. Family affection too was undermined, and the parish had to pay women for rendering the commonest offices of humanity to their sick parents, who were accounted "a great hindrance"; in fact, the general demoralization can scarcely now be realized. Population was artificially stimulated, land began to go out of cultivation, small tradesmen and farmers were ruined by the enormous rates; and in the village of Cholesbury, out of a population of 139 souls, only 35 persons, including the clergyman and his family, supported themselves; the remaining 104 by the assistance of the poor law supported two beer-houses. Favoritism and fraud were rampant; one man received relief in six parishes; the laborer had, as has been well said, "a slave's security without a slave's liability to punishment"; and in many places the paupers began to enforce their demands with threats and violence, and it seemed as if this abominable system of out-relief, with its vain attempts to provide "fair" subsistence, were to prove the ruin of the national character. In the words of the eminent American, Francis A. Walker,

"Such may be the effect of foolish laws. The legislator may think it hard that his power for good is so restricted, but he has no reason to complain of any limits upon his power for evil. On the contrary, it would seem that there is no race of men whom a few laws respecting industry, trade and finance, passed by country squires or by labor demagogues, in defiance of economic principles, could not in half a generation transform into beasts."

Happily, recovery was still possible; a Royal Commission was appointed to inquire into the whole subject, and issued in 1834 a report which deserves to be a classic, alike for the student of human nature and of economics. The fruit of this report was the act known as the New Poor Law, which swept away the worst evils by asserting as a fundamental principle that the condition of those who receive public relief must be less eligible than that of the independent laborer. The workhouse test was, with certain permissive exceptions, re-established, and a central board was formed, which has now become a government department under a president, who changes with the administration, but who is supported by a highly experienced staff of permanent officials.

This central board exercises, through its auditors, a complete supervision of all parish accounts, and can surcharge the local authorities if they incur any illegal expenditure; it sanctions the appointment and salaries of relieving officers and workhouse officials, the more important of whom are directly responsible to it, and are only in a secondary degree under the boards of guardians. Its inspectors pay surprise-visits to the various poor law institutions, and as they have power to examine witnesses on oath, their reports are of great value and interest. The whole machinery of the department is devised with great skill, and under its management a still larger proportion of our pauperism would have been abolished, had it not been for that English dislike of interference which induces local boards to disregard the London authority, and prevents that authority from rigidly enforcing its own rules.

The new law encountered the most violent opposition, not only from the ignorant and depraved, but from employers and others; and partly on this account, and partly in consequence of seasons of depression, such as occurred during the cotton famine, the cholera year, and years of war and of agricultural distress, the progress of improvement, though sure, was very slow. In 1838 there was "an increase of more than 50,000 depositors and of above £1,800,000 in deposits, in friendly societies," chiefly in rural districts, while in the three years that followed the passing of the act there was a gross saving to the country of £4,000,000, much of which was spent in the wages of productive industry. About twelve years later our third great friendly society, the Hearts of Oak, came into existence, and with its famous predecessors, the Foresters and Oddfellows, continues to increase and to display the honorable independence and self-governing power of our wage-earners when they are uninjured by sentimental legislation.

The year 1870 marked a new era; fresh interest was excited by the reports of the poor law inspectors, and the passing of the Education and other acts gave a new impetus to progress. Poor law infirmaries have been provided for the sick, and, at least in London, are often equal to the best hospitals; lunatics are placed in properly inspected asylums, and children of destitute parents are cared for in schools, while those who are orphans or deserted may be boarded out in carefully selected homes, so as to avoid the creation of that miserable product of our civilization known as "the institution child."

All this expenditure presses heavily on the rate-payers, and the question arises whether we are not here and there overstepping the limits of a wise provision and offering inducements to pauperism. It is also alleged that the extreme care bestowed on the insane, the epileptic and otherwise afflicted, promotes the increase of their numbers by prolonging their lives and partially improving their condition.

In one direction a salutary change has been effected. Determined efforts have been made in many places to diminish out-relief, and consequently to lessen pauperism.

The following figures illustrate the effect of twenty years of this policy under the direction of an able and devoted chairman and board of guardians in the union of Bradfield. In January, 1871, there were in that union 1258 paupers, or one in 13 of the whole population; in January, 1891, there were only 149 paupers, or one in 110 of the population. Twenty-nine of these were persons who had been in receipt of outdoor relief in 1871; not a single outdoor pauper belonged to the current year. The money rate had correspondingly fallen from two shillings and a halfpenny to fivepence farthing, and even on a low rental this difference means a considerable addition to the free income of the working classes. The figures are equally satisfactory in the case of the aged poor for whom so much sympathy is felt; some few may be regarded as survivals of the bad old days, for the New Poor Law was almost inoperative in their youth, and these no doubt helped to swell the numbers when 35.5 per cent. of the Bradfield population over 60 years of age were paupers; that figure is now reduced to about 4 per cent.

As one writer has observed, "It is almost entirely a question of poor law administration whether 4 or " (taking the figures from Brixworth Union into account) "56 per cent. of the population are paupers or independent when they die." In some of the Bradfield parishes there are no paupers at all. Charity, too, has become more active and intelligent, and readily provides for cases of undeserved and exceptional misfortune; and lastly, a careful inquiry has shown that it is a mistake to assert that the neighboring unions are unaffected by the spirit of reform, for there is a steady though very gradual improvement in them all.

With such object-lessons before us it might be thought that guardians in general would hasten to institute similar reforms, but unhappily there are signs of a reaction in favor of relaxation of the

poor law, and it may be that the poorer ranks of the democracy
will refuse to profit by the experience of the middle class, and that
the old lessons must be learnt—and paid for—again. Two forces
are on the side of the reactionaries, the Socialists and the mass of
the clergy of all denominations; for so do extremes meet. The
Socialist naturally tempts the improvident with dreams of state-
regulated labor and of state-relief on easy terms, nor is the Liberal
press guiltless of highly colored statements that picture our workhouses as the resort of the deserving poor. It is in part owing to
this mistaken notion that the conditions in many of these institutions
have been rendered incomparably better than in many homes of
workingmen, and that new efforts are being made to modify those
restrictions which still prove deterrent to persons who live habitually
on the verge of pauperism.

The clergy, as of old, exhort their congregations to give, but they
are not trained to understand, and therefore they cannot enforce, the
full responsibility of the giver. By making vice and idleness easy,
an unwise charity directly encourages the pauper spirit; and in all
probability we owe to the Salvation Army alone a large increase in
the number of persons who will ultimately come upon the rates.

Thus, after centuries of legislation we have still an army of paupers
that diminishes but slowly, and an army of vagrants as well. For
these, provision is made in casual wards, where a night's lodging and
a meagre supply of food can be obtained—the performance of a task
of work, and increased detention after each admission within a month,
being the conditions imposed. This system has proved a failure, at
least in London; the pressure of *ill-informed public opinion* has
caused the rule of detention to be relaxed, and the multiplication of
charitable refuges and shelters defeats every attempt of the poor
law to deal effectually with the vagrant class. Greatly as we dislike over-much legislative interference, it is open to question whether
our irresponsible and uncontrolled charity does not create worse
evils; it undoubtedly fosters a class whose existence is not only a
disgrace, but a source of national deterioration; and here we reach
the vital issue on which the administrators of relief, whether legal or
voluntary, differ so profoundly. Are we or are we not to deal with
the needy and the destitute, that is to say, in the majority of cases,
with the incompetent and the drunkard, according to their immediate desires, or in the manner most beneficial to the community at
large?

On one side are the reactionaries, including the host of well-meaning and enthusiastic persons who are swayed by the appeal of the moment, and are able to believe that there are royal roads to happiness and that the latest big scheme is a panacea for human ills.   On the other side are those who take a broader and more carefully reasoned view, and who attach the highest importance to the interests of the nation as a whole.   I venture to think that time will justify the latter, and that the triumph of statemanship lies in applying the experience of the past, with such wise modifications as are required by the exigencies of the present.

For your great nation all things seem possible, yet as your wide lands fill up and your cities increase in size, the old problems will inevitably present themselves, and happy will it be for the world if you can solve them rightly.   It is our hope that out of the failures of the past may grow the successes of the future, and in organizing and moulding your social institutions you may perhaps find helpful material in the records of that old country for which many of you evince so kindly a regard.

Authorities Consulted.

British Encyclopædia, last edition.   Article " Poor Law."
Report of Poor Law Commissioners of 1834.
English Poor Law System.   By Dr. P. F. Aschrott.   Translated by Preston Thomas.
Poor Law Reform, an essay in *Edinburgh Review* of 1841–2.
Report of South Wales Conference (Poor Law) of 1892.
Speech of Mr. Bland Garland of Bradfield at Annual Meeting of the Charity Organisation Society, etc., etc.

POOR LAW PROGRESS AND REFORM, EXEMPLIFIED IN THE ADMINISTRATION OF AN EAST LONDON UNION.

WILLIAM VALLANCE, CLERK TO THE GUARDIANS OF THE WHITECHAPEL UNION, LONDON, ENGLAND.

The history of poor law administration in England is an instructive one, and presents to civilized communities a valuable object-lesson in national philanthropy. It stands as at once the conception of an earnest, as well as civilly prudent, people actuated by humane impulses.

It affords abundant evidence, through the centuries, of a public concern for the welfare of the poor, whilst in its alternations of severity and indulgence is seen the desire to prevent public relief from degenerating into a system of indiscriminate almsgiving, with all its attendant demoralization.

We see in the legislation of the last four hundred years the swaying of the pendulum of popular feeling, the objective in one case being the "sturdy vagabond" or the "valiant beggar" who called for repression, and in the other the suffering poor, who were recognized as having a legitimate claim upon society.

True, mistakes many and great have been made, more especially in the administration of the law ; and notwithstanding the lessons of history, and the stimulation of modern thought upon social questions, we are yet face to face with the unsolved problem—how to deal with the poor.

We know that hundreds of statutes have been passed in relation to the poor, and that these represent mountains of speech and rivers of ink ; and we think we are in a position to take larger views of public and relative duty to our " neighbor " than our forefathers ; but human nature is found to be as frail as ever, and so the best intentions and the best systems fail when the heart is allowed to give impulse to human action without the controlling guidance of the head. In other words, where the administrators of relief fail to appreciate the fundamental principles upon which the law is based, and only see the possibility—without regard to antecedent circumstances and prospective results—of ameliorating existing conditions of poverty, not only are the spirit and intentions of law contravened, but an injury is done to the poor themselves.

Without attempting to trace the history of the English poor law, which is as well known in America as in England, it may perhaps suffice to make bare mention of the Poor Law Amendment Act, 1834, which was founded upon one of the most remarkable reports ever presented to Parliament. The abuses, the rampant evils, which were found to have resulted from a weak policy and a worse administration of poor law relief, so shocked the public sense that Parliament was induced to pass a measure which for nearly sixty years has remained the modern landmark in poor law legislation.

. That it was founded upon sound principles is universally acknowledged by thoughtful administrators, whilst (coupled with the report
of the Royal Commission) it remains with us a mentor and a warning. "The fundamental principle," as stated by the commissioners
in their report upon the amendment of the poor laws, with respect
to the legal relief of the poor, is that

"The condition of the pauper ought to be, on the whole, less eligible than
that of the independent laborer. The equity and expediency of this principle
are equally obvious. Unless the condition of the pauper is, on the whole, less
eligible than that of the independent laborer, the law destroys the strongest
motives to good conduct, steady industry, providence and frugality among
the laboring classes, and induces persons, by idleness or imposture, to throw
themselves upon the poor rates for support. But if the independent laborer
sees that any recurrence to the poor rates will, while it protects him against
destitution, place him in a less eligible position than that which he can attain
by his own industry, he is left to the undisturbed influence of all those motives
which prompt mankind to exert forethought and self-denial. On the other
hand, the pauper has no just ground for complaint if, at the same time that
his physical wants are amply provided for, his condition should be less eligible
than that of the poorest class of those who contribute to his support."

Hence the guardians were restricted to the relief of destitution,
either by receiving the destitute person into a poor law establishment, or (in certain excepted and exceptional cases) by relief in
money, food, or articles of absolute necessity. They were precluded
from the payment of rent; they could not redeem tools or other
articles from pawn; they could not provide at the cost of the poor
rate any tools, implements or other articles, other than articles of
clothing when urgently needed; they could not set up a poor
person in business. In other words, they could only provide for
present existing physical wants, and could do nothing either to prevent the poor becoming paupers or to lift them out of a condition
of dependence. The "excepted and exceptional cases" to which I
have referred are chiefly those in which the destitution has been
occasioned by sickness, widowhood, and old age, and in these cases
considerable discretion has been reserved to the guardians. But
what has been the result? It will be admitted by thoughtful administrators that the legislation for these "excepted and exceptional
cases" has been as disastrous to the poor as it has been injurious to
the community. What was intended to be the exception has become

the rule, and the distinction between the "gift" of charity and the "legal right" of poor law relief has been lost sight of. Without due regard to the causes of destitution, or the consequences of relief, guardians have found the means ready to their hand, not only of distributing alms out of compulsory taxation to the poor who parade their "legal right," but, what has been far worse, relieving the rich from trouble and concern, and churches and religious bodies from the sense of responsibility, in regard to the well-being of the poor. There has also been, proportionately, a relaxation of effort to save and redeem from pauperism; the poor having been left to the relief which brings degradation, and to the degradation which brings the relief. Thus the poor who might have been saved have become paupers, and those who might have been redeemed have remained paupers.

In the case of the Whitechapel Union it has to be observed that it is a district largely inhabited by the poor, and "very poor"; and that (upon the basis of tables contained in "Life and Labour in London," by Mr. Charles Booth, the eminent statistician) the "lower and upper middle classes" of the district number $6\frac{1}{4}$ per cent. of the population; the "regular weekly workers," 71 per cent.; the "irregular and casual workers," $19\frac{1}{2}$ per cent.; and the lowest class, which includes "loafers" and the criminal or semi-criminal classes, $3\frac{1}{4}$ per cent.

In speaking of the poor law administration in Whitechapel it has to be admitted that the policy and practice of the guardians prior to 1870 were neither better nor worse than those adopted in other parts of London and the country. Its relief system may be said to have been that of meeting apparent existing circumstances of need by small doles of outdoor relief; the indoor establishments being reserved for the destitute poor who voluntarily sought refuge in them. Able-bodied men who applied for relief on account of want of employment were set to work, and in return were afforded outdoor relief in money and kind. Under this system the administration was periodically subjected to great pressure, so much so that the aid of the police had not infrequently to be invoked to restrain disorder and afford necessary protection to officers and property. Police protection was even at times required for the guardians during their administration of relief. The experience of the winter of 1869-70, however, was such as to lead the guardians to review their position and earnestly to aim at reforming a system which was felt to be fostering pauperism and encouraging idleness, improvidence and imposture, while the "relief" in no true sense helped the poor. It was seen that voluntary charity largely consisted of indiscriminate almsgiving; that it accepted no definite obligation as distinct from the function of poor law relief; that the poor law was relied upon to supplement private benevolence; that the almsgivers too frequently were the advocates of the poor in their demands upon the public rates; and that both poor law and charity were engaged in relieving a distress much of which a thoughtless benevolence and a lax relief administration had created. This condition of things the guardians resolved to amend. They looked forward to the ultimate possibility of laying down a broad distinction between "legal relief" and "charitable aid," and of interpreting the former as relief in the work-house or other institution for the actually destitute. and the latter as personal sympathy and helpful charity; and so they began by gradu-ally restricting outdoor relief in "out-of-work" cases, until they were able (in 1870) to entirely close the outdoor labor yard, and it has not since been re-opened. In this process of restriction it was found that about one in ten of those who were offered indoor in place of outdoor relief entered the workhouse, and these in turn gradually withdrew themselves, so that eventually the indoor pauperism resumed its normal condition. Following this was a further review of the outdoor relief lists, and the gradual application of other forms of limitation, side by side with efforts to bring the more deserving within reach of helpful charity. The guardians were especially mindful to guard the entrance to the outdoor relief list, and, where the circumstances seemed to necessitate present relief in the home of the applicant, it was sought to make it in the first place adequate to the necessities of the case, and next, temporary in duration; and it was usually given upon some condition of personal effort to avoid future recourse to the rates for support. Sick men with families dependent upon them, if not offered indoor relief, were relieved temporarily in money and kind, upon the distinct promise to join a benefit club. Widows with dependent children were, in some cases, afforded relief out of the workhouse, for a strictly limited period, pending inquiries as to their circumstances and possibilities, com-munication with relatives and late employers, and efforts to place them in positions to achieve independence. In some cases employment was offered in the infirmary as a scrubber or washer at weekly wages; or, failing other means of meeting the necessities of the case, the guardians undertook to receive a portion of the family into the district school, leaving the mother free to enter service, or otherwise to provide for herself and one, or sometimes two, children. The aged and infirm were only relieved out of doors when there was evidence of thrift, and when the guardians were satisfied that there were no children or relatives legally or morally bound to support them and able to do so; but even these exceptions and limitations became non-existent and unnecessary with the organization of voluntary charity, which gradually undertook the benevolent work of saving the really deserving poor from the poor law. Thus the door of out-relief became gradually closed, and, as a fact, no cases, other than those of sudden or urgent necessity relieved by the relieving officers in kind, have now for some twenty-two years been added to the outdoor relief list; and now (in 1893) there remains but one aged woman, the sole remnant of a former system, in receipt of permanent outdoor relief. As illustrating, too, the limited extent to which relief in kind is afforded by the relieving officers under circumstances of urgent necessity, it may be added that the average weekly cost of such relief last year was but 16s. 1d.

Although no written or printed by-laws have been adopted, the guardians have none the less fixed rules of administration, and these fixed rules the poor understand; whilst it has been as clearly seen that to "play fast and loose" with the poor is to do them injury, to encourage reliance upon the poor law, to occasion discontent, and to restrain the flow of helpful Christian charity.

The appended statistical tables will exemplify the gradual nature of the restriction of outdoor relief and its contemporaneous effect, if any, upon the indoor pauperism. Taking the sixth week of the quarter ended at Lady Day, 1870, as a starting-point, that being the week in which the highest pauperism was reached, the first table will be found to show the number of paupers relieved, the percentages of indoor and outdoor paupers, and the amount expended in outdoor relief in that and the corresponding weeks of the intervening years up to 1893, viz:

	Indoor paupers relieved. (1)	Outdoor paupers relieved. (2)	Total number of paupers relieved exclusive of lunatics in asylums. (3)	Percentages.		Cost of outdoor relief (i. e. in money and kind).	
				Indoor. (4)	Outdoor. (5)	During the 6th week of the Lady-day Qtr. (6)	During year ended Lady-day. (7)
						£ s. d.	£
1870	1,419	5,339	6,758 (a)	21.0	79.0	168 17 4	6,685
1871	1,219	2,568	3,787	32.2	67.8	120 14 3	6,073
1872	1,000	1,568	2,568	38.9	61.1	75 18 7	4,730
1873	1,163	845	2,008	57.9	42.1	50 4 5	2,654
1874	1,154	609	1,763	65.5	34.5	36 11 1	2,114
1875	1,170	346	1,516	77.2	22.8	22 9 0	1,406
1876	1,268	186	1,454	87.2	12.8	16 19 7	916
1877	1,203	122	1,325	90.8	9.2	12 2 9	873
1878	1,221	141 (b)	1,362	89 6	10.4	11 0 6	731
1879	1,431	143 (b)	1,574	90.9	9.1	9 15 3	592
1880	1,464	128 (b)	1,592	92.0	8.0	9 7 7	546
1881	1,582	121 (b)	1,703	92.9	7.1	8 17 4	528
1882	1,478	105 (b)	1,583	93.4	6.6	7 6 11	584
1883	1,482	91 (b)	1,573	94.2	5.8	4 8 10	521
1884	1,418	77 (b)	1,495	94.8	5.2	4 2 9	463
1885	1,370	74 (b)	1,444	94.9	5.1	4 8 1	309
1886	1,305	70 (b)	1,375	94.9	5.1	3 3 5	167
1887	1,247	61 (b)	1,308	95.3	4.7	2 7 11	131
1888	1,356	63 (b)	1,419	95.5	4.5	2 10 11	117
1889	1,308	46 (b)	1,354	96.6	3.4	1 15 7	86
1890	1,258	52 (b)	1,310	96.0	4.0	1 16 3	84
1891	1,345	71 (b)	1,416	95.0	5.0	3 5 4	77
1892	1,342	56 (b)	1,398	96.0	4.0	2 14 10	67
1893	1,518	47 (b)	1,565	97.0	3.0	1 19 2	72

It is to be observed that in 1870 the imbecile paupers were maintained in the workhouse and are accordingly enumerated in column 1.   In 1871 those paupers had been transferred to imbecile asylums and had ceased to be so enumerated until 1879, when they were required to be again included in the return of indoor paupers.   This will explain the sudden diminution in the indoor paupers in 1871 and the sudden rise in 1879.

(a) The figures for 1870 may be regarded as exceptional to the extent of about 2000 paupers, there being at that period a severe temporary pressure upon the administration; but it is nevertheless interesting to note that the experience of the winter of 1869-70 induced the guardians to voluntarily suspend the outdoor relief regulation order early in the following year, and to apply strictly the principle of the outdoor relief prohibitory order.

(b) These figures include 30 boarded-out children in 1878, 36 in 1879, 42 in 1880, 52 in 1881, 55 in 1882, 60 in 1883, 49 in 1884, 49 in 1885, 54 in 1886, 48 in 1887, 41 in 1888, 38 in 1889, 42 in 1890, 37 in 1891, 34 in 1892, and 30 in 1893.

The following table will further show the *mean pauperism* of the Whitechapel Union (classified) in each of the 24 years ended at Lady Day, 1893, with its ratio to population, viz :

COMPARATIVE STATEMENT OF PAUPERISM

In the Whitechapel Union, being the mean numbers of paupers of all classes (indoor and outdoor) relieved on the 1st of July and the 1st of January in each of the 24 parochial years ended at Lady-day, 1893; together with the ratio per 1000 of population.

| Year ended Lady-day. | INDOOR PAUPERS. | | | | | | OUTDOOR PAUPERS. | | | | | Mean number of indoor and outdoor paupers. | Ratio per 1000 of population. |
	In work-house and infirmary.	In schools and training ship.	Imbeciles in asylums.	In hospitals, etc.	Vagrants.	Total.	In relief lists.	Lunatics in asylums.	Medical relief only.	Children boarded-out.	Total.		
1870	899	353	..	..	59	1,311	2,797	178	579	..	3,554	4,865	61.6
1871	807	322	45	9	51	1,234	2,597	184	686	..	3,467	4,701	61.8
1872	652	303	121	26	31	1,133	1,848	171	276	..	2,295	3,428	45.0
1873	685	347	117	7	12	1,168	881	169	197	..	1,247	2,415	31.5
1874	718	374	147	13	8	1,260	642	141	176	..	959	2,219	29.0
1875	773	360	150	8	14	1,305	435	136	132	..	703	2,008	26.2
1876	774	376	151	4	16	1,321	190	145	91	..	426	1,747	22.8
1877	801	324	171	15	28	1,339	142	184	73	14	413	1,752	22.8
1878	799	316	177	22	36	1,350	117	210	66	28	421	1,771	23.1
1879	836	302	172	18	32	1,360	84	222	52	35	393	1,753	22.8
1880	807	302	165	25	51	1,350	70	238	73	42	423	1,773	23.1
1881	830	298	164	23	50	1,365	65	228	98	48	439	1,804	23.5
1882	899	271	153	57	51	1,431	46	230	53	55	384	1,815	25.4
1883	934	289	145	23	41	1,432	34	219	38	58	349	1,781	24.9
1884	875	293	139	22	17	1,316	24	214	46	53	337	1,683	23.5
1885	866	247	133	60	44	1,350	22	218	32	53	325	1,675	23.4
1886	810	233	127	18	35	1,223	20	232	44	52	348	1,571	22.0
1887	793	196	125	29	29	1,172	15	228	30	51	324	1,496	20.9
1888	871	186	126	30	40	1,253	8	226	42	42	318	1,571	22.0
1889	890	195	137	25	56	1,303	8	216	41	40	305	1,608	22.5
1890	904	180	138	11	33	1,266	7	212	51	39	309	1,575	22.0
1891	922	172	140	39	38	1,311	13	210	47	38	308	1,619	22.5
1892	901	199	135	34	41	1,310	11	229	38	34	312	1,622	21.4
1893	929	194	124	83	44	1,374	20	242	20	30	312	1,686	22.6

These progressive results, as will be seen, have not been accompanied by a proportionate, nor even an appreciable, increase in the number of indoor paupers relieved. Indeed, there is to be deduced the somewhat remarkable fact—taking into account the increase of sick poor under the separate infirmary system—that the new departure taken in 1870 has resulted in a *diminution* in the indoor pauperism. This is probably owing, in part, to the discouragement which the system has given to speculative applications for relief, and, in part, to the concentration of official and voluntary effort upon the dispauperization of the poor. There is also reason to believe that the policy which has been pursued has resulted in an improvement in the condition of the poor. Rents are said to be better paid, and more money to be deposited in savings and penny banks than formerly, whilst publicans and pawnbrokers are equally lamenting the badness of trade. The poor are certainly more self-respecting than they were, whilst the work of voluntary charity may be now described as more personal service and less almsgiving. So uniform and strict has become the administration of legal relief, and so well understood is the system, that an application for outdoor relief is now seldom made to the guardians.

Simultaneous with the restriction of outdoor relief has been the endeavor of the guardians to reform their indoor administration by making their workhouse a " well regulated " establishment, and contributory as far as possible to character and self-reliance, as well as deterrent to the idle malingerer.

This record of an administration of the poor law in one populous East London Union has been rendered possible only by the consistent adherence of the guardians, during the last 24 years, to the principles which they regarded as sound and in the truest interests of the poor, and by their determined refusal to become either the advocates or patrons of individual applicants at board meetings. They saw that by the out-relief system the working classes were being educated in dependence, being practically told that every recurring misfortune or contingency of life would be amply met out of the public rates, whilst they were demoralized by the knowledge that the adversity which flows from idleness, intemperance or improvidence would be rewarded by an eligible form of relief out of the taxation of the industrious, thrifty, and self-reliant. They saw also that the system of outdoor relief encouraged reckless and thriftless marriages, husbands and wives being in no sense brought face to face with the realities of life. Employment might be precarious and income small, but the lesson of the poor law too frequently bore its fruit, "the parish" being written against all such contingencies as "sickness," "births," "burials," "widowhood," "orphanage," and "old age." It was also found that the practice of awarding from public rates permanent pensions to widows with families, at a rate so uniform that they were readily calculated in anticipation, and so certain that they were received as their due, tended to the relaxation of those habits of forethought on the part of heads of families, which are essential to the independence of the working classes; it was wanting in the elements of a true Christian charity, and induced such a spirit of helplessness that their misery and pauperism became chronic. In Whitechapel the cases of widows with children dependent upon them are invariably referred to the Charity Organization Society, through which they receive present needed help, and they are only returned to the guardians in the event of absolute failure to meet adequately the permanent necessities of the case. And here it is worthy of notice that this policy has not resulted, as might perhaps be assumed, either in the substitution of another form of outdoor relief outside the poor law, or in a very special increase in the number of children maintained in the district school. The present number of children of widows in the district school is 37 as compared with the mean number of 418 widows and 1010 children in receipt of outdoor relief in 1870. And not only has this army of outdoor pauper children disappeared, but, as a fact, notwithstanding the addition of the children of widows to the indoor pauper roll, the number of children now maintained in schools and institutions, and "boarded-out" in the country is less by 36 per cent. than the number provided for in the district school 23 years ago. With regard to the aged poor, whatever the difficulty in applying strict principles in their relief, experience yet points to the corrupting influence of a certain provision, out of public rates, of weekly pensions in old age. The system operates to the encouragement of a life-long anticipation of a "parish allowance" as an eventuality, if not absolutely to be desired, at least not worth a present self-denial to obviate. Nor is this anticipation confined to the pauper himself, but extends to his children, who too frequently regard their payment of poor rates as fully satisfying every claim upon them. In Whitechapel, the entire discontinuance of outdoor relief, even to the aged, has been rendered possible by the establishment of a "Pension Society," which deals with cases of exceptional distress and desert, the pensions going to the old people "by the hands of ladies who are both almoners and friends."

But there are not only classes of poor to be dealt with under normal circumstances; there are seasons of distress arising from a scarcity of employment; and, whether recurrent or exceptional, it is equally important that the administration of legal relief should be uniform and clearly understood. It may be that some relaxation is necessary at times by reason of insufficiency of workhouse accommodation, but it is of the first importance that the poor should know the nature and extent of the relaxation and the circumstances under which it is permitted. There is a public sentiment, especially in times of commercial depression, antagonistic to a form of relief which is thought to have the effect of "breaking-up homes." It may therefore be interesting to state that in the early part of 1887 the Whitechapel guardians sought and obtained, but did not feel it necessary to exercise, temporary powers to deal with applications for relief in such a manner as to ensure the preservation of decent homes, to afford adequate security against a too ready dependence upon the rates for support, and to relieve undue pressure upon workhouse accommodation, namely, by affording outdoor relief to the wife and dependent children of an indoor pauper so long as he might remain an inmate of the workhouse. Under ordinary circumstances, however, the system which seems adequately to meet the necessities of " out-of-work " cases, and to be at the same time conducive to the interests of the community, is indoor relief to the head of a family, coupled with charitable aid to the wife and children, so as to keep a decent home intact. There would, of course, remain a further legitimate work for private charity in saving the more deserving from the poor law, and encouraging and aiding them in their efforts to achieve independence.

· But however conspicuous may have been the results of a strict, consistent and unvarying administration of poor law relief in the Whitechapel Union, the records of the country generally, since 1870, are also those of gradual and continuous improvement. In that year, whilst the ratio of indoor pauperism to population was but 7.1 per 1,000, that of outdoor pauperism was 39.4, and this may be taken to be the then normal pauperism, since there had been little variation for many years.

The movement, however, which sprang up in that year, and in which the Whitechapel Board had the distinction of taking a leading part, in favor of a stricter administration of legal relief has produced the following striking results. Taking the quinquennial periods from 1870, the ratio of each form of pauperism to 1000 of population in England and Wales, the metropolis and Whitechapel respectively stood as follows, viz.:

Years.	England and Wales.			The Metropolis.			Whitechapel Union.		
	Indoor.	Outdoor.	Total.	Indoor.	Outdoor.	Total.	Indoor.	Outdoor.	Total.
1870	7.1	39.4	46.5	11.5	36.0	47.5	16.6	45.0	61.6
1875	6.2	27.6	33.8	11.6	20.3	31.9	17.0	9.2	26.2
1880	7.1	24.7	31.8	13.0	13.7	26.7	17.6	5.5	23.1
1885	6.8	21.8	28.6	13.8	11.6	25.4	18.9	4.5	23.4
1890	6.6	20.7	27.3	14.1	11.8	25.9	17.7	4.3	22.0
1892	6.4	19.2	25.6	13.8	10.8	24.6	17.3	4.1	21.4

It will be observed that notwithstanding the outdoor pauperism in Whitechapel has fallen 40.9 per 1,000 of population, i. e. from 45.0 to 4.1 (as against 25.2 per 1,000 in the metropolis) since 1870, the indoor pauperism has increased but 0.7 in Whitechapel as against 2.3 in the whole metropolis. Indeed, the fact may be accepted that no increase of indoor pauperism has resulted from a strict administration of relief in Whitechapel, since a comparison of figures is not fairly equal, by reason of the almost continuous increase already referred to in the number of sick poor resorting to the separate infirmary in recent years.*

This fact sufficiently disposes of the assertion frequently made, that a rigid administration of outdoor relief has the effect of driving the poor into the workhouse; but if further evidence is needed, it will be found in an analysis recently made of the aged inmates of the workhouse (exclusive of sick under treatment in the infirmary, who were assumed to be in receipt of the only form of relief which adequately and humanely met their necessities), from which it appeared that 92

* During the year 1892 no fewer than 5,155 persons passed through the infirmary by discharge or death, as against 3,202 in 1885.

per cent. were admittedly "homeless," in the sense that they were without home, furniture or relations with whom they could live outside; whilst of the remainder, but two were scheduled in the "classification of causes" under the heading of "destitution apparently arising from misfortune"—as distinguished from destitution of which "intemperance," or "improvidence" had been a contributory cause.

But perhaps the most satisfactory way in which to judge of the administration of relief in the Whitechapel Union will be by a comparison of its pauperism, and expenditure upon relief, in 1870 and 1892. Thus we find that the mean numbers of *indoor paupers* (inclusive of vagrants) relieved in those respective years were as follows :

	1870.	1892.
England and Wales	156,558	186,607
Metropolis	36,441	58,145
Whitechapel	1,311	1,374

thus showing an increase in England and Wales of 19 2 per cent., the Metropolis of 59.5 per cent., and Whitechapel of 4.8 per cent.

Taking next the *outdoor paupers*, the mean number relieved in the above-mentioned years was :

	1870.	1892.
England and Wales	876,000	558,150
Metropolis	114,386	45,792
Whitechapel	3,554	312

thus showing a decrease in England and Wales of 36.2 per cent., the Metropolis of 60.0 per cent., and Whitechapel of 91.2 per cent.

The *expenditure upon outdoor relief* in 1870 and 1891 (being the latest return appended to the Report of the Local Government Board for 1891–92) was :

	1870.	1891.
England and Wales	£3,633,051	£2,400,089
Metropolis	412,817	184,118
Whitechapel	6,685	800

thus showing a decrease of expenditure in outdoor relief in England and Wales of 33.9 per cent., the Metropolis of 55 4 per cent., and Whitechapel of 88.0 per cent. ; or excluding the cost of "boarded-out children" (£543), the decrease of expenditure in outdoor relief in Whitechapel will be found to be no less than 96.1 per cent.

In the foregoing figures there is ample justification for saying that poor law reform is abroad in England; whilst in the earnest and increasingly organized efforts put forth on behalf of the poor, the sinning and the suffering, we see the stimulus which a strict administration of legal relief gives to a real live charity—the charity of personal service.

But after all, how much remains to be done! As yet, the fields of philanthropic service have only been entered. Looking at the giants of evil which have to be encountered, especially in our great cities, we see how weak and impotent is disjointed effort in the cause of the poor, and how increasingly necessary it is that earnest men and women should be found, not fighting alone with puny self-made weapons, but as members of a highly-trained and organized army, furnished with the very best arms which science and experience can devise. In this way alone can the great work of serving the poor be successfully accomplished; and may the two great English-speaking peoples be found in the forefront of the fight, waging war, not against pauperism alone, but also against the various social evils which beget pauperism, misery and despair.

From the standpoint, therefore, of an experience of nearly a quarter of a century in a strict administration of relief, I would in conclusion lay down the following propositions:

1. That the duty of the state in relation to the poor should, in the interest of the commonwealth, be restricted to the relief of actual destitution, and not be extended to the alleviation of the condition of poverty.

2. That legal relief, *i. e.* relief provided out of compulsory taxation, should be at once adequate and humane, and yet in a form which will not tempt the people to rely upon it, or to induce relaxation of effort in making a more eligible provision for themselves.

3. That the only form of relief which meets these conditions, is that of maintenance in some suitable institution.

4. That outdoor relief, or relief afforded in the applicant's home at the cost of the state, and in response to a legal claim, is and must be fruitful of evil results both to the individual and the community.

5. That a strict administration of state relief implies a necessity for organized voluntary effort, in saving the more deserving poor from a recourse to the poor law, and leaves a wide field of service for the individual discharge of man's duty to man.

6. That the work of visiting and befriending the deserving and

suffering poor, not already dealt with by the poor law, is a personal one, and cannot be discharged through the agency of any state machinery.

7. That all charitable relief is, in turn, but part of and subsidiary to organized earnest efforts to raise the standard of existence, and to develop the character and possibilities of the poorer classes.

THE WORK OF THE LONDON COUNTY COUNCIL IN RELATION TO PUBLIC HEALTH AND THE HOUSING OF THE WORKING CLASSES.

JOHN LOWLES, F. S. S., F. R. C. I., F. I. I.

In submitting to the notice of the Congress a few facts connected with the very important branch of the work of the authorities in London which forms the subject of my paper, I may perhaps be allowed to preface them by a word or two concerning London itself. Like Chicago, its growth has been and is extraordinary. Its population to-day borders close on six millions, whilst the yearly addition thereto approaches one hundred thousand.

Originally, London consisted of what is now known as the City proper, an area of 668 acres in extent ; but the present county of London, over which the London County Council exercises jurisdiction, consists of 75,462 acres, whilst if we measure London by the extent of the jurisdiction of the Metropolitan Police, it reaches an area of nearly 700 square miles. Perhaps the latter area affords the best standard for comparison with Chicago as its limits are defined to-day. The population of the larger area exceeds five and a half millions, whilst the smaller area contains four and a quarter millions of people.

Time will not permit me to trace out the growth of the government of London. Suffice it to say that the parish is the unit of local government; and the vestry, whose members are elected for three years (one-third retiring annually), is the local authority. In the case of smaller parishes, two or more are bracketed together for administrative purposes, under the title of district board. In 1855 a great step forward was made by the passing of an act called the "Metropolis Local Management Act," and a body called the "Metropolitan Board of Works" came into existence, consisting of one or two representatives from each of the vestries or district boards, according to population.

In 1888 a still more important step was taken by the creation of county councils directly elected by the people, London being created a separate county thereunder, and the Metropolitan Board of Works was abolished. The London County Council consists of 118 councillors (elected for three years by the various parliamentary divisions), and 19 aldermen (elected by the Council itself), half of whom serve for three and half for six years. Women ratepayers exercise the municipal franchise as they do the educational. There can be no doubt that the creation of this new governing body on a popular basis has greatly stimulated public interest in local government, and has immensely benefited the cause of sanitary reform and promoted the health, comfort and happiness of the people. The various drainage works, executed at the cost of many millions of pounds, and the ample provision for dealing with epidemics and infectious diseases, coupled with the unceasing vigilance of the authorities responsible for the department of public health, and the drastic powers conferred upon them by acts of Parliament, have combined to make London the healthiest metropolis in the world.

Some idea of the magnitude of the work of main drainage alone may be gathered from the fact that 38 325.000,000 gallons of sewage were treated in the twelve months ending March 31, 1892. Extensive pumping stations exist at Barking and Crossness, on the north and south sides of the Thames respectively; and the sewage, after being deodorized by manganate of soda and sulphuric acid, is disposed of by sludge vessels, which deposit the solids in deep parts of the English Channel, whilst the effluent flows out to the mouth of the river, care being taken to discharge it at favorable states of the tide.

Various schemes for utilizing the sewage for fertilizing purposes have from time to time been made, but the mere pressure of the daily task of removal has in itself prevented hitherto any extended experiments in this direction. A most effectual provision for securing local and general supervision in sanitary matters is found in the medical officers, whose fixed departmental appointment in every parish or district is insisted upon. These in turn periodically report to and are practically supervised by the health department of the London County Council, which is fortunate in having at its head a most capable and efficient expert in the person of Dr. Shirley Murphy, whose work is beyond praise.

The Council has recently been engaged in formulating a series of by-laws relating to matters of prime importance in connection with public health (a copy of which is appended hereto); and these by-laws, on being approved by the Government Department (the Local Government Board), will at once be operative and have all the force of the act of Parliament itself.

Further powers entrusted to the London County Council which are intimately bound up with the public health are those which enable them to inspect and license slaughter-houses and cow-houses, to regulate offensive trades, the inspection of dairies and milk-stores, the provision of public mortuaries, the appointment of coroners, the securing of a constant water-supply, the slaughtering and removal of animals afflicted with contagious disease, the prevention of rabies, etc., etc.

The care of the asylums for imbecile and insane (of whom there are some 11,000 under treatment) is in the hands of the County Council; but the provision of accommodation for persons suffering from infectious disease is entrusted to a separate body called the Metropolitan Asylums Board, whose work has materially lessened the mortality of late years and proved of inestimable benefit to the poor in preventing the spread of infection, by immediate isolation away from the houses of those afflicted.

This latter body will at no distant date probably be directly controlled by the Council, with whose officers, however, it works in perfect accord. It will be readily understood that the exigencies of the situations in which administrators have from time to time found themselves in dealing with the needs of such a vast population, with all the accumulated sanitary errors of omission and commission of preceding generations around them, have rather retarded than advanced the practical realization of a perfect ideal in administrative work, inasmuch as the necessity for close attention to the pressing everyday requirements of the present has left little time for perfecting, harmonizing and unifying the multitudinous agencies working at high pressure day by day. The work of reform in every department of the state must ever be progressive and never can be complete, and in no department is this truth more manifest than in that under notice.

It is a matter for rejoicing, however, that such enormous strides in the right direction in matters of public hygiene have been made in recent years. These strides were clearly and profitably demonstrated by the Congress held in London in the summer of 1891, in which so many distinguished American professors of medical and sanitary science took part.

In England the study of sanitary science as a special and distinct subject is now firmly established, and no candidate for appointments in the public service connected with health matters is considered eligible unless he possesses certificates of competency from some recognized institution issuing certificates after examination.

Passing on to the work of the London County Council in connection with the dwellings of the working classes, legislation has for many years been directed to removing the insanitary areas which were at once a disfigurement and a danger to many of our large cities, and especially of the metropolis.

Various Royal Commissions collected evidence of a most appalling kind respecting the condition of the homes of the poor. So huge an evil could not be remedied by a single act of Parliament; but all political parties being agreed that drastic measures were necessary, and public sentiment warmly supporting that view, powers have from time to time been conferred upon the local authorities, which have largely mitigated the evil, and marked the beginning of a new era in this important department of social life. Of course the effectiveness of the remedy very largely depended upon the zeal and energy of those entrusted with its application. Danger of laxity in this respect on the part of the parochial authorities has been reduced to a minimum by the mandatory powers conferred upon and extensively used by the County Council since 1890.

Under the Council's auspices a rapid transformation is taking place in the metropolis. Insanitary dwellings are being rigidly inspected and either completely overhauled at the owner's expense, or ruthlessly closed, while in cases where the closely packed buildings did not admit of adaptation to sanitary requirements, they have been cleared away at the public cost, and new and improved dwellings, with every requisite appliance and a minimum width of forty feet for each street, have risen up in their place. An important movement has been made towards inducing workingmen with families to settle in the suburbs, by providing cheap and speedy means of transit.

The Council, aided by several members of Parliament, have

obtained special concessions from the great railway companies, and on one line it is possible for a workman to live $11\frac{1}{2}$ miles out of London and to be carried to his work and back by train at a cost of twopence (4 cents) for the double journey. It will still be necessary, however, for large bodies to reside near their employment in the great centres of London, and for these the improved dwellings erected by the Council or on the Council's land, where most complete sanitary arrangements are rigidly enforced, will provide accommodation well within their means, at a rental of two shillings (50 cents) weekly for each room occupied.

A most important departure has been taken by the Council in the erection of a Municipal Lodging House in one of the poorest parts of London (Drury Lane), for the accommodation of poor casual lodgers at a cheap rate. The building is perhaps the most perfect of its kind in existence, and is worthy of imitation in other centres where a large transient poor population exists. Its erection cost some £16,000, and accommodation is provided for 320 inmates, at a charge of fivepence (10 cents) per night. This charge includes the use of spacious day-rooms, kitchens and lavatories, of appliances for cooking, and of most comfortable dormitories. Immediately it was opened it was filled with appreciative customers, and it is hoped that its phenomenal success will stimulate the Council to build similar lodging-houses in other parts of London, although it is probable that if they do so they will reduce the capacity of each house considerably, as it is felt to be safer from a sanitary point of view. There can be no doubt that, apart from their superiority in the physical comfort afforded to the inmates, these municipal lodging-houses are destined to play an important part in the lives of their inhabitants from an ethical point of view. They can easily be made healthy, well-conducted clubs for the poor; and their surroundings are such as to bring back or preserve that self-respect, the loss of which, from one cause or another, has in most cases been the chief factor in bringing the poor creatures to poverty and degradation.

From what I have myself personally seen in New York and Chicago I think great room exists in both cities for work in this direction, as also in the whole department covered by my paper, and I am quite sure that I may, while tendering my thanks to this Congress for according me the privilege of contributing a paper (imperfect though it be) on this subject, be allowed to say how delighted I shall be to supply detailed information at any time to any one who

.may be interested on this side, and thus reciprocate in some measure
the uniform courtesy and consideration I have experienced on all
hands whenever I have visited the United States.

LONDON COUNTY COUNCIL.

BY-LAWS MADE BY THE LONDON COUNTY COUNCIL UNDER THE PUBLIC HEALTH (LONDON) ACT, 1891.

BY-LAWS UNDER SEC. 16 (2).

*For prescribing the times for the removal or carriage by road or water of any
fœcal, or offensive or obnoxious matter or liquid in or through London, and
providing that the carriage or vessel used therefor shall be properly constructed
and covered so as to prevent the escape of any such matter or liquid, and as to
prevent any nuisance arising therefrom.*

1. Every person who shall remove or carry by road or water in or through
London any fœcal or offensive or obnoxious matter or liquid, whether such
matter or liquid shall be in course of removal or carriage from within or without or through London, shall not remove or carry such matter or liquid in or
through London except between the hours of 4 o'clock and 10 o'clock in the
forenoon during the months of March, April, May, June, July, August, September and October, and except between the hours of 6 o'clock in the forenoon
and 12 o'clock at noon during the months of November, December, January
and February. Such person shall use a suitable carriage or vessel properly
constructed and furnished with a sufficient covering so as to prevent the
escape of any such matter or liquid therefrom, and so as to prevent any
nuisance arising therefrom.

Provided that this by-law shall not apply to the carriage of horse dung
manure.

As to the closing and filling up of cesspools and privies.

2. Any person who shall by any works or by any structural alteration of any
premises render the further use of a cesspool or privy unnecessary, and the
owner of any premises on which shall be situated a disused cesspool or privy,
or a cesspool or privy which has become unnecessary, shall completely empty
such cesspool or privy of all fœcal or offensive matter which it may contain,
and shall completely remove so much of the floor, walls and roof of such privy
or cesspool as can safely be removed, and all pipes and drains leading thereto
or therefrom, or connected therewith, and any earth or other material contam-
inated by such fœcal or offensive matter. He shall completely close and fill
up the cesspool with concrete or with suitable dry clean earth, dry clean brick
rubbish, or other dry clean material, and where the walls of such cesspool shall
not have been completely removed, he shall cover the surface of the space so
filled up with earth, rubbish or material, with a layer of concrete six inches
thick.

3. Every person who shall propose to close or fill up any cesspool or privy shall, before commencing any works for such purpose, give to the Sanitary Authority for the district not less than forty-eight hours notice in writing, exclusive of Sunday, Good Friday, Christmas day, or any bank holiday, specifying the hour at which he will commence the closing and filling up of such cesspool or privy, and during the progress of any such work shall afford any officer of the Sanitary Authority free access to the premises for the purpose of inspecting the same.

As to the removal and disposal of refuse, and as to the duties of the occupier of any premises in connection with house refuse so as to facilitate the removal of it by the scavengers of the Sanitary Authority.

4. The occupier of any premises who shall remove or cause to be removed any refuse produced upon his premises shall not, in the process of removal, deposit such refuse, or cause or allow such refuse to be deposited upon any footway, pavement or carriageway.

Provided that this by-law shall not be deemed to prohibit the occupier of any premises from depositing upon the kerbstone or upon the outer edge of the footpath immediately in front of his house, between such hours of the day as the Sanitary Authority shall fix and notify by public announcement in their district, a proper receptacle containing house refuse, other than night soil or filth, to be removed by the Sanitary Authority in accordance with any by-law in that behalf.

5. Every person who shall convey any house, trade or street refuse across or along any footway, pavement or carriageway shall use a suitable receptacle, cart, carriage or other means of conveyance properly constructed so as to prevent the escape of the contents thereof, and, in the case of offensive refuse, so covered as to prevent any nuisance therefrom, and shall adopt such other precautions as may be necessary to prevent any such refuse from being slopped or spilled, or from falling in the process of removal upon such footway, pavement or carriageway.

If in the process of such removal any such refuse be slopped or spilled, or fall upon such footway, pavement or carriageway, such person shall forthwith remove such refuse from the place whereon the same may have been slopped or spilled, or may have fallen, and shall immediately thereafter thoroughly sweep or otherwise thoroughly cleanse such place.

6. Where a Sanitary Authority shall arrange for the daily removal of house refuse in their district or in any part thereof, the occupier of any premises in such district or part thereof on which any house refuse may from time to time accumulate shall, at such hour of the day as the Sanitary Authority shall fix and notify by public announcement in their district, deposit on the kerbstone or on the outer edge of the footpath immediately in front of the house or in a conveniently accessible position on the premises, as the Sanitary Authority may prescribe by written notice served upon the occupier, a movable receptacle, in which shall be placed, for the purposes of removal by or on behalf of the Sanitary Authority, the house refuse which has accumulated on such premises since the preceding collection by such authority.

The Sanitary Authority shall collect such refuse, or cause the same to be collected, between such hours of the day as they have fixed and notified by public announcement in their district.

7. The Sanitary Authority shall cause to be removed not less frequently than once in every week the house refuse produced on all premises within their district.

8. Where, for the purposes of subsequent removal, any cargo, load, or collection of offensive refuse has been temporarily brought to or deposited in any place within a sanitary district, the owner (whether a Sanitary Authority or any other person) or consignee of such cargo, load or collection of refuse, or any person who may have undertaken to deliver the same, or who is in charge of the same, shall not without a reasonable excuse permit or allow or cause such refuse to remain in such place for a longer period than twenty-four hours.

Provided (*a*) that this by-law shall not apply in cases where the place of temporary deposit is distant at least one hundred yards from any street, and is distant at least three hundred yards from any building or premises used wholly or partly for human habitation, or as a school, or as a place of public worship or of public resort or public assembly, or from any building or premises in or on which any person may be employed in any manufacture, trade or business, or from any public park or other open space dedicated or used for the purposes of recreation, or from any reservoir or stream used for the purposes of domestic water supply; (*b*) that this by-law shall not prohibit the deposit, within the prescribed distances, of road slop unmixed with stable manure for any period not exceeding one week, which may be necessary for the separation of water therefrom.

9. Where a Sanitary Authority or some person on their behalf shall remove any offensive refuse from any street or premises within their district, such Sanitary Authority or such person shall properly destroy by fire or otherwise dispose of such refuse in such manner as to prevent nuisance.

Provided always that this by-law shall not be deemed to require or permit any Sanitary Authority or person to dispose of or destroy by fire any night-soil, swine's dung or cow-dung.

10. A Sanitary Authority or any person on their behalf who shall remove any offensive refuse from any street or premises within their district shall not deposit such refuse, otherwise than in the course of removal, at a less distance than three hundred yards from any two or more buildings used wholly or partly for human habitation, or from any building used as a school, or as a place of public resort or public assembly, or in which any person may be employed in any manufacture, trade or business, or from any public park or other open space dedicated or used for the purpose of recreation, or from any reservoir or stream used for the purpose of domestic water supply.

Provided always that this by-law shall not be deemed to prohibit such deposit of such refuse for a period of twenty-four hours, when such refuse is deposited for the purpose of being destroyed by fire, in accordance with any by-law in that behalf.

11. For the purposes of the foregoing by-laws the expression "offensive refuse" means any refuse, whether "house refuse," "trade refuse," or "street refuse" in such a condition as to be or to be liable to become offensive.

Penalties.

12. Every person who shall offend against any of the foregoing by-laws shall be liable for every such offense to a penalty of five pounds, and in the case of a continuing offense to a further penalty of forty shillings for each day after written notice of the offense from the Sanitary Authority. Provided nevertheless that the court before whom any complaint may be made, or any proceedings may be taken in respect of any such offense, may, if the court think fit, adjudge the payment as a penalty of any sum less than the full amount of the penalty imposed by this by-law.

By-Laws under Section 39 (1).

With respect to waterclosets, earthclosets, privies, ashpits, cesspools, and receptacles for dung, and the proper accessories thereof in connection with buildings, whether constructed before or after the passing of this Act.

1. Every person who shall hereafter construct a watercloset or earthcloset in connection with a building, shall construct such watercloset or earthcloset in such a position that, in the case of a watercloset, one of its sides at the least shall be an external wall, and in the case of an earthcloset two of its sides at the least shall be external walls, which external wall or walls shall abut immediately upon the street, or upon a yard or garden or open space of not less than one hundred square feet of superficial area, measured horizontally at a point below the level of the floor of such closet. He shall not construct any such watercloset so that it is approached directly from any room used for the purpose of human habitation, or used for the manufacture, preparation, or storage of food for man, or used as a factory, workshop, or workplace, nor shall he construct any earthcloset so that it can be entered otherwise than from the external air.

He shall construct such watercloset so that on any side on which it would abut on a room intended for human habitation, or used as a factory, workshop, or workplace, it shall be enclosed by a solid wall or partition of brick or other materials, extending the entire height from the floor to the ceiling.

He shall provide any such watercloset that is approached from the external air with a floor of hard smooth impervious material, having a fall to the door of such watercloset of half an inch to the foot.

He shall provide such watercloset with proper doors and fastenings.

Provided always that this by-law shall not apply to any watercloset constructed below the surface of the ground and approached directly from an area or other open space available for purposes of ventilation, measuring at least forty superficial feet in extent, and having a distance across of not less than five feet, and not covered in otherwise than by a grating or railing.

2. Every person who shall construct a watercloset in connection with a building, whether the situation of such watercloset be or be not within or partly within

such building, and every person who shall construct an earthcloset in connection with a building, shall construct in one of the walls of such watercloset or earthcloset which shall abut upon the public way, yard, garden, or open space, as provided by the preceding by-law, a window of such dimensions that an area of not less than two square feet, which may be the whole or part of such window, shall open directly into the external air.

He shall in addition to such window, cause such watercloset or earthcloset to be provided with adequate means of constant ventilation by at least one air-brick built in an external wall of such watercloset or earthcloset, or by an air-shaft, or by some other effectual method or appliance.

3. Every person who shall construct a watercloset in connection with a building, shall furnish such watercloset with a cistern of adequate capacity for the purpose of flushing, which shall be separate and distinct from any cistern used for drinking purposes, and shall be so constructed, fitted, and placed as to admit of the supply of water for use in such watercloset so that there shall not be any direct connection between any service pipe upon the premises and any part of the apparatus of such watercloset other than such flushing cistern.

Provided always that the foregoing requirement shall be deemed to be complied with in any case where the apparatus of a watercloset is connected for the purpose of flushing with a cistern of adequate capacity which is used solely for flushing waterclosets or urinals.

He shall cause every flushing cistern that may be of such a kind as to be emptied at one pull of the flushing apparatus to be so constructed that the inlet for water shall be capable of charging the cistern in not less than one minute.

He shall construct or fix the pipe and union connecting such flushing cistern with the pan, basin, or other receptacle with which such watercloset may be provided, so that such pipe and union shall not in any part have an internal diameter of less than one inch and a quarter.

He shall furnish such watercloset with a suitable apparatus for the effectual application of water to any pan, basin, or other receptacle with which such apparatus may be connected and used, and for the effectual flushing and cleansing of such pan, basin, or other receptacle, and for the prompt and effectual removal therefrom and from the trap connected therewith of any solid or liquid filth which may from time to time be deposited therein.

He shall furnish such watercloset with a pan, basin, or other suitable receptacle of non-absorbent material, and of such shape, of such capacity, and of such mode of construction as to receive and contain a sufficient quantity of water, and to allow all filth which may from time to time be deposited in such pan, basin, or receptacle, to fall free of the sides thereof and directly into the water received and contained in such pan, basin, or receptacle.

He shall not construct or fix under such pan, basin, or receptacle, any "container" or other similar fitting.

He shall construct or fix immediately beneath or in connection with such pan, basin, or other suitable receptacle, an efficient siphon trap, so constructed that it shall at all times maintain a sufficient water seal between such pan, basin, or other suitable receptacle and any drain or soil pipe in connection therewith. He shall not construct or fix in or in connection with the watercloset apparatus any D trap or other similar trap.

If he shall construct any watercloset or shall fix or fit any trap to any existing watercloset or in connection with a soil pipe, which is itself in connection with any other watercloset, he shall cause the trap of every such watercloset to be ventilated into the open air at a point as high as the top of the soil pipe, or into the soil pipe at a point above the highest watercloset connected with such soil pipe, and so that such ventilating pipe shall have in all parts an internal diameter of not less than two inches, and shall be connected with the arm of the soil pipe at a point not less than three and not more than twelve inches from the highest part of the trap and on that side of the water seal which is nearest to the soil pipe.

4. Any person who shall provide a soil pipe in connection with a building to be hereafter erected, shall cause such soil pipe to be situated outside such building, and any person who shall provide or construct or refit a soil pipe in connection with an existing building, shall, whenever practicable, cause such soil pipe to be situated outside such building, and in all cases where such soil pipe shall be situated within any building, shall construct such soil pipe in drawn lead, or of heavy cast iron jointed with molten lead and properly caulked.

He shall construct such soil pipe so that its weight in proportion to its length and internal diameter, shall be as follows—

Diameter.	LEAD. Weight per 10 feet length. Not less than	IRON. Weight per 6 feet length. Not less than
3½ inches	65 lbs.	48 lbs.
4 "	74 "	54 "
5 "	92 "	69 "
6 "	110 "	84 "

Every person who shall provide a soil pipe outside or inside a building shall cause such soil pipe to have an internal diameter of not less than three and a half inches, and to be continued upwards without diminution of its diameter, and (except where unavoidable) without any bend or angle being formed in such soil pipe, to such a height and in such a position as to afford by means of the open end of such soil pipe a safe outlet for foul air, and so that such open end shall in all cases be above the highest part of the roof of the building to which the soil pipe is attached, and where practicable, be not less than three feet above any window within twenty feet measured in a straight line from the open end of such soil pipe.

He shall furnish the open end of such soil pipe with a wire guard covering, the opening in the meshes of which shall be equal to not less than the area of the open end of the soil pipe.

In all such cases where he shall connect a lead trap or pipe with an iron soil pipe or drain, he shall insert between such trap or pipe and such soil pipe or drain a brass thimble, and he shall connect such lead trap or pipe with such thimble by means of a wiped or overcast lead joint, and he shall connect such thimble with the iron soil pipe or drain by means of a joint made with molten lead, properly caulked.

In all such cases where he shall connect a stoneware trap or pipe with a lead soil pipe, he shall insert between such stoneware trap or pipe, and such soil pipe or drain, a brass socket or other similar appliance, and he shall connect such stoneware trap or pipe by inserting it into such socket, making the joint with Portland cement, and he shall connect such socket with the lead soil pipe, by means of a wiped or overcast lead joint.

In all cases where he shall connect a stoneware trap or pipe with an iron soil pipe or drain, he shall insert such stoneware trap or pipe into a socket on such iron soil pipe or drain, making the joint with Portland cement.

He shall so construct such soil pipe that it shall not be directly connected with the waste of any bath, rainwater pipe, or of any sink other than that which is provided for the reception of urine or other excremental filth, and he shall construct such soil pipe so that there shall not be any trap in such soil pipe or between the soil pipe and any drain with which it is connected.

5. A person who shall newly fit or fix any apparatus in connection with any existing watercloset, shall, as regards such apparatus and its connection with existing soil pipe or drain, comply with such of the requirements of the foregoing by-laws as would be applicable to the apparatus so fitted or fixed if the watercloset were being newly constructed.

6. Every person who shall construct an earthcloset in connection with a building shall furnish such earthcloset with a reservoir or receptacle, of suitable construction and of adequate capacity, for dry earth, and he shall construct and fix such reservoir or receptacle in such a manner and in such a position as to admit of ready access to such reservoir or receptacle for the purpose of depositing therein the necessary supply of dry earth.

He shall construct or fix in connection with such reservoir or receptacle suitable means or apparatus for the frequent and effectual application of a sufficient quantity of dry earth to any filth which may from time to time be deposited in any receptacle for filth constructed, fitted, or used, in or in connection with such earthcloset.

He shall construct such earthcloset so that the contents of such reservoir or receptacle may not at any time be exposed to any rainfall or to the drainage of any waste water or liquid refuse from any premises.

7. Every person who shall construct an earthcloset in connection with a building shall construct such earthcloset for use in combination with a movable receptacle for filth.

He shall construct such earthcloset so as to admit of a movable receptacle for filth, of a capacity not exceeding two cubic feet, being placed and fitted beneath the seat in such a manner and in such a position as may effectually prevent the deposit upon the floor or sides of the space beneath such seat, or elsewhere than in such receptacle, of any filth which may from time to time fall or be cast through the aperture in such seat.

He shall construct such receptable for filth in such a manner and in such a position as to admit of the frequent and effectual application of a sufficient quantity of dry earth to any filth which may be from time to time deposited in such receptacle for filth, and in such a manner and in such a position as to admit of ready access for the purpose of removing the contents thereof.

He shall also construct such earthcloset so that the contents of such receptacle for filth may not at any time be exposed to any rainfall or to the drainage of any waste water or liquid refuse from any premises.

8. Every person who shall construct a privy in connection with a building shall construct such privy at a distance of twenty feet at the least from a dwelling-house, or public building, or any building in which any person may be or may be intended to be employed in any manufacture, trade, or business.

9. A person who shall construct a privy in connection with a building shall not construct such privy within the distance of one hundred feet from any well, spring, or stream of water used, or likely to be used, by man for drinking or domestic purposes, or for manufacturing drinks for the use of man, or otherwise in such a position as to render any such water liable to pollution.

10. Every person who shall construct a privy in connection with a building shall construct such privy in such a manner and in such a position as to afford ready means of access to such privy, for the purpose of cleansing such privy and of removing filth therefrom, and in such a manner and in such a position as to admit of all filth being removed from such privy, and from the premises to which such privy may belong, without being carried through any dwelling-house, or public building, or any building in which any person may be or may be intended to be employed in any manufacture, trade or business.

11. Every person who shall construct a privy in connection with a building, shall provide such privy with a sufficient opening for ventilation as near to the top as practicable and communicating directly with the external air.

He shall cause the floor of such privy to be flagged or paved with hard tiles or other non-absorbent material, and he shall construct such floor so that it shall be in every part thereof at a height of not less than six inches above the level of the surface of the ground adjoining such privy, and so that such floor shall have a fall or inclination towards the door of such privy of half an inch to the foot.

12. Every person who shall construct a privy in connection with a building shall construct such privy for use in combination with a movable receptacle for filth, and shall construct over the whole area of the space immediately beneath the seat of such privy a floor of flagging or asphalt or some suitable composite material, at a height of not less than three inches above the level of the surface of the ground adjoining such privy; and he shall cause the whole extent of each side of such space between the floor and the seat, other than any part that may be occupied by any door or other opening therein, to be constructed of flagging, slate, or good brickwork, at least nine inches thick, and rendered in good cement or asphalted.

He shall construct the seat of such privy, the aperture in such seat, and the space beneath such seat, of such dimensions as to admit of a movable receptacle for filth of a capacity not exceeding two cubic feet being placed and fitted beneath such seat in such a manner and in such a position as may effectually prevent the deposit, upon the floor or sides of the space beneath such seat or elsewhere than in such receptacle, of any filth which may from time to time fall or be cast through the aperture in such seat.

He shall construct such privy so that for the purpose of cleansing the space beneath the seat, or of removing therefrom or placing or fitting therein an appropriate receptacle for filth, there shall be a door or other opening in the back or one of the sides thereof capable of being opened from the outside of the privy, or in any case where such a mode of construction may be impracticable, so that for the purposes aforesaid the whole of the seat of the privy or a sufficient part thereof may be readily moved or adjusted.

13. A person who shall construct a privy in connection with a building shall not cause or suffer any part of the space under the seat of such privy, or any part of any receptacle for filth in or in connection with such privy, to communicate with any drain.

14. Every person who shall intend to construct any watercloset, earthcloset, or privy, or to fit or fix in any watercloset, earthcloset, or privy any apparatus or any trap or soil pipe connected therewith, shall, before executing any such works, give notice in writing to the clerk of the Sanitary Authority.

15. Every owner of an earthcloset or privy existing at the date of the confirmation of these by-laws shall, before the expiration of six months from and after such date of confirmation, cause the same to be reconstructed in such manner that its position, structure and apparatus shall comply with such of the requirements of the foregoing by-laws as are applicable to earthclosets or privies newly constructed.

16. When any person shall provide an ashpit in connection with a building, he shall cause the same to consist of one or more movable receptacles sufficient to contain the house refuse which may accumulate during any period not exceeding one week. Each of such receptacles shall be constructed of metal and shall be provided with one or more suitable handles and cover. The capacity of each of such receptacles shall not exceed two cubic feet.

Provided that the requirement as to the size of each of such receptacles shall not apply to any person who shall construct such receptacle or receptacles in connection with any premises to which there is attached as part of the conditions of tenancy the right to dispose of house refuse in an ashpit used in common by the occupiers of several tenancies, but in no case shall such ashpit be of greater capacity than is required to enable it to contain the refuse which may accumulate during any period not exceeding one week.

17. The occupier of any premises who shall use any ashpit shall, if such ashpit consist of a movable receptacle, cause such receptacle to be kept in a covered place, or to be properly covered, so that it shall not be exposed to rainfall, and if such ashpit consist of a fixed receptacle, he shall cause the same to be kept properly covered.

18. Where the Sanitary Authority have arranged for the daily removal of house refuse in their district, or in any part thereof, the owner of any premises in such district or part thereof shall provide an ashpit which shall consist of one or more movable receptacles, sufficient to contain the house refuse which

may accumulate during any period not exceeding three days, which the Sanitary Authority may determine, and of which the Sanitary Authority shall give notice by public announcement in their district. Each of such receptacles shall be constructed of metal, and provided with one or more suitable handles and cover. The capacity of each of such receptacles shall not exceed two cubic feet.

Provided always that this by-law shall not apply to the owner of any premises until the expiration of three months after the Sanitary Authority have publicly notified their intention to adopt a system of daily collection of house refuse in that part of their district which comprises such premises.

19. Where any receptacle shall have been provided as an ashpit for any premises in pursuance of any by-law in that behalf, no person shall deposit the house refuse which may accumulate on such premises in any ashpit that does not comply with the requirements of these by-laws.

20. Every person who shall construct a cesspool in connection with a building, shall construct such cesspool at a distance of one hundred feet at the least from a dwelling-house, or public building, or any building in which any person may be, or may be intended to be, employed in any manufacture, trade, or business.

21. A person who shall construct a cesspool in connection with a building, shall not construct such cesspool within the distance of one hundred feet from any well, spring, or stream of water.

22. Every person who shall construct a cesspool in connection with a building, shall construct such cesspool in such a manner and in such a position as to afford ready means of access to such cesspool, for the purpose of cleansing such cesspool, and of removing the contents thereof, and in such a manner and in such a position as to admit of the contents of such cesspool being removed therefrom, and from the premises to which such cesspool may belong, without being carried through any dwelling-house, or public building, or any building in which any person may be, or may be intended to be, employed in any manufacture, trade, or business.

He shall not in any case construct such cesspool so that it shall have, by drain or otherwise, any means of communication with any sewer or any overflow outlet.

23. Every person who shall construct a cesspool in connection with a building, shall construct such cesspool of good brickwork bedded and grouted in cement, properly rendered inside with cement, and with a backing of at least nine inches of well-puddled clay around and beneath such brickwork, and so that such cesspool shall be perfectly watertight.

He shall also cause such cesspool to be arched or otherwise properly covered over, and to be provided with adequate means of ventilation.

24. A person shall not use as a receptacle for dung any receptacle so constructed or placed that one of its sides shall be formed by the wall of any room used for human habitation, or under a dwelling-house, factory, workshop, or workplace, and he shall not use any receptacle in such a situation that it would be likely to cause a nuisance or become injurious or dangerous to health.

25. Every owner of any existing receptacle for dung shall, before the expiration of six months from the date of the confirmation of these by-laws, and every person who shall construct a receptacle for dung, shall cause such receptacle to be so constructed that its capacity shall not be greater than two cubic yards, and so that the bottom or floor thereof shall not, in any case, be lower than the surface of the ground adjoining such receptacle.

He shall so construct such receptacle that a sufficient part of one of its sides shall be readily removable for the purpose of facilitating cleansing.

He shall also cause such receptacle to be constructed in such a manner and of such materials, and to be maintained at all times in such a condition as to prevent any escape of the contents thereof, or any soakage therefrom into the ground or into the wall of any building.

He shall cause such receptacle to be so constructed that no rain or water can enter therein, and so that it shall be freely ventilated into the external air.

Provided that a person who shall construct a receptacle for dung, the whole of the contents of which are removed not less frequently than every forty-eight hours, shall not be required to construct such receptacle so that its capacity shall not be greater than two cubic yards.

And provided that a person who shall construct a receptacle for dung, which shall contain only dung of horses, asses or mules with stable litter, and the whole of the contents of which are removed not less frequently than every forty-eight hours, may, instead of all other requirements of this by-law, construct a metal cage, and shall beneath such metal cage adequately pave the ground at a level not lower than the surrounding ground, and in such a manner and to such an extent as will prevent any soakage into the ground; and if such cage be placed near to or against any building he shall adequately cement the wall of such building in such a manner and to such an extent as will prevent any soakage from the dung within or upon such receptacle into the wall of such building.

26. The occupier of any premises shall cause every watercloset belonging to such premises to be thoroughly cleansed from time to time as often as may be necessary for the purpose of keeping such watercloset in a cleanly condition.

The occupier of any premises shall once at least in every week cause every earthcloset, privy, and receptacle for dung belonging to such premises to be emptied and thoroughly cleansed.

The occupier of any premises shall once at least in every three months cause every cesspool belonging to such premises to be emptied and thoroughly cleansed.

Provided that where two or more lodgers in a lodging-house are entitled to the use in common of any watercloset, earthcloset, privy, cesspool, or receptacle for dung, the landlord shall cause such watercloset, earthcloset, privy, cesspool, or receptacle for dung to be cleansed and emptied as aforesaid.

The landlord, or owner of any lodging-house, shall provide and maintain in connection with such house, watercloset, earthcloset or privy accommodation in the proportion of not less than one watercloset, earthcloset, or privy, for every twelve persons.

For the purposes of this by-law, " a lodging-house " means a house or part of a house which is let in lodgings or occupied by members of more than one family. " Landlord " in relation to a house or part of a house which is let in lodgings, or occupied by members of more than one family, means the person (whatever may be the nature or extent of his interest) by whom or on whose behalf such house or part of a house is let in lodgings or for occupation by members of more than one family, or who for the time being receives or is entitled to receive the profits arising from such letting. " Lodger " in relation to a house or part of a house which is let in lodgings or occupied by members of more than one family, means a person to whom any room or rooms in such house or part of a house may have been let as a lodging or for his use or occupation.

Nothing in this by-law shall extend to any common lodging-house.

27 The owner of any premises shall maintain in proper condition of repair every watercloset, earthcloset, privy, ashpit, cesspool, and receptacle for dung, and the proper accessories thereof belonging to such premises.

Penalties.

28. Every person who shall offend against any of the foregoing by-laws shall be liable for every such offense to a penalty of Five pounds, and in the case of a continuing offense to a further penalty of Forty shillings for each day after written notice of the offense from the Sanitary Authority. Provided nevertheless that the court before whom any complaint may be made or any proceedings may be taken in respect of any such offense may, if the court think fit, adjudge the payment as a penalty of any sum less than the full amount of the penalty imposed by this by-law.

PRIVATE UNOFFICIAL VISITATION OF PUBLIC INSTITUTIONS.

LOUISA TWINING.

I have been asked to say something on this subject from an English point of view, and I have much pleasure in doing so, as I have long been interested in it, advocating its adoption and extension in this country.

It is many years since I read of the plans of the State Charities Aid Association, and they at once commended themselves to me. I wrote a paper about them in the London *Charity Organization Review*, and would gladly have seen them more widely adopted here. But I had endeavored to make a move in this direction long before; for as far back as the year 1853 I had begun to visit our workhouses, or as they would rather be called in America, "poorhouses," under our poor law, supported by rates collected from all classes. The evils of close management, carried out only by paid officials, at once struck me as being inevitable under such a system, in which, at that time, all control and inspection by women was unknown; the paid officers being almost universally of a low, or, at least, middle-class grade. The rate-payers had neither knowledge nor control of anything beyond the election of their so-called representatives, in which, however, little or no interest was taken, and the proceedings that went on inside the "house" were carefully concealed, visitors of any kind, except the friends of the inmates, being unknown. So strong was my conviction of the dangers and absolute evils of such a state of things, that even after my first visit I endeavored to gain admission for other visitors besides myself. This was of course objected to by those whose interest it was to keep out all inquiry and inspection except, what was demanded by law, the occasional visits of gentlemen from the Central Poor Law Board. It has always been a matter of surprise and astonishment to me that these educated and intelligent gentlemen should have had their eyes closed for so long a time to the evils of the system; it has only convinced me of the truth, which has been growing ever since, that men are not intended to control or examine domestic matters and management, and that, as the late Mrs. Jameson acutely remarked in her lectures delivered in 1855, the "female element" being entirely wanting (at least of an educated or refined description), and no "communion of labors" between men and women being even dimly recognized, it is not difficult to account for any shortcomings that may have arisen in the system.

It is not necessary for me to relate the many obstacles that were to be encountered before my object was attained; having made my first efforts to get the daylight of public opinion admitted into abodes that were as inaccessible to outside influence as the strictest of prisons, obstacles had been so far overcome by the year 1858 that a society was started for "workhouse visiting," supported by some of the best men and women of the time, who formed our active committee, while a much larger body gave it their sanction and support. A journal was shortly started, which quarterly or oftener gave interesting information to the outside world concerning every department of pauper life, the schools, infirmaries, the aged and the able-bodied.

This was carried on for some years, till its object seemed to be attained, and the visitors had been admitted into many poor law institutions. The revelations they brought to light, especially as to the condition of the sick, led to many more investigations; and the attention of medical men being aroused, a commission was set on foot by the *Lancet* for an examination of some of the institutions where gross neglect and abuses had been known to take place. In this brief sketch it is sufficient to say that all these private efforts, beginning with those made by visitors who naturally spoke of what they saw, led to the important legislation which was passed in 1867 for the separation of the sick from all other classes of inmates, especially in the metropolitan district, in which there are twenty-four different centres or unions, each with a new infirmary, the largest of which contains over 700 patients.

My object is not to describe workhouse infirmaries, but only the progress of voluntary effort, which has effected so many reforms in all departments of social work. The schools for pauper children are now open to different bodies of voluntary workers, such as the Metropolitan Association for Befriending Young Servants, and the workhouse branch of the Girls' Friendly Society. The infirmaries have been largely improved and influenced by the Association for Promoting Trained Nursing in them, and the committee are now applied to from all parts of England for nurses whom they have either trained or can recommend.

Homes of various kinds are begun by private persons for various classes of inmates, especially for the industrial training of children, and certified by the Central Board, so that payments can be made by guardians for their maintenance. Through an act of Parliament passed in 1863, supplemented by private charity,* "feeble-minded" children are now being thus treated, with every hope of success; and this is chiefly owing to the representations of those who have studied their condition in the schools. Committees of ladies, called "Workhouse Girls' Aid Committees," are authorized to work amongst the fallen girls, and endeavor to help those who are capable of being

---

* The now well known plans of the Association for Boarding-out Orphan and Deserted Children in Families should also be named, as having been begun in 1870, by some ladies in Westmoreland, and sanctioned by the last Government Board, and which now numbers thousands of children under the care of such committees, who are thus removed from the atmosphere and surroundings of pauperism.

raised from their degradation. The beneficent aims of the " Brabazon Scheme" are too well known in America for me to describe them; but the boon that they bestow on the apparently helpless and hopeless objects in the sick and infirm wards can be appreciated only by those who have witnessed them. Temperance work is carried on by outside bodies in many poor law institutions for young and old. Then, as the last proof of the progress of this movement of voluntary action co-operating with official work, I name with great satisfaction the order that was issued in January of this year by the Local Government Board, authorizing the appointment of "ladies' committees, who need not be guardians, with authority, subject to rules framed by the guardians, to visit the parts of the workhouse in which female paupers or pauper children are accommodated, with the view of their reporting to the guardians any matter which appears to them to need attention."

This is in fact carrying out the suggestions of the Workhouse Visiting Society thirty-five years ago, with the additional powers of authority to report upon what they see and inspect.

I can hardly leave this subject without reminding my readers of the most remarkable instance of voluntary work resulting in beneficent reforms by the self-imposed labors of Elizabeth Fry and Howard in the last century, and later, by Sarah Martin, when the condition of prisons and prisoners was too terrible to be described. All improvements that have since taken place may date from those efforts of self-denying humanity.

Visitors are now permitted and appointed for all prisons.

Outside inspection has not yet been provided for hospitals, but it is earnestly desired that ladies should at least be allowed to act on the various committees of management. Visitors to the sick are allowed to cheer them by reading or conversation, but for no other purpose.

IMMIGRATION OF ALIENS.

ARNOLD WHITE, LONDON.

I owe an apology to every American citizen who may do me the honor to read this paper. That an apology is due will appear from the two postulates underlying the whole argument that follows, i. e.

that men are born neither (1) free nor (2) equal. There is of course a diplomatic and even a theological sense in which men are both equal and free; but if casuistry be laid aside, and the vernacular of plain business alone employed, the equality and freedom of mankind are restricted to iron-clad limits of narrow compass. The yellow man propelled from the valley of the Yangtse-Kiang by the expulsive force of over-population and of want; or the poor Jew of Moscow or of Kiev who is "moved on" by the piety and police of Pobiedonostzev or the anger of Alexander, is in each case free to lie down and die, and they are equal in "natural rights," whatever they may happen to be. The fact is that, as regard individuals as well as regards nations, in respect to freedom and equality there has been a vast quantity of gaseous cant floating about this planet ever since the bovine stipulations of George the Third and his advisers broke up the effective and permanent union of the Anglo-Saxon race; and more especially since the peasants of France, not without bloodshed, successfully asserted their right not to sit up o' nights flogging the ponds, so that the *seigneurie* at the château might slumber in peace undisturbed by the croaking of frogs.

Both the States and Great Britain are just at present puzzled by the immigration riddle. They are affected by much the same causes, if in a different form. Russian persecutions have directed, both to American and British shores, an army of excellent people, whose chief qualification for citizenship is want, and whose hereditary ignorance of, and muscular incapacity for, the more elementary conditions of success in a new country are better calculated to stir the benevolence of philanthropists than the admiration of statesmen. Nor is the reason far to seek. The duty of statesmen is not fulfilled when they have given attention to the current problems of political necessity. They are, in addition, trustees for posterity. From this task they may shrink; they may evade it; but the duty remains. To regard the welfare and destiny of unborn millions may raise no applause, make no reputations, and excite no emotions of gratitude; but the interests of that silent multitude that mutely waits round the corner of the century to receive what we relinquish are interests that cannot be ignored by an honest statesman, and will be safeguarded by a great one.

Much dispute is raised in these days of Irish controversy as to what it is that constitutes a nationality. Without attempting a complete answer, it may be admitted that oneness of race is at all events an elementary condition in a full-grown nation. Nothing strikes a stranger more in the United States than the fact that the German of Cincinnati, the Swede of Milwaukee or the Irishman of New York is in each case more intensely Teutonic, Scandinavian and Hibernian than in their respective fatherlands. In point of fact, race is in process of making in North America ; you have not yet struck a type. It is true that to most European minds the typical American is successfully produced by the Atlantic States. California, Virginia and Ohio demur to this assumption. In point of fact, the American type is forming ; it is not yet formed, and may well take a few centuries to evoke a type that will be recognized throughout the whole of the States themselves as racially and distinctively American.

If my proposition be true, that the American nation, however completely equipped for all practical purposes in its struggle for existence in the world of to-day, is not yet racially blended, perfected, complete, or developed, then the duty of your rulers to exclude all that may tend to deteriorate your type becomes a duty of the most impressive nature—that is, if men are not born equal, a proposition with which I set out. The difference between a philanthropist and a statesman is the difference between one who looks to all the results following the movement of a given piece of machinery, and one who looks only to the specific phenomenon which has touched the striated muscle he is pleased to call his heart. The philanthropist is known to exhibit imperial indifference towards the direst sufferings when they are the result of the noble emotions. It is enough for him that the evil he has set himself to redress really is destroyed. The generation of a cloud of other and greater evils is a matter of indifference. The bear who watched his sleeping man-friend being disturbed with buzzing flies, and thereupon sympathetically destroyed the flies and killed the man with one and the same blow, it always struck me, must have been an Anglo-Saxon philanthropic bear.

In point of fact, in statesmanship there is never a clear road. Every conceivable course is open to objections. The wisest and the greatest statesman is he who, having resolved on his goal, takes the line open to the fewest objections. Apply this principle to the maintenance and improvement of the respective types of American and British nationalities, by what considerations will Washington and London be governed in dealing with the question of the immigration of aliens, and more especially of destitute aliens—aliens destitute not merely of money and of muscle, but of character, purpose, knowledge, and everything that separates a man from the unclean beasts of Gadara.

In the solution of this problem, the government of the States enjoys a marked advantage over that of Great Britain. The port of New York is the gate through which, for practical purposes, every sea-borne immigrant must pass before he can enter the land where all poor men want to go at some time or other during their lives. The facility with which regulations can be framed is not much less than the ease with which they can be enforced.* A given physical, mental, or propertied standard, once prescribed, can be effectively maintained under the shadow of the statue of Liberty. It is otherwise in England. We have many ports. The distances from other lands are measured by hours and not by days. The steamship companies, which are under effective control by the United States, elude the administrative capacity of any President of the Board of Trade yet born in England. The first consideration, therefore, is that of the executive powers with which the immigration authorities are to be endowed. As in so many other cases of new developments, the United States is acting, while Great Britain is weighing the objections to every conceivable course and pronouncing, with all the weight of inspiration, against the adoption of any of them. The result is that not only do we receive the scum of Europe, but we get the back-wash of the American scum, besides the good folk who, from mental and physical disabilities, do not attempt to ring the bell at Ellis Island in New York harbor.

Next to the executive difficulties in the way of restriction and discrimination, the main consideration is the democratic lines on which restriction is now advocated both in the States and in England. The persons who deprecate interference with the free inflow of the destitute alien are either pure sentimentalists or capitalists who have everything to gain by the fiercest competition between wage-earners. Because England once received the skilled and useful Huguenots after the revocation of the Edict of Nantes, when the population of these islands was under eight millions, therefore she should now receive, they argue, the destitute population of Eastern Europe, when her population is thirty-nine millions, and the struggle for life so fierce as to crush out the dignity of manhood, the grace of womanhood and the merriment of children. These wiseacres, who can

* I do not speak of the misuse of the Canadian back-door, which constitutes a real American nuisance, to be removed by diplomacy.

afford to indulge in the luxury of traditions for which they do not pay, but from which they profit in the form of wicked cheapness, have no eyes to see that for all nations there are other and nobler traditions, which bear upon the nearer duties of regard to brothers in blood, color, race, before exercising vicarious hospitality to strangers without racial claim to generosity at the expense of justice to their own people. Mr. Gladstone himself has fallen into this error. We are, he says, a colonizing nation. We dispatch to other countries many more than we receive from them. This is true enough, but the quality of the human material received, must be compared with that sent. The latest witness on this subject is Mr. N. S. Joseph, whose labors as Honorary Secretary to the Russo-Jewish Committee reflect lustre not only on the community of which he is one of the most gifted sons, but also on the country that is so fortunate as to reckon him among her citizens. Mr. Joseph delivered an address on January 26th, at the inaugural meeting of the visiting and bureau departments of the London Russo-Jewish Committee.

After saying that there remain in London at present an enormous number of Russian immigrants constantly demanding sympathy and assistance, he continues as follows :

"I purposely abstain from giving any estimate of that number, but it suffices to say that the lowest estimate is alarming enough to us as a community . . . . . . The first difficulty arises from the heterogeneous nature of the refugees. There are some thoroughly capable and industrious, who only need a friendly directing hand to guide them to the means of earning a livelihood ; others wholly incapable and idle, and who, perhaps, rarely did a day's work in their own country. There are some fine, sturdy specimens of humanity, physically and morally fit subjects for emigration ; others, perhaps fully as deserving of a fresh start in a new country, but so attenuated and weakened by privation and suffering as to be physically unfit for emigration. There are, unfortunately, a large number of poor widows and orphans, and to our disgrace it must be added, there are many deserted wives and children. There are many men who occupied high social, professional or commercial positions in their own country, and who have arrived here wholly without means, and there are thousands of immigrants who cannot be called refugees at all, but who, chronic incurable paupers, have come from Russia or Poland in the hope of getting something from the Russo-Jewish Fund, of which they have heard exaggerated accounts. Then there are many who, in Russia, belonged to trades which have practically no existence here, and a still larger number who were only hawkers and petty dealers. Then there are the sick and aged, who might or might not have been driven out of their native place. Moreover, there are, as might be expected, the differences arising from variations in mental and moral constitution and development—the cultured and the semi-barbarous, the truthful and the untruthful, the honest and the dishonest, the intelligent and the unreceptive."

It may fairly be claimed—both by working men and women who are subjected to the searching fire of furious competition, and the rate-payers who are responsible for maintaining invalided and superannuated workers, disabled in the struggle for life—that immigrants of the class described by Mr. Joseph may be rigorously excluded from our shores. If they are not wanted in the States, with your millions of fertile but still neglected acres, they are still less wanted here, with our myriads of unproductive but naked and hungry babies.

The political refugee argument will not bear examination. The Mazzinis, Volkokies, Somersets, Krapotkines, and Garibaldis have always paid their hotel bills, or found friends to discharge their obligations for them, and will always succeed in obtaining sympathy and cash from lovers of freedom. To speak plainly, after an experience of nine months in Russia during the height of the Jewish persecutions, the true expulsive force is as much economic as political. The struggle for life in a town like Berdichev, where 70,000 Jews are huddled together under the saddest conditions of want, pressure and squalor, can end in one of two ways only. Either the poor souls must die or they must depart. In England we have no room for them except by lowering the general rate of wages in the trades in which the immigrants compete, and thus reproducing in London itself the tortures and tragedies of Berdichev. (Michelet said, "*La liberté serait un mot si l'on gardait des mœurs d'esclaves.*") The refugees from economic conditions that are insupportable do not gain, and still less impart, the liberty they seek, when they are accompanied by the very conditions from which they fly. To exchange the religious serfdom to the Czar for the economic serfdom of the sweating-master of Whitechapel is at least a doubtful advantage to the serf himself. But when he spreads the contagion of serfdom in his new home, the hour has struck for the rulers of a free people to look first to the welfare of their own people and their own race, before admitting the inefficient surplus of a lower nation.

There is little sentiment in this matter of immigration. It is a business matter. Since the home is the unit of the nation, celibate immigration should be discouraged by adequate restrictive means. The anti-Chinese movement arising in your Pacific Coast was justified by this consideration alone. Any nationality should be carefully watched when the female immigrants fall below thirty-five per cent.

of the whole. On this basis Russia, Italy and Hungary furnish unsatisfactory records, as in each case these nations contribute more than sixty-five males out of every hundred immigrants of their respective races to your shores.

To recapitulate. The first duty of the statesman of a great nation, is to maintain and improve the best standard of his race; to free it from those elements that tend to degrade or deteriorate the community; and to control the influx of human beings so as to raise rather than lower the conditions of life under which the new generation of hand-workers is born. Mixture of two races may either improve or degrade the character of both. The fusion of incongruous blood results in the generation of a mongrel type. The mixture of congruous and harmonious types results in the production of a race combining the characters and virtues of both, and the vices of neither. What higher aim can the leaders of our common race pursue than the purification and development of the Anglo-Saxon type?

If these things be so, the grounds therefore for excluding unsuitable immigrants from America and England are:

1. The degradation of the racial type.

2. The unfair competition forced upon the class of unskilled wage-earners, who are too poor and too numerous to combine against unscrupulous capitalists.

3. The lowering of the standard of life among the classes with whom destitute aliens compete in the unskilled labor market, and the consequent contamination of character of the native-born.

4. The diversion of the charity fund from existing national distress.

5. In the case of the Russian exodus, the free admission to the States or Great Britain of destitute multitudes of what Mr. N. S. Joseph calls "chronic incurable paupers," is the best incentive to the Czar and his ministers to persevere in their policy of extermination.

To a savage or a child the surgeon's knife is indistinguishable from relentless torture. A great nation, no less than a great family, is bound by duty to those that come after us, no less than to the generation of to-day, to do nothing, and to spare no one, who imperils the realization of the national or family ideal.

CHARITY IN BELGIUM.

PROSPER VAN GEERT, BUREAU DE BIENFAISANCE, ANTWERP.

The Charity Board.

The Charity Boards were created by the decree of 7th Frimaire, year V of the French Republic (November, 1796), after the incorporation of the Belgian provinces. The purpose of the present notes not being the narration of the history of the legislation, but merely that of the facts connected with the Charity Board, we shall simply refer to the act sanctioning its institution. This act contains in its tenth section a provision well worth remembering, namely, that all *assistance given at home* shall as far as possible be *in kind*.

What is the Charity Board? The aim of the Charity Board is to assist paupers *at home*. So that so long as there can be no question of complete support, so long as the pauper can within certain limits provide for his personal needs, he is to be considered indigent and as having a call for support upon the Charity Board. On the other hand, if there be any reason for committing the pauper to an asylum, in case he cannot find the means for self-support, he must needs fall back upon the civil asylums, which are themselves managed by a special board, entirely different from the management of public charity.

This difference forms the line of separation between the two official ways of practising charity in Belgium. The home assistance is divided into: (*a*) Assistance in money, in kind, or in rent; (*b*) Medical assistance; (*c*) Assistance given to abandoned children.

Assistance in Money, in Kind, and in Rent.

According to law, assistance in kind should be the rule. Logic, reason and experience fully corroborate this. In fact, how often is public charity defrauded by a pauper or a pseudo-pauper. Consequently there can be no doubt but the chance of making a bad use of the gift received will be lessened by assistance granted *in kind*. Gifts in kind are of different sorts; they may be in garments, bedding, food, or fuel (coals).

The Antwerp Charity Board possesses a central store for garments. The prices of the various articles are posted up for inspection. Besides this main store, three branch stores are kept in the populous quarters of the city, or four places in all where paupers may procure food or fuel. As for garments and bedding, these are specially delivered upon remittance by the pauper of tickets *ad hoc*, filled up by the *visitors of the poor*, and countersigned by the chairman of the committee. They may, however, also be delivered by the central committee itself, if such be the' pauper's desire. Such is also the case with food and fuel.

We shall now take the liberty of entering into a more minute inspection of the methods of work of a Charity Board.

The Charity Board is placed under the guidance of five directors, appointed by the town authorities out of a double list of candidates presented by the Charity Board itself. The directors are appointed for a term of five years, unless they be elected to fill the place or finish the term of a deceased director or of one who may have renounced. The burgomaster is by right a member of the board, exclusive of the five directors ; he has a deliberating vote and is chairman of the council. However, the burgomaster is not called upon to fulfill this mission except under very serious circumstances.

The members of the council elect among themselves a president, an ordonnator, and a secretary, dividing any other kind of functions or departments among the rest of the members.

The work of the board being rather extensive at Antwerp, the secretary is elected outside the council; a salary is granted him, but he has neither a deliberating nor a consulting vote. He is the chief of the corps of officials employed by the board. The council is entitled to deliberate when three of its members at least are present. General or permanent assistance is granted by the directors during the Friday meetings. The pauper then appears before the committee ; if he be known, which is ascertained by the inscription of his number in his marriage certificate, his state is looked up and the reports sent in about him by the inspector or visitor are consulted. As the case may be, a gift is allowed him once for all, or a permanent tax is granted him, according to the wants of his family. The latter allowance is generally in kind, as for instance *two francs a week* in kind. The pauper himself chooses what he is most in want of. All the prices are posted up by quantum of 25 centimes (five cents).

What is the part of the inspectors and visitors? The visitors of the poor are not paid, devotion alone urging them to practice charity; they take the tickets home to the poor and verify whether the assistance allowed continues to be necessary. They also carry about with them a number of cards or tickets for all kinds of relief, which they are entitled to grant under sanction of the Committee of Charity. There are eleven such committees at Antwerp, each of them composed of an unlimited number of visitors. Each visitor has a circumscription of a certain number of streets. The inspector (one for each committee) helps the committee; he sends in reports about the cases which have come to his knowledge, consults the states and registers for the booking of the sums or quantities granted, and keeps the committees and the directors informed. The inspectors are paid.

All this is perfectly democratic. The pauper is quite free to choose what he likes, and thus receives what he is in want of. One thing, however, must disappear, and is condemned to disappear ere long, *i. e.* the allowance of assistance by the visitors and directors as well as the Friday meetings.

These meetings are a disgrace. Fifty or sixty persons flock together in one room at a certain moment and are there compelled to lay bare their shame, thus throwing more shame upon society. However, not for a long time to come; for, as we said, these meetings are condemned to disappear.

According to the new regulations now in course of elaboration, the pauper will apply personally to an official *ad hoc* who will be in attendance at the office, or to his visitor, or even to the director. All operations will be transferred to the central office every day. The next day the inspector will send in his report, which will have to be submitted to the local committee after the visit by the visitor; the committee will then allow the assistance, unless the council of directors, who are to ratify the allowance, decide otherwise. This will be a thoroughly useful reform, as it will avoid giving twice and will cause the assistance to turn out useful; but above all, it will spare the pauper the mortification of being obliged to apply for support in public, an obligation which now makes him devoid of all shame and restraint and almost teaches him pauperism.

The work of the Charity Board should be a regenerating work as well as one of assistance, and for this very reason it should avoid hurting any feeling of shame and fear in the breast of the wretched pauper, lest this feeling be caused to wear off and the pauper urged to seek a maintenance in pauperism.

With regard to the above statement we venture to point to the line of working now being followed by the Antwerp Charity Board, whose great aim is to try to regenerate the pauper by allowing him assistance *once and for all*, but in sufficient quantity. For indeed it cannot suffice to say, "We give you two, three or four francs a week, your state being a wretched one; go and make the best of that sum." The individual's position should be examined and the proper way of assisting him ascertained. We therefore feel sure a single gift of five hundred francs, well employed, is far preferable to weekly gifts of say *two* francs.

By means of the two francs a week a focus of pauperism, wretchedness and mendicity is created, fatally leading to an increase in the number of persons kept at the pauper's asylum at Hoogstraeten, where charity colonies are formed; whereas when, for example, a man has a small business which he can no longer keep up, he may work himself out of misery by means of the sum he is in need of; if he be an artisan, some tools may be bought for him and work given him. It also often happens that assistance is given to wives whose husbands have left for America, the passage money being paid by us. After a lapse of time the great country of labor generally regenerates them, and very seldom do any of these people return to Europe. The most beautiful task of the director is the regeneration of the pauper by means of one single gift in money.

Relief in the form of rent comes next, and however rare its practice may have been up to the present moment, the city of Antwerp is about to make a trial by procuring a hundred rooms for aged people. In fact, why should old people, husbands and wives, be kept separated in asylums, where they have to mess at a common table and are obliged to lead a convent life?

Our dream, now about to be realized, is the construction of a building for old paupers, male and female, where the sexes are not kept apart, where every one can live as if he were at home, in his own large, airy room, cooking his own food, as long as they do not dine out at their children's, which will be the rule as much as possible. Thus we hope to prevent the breaking-up of family life as well as the respect due to aged people. The asylum, indeed, only becomes necessary when the old pauper is impotent, and in such a case he has to fall back for entire support upon the Board of Asylums.

Here ends the first part of the task. I might, indeed, add a few words about the desirability of uniting the two Boards of Charity, with a view upon the budget as well as with regard to the paupers. But *hic non locus est.* So let us analyze the facts.

Medical Assistance.

The sick pauper does not always go to the hospital. If he be under treatment at home, or rather if his sickness is of such a nature that he can walk about and leave his house, he has to look to the Charity Board for assistance. The pauper then goes to the dispensaries of the board, where he finds two doctors in attendance for two hours every day, with all the instruments for practising chirurgery in case of need, in so far as small operations may be required. The pauper receives a doctor's ticket, which is never refused him except in case of duly stated abuse. For, sickness being the shortest road to misery, given medical assistance should always be given promptly, as we cannot be too lavish in distributing the benefits of medical science.

Sixteen physicians are attached to the board service. They also visit the pauper at home if he cannot go out, for notwithstanding the admirable organization of the Antwerp hospitals, many a poor patient persists in his erroneous notion that "the hospital is a place to be shunned." So deeply is the spirit of antipathy against hospitals still rooted in the working classes.

We know full well it may seem hard to have to leave your family with the prospect of never seeing them back again. How humane would it be if we could find means to have every one treated at home; but how could we do so now, in the present state of the homes of our working people, without the proper quantum of air and space? Consequently, for the patient's sake as well as for that of health he should be taken to the hospital. And that is what we should endeavor to make our working people understand.

Our new rules are essentially democratic. The pauper chooses his own doctor as well as his own method of treatment. Recovery is very often dependent on confidence. Do we not choose ourselves Doctor So-and-so because he has our confidence? Why should not the same latitude be given to the pauper, if he thinks more of the doctor of another section than of the physician of his own? Why refuse him that satisfaction? On the other hand, if the pauper believes in homœopathy, why should we refuse him the aid of that school, which the rich are free to call in?

The Charity Board has no right to proclaim the excellence of any system; its only task is to look after the common possession of the poor; by means of its revenue it is to see that the pauper obtains the greatest possible source of welfare, the greatest number of means apt to relieve him in his misery. Therefore we have considered it to be our duty to grant the pauper these two liberties: that of choosing his own doctor as well as the method of treatment.

Such is the constitution of the two first branches of the Charity Board. We could also add a great many different departments: we could explain the way in which our offices are kept, what is our position with regard to the provincial government, to the state; what is the sense of the *law on home support*, and what relations we entertain with the various commons of the country. We might also treat of the service of funerals for paupers, which is now done by order, whereas formerly the pauper was interred by the lowest bidder, just as if he had been a parcel. It might be useful to explain what our colonies of Hoogstraeten Merxplas are, and our depot at Bruges; the suppression of these institutions might form the subject of a discussion, as also their eventual disappearance through the foundation of charity colonies in the Congo Free State, as it was proposed during the National Conference in 1891. We might also mention the various resources of the board, the produce of balls, theatricals and concerts, as also the objects which ought to be taxed with a view of supporting public charity. But all that would lead us too far; our object was the exposition of the above facts, which we venture to hope have been exposed with sufficient clearness and concision.

Abandoned Children.

Section 2 of the act of July 30, 1834, places the abandoned children under the charge of the Charity Committee, and although the above-named act has been cancelled by the subsequent law of March 14, 1876, in its section 43 the obligations of the Charity Committee have not been altered and their position is left quite identical.

Abandoned children (see the imperial decree of January 19, 1811) are those who, born of father and mother who are known to have brought them up, or who have been brought up by other persons having those children in charge, have subsequently been left alone, the persons who had them in charge having disappeared, and no call upon the parents being possible. It would seem that such a definition could only refer to parents having absconded from their natural obligations by flight. This is not so, however. It has been decided (see royal decree of November 22, 1861) that an asylum may receive children although the place of residence of the parents be known since the origin. In fact, it is concluded that in using the expression " when no call upon the parents is possible," the law has meant an " efficacious " call, the effect of which would be to put an end to the necessity of supporting the child. And in consequence of the above interpretation, children whose parents were at the hospital or in prison have been admitted ever since the law has been in force.

Wishing to work according to the true spirit of charity, our committee has also decided that after a special decision of the council of directors, the board could also admit " morally abandoned children." Several cases have occurred under exceptional circumstances, and the decision of the committee has always been favorable.

The guardianship over children abandoned by their parents is regulated by the act or decree of 15–25 Pluviose, year XIII (February 4–14, 1805). One of the members of the directing committee is to be the guardian, the others forming the family council. It is, however, very doubtful whether this decree also refers to the members of the Charity Board, the law being very incomplete. The guardianship therefore is merely temporary and only lasts until the return of the parents.

A law should be carried taking this guardianship from the parents by a decision of the court, after consultation of the Charity Board, and transferring it to a member of that board. As matters stand now, all is vague and the greatest conflicts are possible. For instance, the reimbursement of the sums spent in supporting the child is permitted in case of return of the parents, according to the text of the act of January 19, 1811, section 21.

Everything remains to be done in that quarter. However, in the meanwhile we have gone forward as far as possible. We have studied what could be done for abandoned children, opinions having widely differed on that subject.

Section 9 of the decree of January 19, 1811, authorizes children over six years of age to be bound apprentices to countrymen and artisans, as far as may be found possible. But far from being possible, this is much rather barbarous ; for who would think of sending a child of six to the workshop or the plough ?

Several members have expressed the wish of seeing the children sent into family life in the country, under the survey of an inspector. That was the old system and has its supporters even now. A very good pamphlet was even published on the subject by the honorable ·

alderman of finances of the city of Ghent. But experience has taught us that this system could lead to nothing but one vast swindle. Besides, how could the moral education of the children be looked to ; and is not moral education the great point when you are to lose sight of them?

Other members were for sending them into the country to our farmers. This was better, no doubt, but you cannot make a farmer out of every child ; moreover, the instruction to be found in the rural schools is far from answering the desiderata of our board. Oversight, too, is difficult.

It has therefore been necessary to make a call upon the resources of modern society to find the best system. Up to the age of twelve the child is now left in charge of the teacher. Asylums are to be built for such children, where they can find family life and go to school every day just like the children of our working people. These asylums will have to be double; one for girls, another for boys. The asylum for girls will also accept girls of over twelve years of age, and the children will be kept there until some situation is found for them outside.

In the meantime all the occupations of a woman of the people will be taught them, as sewing, knitting, washing, ironing and cooking. A nursery will be opened for babes less than four years old. According to physical strength the girls will consequently be formed as cooks, chambermaids, nurses, washerwomen or seamstresses. All the work is done at the establishment, so that the girls will find complete instruction as well as the example of greatest economy, which will be the rule at the asylum.

After school years are past the boys find our baker's shop, where the bread for paupers is baked, as well as buns, cakes, etc. The bakery is now in existence, as well as a shoemaker's shop, where the shoes for all the boys and girls are made. Moreover, the shoemaker also works for his own account, even for families in town ; we now possess about a thousand houses in the city as property of our fund ; we therefore opened a joiner's, a painter's and a plumber's workshop to keep them in repair. In every workshop we have placed two, three or four boys, living there with the master, and thus finding a family life ; in the evening the boys go to the schools for adults; on Sundays they repair to what we call the " Patronages " in such a way that they are learning their trade and finishing their primary instruction at the same time. We have, moreover, come into connection lately with the Ostend school for sailor-boys and with the military authorities, so that we hope to find there another couple of ways out by the formation of sailors or soldiers, for instance when some of our boys are sons of shippers, or when through some circumstances over which we have no control other boys may have had no time for learning a trade and express a wish of joining the army.

Last, not least, and to crown the work, plans have now been adopted for the creation of a large model farm at Schilde near Antwerp, with lands covering an area of about 200 acres, so that those amongst our boys who are not willing to become artisans will have a chance of being excellent husbandmen one day, capable of turning to profit the numerous rural possessions belonging to the Charity Boards.

This farm will, moreover, produce all the food generally drawn from our soil for the use of our charity institutions and that of our poor in general, so that the Charity Board will become a kind of collectivity managed by *all* for the profit of *all*, to the greatest benefit of those dependent on it, and causing the least expense possible to those who are obliged to maintain it.

Such is in raw outlines the service of abandoned children at Antwerp. Still above all that, stands a new principle based upon the whole and which we feel must be put forward here. For indeed the Antwerp Charity Board has been the first to introduce farming into the management. A committee has been formed of lady patrons who undertake the oversight and economy of our two institutions.

The care of a good father would not suffice in this instance and woman's task is called for. Here, in this continuous work of the formation of the child's character, woman can, if she will, show all the devotion she is capable of, together with her full power of education and household management. At Antwerp a beginning was made; five ladies, the directors' wives, being incorporated into the board, together with another lady member, the wife of one of our colleagues of the Asylums Board, noted for her devotion and compassionate nature. Moreover, the Burgomaster's wife was elected honorary president. The precedent thus established, this committee will require to be extended considerably, so as to be able to find as many good situations as possible for our pupils.

Meanwhile the Charity Board has great hopes of seeing this innovation crowned by success.

RELIEF BY WORK IN FRANCE.

M. GROSSETESTE-THIERRY, PARIS.

[TRANSLATION.]

Relief by work in France is not an innovation due to the initiative of private individuals.   From the most remote period of our history it has been practiced by the state towards mendicants.   The deprivation of liberty and confinement in workshops, where they were compelled to work from twelve to thirteen hours a day, superseded corporal punishment for all able-bodied persons found begging in city or country.   Louis XVI. opened " houses of charity " (*maisons de charité*) for them.   The National Assembly and the Convention, " thinking that labor is the only means by which wise and enlightened nations can relieve poverty," distributed considerable sums of money among the departments, to be expended in drainage, the clearing of land, the digging of canals, etc.   The Empire established " depots of mendicity," in which " all persons asking aid, or having no means of support, shall be detained until they have learned to earn their own living at some kind of work."

It would seem as if such measures ought to have exercised a salutary influence upon vagrancy and mendicity, and yet their failure was complete.   In analyzing the result obtained by private action, superseding that of the state, we find the cause of this failure.

I.

If we study the poor as a whole, we are soon convinced that the best argument in favor of work is that the professional beggar dreads it.   Private action makes use of this very repulsion to unmask imposture and aid the truly unfortunate.

A Parisian was the pioneer in this movement.   Under the very suggestive name of *Pierre de Touche* (Touchstone), M. Mamoz has created a work which has been of signal service to all who were formerly the victims of epistolary begging.   A person receiving a letter, in which the most bitter misfortunes are related in the most delicate terms, and which ends in a demand for help, has only to send the name and address of the writer to M. Mamoz to have any doubt dispelled.   The *Pierre de Touche* makes inquiries, gives the results to the inquirer, and, at his request, gives aid to the applicant in the form of sewing. The articles made are bought by charitable persons and distributed among the poor. "Make the poor work to help other poor people" is the motto of a work which has attracted general sympathy. This for the women. For the men M. Mamoz has established an intelligence office (*office de publicité*), and is constantly exercising his ingenuity to find employment suited to their ability. Twenty years' devotion to this delicate and often difficult work has made of this good man a veritable apostle of relief by work.

In 1880 Pastor Robin founded at Belleville, the most populous quarter of Paris, the *Maison Hospitalière*. Here we find the work ticket (*bon de travail*) in use in nearly all French institutions. A work ticket of 1.5 francs torn from a sort of coupon-book permits its supporters to send to this institution the poor and unemployed, who find there "a kind reception, cordial and comforting words, food, shelter, and a place in the workshops, with liberty to go out in the morning to look for work at their own trades." Assisted persons are employed at making small fagots called *margotins*. They are not paid in money; but in this way they meet their daily expenses, and, if they are skillful, can have something to their credit when they leave. They are required to make fifty *margotins* a day, which entitles them to 1.5 francs, represented by two meals and a lodging. All they make above this goes to their credit.

The results for 1892 are as follows: Of 959 admitted into the *maison hospitalière*, 695 worked on an average 14½ days; 14,275.95 francs were expended and 13,270.25 francs received—a cost of ten centimes per day per man, a very satisfactory result when compared with similar work. 264 men were dismissed for refusing to work or for insufficient work.

The object which Pastor Robin has sought for thirteen years is to provide the workingman gratuitously with an outfit of tools and to make him the beneficiary of all his labor. Charles Robert has said of the *Maison Hospitalière*, "the work is beautiful and the idea which it realizes is a grand one." So it is not surprising that the assistance of the government and of the numerous friends of the work has enabled Pastor Robin to construct a building which will accommodate from 45 to 50 inmates.

The *Hospitalité par le Travail* (lodging and food for work), which is under the direction of a religious body, receives annually about 1,500 women, who are employed at washing and ironing for schools and for private families; they also make artificial flowers.

These women remain here about twenty days; they receive no wages, but are fed and lodged, and places are found for them when opportunity offers.

The gift of a considerable sum enabled an institution, known as the Central Office for Charitable Works, to construct in 1891, on land contiguous to the property of the *Hospitalité par le Travail*, some buildings designed to receive the unemployed. This refuge has been confided to the care of Sister St. Antoine, who has charge of the woman's establishment. Here, in very rudimentary workshops, with the help of inexperienced assistants, she has in a few months established a centre of considerable production, and one which satisfies the demands of an exacting clientèle.

The men, coming from all parts of Paris, soured by poverty and employed at work of which they are generally ignorant, are separated into groups of ten under charge of overseers, and make common furniture—tables, wardrobes, sideboards—which is sold at a low price in the large stores of the capital. There are about 70 of these men, and their stay is limited to 20 days. Their wages are 2 francs a day; of this they receive 80 centimes in cash in the morning for their food, which is supplied by the establishment, and also a lodging ticket, worth 40 centimes, which entitles them to a lodging out of the house. 45 centimes are reserved to defray their expenses when they are looking for permanent employment. Two days a week are allowed for this purpose. The central office has established a regular bureau of information, through which it obtains knowledge of the shops where there are vacant places.

These institutions are in operation all over Paris, and undoubtedly exercise an ameliorating effect upon the unfortunate. But their influence upon street beggars is not so direct as that of the Relief Unions (*Unions d'Assistance*), whose sphere of activity is more restricted. These have made the profession of begging a very difficult one by means of the food-ticket, which puts a stop to indiscriminate charity, and forces the beggar to present himself at some place where he is subjected to a summary questioning, which it is generally his interest to avoid.

II.

The municipal council of the city of Paris has created—on land belonging to the department of public relief, in the department of the Marne—an agricultural colony, which is intended to find for working men who have fallen into poverty definite occupation in rural labor, after their moral and material restoration has been effected by regular and suitable work.

This colony, which has been in existence since January, 1892, at the hamlet of Chalmelle, receives, after inquiries made at the Hotel de Ville, unmarried men, to whom are given clothing, food and lodging. These men are formed into squads, according to their aptitudes or the necessities of work, under the orders of superintendents of farming or of shops, and receive 50 centimes a day. Some perquisites are allowed them in the form of savings-bank books. Their stay in the colony is not limited, but it was observed that between January and October, 1892, the entire personnel had changed.

The disciplinary measures employed are: first, a reprimand; second, withholding wages and transferring them to fund for perquisites; third, consignment to the farm on Sunday; fourth, expulsion. The labor consists in improving a section, which has been neglected for years, by drainage, cleaning and various kinds' of cultivation. The winter is employed in repairing farming implements and in the little farm work that is necessary.

This labor is not very productive, because it is unskilled and changes are so frequent. This institution will not be a success until it is under the direction of earnest men who know how to excite a spirit of emulation and a love of work in the colonists.

In 1892, 57 colonists were received at Chalmelle, of whom 18 were from 20 to 30 years old, 17 from 30 to 40, 16 from 40 to 50, and 6 from 50 to 60 years old.

Of the 31 who left the establishment, 4 were expelled for drunkenness or insubordination, 12 left voluntarily, and 15 were placed by the directory.

The actual sum expended was 15,000 francs, but the commission hope that three years of good work will be sufficient to balance receipts and expenditures.

In an agricultural country like France these colonies are needed to regenerate the mass of farm laborers who, having been tempted, not only by the mirage of a great city, but also by the number of charitable institutions found there, believe that they can obtain better or less'laborious situations. These men, having wasted their small savings, are fatally tempted to join the often formidable hosts of the abodes of night, and become beggars, and at last criminals.

The agricultural colony draws them out of this morbid atmosphere, restores their confidence in themselves, which the disillusions of life and contact with vice have destroyed, and prepares them, by a sustained activity of several months, to resume an honorable place among their fellow-men.

III.

The magnificent outburst of charity provoked by the rigorous winter of 1890 gave a fresh impetus to private initiative. All the asylums overflowed with mendicants, who crowded the streets. The Champs de Mars was transformed into a vast caravansary of idle men, who excited a feeling of insecurity everywhere, and who did not disappear until they were required to establish their identity or go to work.

It was at this time that societies or unions for relief by work were established. This form of relief results almost immediately, in those districts where it is in operation, in a very perceptible diminution of the number of its idle or pauper impostors. In fact, thanks to its restrictions and its almost daily communication with the Bureau of Charitable Relief (*Bureau de Bienfaisance*) of the municipality, the Union for Relief has been able to establish a local clientèle ; for by means of the work-ticket it gets rid of the professional beggar. We find such a society in the XVII arrondissement, under the title of "*Société d'Assistance de Batignolles-Monceau.*"

This society opened its workshop on the 15th of February, 1892. Its founder, like Pastor Robin, chose the making of kindling-wood, an occupation at which any well person can work without serving an apprenticeship. The assessment made on the patrons of the society is six francs a year. A grant of 15,000 francs from the Mutual Pools (*Paris Mutuel*) has enabled it to erect a building in which, in six months, 160 paupers found refuge. They worked 1844 days and earned 2,781.25 francs, at the rate of 1.50 francs per day. The society pays their wages in cash, for it does not provide for them in the house. A committee of lady managers superintends the work of the women. 266 women passed through the workshop this year ; there were paid to them 3,427.90 francs, and the finished work was sent to the school board to clothe poor children, or was distributed gratuitously to the needy.

The *Bureau de Bienfaisance* of the XVII arrondissement, which is the organ of the department of public relief, has adopted one measure which does credit to its members and shows how great is the desire to deprive impostors of official aid. It gives to the assisted tickets of seventy-five centimes, payable after three hours' work in the shops of the society. It is evident that this change in the form of official relief will, if it becomes general, have a considerable influence on the mass of pauperism and on the apportionment made to the honest poor. This work-ticket in use in every ward of a large city must be considered one of the most powerful agents against *professional* begging.

This society aims to assist only those who are worthy of help ; to give aid only by finding work for those who are well, and by relieving the necessities of the unfortunate whom stoppage of work, sickness or reverses prevent from taking care of themselves. Its operation is assured by an assessment of ten francs a year, by subsidies and by donations. It issues two tickets. One is green, of the value of ten centimes, which any one can obtain from the agent of the Union ; this "ticket" cannot be used by the recipient until it has been exchanged for a food-ticket ; it represents pressing need. The other ticket is gray, folds up like an envelope, and is worth what the giver pleases. It may contain a simple request or recommendation for aid either in money or work.

If the person assisted is a well person, this ticket is earned by sweeping the streets at 2 francs a day of six hours, by making *margotins* in the shop of the society of Batignolles at 1.50 francs, or by working in the carpenter's shop of Sister St. Antoine at 2 francs a day. Women are paid for sewing or knitting, which they do at home or in shops affiliated with the Union, at 1 franc or 1.75 francs a day according to their skill. The work of the women has produced over 3000 francs in ten months.

The Relief Union of the XVI arrondissement, having no workshops of its own, is associated with others which have them, and employs its beneficiaries and carries their wages to the credit of these latter Unions. These wages are the aid inscribed on gray tickets transformed into work. All sums charged are collected every quarter from subscribers. In this way the Relief Union of the XVI has, during the last year, exchanged 6315 green tickets for food-tickets, procured regular work for 231 persons, and assisted 327 with temporary work and 169 with money.

The Union of the VI arrondissement, established in a vast building in the St. Germain market, issues work-tickets of 10 centimes without limiting the time of stay ; and the total is collected only after they have been worked out. Besides the assessment of the members, it has received two grants—one of 10,000 francs from the Mutual Pools, and the other of 2000 francs from the city. The average number present in the workshops is 30, who pick tow, prepare pumice-stone, or pick old corsets to pieces; they remain on an average 12 days. They receive no money, but tickets for food and lodging are given them. By an agreement between the Union and a neighboring restaurant-keeper they can get two meals and a good room for 1.70 francs.

This work, which meets with much sympathy, has produced a very sensible diminution of mendicity in the arrondissement. On March 31, 1893 (the Union was founded in March, 1892), it had found situations for, entertained, helped or sent back to the country 758 persons, of whom 335 were directly placed by the Union, 25 aided through their families, 124 returned to the provinces, 26 cared for in the house, and 18 sent away for various causes ; 133 found situations for themselves, and 97 left without any reason given. Say 45 per cent. were placed by the Union, and 65 per cent. if we add those who were returned to the provinces and those cared for in the house. The Relief Union and the free municipal bureau render signal service to the VI arrondissement.

IV.

The provinces have largely shared in the movement of private beneficence which resulted in the establishment of relief unions. Marseilles, Lyons, Besançon, Hâvre, Nismes, Rouen, Melun and other cities have similar institutions, with work as the basis of relief; these also find situations for those whom they assist. Two of them may be considered types of rational assistance.

1. *Assistance by work in Marseilles.*—On the 23d of February, 1891, there was established at Marseilles, under the title of "*Assistance par le Travail,*" a work which, thanks to the energy of its founder, M. E. Rosband, and the devotion of his fellow-laborers, made rapid progress. His aim was not only to procure temporary work for the unemployed which would give them the necessaries of life, but to seek out the worthy poor and to unmask imposture ; to bring the benevolent and the wretched together ; to find regular work for the unemployed ; to give immediate help in urgent cases ; to make loans upon honor ; to give free advice ; to protect children in physical or moral danger, and to protect discharged convicts.

The results of two years' work are considerable, but the limits of this paper will permit only the report of the section on relief by work. February 27, 1891, an account of 4000 francs, allowed by the savings bank, formed its first capital. Subscriptions were fixed at 5 francs; and on December 31 of the same year, thanks to the donations of private individuals, of the Minister of the Interior and of anonymous benefactors, the institution showed nearly 65,000 francs received and 50,000 expended. A certain number of tickets, each of the value of 25 centimes for one hour's work, are given to the patrons in the form of a coupon-book. One of these tickets detached from the book is given to the applicant, who goes to the agency, whence he is sent, according to his ability, to the work-yard, or the addressing office, or if the applicant is a woman, she is set to packing or sewing. The applicant gets very little remuneration, essentially temporary and assuring him a bare living, in order to excite him to an effort to find regular occupation.

Under these conditions, 2545 persons presented themselves at the institution 26,478 times in 1892, and worked out 60,601 twenty-five centimes tickets, of which the supporters gave 47,099 against 6235 from other sources, such as the *bureau de bienfaisance*, savings-bank and deaconates. Besides this, 7267 extra tickets were given out and paid for in work by bearers of single tickets who were desirous of obtaining more work to supplement the meagre wage of 25 centimes. Of the 2545, 1948 men and 335 women were helped at the wood-yard and 262 men at the addressing office. These results show the interest which the people of Marseilles take in this work.

It is to be noted that most of those assisted in the wood-yard bring in a return of only 9 centimes for a ticket of 25 centimes; that is to say, the object of the institution is to offer at all times, through the payment for the work by its supporters, temporary work to the unemployed.

The addressing office received 262 persons, mostly unemployed clerks, who did 2868 days' or 9010 hours' work. Their writing brought in 1407.20 francs, which was entirely absorbed by the expenses. 157 women, present 5876.95 times, did work corresponding to 1533.20 francs wages.

No assisted person can remain more than four hours a day in the shops of the society, and if he shows a disposition to remain longer, he is temporarily excluded. The workman receives a book which indicates the number of days present and serves as a recommendation and protection; it also insures a reserved place in the lodging-house (*Hospitalité de Nuit*). Finally, these tickets when used are returned to the benefactors, who can verify their use and pay their value to the treasurer of the work.

2. *The work at Lyons.*—This work, established in 1890, permits a prolonged stay with remuneration in kind and in work-tickets of 1.50 francs, which represents the first day's stay. Though the system is diametrically opposed to that of Marseilles, the results are no less important. Experience has demonstrated to the founders of the Temporary Home that the more prolonged the work is the more favorable is the result in all respects, and they have never hesitated to keep beyond the regulation time any whose earnest work might stimulate the zeal of their companions.

The work-ticket of 1.50 francs permits a person to remain a week at least in the workshop, where he receives three meals a day and his lodging; he is obliged to make 50 *margotins* in an afternoon, and he is allowed a premium (one centime) for every one over this number, which he receives at the end of his stay. Under these conditions the work has been able almost to balance its budget from its own resources, and in 1892 to take care of 890 men who remained 6974 days, making an average of nearly 8 days. These results are excellent, when it is considered that they have been obtained with absolutely inadequate facilities.

The distributing committee of the Mutual Pools, wishing to recognize the effort and the sustained devotion of the promoters of this work, has allowed them the sum of 40,000 francs for the purchase of property, and there is no doubt that the Lyonnaise foundation will in a short time realize the dream of its sympathetic president:

"Mendicity is forbidden here, but we receive with cordial sympathy and profound joy every one who wishes to regain his manhood, to be regenerated, to be saved by work."

V.

The French conception of relief by work presents certain peculiarities which reveal its spontaneous origin. A few citizens, in places widely separated, and without any appeal to the public or to the government, and often with very insufficient funds, established institutions having for their foundation the temporary occupation of the unemployed, which is freely offered and freely accepted. No common rules govern their action. In one the assisted person

receives payment in money, in another in food, and in a third wholly
in lodging. At Marseilles, his stay in the workshop is limited to
four hours a day ; at Lyons, he may remain a week, or longer, if he
gives evidence of energy and good intentions; at Paris, some institutions take care of him fourteen days, others twenty ; and wherever
these unions are in operation they struggle successfully against professional beggary. Public charity seconds their efforts by active
co-operation, by subsidies, and by credits allowed by the bureaus of
charity. Hardly had they been organized when unhoped-for results
were obtained ; because it is recognized that the change from indiscriminate individual charity to a form of relief which is paid for in
work, and the union of private initiative with public relief, with a view
to reviving the energy of the able-bodied poor, raise in an agricultural country like France a much more rational obstacle to the
revival of vagrancy and mendicity than increased severity of the
repressive system.

When the public authorities, completing the work already begun,
shall endow the country districts with shelters of a preventive character which will excite emulation, such as the large centres now
have, the city will no longer absorb the population of the country ;
the unemployed, who first become beggars and then dangerous
criminals, will furnish agriculture with the hands it now lacks, and
will co-operate in national saving, instead of imposing taxes which
are as burdensome as they are useless.

THE AUSTRIAN POOR LAW SYSTEM.

EDITH SELLERS.

The Austrian poor law system differs widely from that in force in
any other country. While elsewhere poverty is regarded officially
as a crime and dealt with accordingly, in the Eastern Empire it is
held to be merely a misfortune. In the eyes of Western legislators,
the destitute, whether little children, strong men, or infirm old
people, are all on the same level. By their laws, the same treatment is meted out, in the hour of need, to sturdy beggars and loafing
vagabonds, as to industrious men and women whose life has been
one long fierce struggle to keep the wolf from the door. Austrian

statesmen, however, hold different views both as to expediency and humanity. They classify their poor most carefully, for they maintain, and with some show of reason, that it would be just as absurd to club together all criminals—libellers, thieves and dynamiters—as all paupers. They even discriminate in the use of the term, reserving it exclusively for able-bodied men and women. Throughout the empire, the young who have no relatives to support them are the adopted children of the state; the aged destitute are its worn-out industrial pensioners; and the whole population would be horrified at the thought of treating as paupers the one class or the other.

The first Austrian poor law was drawn up by the Emperor Joseph II., and is strongly imbued with the personal characteristics of its author. It came into force in the year 1781 and is the basis of all later legislation on the subject. Its fundamental principle is that the responsibility for the relief of distress rests not on the state, but on the town or commune. The imperial exchequer is under no obligation to contribute towards the support of the poor, although it may, and frequently does, make a grant to some one or more districts in case of special distress occurring there. Each town or commune is required to provide food and shelter for such of its inhabitants as are destitute, and to take charge of idiots, cripples and invalids. The local authorities are exhorted to show special consideration for the aged, and to secure for them the means of passing their declining days in comfort. On the other hand they are exhorted to deal sternly with the able-bodied, and to refuse all help to those who, having the strength to work, are lacking in the will. A marked feature of this first poor law is the importance of the rôle it prescribes for the clergy. The Emperor Joseph, holding that the very *raison d'être* of the church is to relieve distress, placed the administration of his law in the hands of the priests. He insisted that they should become guardians of the poor in all the meanings of the term. This arrangement did not work satisfactorily. In many districts these clerical guardians proved themselves at once negligent and corrupt, with the result that it soon became necessary to replace them in their office by laymen. From time to time other alterations in this law were made by the provincial assemblies, with a view to adapting it to their special local requirements, so that the old imperial measure has undergone many transformations, and to-day almost every province and large town has a relief system of its own.

All these systems, however, are founded on the same principle and are characterized by the same spirit. The one in force in Vienna, therefore, may be taken as a type of the rest.

In Vienna, the responsibility for the relief of the poor is vested in the *Armendepartment*. This department administers the municipal charities, manages the public benevolent instituticns, and decides all questions relating to the relief of the poor of the city as a whole. It consists of 537 guardians of the poor ; 233 *Waisenväter* (fathers of orphans) ; 54 *Waisenmütter* (mothers of orphans), and a certain number of paid officials. The guardians are elected by the rate-payers ; the *Waisenväter* and *Waisenmütter* are appointed by the burgomaster. In addition to this central authority, each of the nineteen districts into which Vienna is divided has a board of guardians of its own. The members of these boards are elected by the rate-payers of their respective districts, to whom they are responsible for the administration of the relief granted in these districts.

The recipients of relief are divided into three classes, viz. children under sixteen, able-bodied men and women, and the aged and infirm. Vienna boasts, and not without reason, that it takes better care of its destitute children than any other city in the world. All children, whether orphans or not, whose relatives are unable to provide for them are adopted by the city. They are never allowed to enter a workhouse or any place where they would be brought in contact with paupers, and the greatest care is taken to prevent any stigma being attached to them on account of their friendless condition. If under ten, they are generally boarded-out with well-to-do peasants, who must undertake to care for them as if they were their own sons and daughters. They attend the village school, where they mix with their companions upon terms of perfect equality ; and thus grow up without ever experiencing that parish feeling which is often so painful a feature of the lot of such children in other countries. Each one of them, if a boy, is under the special care of a *Waisenvater*; if a girl, of a *Waisenmutter*. These official fathers and mothers are held responsible by their fellow-citizens for the welfare of their charges. They must visit them regularly, see that they are properly fed and clothed, that they are treated kindly by their foster-parents, and that they are being trained in such a manner as to fit them to make their own way in the world. As no one would accept the office who was not fond of children, a warm feeling often springs up between these guardians and their protégés, to the great advantage of the latter, who thus start life with a friend at their back to whom they can turn when difficulties arise. When the children are old enough to benefit by more careful teaching and supervision than can be secured for them whilst boarded-out, they are either placed in orphanages or sent to training-schools, where they are fitted for the calling for which they show most natural aptitude. Every precaution is taken to prevent their going to swell the ranks of unskilled labor. The boys are carefully trained in some well-paid handicraft—carpentering, bricklaying, shoemaking, etc.—whilst the girls are taught to cook, wash, clean, sew, to perform in fact all the duties of housewives. If any of them show signs of special talent they are given an opportunity to cultivate it; for attached to the public schools are scholarships for which only pauper children may compete. Even the University throws open to them *gratis* all its lectures and examinations—a noteworthy fact considering the exclusive spirit which generally characterizes such institutions.

Vienna has under its care at the present time some 7000 children, of whom one-third, roughly speaking, are in schools and orphanages, while the rest are boarded-out. The average cost per head in an orphanage is 79.96 kreuzer a day. This is certainly a liberal allowance for a child—more than half as much again as that granted for a man; but the money is well spent, for the adopted children of the city turn out as a rule useful men and women, self-supporting, law-abiding, and capable of doing good service in the world.

For the relief of the able-bodied a sort of modified Elberfeld system prevails in Vienna. Each district guardian has under his care some twenty families with whose character, habits and circumstances he is expected to be personally acquainted. Unfortunately, however, like other honorary officials, he sometimes neglects his duty in this respect. He has at his disposal a small sum of money for the relief of cases of temporary distress. His special duty, however, is not so much to deal with distress himself as to supply the information necessary for enabling the *Armendepartment* to deal with it effectually. He, therefore, unless the circumstances of the case be exceptional, passes on all applications for help to the officials of the central department in charge of the public institutions for paupers. These institutions are arranged on a sort of descending scale of comfort. There are *Asyls* for those who are anxious to work but have no work to do; a workhouse for those who will work if they must, but would rather play; and a *Zwangsarbeithaus* (forced labor colony) for those who can only be driven to work by threats and blows. By thus keeping the three classes distinct, the authorities are able to deal out to each one of them the precise treatment it merits.

An *Asyl* is a municipal boarding-house to which a workman who, owing to loss of employment or some other misfortune, is in a state of destitution, may claim admittance. There he is provided, free of charge, with a supper, bath, bed and breakfast every day for a limited time, upon condition that, during that time, he makes every possible effort to obtain employment. The *Asyl* officials are in constant communication with the great employers of labor, and have a labor-bureau of their own. Thus they know to a nicety where work is to be found, and are able to save the unemployed from many a weary tramp. So long as a man is honestly doing his best to become self-supporting they give him every help; but they keep a sharp watch on his proceedings, and if he shows signs of a taste for loafing they treat him with scant toleration. In no circumstances is he allowed to return to the *Asyl* too often or to stay there too long. Three days is the average length of a visit. At the end of that time, unless he has either found work or can prove that he is on the way to do so, he must leave the *Asyl.* Another refuge, however, is open to him; he may go to the workhouse.

In Austria a workhouse is something entirely different from the institution which bears that name in America. Vienna with its population of 1,500,000 has only one workhouse, and of this the number of inmates is rarely more than 170. Yet it is by no means an unpleasant abode. The food is good, the rooms are comfortable, and there is a decided air of life and gaiety about the place. The inmates are required to do a certain amount of work, to keep regular hours, and to be peaceable and orderly in their behavior. So long as they conform to these rules they enjoy considerable liberty, for the officials never interfere unnecessarily with their proceedings. On Sundays and *fête* days they do no work at all, and once a week they are free the whole day to go out in search of employment. Thus, in certain circumstances, a sojourn in the workhouse may be almost enjoyable; it can, however, never be prolonged. The workhouse, like the *Asyls,* is designed to tide over temporary distress, and the authorities are always on the alert to prevent its inmates regarding it as a fixed residence. They may stay there for a few weeks, for months even, if it be a time of industrial depression; but sooner or later, unless they find work for themselves outside, they will be sent to the *Zwangarbeithaus*.

Loafers, vagrants, and all those who wish to live on the labor of their fellows have a wholesome dread of a visit to the Viennese *Zwang-arbeithaus*. And well they may, for it is an eminently unpleasant experience. In the *Zwangarbeithaus* the strictest prison discipline is maintained, and all who are there must earn their rations before they eat them. This is as the law of the Medes and Persians. Nor can the inmates leave at will; the length of their stay depends on their conduct, not on their wishes. The treatment to which paupers are subjected in this institution is undoubtedly harsh, but few will be inclined on that account to condemn it. For it must not be forgotten that decently industrious men and women are not sent there; it is set aside entirely for those whom gentler means have failed to redeem. And certainly public opinion, especially among the working classes, is decidedly on the side of the authorities in putting down, with a firm hand, professional loafing. No one thinks the worse of a comrade for going to an *Asyl;* he may even pass a few weeks in the workhouse without losing caste; but if he has once crossed the threshold of the *Zwangarbeithaus* there is a mark against his name for ever.

The Viennese poor law regulations with regard to the aged and infirm are essentially humane in character. Not only are the old people well fed, well tended and well clothed, but their feelings, tastes and prejudices are carefully consulted. It would be difficult for Americans to form any idea of the respectful consideration with which the aged poor are treated in Austria. The unusual privileges they enjoy result, perhaps, in some measure at least, from the unsatisfactory financial conditions of the country. Austrian legislators have always been compelled to recognize the fact that, for a certain percentage of the population, pauperism is as inevitable as the grave. No amount of economy or self-denial will enable peasants whose average earnings are at most three florins a week, or town laborers who gain perhaps five or six, to lay by a provision against old age. The relief such people receive when their strength is spent can, therefore, carry with it no disgrace. More than a hundred years ago the Emperor Joseph proclaimed the principle around which the battle to-day is raging so fiercely. "Old age relief is a right, not a charity," he maintained. By his law any person who had completed his sixtieth year, and was without means of support, might claim from his commune an annuity equal in amount to one-third of the average yearly wages he had received. The annuity was to be regarded in precisely the same light as a soldier's pension, namely, as the reward of past services. Since that time the amount of a superannuation pension has often been changed and is now miserably small; still the right of the old and feeble to be supported by the community has never been questioned.

The city of Vienna is now supporting partially or entirely about 21,000 persons who are aged or infirm. To some 16,000 of them it grants pensions of from two to six florins a month, and also in many cases rooms, firing and lights. For the rest it provides homes in charitable institutions of one sort or another. Of these the chief are the *Armeninstitute* and the *Versorgungshäuser*. Any native of Vienna, if he be above sixty years of age, of good character, and without means of support, may claim admittance to a *Versorgungs-haus*. If there be no vacant room at the time, the authorities must grant him a pension, or admit him to an *Armeninstitute* until a place can be found for him in a *Versorgungshaus*. Both these institutions are supported by the city. The former are simply poorhouses which are reserved for the aged and infirm ; paupers, that is the able-bodied destitute, being rigidly excluded. They correspond so far as their aim is concerned to state-provided almshouses in America, but are arranged with much more regard for the comfort of the inmates. *Versorgungshäuser* are an institution peculiar to Austria and one of which the nation is justly proud. Vienna owns five, one in the city itself and four in the suburbs. They are fine large buildings standing in pleasant gardens, and they are regarded by the whole community as the special property of the aged poor.

There is no pleasanter spot in all Vienna than a *Versorgungshaus*, the inhabitants are so delightfully contented and happy. They feel there, as they say, in their own home, in the old folks' home, and they assume quite an air of proprietorship as they go about the place. Their rooms are most cosy little apartments, with bright colored prints on the wall and plants on the window-sill. All sorts of old family relics, too, are dotted about, for these lucky old people are not required (as they would be if they lived elsewhere) to part with their most cherished possessions when they accept a home from the state. A *Versorgungshaus* is divided into two parts, the men living on one side and the women on the other. As, however, the hall, the dining-room, the corridors and the gardens are equally

open to the two, husbands and wives, if they wish it, can pass the
whole day together. They may also go out for walks together every
afternoon, and may, if they choose, once a week spend the whole
day with their friends. Their friends, too, are encouraged to pay
them visits, and on a fine afternoon there is often quite a lively
assembly in the gardens. The women are expected to help to keep
the house neat, and the men to give a hand in the garden from time
to time. Beyond that they are free to employ their leisure as they
choose ; so long as they are orderly in their ways and keep regular
hours, the officials never interfere with them. Far from encroaching
on their liberty, they seem anxious so far as possible to humor their
prejudices. Of this their treatment of the clothes difficulty is a proof.
The authorities provide warm comfortable clothing of an uniform
pattern for all the inmates, but if some of them prefer (as many do)
wearing their own old tattered garments, they are free to do so, at
least so long as they can keep them clean.

In some of the *Versorgungshäuser* the commissariat arrangements
are on the restaurant principle. Attached to the building is a
restaurant, managed by a private company, but under the supervision of the *Armendepartment* officials and the guardians. Here
the old people, excepting in case of illness, have their meals. They
are each given 38 kreuzer a day for food, and this they may spend
as they choose, although the guardians reserve the right of with-
drawing this privilege if it be abused. The food supplied is thoroughly good and beautifully cooked, great care being taken to
provide a variety of dishes every day. A doctor and two of the
guardians are always present when the dinners are being served out,
to insure the old people receiving good value for their money, both
in the quantity and in the quality of their food. These restaurants
are marvels of good management, for, although they supply their
guests with as much wholesome appetizing food as they can eat, at a
maximum charge of 39 kreuzer per head a day, they are self-supporting.

The average cost of the inmates of the *Versorgungshäuser* is only
52.87 kreuzer a day. This is the cost of maintenance only, and does
not include any allowance for interest on the capital outlay on the
buildings. In spite of this, considering the high standard of life
maintained, they must certainly be classed among the most economically managed institutions in the world.

The public hospitals in Vienna are all under state supervision.

Any patient who presents himself at one of these hospitals is at once admitted, provided his condition be such as to necessitate medical or surgical treatment.   No questions are asked as to his status or means until he is cured or pronounced incurable; then the hospital author- ities claim a fixed amount for every day he has been under their care.   This he must pay unless he can prove that neither he nor any of his responsible relations have the money to do so.   In that case the *Armendepartment* defrays the cost of his treatment.   If, how- ever, he be not a native of the city, the commune to which he belongs must refund the money to the department.

It is impossible to ascertain the exact cost to the municipality of the relief of the poor of Vienna.   The money is not raised by means of any one rate, but is largely derived from sources which vary in the amount they yield from year to year.   It is not until the fund obtained from the old foundations, confiscated church lands, lega- cies, etc., is exhausted that the rates are resorted to.   Roughly speaking, however, exclusive of the hospitals and orphanages, the city spends six and one-half million florins annually on its poor.   Of this sum only one million, in an average year, falls on the rates.

POVERTY AND ITS RELIEF IN AUSTRIA.

DR. MENGER, VIENNA.

[TRANSLATION.]

As in other countries, so preëminently in Austria, there are two kinds of poverty to be considered, namely, poverty which is due to the inability of the person himself to provide the necessaries of life, and that which is due to the inability of those whose duty it is to support him.

Poverty in the first form is the result of inability to procure by one's own means the indispensable necessaries of life.   It befalls indi- viduals or families through sickness, death of the breadwinner, the consequent destitution of those left behind, other misfortunes, thrift- lessness and the like.   In many parts of Austria the collective wealth as compared with the population is not large, its general distribution being often very unequal.   This, together with the heavy demands made by the very high and often unequally imposed state taxes and duties, direct and indirect, and the fact that states, districts and communes are all anxiously striving rapidly to make amends for the unfortunate lack of development in the first half of this century, multiply in many regions the number of poor beyond what would otherwise be the case. The very grave political problems which Austria-Hungary has had to face because of wars and preparations for wars against the enemies of European civilization (formerly against Turkey, now against Russia, with both of which powers France joined hands), have not only called forth numerous difficulties of internal policy, but have affected in many unfortunate ways both the state finances and the accumulation of capital, the distribution of public wealth and the development of business possibilities. The spirit of enterprise is comparatively little developed in Austria. The problems of poverty in Austria are, therefore, for reasons of universal experience, far more difficult of solution than those of civilized countries with larger and better distributed public wealth, greater capital and business possibilities, and, above all, a greater spirit of enterprise in the domain of economics, such as France, North America, and even Germany.

In addition to the general causes of pauperism, which are met with everywhere, but which in Austria, as stated above, operate much more powerfully than in many other countries, there are certain far-reaching economic and social phenomena which have brought whole classes, or at least considerable portions of the population, to an exceedingly distressing economic condition.

Before industrial production made steam power, the steam engine and railways subservient to its use to such an extent as it does now, much of the manufacturing in Austria was done in the homes of the laborers; this supplied the country with a great variety of goods, such as textile fabrics, many kinds of hardware, etc., and there was some manufacturing for export. There often resulted from this state of affairs in places which were not very productive, as in sterile mountain regions, a very dense population. Considerable portions of Galicia, a great part of Silesia, Moravia and Bohemia, some districts in Lower Austria, many valleys in Styria, Carinthia, Carniola, Vorarlberg and the Tyrol supported themselves by these domestic industries. In the northern part of the empire they consisted principally in the spinning and weaving of wool, flax, and later of cotton; the south was especially the home of the metal industry. Even now

the textile manufacture of wool, flax and cotton is carried on in the
northern states of the empire, particularly in Bohemia, Moravia and
Silesia, also in Lower Austria; while metal-working prevails in the
southern and Alpine states. But the competition of large factories
has overthrown home manufacturing and the smaller producers.
Of course there might have been such a development in Austria
as in many other countries, where the different kinds of domestic
manufacture were replaced by the large modern factory which gave
work and bread to the laborers in the smaller trades, to the modest
employer and employees engaged in manufacture at home. This
line of development was hindered by the circumstance that in the
first half-century after the establishment of the first railway in
Austria, hardly any lines except the so-called trunk-lines were built,
whereas branch roads received but little attention. The main lines
ran chiefly through the large valleys and plains. Along these lines
the great manufacturing establishments settled. Many districts
where home manufacturing flourished remained for decades without
railroads. There are still extensive and thickly populated regions
which have none.

To the other causes of the economic superiority of the large
manufacturing enterprises there was added cheap and safe transportation by the railroads. The result was that the small manufacturers suffered the greatest losses; but competition could be
maintained only by constantly reducing wages. The distress of the
weavers has become almost proverbial. In many of these districts,
wages per week amount to from 1.70 to 2.00 florins (about 85 cents
to one dollar). Only by the completion of a network of railways
with numerous branch roads can this great evil be lessened to any
considerable extent, if indeed it is not already too late.

A second cause of the poverty to which a large part of the population of whole districts is succumbing, is the too minute parceling of
land, without a corresponding development of other business which
would help the smaller holder. This happens in those districts in
which this division is not accompanied with increased activity in
agriculture. The reason for this is generally the fact that in these
districts capital, education and the spirit of enterprise in industrial
pursuits stand on a low plane. Wide-spread poverty is found also
in many regions where a very large portion of the land is tied up in
entail, while the proprietors gladly buy up such peasant holdings as
are for sale. Similar phenomena appear in extensive tracts of land

in Galicia and in some parts of Bohemia and Moravia. The rural pauperism in South Tyrol has its chief cause in the diseases of its vines and the consequent failure of the crops, and in the great fall in the value of silk, due to the competition of China and Japan.

The far greater part of the Jewish population of Galicia presents a peculiarly pitiable form of pauperism in mass. Too early marriages, premature and numerous offspring—phenomena connected with the religious views of widely extended Jewish sects—increased living expense due to the Hebrew dietary laws, the echoes of hard oppression under which the Israelites have suffered for centuries even in their economic relations, have produced phases of poverty such as it would be difficult to find elsewhere. A large part of the Jewish population of Galicia does not live from day to day, but, as may be said without exaggeration, from meal to meal. From three to four Jewish families often live in one room. The territory belonging to each family is outlined with chalk. Disease and superstition thrive with extraordinary luxuriance under such conditions. Here also the lack of opportunity for work, due to lack of enterprise and the shyness of capital to embark in industrial enterprises, is one of the chief causes of this misery and its deplorable consequences in social and economic relations. It is not true that Galician Jews in general abhor all physical labor. They engage in a great many manual trades. They serve even as porters * in many cities. But in many parts of Galicia there is not a sufficient supply of even moderately paying labor for the Christian laborer.

The relief of poverty in Austria, as elsewhere, falls first upon endowed religious institutions and voluntary associations, but chiefly upon the communes, and to some extent upon the states. The Austrian institutions for the poor suffered very much from the large state bankruptcies in the beginning of this century, their capital suffering quite a heavy reduction. To this must be added the very great rise in the prices of the necessaries of life, so that it may be said without exaggeration that the spirit of benevolence will have to multiply the existing institutions greatly, if they are to attain the importance which they possessed toward the end of the last century. The religious societies—the Catholic church to the greatest extent, but the Protestant and Jewish congregations as well—dispense charity

----

*All through Poland men are employed as we use horses, to deliver goods from stores, such as sacks of flour, salt, potatoes, etc. It is very hard work.— *Translator.*

on a large scale. The fundamental factor in poor relief in Austria is, however, the commune. In contrast with former legislative efforts, for instance that of 1754, charity now rests upon the following principles: Every Austrian subject, in case of impoverishment, is entitled to receive the indispensable necessaries of life from that commune in which he has the *right of settlement*. This right, however, except in case of a voluntary admission into a commune, or an appointment to a state office in a specific place, is acquired only by inheritance or marriage. The principles of the older Austrian egislation, which as late as in the imperial patent of 1804 allowed the right of settlement to be acquired by a four years' residence, continued without certificate and permitted by the community, were done away with by the law of December 3, 1863, which regulates the power of granting settlement and the right of settlement itself.

While the Prussian settlement laws which reached their climax in the institution of a relief-domicile have been recognized in all Germany, with the exception of Bavaria and Alsace-Lorraine, the older Austrian laws, which also contained a provision for relief-domicile, have been invalid since 1863. Every citizen must have a right of settlement in some commune. The right of settlement in a commune gives a claim to charitable support. This is obtained by birth (descent from a domiciled father, or, in case of illegitimacy, from a domiciled mother); by marriage, when the groom is domiciled; by admission into the commune; and lastly, by appointment to an office the headquarters of which are located in the commune. These legal regulations have produced a very peculiar state of affairs in the domain of charity, and from our experience thus far we have no hesitation in saying a very deplorable one. Since in the main the right of free migration obtains in Austria, and the movement from the open country to the larger cities, from the purely agricultural districts to the manufacturing centres, is very great, the ratios between residents entitled to right of settlement and residents who are not, and between residents and non-residents entitled to the right, are becoming every year in many important communes more and more unfavorable to the former class in both cases. The time is not far distant when most of the people entitled to settlement will live away from their places of domicile, and such as do not possess the right of settlement in a place will form the majority of its population. With each generation this disproportion increases, and with it the great evils that follow in its train.

The confused condition of the Austrian settlement laws exercises a most baneful influence over poor relief. Families whose heads have worked in a place for decades are obliged, when death or disability of the father occurs, to claim their right of support in some distant community whose name they often scarcely know. German poor are removed to Slavic communes, and Slavic poor to German communes. The beneficiary of the poor law often does not know even the language of the commune in the midst of which he must live and which must care for him. All the evils which modern German writers urge against a relief-domicile do not compare with the bad influence which this principle of the right of settlement, driven as it has been to the extreme, has exercised upon Austrian poor relief.

These great evils have made the need of reform in settlement laws in the interests of Austrian charity clear in almost all of the states. Some of these, especially Lower Austria, have passed reform laws which as far as possible minimize the defects in Austrian poor relief. Some branches of poor relief—for example, much of the care of the sick—have been assumed by the states and districts, partly as a result of legislation, partly as a result of mere custom. The introduction of *Naturalverpflegungsstationen* has diminished vagrancy to some extent, as well as the practice of forcibly moving the vagrant on, which had in Austria degenerated into a lamentable abuse. Yet few branches of Austrian legislation are so much in need of reform as the laws concerning right of settlement in its relation to poor-relief.

The question of the duty of a commune to relieve its poor arises, of course, only when there is no person or society whose duty it is to support the pauper. Persons entitled to the benefits of the poor laws, have, however, in Austria no right of complaint against a commune.

SKETCH OF THE ORGANIZATION OF PUBLIC POOR RELIEF IN AUSTRIA.

DR. FRIEDERICH PROBST, OF THE IMPERIAL CENTRAL STATISTICAL COMMISSION.

[TRANSLATION.]

I.—*Agencies of Public Poor Relief.*

The foundation of the poor law of Austria is contained in the statute of December 3, 1863 (*R. G. B. No.* 105), relative to the regulation of settlement. In §§ 1–22 it is enacted that settlement (*Heimathsrecht*) in a commune establishes a person's claim to support, and that it is the duty of a commune in case of poverty to provide for the support of paupers who have the right of domicile there.

The origin of the poor law on which, as explained above, the jurisdiction of the commune rests, is found far back in the establishment by Emperor Joseph II. of organized parish institutions for the poor (*Pfarrarmeninstitute*) in all German-Slavonic countries.

These institutions, carried on under the guidance of the clergy and with the co-operation of almoners (*Armenväter*) chosen from the parish, were dependent for pecuniary support on the bounty of the commune. But certain other legal means for increasing their income were also at their disposal, namely, the half of the income of disbanded brotherhoods, the property of dissolved guilds, all capital which had accumulated for the release of poor Christian slaves, all fines, a percentage on public auction sales, and all sums bestowed upon the poor by will, and a third of the intestate estates of secular priests. In the year 1789 an order was issued to these parish institutions that before dispensing aid investigation should be made as to whether the applicant had resided for ten years in the given place; if he had not, no aid should be given. Thus the principle that settlement alone entitled one to a claim for support was established, and the parish institutions became the agencies for conducting poor relief in communes.

Under the laws proclaimed since 1861 the enunciation of the general principles for the regulation of poor relief is under the control of the state legislatures. These bodies have legislated in two directions. After the political communes had, under the law of settlement (*Heimathsgesetz*), been entrusted with the direct management of poor relief, the parish institutions for the poor were entirely abolished in several states—Lower Austria, Upper Austria, Carinthia, Croatia, Carniola and Silesia. The property which they possessed at the time was turned over to the communes, and even the legal revenues allotted for their support were transferred to the communes. In those countries in which parish institutions were not abolished, the communes, by virtue of the imperial law mentioned above, became the agencies of public poor relief, and parish institutions for the poor lost their official character.

In a number of states—Lower Austria, Upper Austria, Salzburg, Styria, Carinthia, Carniola, Bohemia, Vorarlberg and Dalmatia—legislation went still farther and by local poor laws prescribed certain limits within which all agencies for poor relief in a commune must act. These laws, however, allowed great latitude to the communes in the matter of organizing their poor relief; for this, in the last analysis, always remains a matter of peculiar concern for the commune. So as to poor relief, the local council (*Ausschuss*) is the determining and supervising body, while the local executive (*Gemeindevorstand*) has the administrative and executive power.

In dispensing material relief to the poor the communal council has the right to avail itself of the services of certain subordinate agencies. It can choose almoners or appoint an overseer (*Armenrath*); in fact it can provide itself with the necessary subordinates, who act under its control and superintendence, and for whose acts it is responsible. It can, when necessary, regulate the sphere of activity of almoners and overseer by general instructions and directions, and, within the limits prescribed by the state laws, make its own poor laws.

According to the statute of February 26, 1876 (*L. G. B. No.* 13), Dalmatia possesses its own charitable commissions (*commissioni di publice beneficenza*), independent of the communes, on which devolves the administration of poor funds and the direction of outdoor and indoor relief. Bishops, provosts (*Pröbste*) of cathedral and collegiate chapters, and pastors of different denominations represented in the commune, are by law members of the charitable commission. The remaining members are nominated, half by the common council (*Gemeindcrath*) from persons not belonging to it, the other half by the committee of state (*Landesausschuss*), with the consent of the communal executive. In spite of the independent position of the charitable commissions, it is the duty of the common council, even in Dalmatia, to procure means for the maintenance of the poor whenever the resources of the charitable institutions and the poor funds are not sufficient.

If the question be asked how the organization of poor relief has actually developed in single communes according to the principles expressed in the laws above mentioned, it is at once clear that in rural communes a more extended organization of the authorities and official agencies entrusted with the care of the poor is not to be expected, because of the smaller population and the smaller number of poor persons to be supported. This inference corresponds with the actual facts. The case is entirely different with respect to poor relief in cities, and this topic, therefore, will be only briefly considered here. It is necessary in examining this branch of the subject to separate cities into different groups from the point of view of the historical development of their poor relief, the influence of which is felt at the present time.

Among the German-Austrian cities there are some, for the most part small ones, which do not have distinct agencies for poor relief, as their administration of poor relief is not distinct from the general administration of the commune. Poor relief is carried on according to old customs and by very primitive methods; usually one special branch of the common council is appointed as the committee for the poor (*Armensektion*), to which a civil officer is added as a poor official. A special poor-commission (*Armencommission*) is found only in large cities, and there are only a few almoners.

In a second group of cities, including the large cities and the cities of the Alpine provinces, and of Moravia and Silesia, poor relief is so organized that the supreme power rests with the executive of the city and its legislative body. These bodies reserve to themselves the issuing of regulations only and a general superintendence and the management of the funds for the poor, or very rarely it happens that at the same time they undertake regular poor relief. This is the case in Vienna, whose magistracy acts as a board for the administration of indoor and outdoor relief. Besides there are the honorary offices of poor commissioners (*Armencommission*), poor councillors (*Armenräthe*), poor directors (*Armendirektionen, Armenausschüsse*) or guardians (*Pflegeschaftsräthe*), who act as corporate bodies with power of decision. In large cities, however, decisions in ordinary and extraordinary cases of actual poor relief have remained under the jurisdiction of the common council or magistracy. In Vienna there is no central poor commission, however, but the authority is decentralized among the different boards of district almoners. The chairmanship of the poor commission is almost everywhere taken by the mayor or his representative. The other members are members of the common council, and in rare cases trustworthy citizens are added to it. Frequently a member of the magistracy (*Magistratsbeamter*) acts as referee. In large cities, such as Prague and Graz, there are under the poor commissions special subordinate boards whose sphere of activity is partly identical with that of the poor commission, partly with that of the board of almoners. Almoners are the executive authorities proper of the communal poor relief. Their functions include investigations, suggestions, raising money, keeping the poor register, making disbursements and the like. They are organized in one or more boards with fixed territorial limits, which have essentially the same duties as belong to their individual members.

These agencies administer either all poor relief, or sometimes—and this is the more frequent—only outdoor relief. For indoor relief there are very often special agents, some honorary, some filled by municipal appointment. The former are either members of the town council (*Gemeinderäthe*), almoners, or persons chosen for this especial purpose. Sometimes the administration of charitable institutions is under the control of a supervising committee (*Aufsichtsausschuss*), or of a portion of the poor commission.

Poor relief is organized on an entirely different plan in the towns situated in the southern part of the empire. In Trent, which may serve as a type of them all, poor relief is under the direction of the *Congregazione di Carità*, a half-official corporate body which had its beginning in the old brotherhoods and which still shows traces of a religious origin. This body is composed of a president, vice-presidents, an ecclesiastical member, the three local pastors, and six other members (one of whom must be a lawyer) selected from the inhabitants and having the rank of members of the magistracy (*Magistratsräthe*). All these offices are honorary and filled for four years. At the quarterly general assemblies the bishop and a member of the magistracy take the chair.

The *Congregazione* appoints its own deputies to supervise its own charitable institutions. There are three select committees on relief (*Almosencommission*) of the *Congregazione* whose special duty is outdoor relief, and the *Congregazione* acts quite independently of the city magistracy. When compared with the activity of the *Congregazione*, the special work of the city magistracy falls far behind.

In Galicia, where the charitable institutions and societies have, up to the present time, succeeded in defending themselves from the ignorance of city governments, the communes have not established any systems of poor relief worthy of mention. Cracow does not even have a separate committee on poor relief, but the necessary work is done in the city council and in the magistracy, by the committee on registration and military. In Lemberg a committee of the common council and special commissions superintend all poor relief, with help from the magistracy. Besides, the city presidents possess, in both places, unusually broad legal powers as to granting support, alms, etc. There are also in Lemberg several subsidized semi-municipal institutions for indoor relief which are strictly denominational.

Of all the Austrian domain, Buchowina is the province which has advanced least in the organization of its poor relief. With the exception of the chief city, this province lacks even the necessary agencies for administering poor relief. In Czernowitz there is, beside the poor relief maintained by the city with the help of the poor council and almoners, a so-called Christian Charitable Institution (*Armeninstitut*), under the supervision of a purely honorary commission. This commission is composed of the mayor, all Christian ministers, and five Christian citizens, and meets under the chairmanship of the Greek-Oriental archbishop. The object of this institution is the assistance of all needy Christian inhabitants of Czernowitz (whether entitled to settlement or not) from income derived from its funds and from voluntary contributions. Besides, Czernowitz has a hospital erected jointly by the city and the savings bank, and under the joint management of a mixed commission.

After this short survey of a hundred years' development of the organization of poor relief in communes, it will be necessary only to mention the fact that lately, in 1889, the Elberfeld system, which is of such inestimable benefit in the German empire, was introduced in Trautenau and Reichenberg. This system has been eminently successful in its attempt to call forth in the citizens themselves a lively interest in the management of their poor relief; and beside the individualization of special cases, it has secured a more rational employment of available means and thereby relieved the charity budget of the commune.

The relative functions of the higher units of government, namely, districts, states and empire, in the organization of poor relief, will be treated later.

II.—*The Law of Settlement.*

The right to claim support from a commune depends on two conditions : first, poverty, and second, settlement (*Heimathberechtigung*) in a commune. The state laws call those persons poor who are not able by their own efforts or means to procure for themselves and their families the necessaries of life. It must be stated here that the duty of a commune to support its poor who are entitled to settlement is conditional only, and can be assumed only when no one else is obliged by law to take it upon themselves. If these persons have means and decline to fulfil their obligations, they are liable, in case of refusal, to be compelled to do so by legal measures. But in the meantime the commune must assume the care of the poor, retaining the right to demand reimbursement for its expenditure from those whose duty it is to pay. The law of settlement of 1863 makes the following regulations in regard to obtaining the right of settlement. Only citizens of the empire can acquire the right of settlement in a commune. Every citizen of the empire may become entitled to the right of settlement in a commune, but it can belong to him in one commune only. This right is based upon (1) birth, (2) marriage, (3) admission into a commune (*Heimathsverband*), or (4) appointment to public office.

Legitimate children are entitled to the right of settlement in that commune in which the father was entitled to it at the time of their birth, or in case he had died previous to their birth, in that commune in which he had obtained this right at the time of his death. Illegitimate children have the right of settlement in the commune in which their mother had the right at the time of their birth. Legitimized children, in so far as they have no right of settlement of their own, acquire the right in the commune in which their father at the time of their legitimation held it. The right of settlement is not established by the adoption of a child or by assuming its care. By marriage women acquire the right of settlement in the commune in which the husband has acquired the right.

The right of settlement is also acquired by admission to domicile in a commune. The commune itself decides upon applications for admission without appeal. Admission to domicile, however, cannot be limited to a certain time, nor can it be granted under conditions limiting the privileges granted by the law of settlement. The special object of this is to prevent waiver of right of support which may, perhaps, be claimed later.

Duly commissioned court, government, and public treasury officials, ecclesiastics and public instructors acquire this right of settlement, at the time of their entrance upon their public duties, in the commune in which they have been assigned a permanent official residence.

In case of change of settlement, a married woman, if she has not been divorced, follows the husband, and retains, even as widow, the right of settlement in the commune in which at the time of his death her husband had acquired his right. Married women who have been divorced or separated by law retain the right of settlement which they held at the time of the legal divorce or separation. If a marriage is declared illegal, the woman is restored to the right of settlement to which she was entitled at the time of her marriage.

In case of change of settlement of parents, legitimate and legitimized children follow the father, and illegitimate the mother, if they have no right of settlement of their own. The children, however, who have a right of their own retain the right of settlement in the commune in which they acquired it. Illegitimate children who have not been legitimized at the time of the marriage of their mother retain the right of settlement which they had at the time of the marriage, provided they had not then acquired a right of their own. The right of settlement in one commune becomes invalid when settlement is acquired in another.

Under provisions mentioned below, persons without settlement, that is, those whose right of settlement cannot be proved at once, are assigned to a commune in which they may have a quasi-right until their proper place of settlement has been ascertained or until they have acquired a right elsewhere. This assignment to other communes takes place in the following order: 1, to the commune in which the pauper was living at the time of his assignment to or voluntary entrance into the army; 2, to the commune in which he lived, uninterruptedly and at liberty, at least a half-year previously, or if he has lived within that period in several communes, to the one where he last lived; 3, to the commune in which he was born; or in case of a foundling, in the one in which he was found; or in case of a person who is or has been under the care of a public foundling institution and whose birthplace or place of finding is unknown, to the commune in which the institution is situated ; 4, to the commune in which he was at the time of claiming the right of settlement.

Wives of men without settlement and such of their children as have no right of their own, but live with them as members of the family, are assigned to the same communes as the men themselves.

The claim to support which the right of settlement gives to a poor person cannot by law be enforced against his commune. If by reason of refusal of aid, or of the method of dispensing relief, he considers himself ill treated, his only resource is to go to the council of state for help. A commune may make a grant of aid dependent on residence in its territory ; but by the laws of certain states this condition is waived if the pauper is confined to the commune in which he is living in order to gain a livelihood, or if on account of sickness he is unable to travel, or if it is merely a question of temporary assistance, or if to support him in his own commune would be more expensive.

III.—*Provisions for Public Poor Relief.*

A commune is required to wholly support its own poor or to give them aid. Support (*Versorgung*) includes the entire maintenance of a poor person, and must begin when there is a total inability, through absolute lack of means, to obtain a livelihood or to pay for the necessaries of life. Aid (*Unterstützung*), on the contrary, includes such necessaries of life as a poor man cannot obtain for himself by his own exertions or means, or by help from other sources. Support and aid are continuous or temporary according to whether a poor man's inability or need of assistance is permanent or occasional. A poor man cannot demand a particular kind of support or aid ; but in the selection of different methods of relief considerations of humanity must be taken into account. The following different methods of poor relief are in operation : 1, placing in almshouses; 2, aiding with money or in kind ; 3, boarding-out (*Privatpflege*) ; 4, billeting of paupers (*Armeneinlage*) ; 5, care of the sick ; 6, providing transportation. With children, the care of their education is assumed.

By state laws, poorhouses are declared to be an urgent necessity in an organized system of poor relief, and their erection is distinctly enjoined upon the commune as a duty. The internal arrangements of these institutions are left to the judgment of the commune, but entire separation of the sexes, prevention of overcrowding in wards,

cleanliness, separation of the sick and of those afflicted with loathsome infirmities, and the obtaining of proper employment for those
still capable of light work, must always be provided for.   Treatment
must be humane, but discipline firm.   In cities a distinction is often
made between city poorhouses (*Bürgerspitäle*) and poorhouses
proper; as the former are intended for the reception of persons who
possess the right of a citizen, the latter chiefly for the reception of
persons having the right of settlement only.   Want of space in these
institutions has led to the custom of paying a money equivalent for
the indoor relief to which they are entitled to persons who are
adjudged eligible for admission into a poorhouse, but for whom room
could not be provided at the time.

Permanent aid in money can be granted only to old and infirm
persons.   This constitutes a kind of poor relief for invalids and the
aged.   Aid in kind is almost entirely limited to temporary aid.   It
consists in clothing, shoes, firewood, food, and sometimes in cities,
tickets for a people's kitchen.

When a poor person is boarded-out at the expense of a commune
he enters the family of the person who supports him, and owes the
latter reverence and obedience.

Billeting, or placing with first one family and then another, still
exists in the Alpine communes where it was formerly the custom.
Those not allowed to receive such aid are: 1, children under fourteen years of age, except when accompanied by a parent who is the
recipient of similar aid ; 2, insane persons, and such blind and sick
persons as are prevented by their infirmities from moving about;
3, married persons who, by accepting such relief against their will,
would be prevented from living together; 4, poor persons afflicted
with a loathsome or contagious disease.   Inmates are obliged to
work in their places of shelter at such occupations as their strength
permits.

The care of the sick incumbent upon a commune includes the procuring of medical aid, of necessary remedies, and providing the course
of treatment prescribed by a physician and adapted to the needs of
the patient.

The care of orphans involves also the appointment of a legal
guardian and supervising the appropriation for education.   The
state administration frequently unites with the communes in the care
of orphans.

Naturalverpflegsstationen instituted lately—in Lower Austria in 1886, in Upper Austria, Styria and Moravia in 1888, in Vorarlberg in 1891, and in Silesia in 1892—come under this head. Their object is to check house and street begging and to lessen the number of tramps, by giving shelter in return for suitable work to the travelling poor who are able-bodied but without employment. As a rule, these stations are erected on the principal highways, and are under the immediate supervision of the commune in which they are situated.

IV.—*Sources of Public Relief.*

The expense of public relief falls mainly on the commune, that is, upon its poor fund, which is administered separately from the other funds of the commune. The revenues of these poor funds may be placed under the following heads:

1. Revenues from the real estate of the poor funds.

2. Income from investments and endowments.

3. A percentage of the gross proceeds of all voluntary public auctions.

4. Fees for admission to membership in the commune in case the commune has the right to charge such a fee.

5. Certain other fees, *i. e.*, fees from licenses for public amusements, for hunting privileges, the dog-tax, fines for keeping coffee and wine rooms open after the legal time of closing, etc.

6. Fines imposed by the commune itself, by the state government or by other public authorities, and merchandise which has been declared forfeit, unless the law has made other provision for their disposition.

7. A third of the property of secular priests or of members of secularized religious orders who have died intestate.

8. Donations, bequests and inheritances.

9. Collections and voluntary contributions.

10. Assessments, taxes for purposes of poor relief.

11. Appropriations by the communes. For if all of these voluntary and legal revenues do not amount to the sum necessary for poor relief in a commune, it must be made up by means of taxes, just as in the case of other expenses of a commune.

It is left to the option of the several communes of the same political district to unite for poor relief with the approval of the political head of the state (*Landeschef*) and of the council of state (*Landesaus-*

schuss). Such a union may embrace all departments of poor relief, or only special branches of it, as poorhouses or hospitals.

In Styria, where, as in Bohemia and Galicia, there are certain autonomic unions of communes under the name of districts* (*Bezirke*), it is the duty of the latter to contract for and pay the charges of a physician or an accoucheur and the cost of remedies for such indigent sick persons as have a right of settlement in a commune of the district and have not been sent to a public hospital.

A district must advance the expenses of sick strangers, with the right to reimbursement from their native commune.

To defray the cost of poor relief, districts have at their disposal: 1, income from capital devoted to poor relief in the district or for certain branches of it, and from endowments of institutions available for such purposes; 2, donations and legacies expressly given for the purpose of district poor relief; 3, legal revenues; 4, voluntary contributions.

In Bohemia, when the necessary expenses of public relief are so great that the commune cannot possibly meet them without straining the resources of its taxable inhabitants, the commune is allowed to resort to the district authorities for payment of the required deficit.

The expense of the relief of the sick poor is chiefly borne by the state treasuries.

The treasury of the state in which the commune of the poor person is situated must be called on to pay expenses incurred for him in a public hospital or in a public foundling institution, when they cannot be collected from his commune. The state treasury must besides compensate a commune for its expenditure in the case of poor persons who have been assigned to it because of their birth in its public lying-in institution. By the laws of several states, the state treasury must pay either in part or entirely for the support of poor persons who are sent to live in a commune pending the establishment of their claim to the right of settlement.

In Lower Austria a special state poor association (*Landesarmen-verband*), with a state poor fund, has been established for the purpose of making restitution to the communes. (Law of February 1, 1885, *L. G. B. No.* 240.)

This includes also, besides the repayments required by the state laws, indemnity in the following cases:

---

* These are to be distinguished from political districts.

1. For the aid and support of the poor who belong to Lower Austria and yet have lived away from their native commune for ten years consecutively, or have never lived in it; in the latter case, however, they are supported only when by birth or marriage they have acquired the right of settlement.

2. The state's poor fund contributes to a sum raised by a combination of communes to defray the common expenses for certain branches of poor relief, especially for the erection and support of poorhouses and hospitals.

By the same law of Lower Austria there was created in every political district an honorary district poor director who superintends the administration of poor relief. By order of the council of state, the duty of reporting and advising on all matters pertaining thereto falls upon this director.

The expenses of the *Naturalverpflegungsstationen* mentioned at the end of the last section are sometimes, as in Silesia, borne immediately by the state; or the communes of a judicial district (*Gerichts-bezirke*) are combined in a union which is responsible for all expenses incurred by its stations.

POOR RELIEF IN VIENNA, AND ITS REFORM.

DR. RUDOLPH KOBATSCH, VIENNA.

[TRANSLATION.]

Prefatory.

A good system of poor relief is the beginning of every earnest social policy.

Vienna is confronted with an event of great significance to its inhabitants, as well as to its administration, namely, the reform of its system of poor relief. It is intended to do away with the antiquated idea of the right of settlement (*Heimatrecht*), the insufficiency of the present charitable institutions, and the perceptible lack of competent charity overseers, and to abolish the scattering of the charity funds and the old order of relief. In their stead a system of poor relief is to be adopted which will be more in accord with modern requirements. There is a pressing need for regulating the relation between communal aid and private charitable societies, of which latter, the imperial city, with its "Viennese golden hearts," has a large number.   This is necessary in order to properly guard against pernicious duplication in charity.   Finally, it will also be necessary to give intelligent attention to preventive measures against pauperism and beggary, and to better provide for the care of pauper children.   Thus an effective and well organized system of poor relief is to be instituted.

In view of this thorough reorganization, which, though it may not be entirely planned, ought nevertheless to be carried to completion, it appeared to the author to be no idle undertaking to bring the present poor relief system to the knowledge of the general public by means of short sketches, and to place before them in the clearest light the individual points in which reform is needed.   The state governments, the magistracies and the communal governments of Austria will also take a lively interest in the approaching reorganization of poor relief in the metropolis of the Empire ; for it may serve to discover a better *modus vivendi* in the intercourse between local poor administrations, wherein the question of support of persons coming and going, and the apportionment of the consequent expense, cuts so important a figure and constitutes a source of constant litigation.

Opportunity was given the author, who has been occupied for a long time as *Conceptsbeamter* in the poor department of Vienna, to obtain an insight into the various branches of poor relief that require reform, and to weigh and criticize the present status of affairs.   As a result of his comparative studies, especially in relation to conditions in Germany, he has come to the conclusion that the evils of the settlement principle (*Heimatsprincip*) cannot be checked by the introduction of domicile relief (*Unterstützungswohnsitz*), in whatever form ; because under domicile relief the question as to whether the pauper should or should not be assisted would depend on other reasons than the simple fact of his known poverty and need, which should be conclusive ; while the cost to those under obligation to give relief would not be less, nor would the work be any simpler.

It follows from this that a radical, effective solution of the pending questions can be effected only by a complete concentration, a nationalization of the charity funds—maintaining, however, a strictly individualizing and more preventive poor relief policy ; and that in the place of the present contributions of communes and states, the actual burden of poor relief should be borne by a general, elastic and progressive poor rate, which, as will be seen in this paper, would entail only a slight advance in the present taxation.

As an important argument against this plan of reform, it will be claimed that, if adopted, still more indigent persons would flock to Vienna from the open country; that as a result the poorer strata of the people would be increased in number; that the opportunities for obtaining work would diminish, and that the expenditure for poor relief would be swelled considerably; that at the same time the smaller communities would obtain a disproportionate relief from the burden, and that the question of the unemployed would assume a still more critical aspect.

At present we are confronted with two opposing policies: the complete adoption of the humanitarian idea, and the policy which considers the community rather than the individual.

In pursuing the former policy, one is obviously guided by the consideration that a measure which involves great loss to a portion, and that a large portion, of the community cannot possibly redound to the real and permanent advantage of society as a whole, especially when this loss means economic and social death; whereas the sacrifice which must be made to prevent or repair the loss requires nothing more than the giving of a small portion of one's worldly goods.

Finally, at the present day, in theory at least, every pauper must be assisted, and it will not be otherwise in the future; but the transportation to the domicile, the pushing from one place to another, the wrangling over indemnities, and the more easy giving of money rather than relief in kind, and other inadequacies of the charity system, might be removed. And to do this, would not any one be willing to pay the slight cost and to pay it gladly?

Löning has truly said in Schönberg's *"Handbuch"** that the experiment of dividing the burden of poor relief according to the principle of equivalents for profit gained must be abandoned, because the basis of public poor relief does not consist in letting such persons as have brought profit to a community by their economic activity receive when disabled an equivalent therefor; furthermore, that it is the state which directs poor relief and is best fitted to intrust its administration to the proper agencies.†

* 3rd edition, Part III, p. 995.

† Compare relief of pauper children, asylums for the insane and feeble-minded, etc. See also the very instructive article by Dr. Rauchberg, "*Zur*

If the state would apply itself to a good and straightforward policy in all the spheres of social activity, it would be possible for a city to prosper and grow stronger even with the increased .influx of the rural population (who are mostly of the better kind) in search of work. Why should Vienna fear an eventual rapid increase in population, when Budapest is being pushed forward by every possible means to the rank of a metropolis, when Paris and Berlin are growing by an influx of population,* and when in all other places where no crusade, open or secret, is carried on against free emigration, nor a European Chinese-wall system advocated, the expenditures for poor relief are not relatively increasing.

As to the details of the reform, attention is invited to the paper itself. That it contains more censure than praise must be explained by the fact that the existing conditions create an urgent need of criticism. Therefore we want no superficial policy, but a combat with visor open.

I.

General bases of the Austrian Poor Law ; Settlement ; Domicile Relief ; Lower Austrian Law of February 1, 1885 ; Nationalization and a general Poor Tax.

It is rumored—and the newspaper reports about it increase from day to day—that steps are again being taken to reform the poor relief system of Vienna. To judge from what has been published,† it appears that at this time also only a partial reform of the poor laws is contemplated, namely, an application of the Elberfeld, or as far as I can learn, of the Berlin system to Vienna. The entire reconstruction, however, of these important social institutions, and above all the thorough revision of the settlement law of 1863, the question of providing work, workhouses, newly framed poor laws, consolidation of the many large and small funds, etc., all these will for the present remain in suspense.

But even if the proposed reform were effected, which is earnestly to be desired, only one, though a very important feature of the German system would be adopted, namely, the individualization of poor

---

Kritik des österreichischen Heimatsrechtes," in the *Oesterreichische Zeitschrift für Volkswirthschaft, Socialpolitik und Verwaltung*, Vol. II, part I, p. 87 ff.

  * The natural increase of population in Vienna from 1881 to 1890 was 9.54 per cent. ; the increase by immigration only 6.15 per cent.

  † See, for instance, the *Neue Freie Presse*, March 30, 1893.

relief, with obligatory gratuitous service on the part of overseers. It is doubtful whether all the other deficiencies of the present relief system will be removed by this means.

To be sure, it is not possible to determine beforehand with absolute certainty which system of poor relief would be the best and would serve as the only perfect model for all poor laws.

The best of all would probably be no poor relief at all; that is to say, such a perfect social policy as to all the economic conditions closely allied to poor relief—protection and insurance of artisans, manual and intellectual laborers, complete development of benefit societies (*Genossenschaften*), guardianship laws (*Entmündigungs-gesetze*), etc., that the causes of poverty would disappear. But these ideals can hardly even be approached in the present state of society. We can see besides that in every country and city—in each according to its respective national and traditional local customs—the same end may be striven for, and if at all possible, attained. It will, however, scarcely be denied that in order to secure the prosperous development of the energies and the desired application of the means which are now and then given to the service of poor relief, certain general requirements are absolutely essential—requirements which may be stated about as follows : that poverty which is known (inability to work, lack of employment, incapacity for self-support, sickness, loss of parents, etc.) entitles to aid as such, regardless of settlement or duration of residence; unity and comprehensiveness of administration, support and aid ; adequate funds and a sufficient number of charitable agencies ; special fitness of persons who come into immediate contact with the poor for their calling ; the differentiation of persons totally unfit to work, whether permanently, temporarily, or both, from those who are only partially disabled, as well as from those who are afraid of and unwilling to work on the one hand, and from those able to and anxious for work, but who for reasons beyond their control are out of employment, on the other ; furthermore, strict individualization, direct investigations as often as possible as to the means and income of the pauper, the causes of his poverty, possibly his illness, etc. ; constant guarding over, and the strictest measures that may be socially justifiable, against "afraid-of-works" and professional beggars, and especially exhaustive care of pauper children of every kind and of indigent young persons.

For many reasons, Vienna poor relief, with its abundant means and countless private benevolent associations, has not been able to take this position.

In order that we may judge as to these deficiencies and the thorough reforms that are necessary, the following sketch of the existing provisions governing Vienna poor relief is given.

The excellent and exhaustive description of the Austrian poor relief system in the *Handwörterbuch der Staatswissenschaften*,* by Baron von Call, relieves us of the task of explaining the Viennese municipal poor relief. It will suffice to say that in Austria the right of a citizen of a state to poor relief or aid follows from his right of settlement in any Austrian commune. The duty of the commune extends only to persons entitled to the right of settlement therein, whether they have made their residence ("the centre of their economic energy") there or not. The only conditions are that the person must have no relatives (parents, children or husband) who are able and in duty bound to assist him, and that he has no other private or legal claims that may be made good. In the latter case the commune is bound to care for the pauper until his possible claim may be settled. The commune itself has the right of determining the kind and amount of aid to be given, and this may be limited to the relief of urgent wants only. The commune may legally compel unemployed able-bodied persons without means of support to work according to their physical ability, as a return for the aid extended, whether in money or in kind.

The communes must provide for sick persons either in public institutions or private houses, and provide medical aid, attendance and medicine. Orphaned and deserted children must be raised and taught a trade at the expense of the commune, the latter appointing a guardian over them. In case the child afterwards comes into the possession of an estate, the commune has a right to enter a claim against it for expenses incurred. The commune may prosecute this claim to indemnity in the state courts and not before a civil tribunal, although the rulings of the supreme court of Austria in this matter are not definite. In this respect also there would have to be a change in the new settlement law, or better still in the poor law, so that there would be a shorter way to the settlement of claims for indemnity on the part of communes or, in case of nationalization of poor relief, on the part of the state. For social political reasons, however, this would apply only in case the estate in question is of sufficient importance, and not when such an estate devolves upon

* Vol. I, pp. 862 ff.

the assisted person; then it would only be necessary to discontinue the relief.

Let us now turn to the discussion of points requiring reform in the Austrian settlement law (of 1863) as far as they relate to the duty of communes to extend relief to the poor. First of all, it must be remarked that the social-economic conditions upon which these regulations are based have changed, and one might say, broadened, perceptibly. The former close connection between a commune and its members has not existed for a long time. Since the right of unrestricted emigration has been recognized, since the enormously increased industrial activity has driven the rural population into the cities, and industrial competition, on the other hand, requires the people to remove from one city to another, the traditional attributes of communes have disappeared and have given place to a new order of things. It would be digressing to speak in this connection of the effects which this inland migration has exercised and still exercises over the well-being of the individual districts. It must be acknowledged as a fact, however, that poverty and its attendant conditions, particularly in large cities, are caused by the economic life there and do not, therefore, affect small communes which send their inhabitants year after year to the centres of trade and industry.

As, therefore, the poverty in cities is bound up with their economic life, the burden of poor relief should fall on the cities.* Instead of this natural order of things, the duty of giving poor relief devolves in Austria upon the place of settlement. For instance, community A may be obliged to aid, and even receive in its poorhouse, husband, wife, children and grandchildren, even though they have lived for decades in community B. The few departures from this ancient principle which the settlement law recognizes (§§18 ff.) come up very rarely in practice. Thus arise the cruel vexations instead of benefits, the nonsensical and often tedious negotiations, after which the commune of settlement either refuses all aid to the pauper, or if his right of settlement can at all be proven or is acknowledged, requires his removal (*Abschiebung*) or transportation home (*Heimbeförderung*). We then witness the disgraceful settlement proceedings, during the progress of which the applicant for aid may either die of starvation or become a beggar, vagabond or criminal, or at best may obtain temporary aid of the most trifling nature out

---

* Not exclusively, for the country and state are as much interested in the economic destinies of large cities as the cities themselves.

of funds provided for the purpose by such sensible philanthropists as have devoted their donations simply to the poor of Vienna without regard to rights of settlement.

It need not be demonstrated how perniciously these things act upon the so-called *morale* of charity. But among the people the opinion prevails that one can, by many years of residence, attain a real natural right—and more than this, a social right. Let us illustrate the sad consequences which this system of poor relief carries with it. A man, otherwise honorable, will not marry a girl whom he loves and with whom he is living, because she and her children would thereby lose their precious right of settlement in Vienna. In another case, two persons will not marry for the reason that the man or the woman draws a pension from the municipality of Vienna, and the marriage of the pensioner would cut off the allowance. Why is this so? The *rationale* of these grounds for cancellation is difficult to understand. It may have been thought that marriage might be used as a means of obtaining settlement privileges, or it may have been thought that if persons marry they ought to have the necessary means. These are certainly no valid reasons. Let us examine more closely. In 1890, out of a total population of 817,299 in Vienna, only 301,035, or about 36 per cent. were entitled to right of settlement. In 1890, 5157 persons were sent away because they were not entitled to right of settlement. Of these, 2953 were over 24 years of age, and 2110 were sent away on account of lack of means of subsistence.

The expenditures incurred for all this were certainly not justifiable, and the social effects of these measures were exceedingly doubtful. There was not wanting a perception of these unhealthy conditions; they simply acted *praeter legem*, or even *contra legem*, rightly remembering, "*summum jus, summa injuria.*" But the result was that matters only became more complicated and complaints universal. The somewhat stereotyped poor law of Vienna (we shall return to the needed reforms in detail later on) was to a great extent made practically inoperative, and most of the corrections were made in order to repair to some extent the injury done by the settlement law. Pending the trial of a claim for settlement, the claimant was given financial aid at regular intervals out of general funds, etc., although this could be given only once in six months. If a pensioner married notwithstanding the prohibition of marriage, his allowance was cut off for a month or two and then resumed.

Those not having the right of settlement were gladly sent to their homes; as far as the law affecting removals (*Schubgesetz*) did not prevent, they were even given money to pay their travelling expenses —only to be found back in Vienna again in a short time.

Even the Lower Austrian law of February 1, 1885, regarding the establishment of a national poor association did not have the desired effect. Vienna was especially to be relieved, in that the national association was to reimburse communes for expenses incurred, especially in case of persons who were sent to a commune by virtue of their birth in a public lying-in hospital situated within its boundaries, or of their having resided there in accordance with §19 of the settlement law, or who, on account of an uninterrupted absence of over 10 years from their (Lower Austrian) commune, practically never lived there. But cases of the first kind rarely occur, and even the provisions for the latter, well worked out as they were in theory, resulted in no important relief to the poor funds of Vienna; for the number of cases where assistance was granted in accordance with the law of 1885, that is, transferred from Vienna to the national association, amounted to only 3040 during the first half of 1891, with an expense of 103,563 florins, and 3190 cases costing 107,185 florins during the first half of 1892. This is scarcely 5 per cent. of the sum which the city of Vienna expended in 1890 (2,244,520 florins) for pensions, orphans, etc., and homes for the aged. It is considerably less than the money distributed by the municipality of Vienna to pensioners residing outside the city, but who have not lived away from it continuously for ten years, and therefore still retain their right of settlement in Vienna. There were, of this class, 5845, receiving 225,008 florins.

But this law was not beneficial even to the poor themselves. Of 817,299 persons living in Vienna in 1890, there were 301,035 (36.8 per cent.) natives, and only 87,978 (10.7 per cent.) persons belonging to Lower Austrian communes. On the other hand, there were 428,286 (52.4 per cent.) whose settlement, that is, right to relief when destitute, was in other parts of Austria or in foreign countries. The number of paupers among the 87,978 Lower Austrians was relatively smaller than among the 428,286 individuals belonging to Bohemia, Galicia, Hungary, Croatia, etc.; it therefore follows that in order to really alleviate the hardships of the settlement principle and to relieve the city to any appreciable extent, this law would have to be extended to cover the rest of the crown lands, and the number of years would have to be reduced from ten to five (as in the German empire it is desired to raise the period necessary to acquire the right to domicile relief from two to five years), if the settlement principle is to be maintained. Furthermore, it would not be necessary to be so strict in regard to the proof of uninterrupted residence of the ten or five years, as the Lower Austrian committee of state has been.

The important question now arises, what system can be adopted in place of the settlement principle? There are several ways of proceeding. The one which we would most naturally adopt in Austria would be the German method, that is, the system of domicile relief. Let us first see what objections have been made to this system.

It is quite evident that everything did not at once change for the better with the enactment of the German law of June 6, 1870, whereby the Prussian system of relief at place of residence was extended to Saxony and the South German countries. First of all, demands were made that instead of domicile relief the burden of poor relief should fall upon the larger autonomous bodies, the states and the empire.

The defenders of the existing German poor law* were opposed by the claim that the communes of domicile try to evade the duty of giving relief by transporting applicants, because the two years' term of acquiring residence with poor relief privileges often leads to great expense which is generally not economically justifiable; for there is no due proportion between a sojourn of only two years in a commune and a presumably unlimited obligation to aid. It was claimed that the period necessary to acquire the right to relief should be generally a longer one. Furthermore, it was maintained, as was emphasized in the recent debates in the Reichstag on the amendments to the present law, that no one could become entitled to domicile relief in his own right until after his twenty-fourth year. Against the nationalization of poor relief is urged the injustice to the pauper, in that in case of continued inability to earn a livelihood he may be returned to his commune of residence, is accompanied by disproportionate expense. It is claimed that the poor who are supported by the state are just the ones who have contributed toward the increase of the spirit of restlessness.

Of the many amendments that have been proposed, varying from the reintroduction of the settlement principle to the complete adop-

---

* See Löning *a. a. O.* and the *Handwörterbuch für Staatswissenschaften*, "*Armenwesen*."

tion of relief at place of residence, the most practical appears to us to be that which seeks to draw on the larger political bodies for the entire or partial burden of expense, whether it be with reference only to persons permanently disabled, or to all persons receiving relief outside their poor law domicile. In general, it might be well to try to avoid as much as possible the intricate system of dividing the expenditures into fourths and thirds, and to levy a poor tax on the commune, district, country, and eventually even the state, according to the *per capita* of population, the proportion to be determined by the average number of persons assisted during a term of years. And this leads us to the consideration of another way of reforming the Vienna poor relief (one which we can think of only in ' connection with the Austrian relief system as a whole), namely, the question of putting the burden of contribution on the states and the empire, as well as to the question of the poor rate.

If we look at England, Sweden, and other countries which cover their expenses for poor relief by means of a poor rate (besides state contributions, funds, bequests, etc.), the thought of an elastic poor tax will not seem so dreadful as may at first appear. The right to poor relief should not be established against a commune either by reason of settlement or of a long or a short residence there, but because it had its origin in a social economic disease which consumes state, province and commune; it should be based solely upon actual want. The duty of poor relief is incumbent upon the people as a whole, and as such they should raise the means.

The poor statistics of Austria are too incomplete to make it possible to ascertain the amount expended annually for the poor in the whole empire. The publications of the Royal Imperial Statistical Central Commission show only the expenditures for maintenance, and those only for special cases of poor relief. We find the following expenditures for the year 1889:

For orphanages, children's asylums, etc.............. fl.	1,067,381
For (3) workhouses (*Arbeitsanstalten*)	41,080
For homes (*Versorgungsanstalten*).....................	3,067,203
For poorhouses (*Armeninstituten*).....................	4,682,996
Total .... fl.	8,858,660

This is evidently much too small an amount; and to be convinced of this one need only compare it with the Vienna charity budget. In

1890 the expenditure from public funds for poor relief amounted, in round numbers, to 5½ million florins, or over 65 per cent. of the sum for the whole empire.

It will therefore be hardly possible by such an inductive method to fix even approximately the total expenditure for poor relief in Austria. We shall therefore endeavor to supply the figures by deduction or analogy. The following table will serve this purpose:*

State and Year to which figures relate.	Total expenditure for charity purposes.	Per 100 inhabitants.		Cost *per capita* of persons aided.	
		Amount.	Number assisted.	Absolute.	Omitting cost of administration.
Germany (1885).......	90,282,160 M.	190 M.	2–5	36–57 M.	
Berlin	7,318,760 M.	556 M.		91.5 M.	
Italy (1880)	81,496,000 l.	260–302 l.			
France (1881–1885): *Bureaux de bienfaisance* Hospitals and alms-houses (*Établissements hospitaliers*)...........	33,620,000 fr. 108,985,000 fr.	89 fr. 288 fr.		22 fr.	18.7 fr.
Total..............	142,605,000 fr.	Av. 189 fr.			
England (1881–1885) .. Direct expenditures.	£15,080,168 8,316,000	£30	2–3	The poor rate in 1883 was 6 per ct. of the revenue from real estate.	
Austria (1881–1885), maintenance........	6,213,000 fl.	30 fl.	1–2		16.5–65 fl.

The above data, especially the comparative figures, do not of course admit of any very conclusive deductions as to a greater or less degree of poverty, or as to the greater or less expense of charity in the countries mentioned. But for Austria, whose expenses are reckoned far too low at 6¼ million florins, an approximation may be made from the German budget. The figures relating to England and France cannot well be used for comparison on account of the great economic differences between those countries and the empire on the Danube.

The population of the German empire is about double that of Austria (50 as against 24 millions). There would then be for Austria

* Compiled on the basis of statistics given in the *Handwörterbuch für Staatswissenschaften.*

a total expenditure of 45 million marks or 27 million florins for charitable purposes. Of course the inhabitants of Austria would then be taxed 0.95 mark or 0.57 florin *per capita*, instead of 0.30 florin. But 0.30 does not by any means represent the true quota, as it is obtained only from the amount spent in relief; and if the cost of administration, with the present division of means and energies, were added, we should have to increase the quota to at least 0.50 florin.

But we do not recommend the introduction of the system of domicile relief, and we rather believe that with the centralization of the poor funds as suggested, the cost of poor relief would be considerably reduced and the pauper would be assisted promptly and thoroughly.

At any rate, the resulting total amount (after deducting all existing funds, trusts, investments, etc., which would have to be converted into national property administered by the communes under the control of the states), would be allotted as a poor tax among the states and communes according to the abovementioned criteria. These would then levy upon the inhabitants in the shape of a progressive income tax, leaving a considerable minimum exempt from taxation. In Vienna where the community must annually expend from 900,000 to 1,300,000 florins for poor relief, this would mean for the inhabitants an increase of 3.3 per cent. in the tax rate—certainly an endurable "tightening of the taxation screws." And this might be reduced if the charity system itself were more rational and the management of it more simple.

II.

Poor Relief Regulations in Vienna ; Overseers of the Poor.

While considering the subject of comprehensive changes in the Austrian charity system, before we discuss the actual administration of poor relief and the charity budget of Vienna, it is proper, in my opinion, to present first the concrete details of the Vienna poor laws, and the complete mechanism of the various forms of relief work, especially as an early reform of parts is far more probable than the reform of the whole.

By virtue of the provisions of the settlement law, the municipality of Vienna has drawn up its own " Regulations for poor relief in the charity districts of Vienna " (last edition, 1888). By their aid we shall now enter upon the discussion of the details of Vienna poor relief.

The city of Vienna forms a charity district, uniformly governed by magistrates, who are controlled by an elective municipal council (*Gemeinderath*). The business management of every municipal district (there were formerly 10, now 19) is conducted through the "charity office." Each charity office divides its activities among several precincts, and the affairs of each precinct are entrusted to the care of an overseer (*Armenrath*). The office is in charge of a general manager (*Institutsvorsteher*), assisted by from one to three officials. The services of the overseers of the poor are given voluntarily and without compensation. Any male resident having a right of settlement in Vienna, and of unblemished character, of whom it is known that he would like to hold this office from a philanthropic feeling, and that he is capable of discharging it, may be elected. Guardians for orphans are elected in the same way.

The overseer of a precinct, who is elected by the district board (*Bezirksvertretung*), is required to recommend for aid only such persons as are really in need, and he must avoid any improper taxing of the relief fund. If a pauper applies for aid to his proper overseer, it is the duty of the latter to convince himself by personal investigation, made "with tact and kindness," that the applicant is in need. In cases of pressing necessity he is to take proper action as promptly as possible. To impudent, lazy, and professional applicants he must firmly refuse assistance. At intervals, but at least twice a year, he is to look after all the poor in his district.

Aid may be given once without an examination of the applicant. If, however, it is a case of a person returning periodically, or a temporary or permanent pension, the overseer must make an investigation and enter the result upon a special blank form. This, together with other documents and reports relating to the case, he must lay before the next charity conference, which must be convened at least once a month, or if there is danger in delay, he must at once turn the papers over to the chairman of the charity office of his district for further action. The decisions of the conferences are transmitted monthly, the single cases at any time, as special reports, to the charity department of the magistracy. This department has power to determine the legality of all grants of pensions, etc., or of admissions into asylums; so the decrees of the magistracy have to pass through a rather long course, as follows: after they have been signed by the poor commissioner they pass through the charity register for entry or revision of the registry sheet; then having passed through the bookkeeping department for entry upon the records kept there by districts, and for the issue of pension books, which are evidence of the right to pensions, they finally arrive in the engrossing room, whence they are sent to the respective charity offices. The actual payments of pensions take place at the district charity offices near the end of each month. The time therefore which elapses between the first application and the final settlement of the matter amounts to an average of from two to three months under the most favorable conditions, and even in cases of special reports, which are rare and fall to the lot of only the more fortunate poor, it takes three to four weeks.

This exact presentation of the course of business will certainly not seem entirely superfluous, for it shows, in the first place, the bureaucratic methods of Vienna poor relief, and then it furnishes a negative illustration of the old proverb, "*Bis dat, qui cito dat.*" The process of engrossing, and even the recording of the decisions, could be dispensed with without injury; the filling in of the convenient pension book would be quite sufficient.

Now as regards poor relief itself, the law defines as "poor" such persons as can no longer meet the most pressing needs of life.

This legal minimum of existence is even specified in figures—an unjustifiable application of arithmetic in social legislation. It is specified that in order to obtain a permanent pension, the applicant must not be in receipt of any income whatever the total amount of which equals or exceeds 5 florins a month or 60 florins a year.

But a pauper cannot make good his claim for assistance as a matter of right except through the tedious course prescribed by municipal ordinances. These declare poor relief to be a public legal right,* whereas we have already alluded to decisions to the contrary by the supreme court. The latter has declared the granting of a pension to be "in the nature of a wasteful loan" (*vorschussweise geleisteter Aufwand*) according to §1042 *a. b. G. B.*

The second requisite for obtaining a pension, etc., is, as was shown, the settlement right. It is just in the largest city of the empire that the hardships which the settlement principle carries with it are most sharply brought to light. Those who are not entitled to settlement

---

* In like manner the German law recognizes the duty of the charity unions to give relief, and consequently the right of the state to compel these unions (*Verbände*) to fulfil that duty.

rights (immigrant laborers and artisans) are among the poorest classes of the capital. They cannot acquire settlement because they cannot afford to pay the necessary taxes, which vary in amount according to the duration of residence in Vienna,* and are relatively very high, and would occasion besides much trouble and loss of time.

The settlement law, cited in the above paragraph, is rarely applied where certain conditions under which homeless persons may be referred to their places of settlement are prescribed; and when it is so applied it is done under protest. It even happens that for a short time aid may be refused to a pauper who has only recently acquired the right of settlement. The idea appears to be, that if one has lived a considerable time in Vienna he should acquire a right of settlement. But how can a person without means do this, when there is no gradation in taxation? And if a poor person has finally acquired settlement he is, forsooth, turned away because he has only just gained his right. The municipality acts from a correct standpoint, economically—for the settlement law amounts to very little socially.

But there are serious faults also in the organization of the overseers of the poor. First of all, the number is too small. The table opposite will show the necessity for reform in this respect.†

It appears, in the first place, from the above data, that 3.91 per cent. (maximum 5.32 per cent., minimum 1.64 per cent.) of those having the right of settlement were assisted by means of pensions, education and orphans' allowances, not including those receiving financial aid on single occasions, or who were admitted to homes for the aged, or placed under medical care. If we add the 4,072 persons in the various homes, the proportion will be raised to six per cent. The figures for those receiving medical attention or financial aid on single occasions cannot be used here because, as they appear in the Vienna statistical annual, there is no way of determining how often assistance was given to the same persons and making the necessary deductions.

We find furthermore in the above table‡ that, on an average, there

---

* For 20 years residence, 10 florins; for 10 years, 50 florins; for 5 years, 100 florins; and for immediate acquirement, 200 florins.

† The data for the new districts, which are not yet officially published, would scarcely alter the result for the better.

‡ The forms of assistance enumerated in the table do not cover the whole, but include at any rate the most important work of the overseers.

Districts.	Population, December 31, 1890.	Persons having settlement in Vienna.		1890. Persons receiving		Recipients in general.		Area in Hectares.	Number of regular overseers.	Under one overseer.	
		Number.	Percentage.	Pensions.	Orphans' pensions and allowances for education.	Total number.	Percentage of total having settlement.			Number of recipients.	Hectares.
I	67,029	26,625	39.72	405	31	436	1.64	283	32	13.6	8.8
II	158,372	39,582	24.99	942	261	1,203	3.04	2,940	65	18.5	45.0
III	110,279	40,499	36.72	1,266	220	1,486	3.67	604	72	20.6	8.3
IV	59,135	24,678	41.73	655	132	787	3.18	179	47	16.8	3.8
V	84,031	34,494	41.05	1,390	405	1,795	5.20	254	58	30.9	4.4
VI	63,901	28,737	44.97	1,013	191	1,204	4.18	138	43	28.0	3.1
VII	69,859	33,608	48.11	1,178	212	1,390	4.13	145	59	23.6	2.4
VIII	48,976	22,438	45.81	981	214	1,195	5.32	104	46	25.9	2.2
IX	81,170	32,864	40.49	1,142	297	1,439	4.38	264	57	25.2	4.6
X	74,547	17,510	23.49	512	272	784	4.47	625	47	16.6	13.3
Citizen Pensions,	..		..	2,295	..	..	..	..	..	..	
Total....	817,299	301,035	36.83	11,779	2,235	14,014	3.91	5,540	526	26.0	10.5

are 26 assisted persons (the extremes being 30.9 and 13.6) and an area of 10.5 hectares to one overseer. This figure is decidedly large. About the same averages appear for the years 1891 and 1892, although nine new precincts have been added, among them being those with a poorer population.

There is an urgent necessity for an increase in the number of charity overseers and orphans' guardians to at least 2,000, or about fourfold, so that in future there will be seven assisted persons to one charity overseer. Aside from the absolute increase in number, the present inequalities in regard to the area and population of the precincts would have to be obviated. In small District I one charity overseer looks after 13 to 14 persons, while in District II, which is ten times as large, 18 to 19 are under the care of one overseer. In District V, which is about as large as the inner city, 31 persons fall to one overseer, or three times as many as in District I. Again, when an overseer becomes ill or leaves the service the business is blocked, because the election of a successor cannot be held promptly and another overseer cannot be doubly burdened. The question, therefore, arises, what shall be the future position of overseers of the poor and guardians of orphans? Shall it be obligatory? Shall compensation be provided? Shall there be a penalty for a refusal to accept the office? In my judgment, there would be no need of compensation if a sufficient number of overseers were provided for—say one for 6 to 7 individuals or families, especially as each overseer would be relieved of part of his burden through such a reform. On the other hand, if a person had any scruples about accepting this honorary office, he could be punished by an increase of his municipal taxes (*Gemeindeumlagen*), or a limitation of his right of suffrage. Of course, these reforms must be made without affecting rights of citizenship in the state, but in a strictly legal way, quite apart from the fact that they would otherwise meet with much opposition in the municipal council.

The Berlin system could thus be imitated. There, any voting citizen is in duty bound to accept a position in the municipal administration without pay, and to hold office at least three years. If he retires from the same without having a legitimate excuse,* he can be made to forfeit his rights of citizenship for from three to six years and to pay a higher rate of municipal taxation.

---

* Such would naturally have to be specified in the Vienna law also.

It may be remarked that with the fourfold increase in the number of overseers (6 or 7 paupers to one overseer), we should still fall far below the Elberfeld ideal; for the latter assigns only four persons or families to one overseer, and, in fact, often entrusts only two or three persons to his care.

Finally, we ought also to reflect whether we should not draw women into the charity service, especially for the care of women and children. We find the same deficiency in the number of orphan-mothers (*Waisenmütter*), while outdoor relief (orphan pensions, education allowances) is exclusively undertaken by men.

There should also be some regulation as to the occupations of the charity overseers. Of the 850 charity overseers (in round numbers) for 1893, 220 are engaged in supplying necessary food products (dealers in produce, milk and meat, innkeepers, coffee merchants, etc.); 143 in the manufacture and sale of articles of clothing and furniture; while only 104 belong to the higher professions. In consequence of this there is a possibility, and there seems to be even a probability, of the employment of paupers at insufficient wages payable in kind, of which the poor themselves as well as disinterested persons have complained.

The number of physicians for the poor (in 1890, 19, and in 1892, 54) should also be considerably increased; the physicians should be better paid, and they should be placed under the control of the city health department and so under the disciplinary power of the magistracy. Physicians should be permitted to express an opinion only in cases of sickness and consequent inability to work, and as to whether the disabilities are permanent or only temporary, total or only partial. The question of ability to gain a livelihood being closely allied to indigence, and a social-economic one, would better be left to the overseers.

One advantage of the individualization of poor relief would be that in cases where poverty was the result of drunkenness, dissipation or want of character of the head or some other member of the family, the facts could be easily and clearly proved; and it would. therefore, be easier to put the paupers at work in a well organized workhouse, as well as to place them under supervision and guardianship. On the other hand, in cases where poverty is due to no fault of the pauper, or if so, in only a slight degree, and where indigence results from a lack of appreciation of the economic conditions, or from direct misfortune, the relief work must be conducted on a broader and especially on a preventive basis.

III.

Temporary Relief.

In regard to poor relief for adults, the law specifies that the aid given shall be in money, provisions, shelter, or employment, according to the peculiar needs of the applicants. In reality, however, the assistance rendered is almost exclusively in the form of money, pensions, or admission to asylums. Relief in kind* or by providing work scarcely ever occurs. This is a decided mistake of the municipal poor relief, for the only refuge† which any one may voluntarily enter is far from being complete enough in its arrangements to serve as a real and sufficient agency for giving work ; and the asylums, the capacity of which is acknowledged to be insufficient, are rarely open to homeless, unemployed young men. As regards financial aid extended on single occasions, there are peculiarly rigid regulations, which must be daily violated if the misery of the numerous applicants is in any degree to be alleviated. This form of assistance can be used only when the distress prevents the gaining of a livelihood by the pauper and his family. The recipient must not enjoy any other income (pension, etc.) beyond an exceedingly small amount. In giving relief it must be noted whether the pauper received any assistance during the last half year for any reason, because the amount given for this form of relief in any one year cannot exceed altogether 15 florins to any one person, man and wife in this case being counted as one. The approval of the magistracy must be obtained by the charity office in every case before this amount can be exceeded. But financial aid is not only given at the charity offices, but also in the charity department of the magistracy, at the mayor's office, at the imperial police headquarters, and at the hospitals. These offices do not come in contact with one another, nor do they have, in general, sufficient opportunity for personal investigations as to the worth of the applicants. No one will doubt that in this way the door is opened to professional beggary and fraud, as well as to

---

* The statistical annual for 1890 states that 3,292 persons received aid in kind at the charity offices, but it does not insert this figure in the tables because "the census is not reliable." In addition to this, there are 300 to 400 persons who annually receive orders for wood to the value of 3,000 florins from the mayor's office ; a further sum of 9,000 to 12,000 florins is annually expended for relief in kind distributed at the precinct agencies.

† See the *Werkhaus,* below, pp. 273 ff.

the refusal of the really worthy but modest poor, and the prohibition
of beggary on the streets is rendered quite illusory. There are,
besides, numerous private charitable societies, which shameless applicants for aid visit as often as they do the municipal or rather public
charity bureaus. Finally, we must remember that there are many
aristocratic and princely personages who are applied to, and sometimes successfully, for alms, and then we can form an idea of how
greatly professional beggary, laziness and vagrancy have been
fostered and constantly kept alive.

The reform in this respect would chiefly consist in giving more
importance to relief in kind and procuring shelter. It is rarely known
what is done with money that is given away. It is not known in the
charity offices, because there are too few overseers, nor in the other
bureaus, because there is there no personal supervision whatever. At
any rate, money and provisions should be delivered only at the resi-
dences of the applicants.* If they have no home, to supply things
that may be moved on single occasions does no good at any rate, the
need in that case being chiefly a safe shelter. One need only look
at other great cities to see how carefully and economically their poor
relief is managed. While, for example, Vienna in 1886 expended
400,000 florins for relief in money, this item in the larger city of
Berlin amounted to only 116,000 florins. The Paris *Bureau de
Bienfaisance* in 1889 distributed altogether 6,800,000 francs.

Of this, the expenditure for bread was	583,900
For other kinds of food	58,570
Total for food	642,470
For fuel	40,940
For clothing, etc.	98,850
Total, in kind	782,260
Relief in money	1,827,540†

The relief in money, therefore, amounted to only 26.8 per cent.
and the relief in kind to 11.5 per cent. of the total expenditure. In
German cities, also, these figures are 35 and 12 per cent. respectively.

* See Dr. L. Kunwald, *Ueber Communalverwaltung und Armenpflege*. Vienna,
1885.

† See *Compte Moral de l'Administration de l'Assistance Publique pour l'Exer-
cice*. 1889. Paris, 1892.

An interesting result of the Vienna system of giving relief in money is the fact that of 27,191 persons assisted by the charity department and the charity offices in 1890, 420 were 20 years of age and under, 1,802 between 20 and 30, 3,946 between 30 and 40. Altogether 5,158 (18.9 per cent.) were of an age when men are usually capable of doing work, and were therefore decidedly not entitled to aid from a social political standpoint. Again in 1890 relief in money was received by 3,375 single, 6,322 married, 2,029 widowed and 54 legally divorced men; and by 2,928 single, 3,491 married, 10,744 widowed and 87 legally divorced women. Unfortunately we are not able to give the reader still further individual statistical data, especially in regard to the personal circumstances of persons temporarily aided in other bureaus, or as to personal facts such as age and family status, because the respective enumerations are missing in the statistical annual.*

An example worthy of imitation is that furnished by the Vienna Society for the Prevention of Pauperism and Beggary (*Verein gegen Verarmung und Bettelei*), which not only gives presents of money, but also makes loans without interest, of which about 40 per cent. are returned annually.

IV.

Pensions; Reasons for Discontinuance; Relief of Pauper Children; Food Distribution; Relief of the Sick; Indemnification; Berlin City Dispensary and Similar Institutions.

On what conditions, then, may a poor man obtain a pension, or admission into an institution? Here the "Regulations" contain some provisions which have to be evaded in practice.

It has been stated that aid amounting to not more than 15 Austrian florins may be given once. If in case of "long-continued illness" of the poor man or of his family, or in other cases of "prolonged distress," this aid proves inadequate, and if he is not entitled to receive a permanent pension, a temporary pension for the probable duration of his need, and amounting to from 2 to 4 florins a month, may be granted.

Larger temporary pensions, equal in amount to permanent ones (8 florins at most), may also be granted, but only in case of special physical infirmities; and then the chief condition precedent to

---

* See particulars later, regarding their significance as poor statistics.

obtaining a permanent pension, *i. e.* that the candidate should be at least 60 years old, may be waived.

The magistracy is required to provide lodging for persons who cannot find a place of abode even with the aid granted them. The question is, " Where?" The institutions are almost full ; certain hard conditions must be complied with in order to procure admission, and no actual rent is paid. Nothing remains except to assist again in money.*

This faulty condition of things shows that an increase in the number of charitable institutions and of wayfarers' lodges, and an extension of indoor poor relief, are absolutely necessary.

Any one wishing to obtain a permanent pension must comply with still greater requirements. Generally he gets it only in case of severe illness ("total inability to make a living ") and at an advanced age (minimum age 60 years—"inability to work "); and if the pension proves insufficient he may be admitted into an institution. Besides this, neither the applicant nor his wife may be any longer a taxpayer in any way, and his yearly income must not amount to more than 60 Austrian florins. At the age of sixty an applicant receives the lowest pension, 2 florins a month, on the express supposition that " he is not yet destitute of all other aid or left entirely to his own resources, but receives some assistance from relatives." At the age of sixty-four his pension is raised to 3 florins a month, at the age of sixty-eight to 4 florins ; 5 florins a month are paid to people of seventy, 6 florins to octogenarians and to those who are blind, cripples, in short to all who are entirely and hopelessly unable to work or to make a living, and to these admission into an institution is offered as an alternative. These institutions may also admit pensioners for pay ; and even persons who are not entitled to the right of settlement on the same basis. The best criticism on these principles is furnished by the practice ; for in practice they have never been carried out to the letter, and never can be. How far in this respect the Vienna poor relief is behind that truly good provision of the Elberfeld system, by which aid is granted on principle for only two weeks! After this time has elapsed a new application or a new request must be made. This

---

* That the private associations for warming-rooms (*Wärmestuben*), shelters, tea and soup-houses, etc., do not provide dwellings for even a single person or family, but only herd the poor people together as in a stable for a few hours or nights, is well known ; these conditions can be improved only by an honest and thorough treatment of the question of improved dwellings.

is one of the points which will need reform when the poor relief of Vienna is freed from the iron bonds of bureaucracy and red tape ; and for this the present head of the community, and councillor Trabauer, the present poor commissioner, are working with great zeal and clear wisdom. Money should not be given to the poor for months and years at a time, subject only to a semi-annual investigation by the overseer,* but only for a short time. For invalids or persons entirely and hopelessly unable to earn a living, institutions are the proper place.

And at the special instigation of the persons mentioned, the city council (*Gemeindevertretung*), either tacitly or by formal resolutions, has done away with the worst red tape and has given scope to freer movement. The 2 florin pensions will be gradually stopped ; for some time, permanent or temporary aid, amounting to from 7 to 8 florins a month, has been given to people under eighty ; and, thanks to the untiring and judicious efforts of the present poor commissioner, the age schedule is beginning to be considered of less importance than the judgment of the city physician for the poor (*Armenarzt*) and the report of the overseer. The latest improvement, for which we are indebted to the same persons, is the addition of 10 and 12 florin pensions to the regular list, though so far this improvement applies only to persons who have been in an institution more than a year, who are entirely unable to work or to make a living, and who are otherwise worthy of the larger pension.

Only citizens of Vienna can receive a pension of 15 florins a month in cases of destitution, and only at a very advanced age and when entirely unable to earn a living ; unfortunately there is only a limited number (600, 400 and 100) of these larger pensions, as of all citizens' pensions (6, 8, 10 and 12 florins a month). We have still to speak of the reasons which may cause the discontinuance of a pension or dismissal from an institution. Eight are enumerated in the " Regulations," five of which, namely, giving up one's claim voluntarily, death of the pensioner, not claiming the pension for three months, commitment to a penal institution, admission into a charitable institution, immoral and indecent habits,† speak for themselves and need no commentary. Not so the other three reasons for discontinuance,

---

* Temporary pensions are generally granted for one or two years, evidently from a desire to escape work.

† In this case, commitment to a penitentiary, a home for drunkards, or a house of correction (*Zwangsarbeitshaus*), etc., must take the place of the pension.

which are in urgent need of being reformed. First of all there is the regulation which provides that on the acquisition of property, or of any source of income, the yearly proceeds of which equal the highest pension (6 florins a month or 72 florins a year), the pension must be stopped at once, and should the pensioner have continued drawing it, he must refund whatever amount he may have drawn after he acquired the other source of income. Here every unprejudiced person will wonder why this minimum of existence which is prescribed by law, and which is somewhat higher than the limit required for aid, was not raised when the seven and eight florin and the recently introduced ten and twelve florin pensions were created.

In the practical application of this economic arithmetic, an evasion, or a rather broad interpretation of the "Regulations," often becomes a matter of necessity. The unconditional obligation to refund is decidedly open to severe criticism ; if any one has continued to draw his pension in addition to the income of his newly acquired property, or in addition to his other sources of income, he should only be deprived of the pension in case of bad faith ; a slight improvement in his economic condition, the acquisition of a few florins, whether as capital or as interest, ought to make no difference in his already very moderate fortune.

It would be different if a pensioner's stipend were stopped because it could be proved that he had some property at the time the pension was granted, even if the income from it amounted only to the lowest pension given (2 florins a month), and that he concealed this fact. No objection could be made to this provision, because any one who owns a very small amount of property, yielding from 2 to 3 florins interest a month, may receive a pension in addition to this, even if he states what he owns, and that it is much too little to supply him with the necessaries of life.

"Marriage of the pensioner" is recognized by the poor regulations as another reason for stopping a pension.

Rarely has an idea, incorrect in itself, been more unfortunately expressed. We have tried before to explain the reason of this law, which turns the very moment that is considered one of the happiest in most men's lives, into a most unfortunate one for a pensioner; it was made to prevent the acquisition by marriage of a right of settlement and so of a claim to poor relief, or to keep down the number of improvident marriages. But are illegitimate relations more provident? And do they not also result in offspring ?

In short, as soon as the law of settlement is revised, this provision will become meaningless, and may be done away with without disadvantage.

Experimental cases, such as saving, if possible, members of the middle classes who are on the verge of ruin, and ought to be aided by larger amounts, are provided for only by endowments in the Vienna poor relief, and these afford a remedy for the unbearable condition brought about by the settlement law only if their bestowal is not dependent on right of settlement.

In connection with this discussion of the pension system we may consider the often analogous outdoor relief of pauper children. Children of poor parents receive aid and contributions for education, amounting to 2 florins a month, as long as they are under fourteen, *i. e.* as long as they are subject to the compulsory education law. Only children who have lost their father, or natural children whose mother is dead, can receive an orphan's pension of 3 florins a month, or in exceptional cases 5 florins a month.*

If children have lost both parents through death; or if the whereabouts of their parents is unknown; or if through "a combination of exceptionally unfortunate circumstances" they can no longer provide for the support of one or of several children; and finally, in the case of foundlings, the provisions for board (*Kostgeld*) apply, *i. e.* these children, if they have settlement rights at Vienna and have no grandparents able to support them, are boarded by the community for 8 florins a month, with people whose dwellings are officially certified to be sanitary and of whom "it is not to be supposed that they take children merely in order to improve their own condition." Children who are not provided for by parents or in some other private home, and who are at least six years old, intelligent and healthy, and who have been vaccinated, are admitted into the city orphan asylums; those who are blind or deaf-mute, into the state asylums for the blind and deaf-mute, where the Vienna relief fund pays for their maintenance. Entirely neglected orphans are placed in a "Home of the Friendless" (*Rettungshaus*), of which there are at present three under private management.

---

*The poor law concerning the granting of these pensions follows a most astonishing principle, namely, that a mother should be able to maintain at least one child without assistance (for why did she give birth to the child?), and therefore contributions for support, money for board, and orphans' pensions are generally granted only when there are several children under fourteen.

Compare with the above requirements for persons willing to receive children as boarders, the curious fact that among the 780 people (average number from 1885–1889) taking boarders, 470 were tradespeople, about 30 were janitors in offices, schools and other places, about 50 day-laborers, women who sew for a living, etc., and about 100 private citizens or officials retired on a pension. Considering these figures, we shall feel tempted to regard the arrangement of boarding children as a kind of Sisyphean task, and, although statistical proof is wanting, this is confirmed by people experienced in such matters, who say that many of these "boarded children" later in life swell the ranks of pensioners, inmates of charitable institutions, wayfarers' lodges, etc.; which proves that they cannot have had a sufficiently steady educational training, and that they develop physical infirmities early in life—in a word, they are not worth the cost.

What we have said about the business management, economics, etc., of pensions applies to orphans' pensions and contributions for their education. But we must say that relief of children, and poor relief generally, should be classified according to the cause of destitution and the condition of the paupers, as follows: 1, relief of orphans proper (including the care of whole orphans and of entirely abandoned children); 2, measures for reforming neglected and delinquent children; 3, aid for children of poor parents—this third class to be transferred generally to the department of poor relief if a corresponding increase in the number of overseers can be obtained, as in that case poor relief would individualize the poor and treat them in single families; 4, admission of all feeble-minded children into proper institutions. It goes without saying that the persons entrusted with relief of children, which is pre-eminently preventive poor relief, especially with the second and fourth classes, need particulariy pedagogical qualifications, coupled with economic insight.

In the relief of the sick, especially in hospitals, the community of Vienna is more interested financially than in any other way. This is also the province where the true bureaucrat feels at home and happy; here, where the complicated quotation of expenditure and of compensation are the order of the day, we find crowds of notes and counter-notes, indorsements with, or often unfortunately without explanation, reports, duns—*bis, ter, quater urgetur*—counter-claims, registers; fortunately for the poor, medicines and small bandages, if they are to fulfil their purpose, must be given out immediately, before a reimbursement of the cost is even promised.

On this very point of sick relief, through a lack of clearness in the Austrian settlement laws, an unnecessary amount of writing has crept in. For paragraph 29 of this law declares that a commune must take care of the poor from other places who fall sick within its district, until they can be dismissed without injury to their health. According to paragraph 30, such a commune is, moreover, bound to inform the commune in which the sick person has settlement rights if it is known or can be found out by investigation without much difficulty; and if such information be delayed, it is responsible for any consequent loss. This paragraph might, with a semblance of justification, be interpreted to mean that the commune in which a sick person is loses all claim to indemnification if it fails to give immediate notice of the case to the commune of settlement when known. And many communes take their stand on this very free interpretation, although ministerial decrees and decisions of the court of administration (*Verwaltungsgerichtshof*) admit of no such reading of paragraph 30 of the settlement law. Even if the expression "without much difficulty" makes this narrow interpretation appear the right one, it would be desirable that in a possible revision of the law this paragraph should be more clearly worded, if there is to be any indemnification at all from communes where the person in question may have been settled perhaps for from two to five years. But this mistaken, though possible, interpretation is not all; there are communes which apply paragraph 30 to paragraph 28 of the settlement law, *i. e.* which require that the commune which gives aid, if it wishes them to hold themselves responsible for indemnification, should without delay notify them of the aid given "in case of immediate need," as paragraph 28 expresses it, referring to medicines needed at once and the like. It will be seen that here is an excellent chance for an endless exchange of notes, and we cannot resist the temptation to describe the particulars of such a correspondence. The physician of the poor has prescribed for N. N., whose settlement is in a small Bohemian commune G., medicines costing one florin or a florin and a half. Prescriptions, bills, in short all documents are respectfully submitted to the local governor of the district for collection. The document is generally returned to Vienna without the amount. The commune G. does not recognize the settlement right, so the bundle goes back to the charity office to collect the settlement documents to be sent to G. Meanwhile N. N. has perhaps moved to another district, often without informing the police of his change of address; to procure indemnification is impossible; the florin must be deducted from the accounts. If N. N. is still found, and if he happens to be in possession of a settlement document, the bundle may go back to the district with the respectfully submitted request to collect and remit the money at last. The bundle actually comes back again without the money. The office at G. says that, according to depositions made by his brother, N. N. earns enough to make it probable that he could pay for the medicines himself; or the question is raised whether N. N. "ought not to have been insured against sickness." After further deliberations at Vienna, the document is sent to G. for the third or fourth time, and returns with the indorsement that the commune G. refuses to refund the expenditure for medicine, because they were not notified according to paragraph 30 of the settlement law, or because N. N.'s parents, who live at G., are able to pay and ought to be applied to. The document is then returned with an interpretation of paragraph 28, to the effect that Vienna had the alternative between N. N.'s home commune and those of his relatives who come under the obligations imposed by civil law, and was therefore bound by law to apply to the former. It may also happen that no answer is sent from G. for a long time, and in that case other notes urging payment are sent. If these produce no results, the state government must be written to. So far, these reports also have remained unanswered; remain to be appealed to the ministry and the court of administration, unless by that time the legislature has forestalled the administration by a new law. This may at any rate serve as an example of the much criticised bureaucracy in the administration of poor relief, and it is to be hoped that it may act as a stimulus towards active reform.

If only the radiant sun of the new settlement and poor law would soon rise on the present gloomy horizon of poor administration, to drive away with victorious power all the dark spectres of red tape and bureaucracy which are clothed in a garment made of a hundred kinds of print, and whose soul is the dust of moldering documents! At least a regular procedure should be prescribed and made obligatory upon the officials both in claiming indemnification and in answering claims.

From what has been said it seems self-evident that the community itself could do much towards simplifying and lowering the cost of poor relief, especially as regards sick relief. With a little "municipal socialism," much more might be gained; the city might take the large corporations for traffic, for lighting, etc., under its own management, and so more work could be provided, etc.

In smaller communities the same principle could more easily be carried out. As to the expenditure for the sick poor, it is worth while to consider the example of Berlin, where a drug-store under the direction of a regularly appointed druggist furnishes the medicines for the city hospitals and institutions for the outdoor poor relief, and even for the sick poor admitted into private charitable institutions. And although the number of prescriptions filled in 1891–92 amounted to 89,760, against 83,810 in 1890–91 and 79,732 in 1889–90, the profit, after deducting the medicine tax, has increased from 65,650 marks in 1889–90 to 78,591 marks in 1891–92. The expenses for the drug-store amounted in the last three years respectively to 40,588 marks, 41,080 marks and 40,886 marks ; the average cost of a prescription was 40–50 pfennigs.*

Other economic industries† are managed with equal success by the Berlin poor commission, such as the " voluntary workhouse," in which only independent artisans are employed to make up raw material furnished by the poor commission, and which furnishes articles of clothing to poor apprentices, school children and to the poor generally who come under indoor or outdoor poor relief; a special bakery makes bread for the charitable institutions, and a cooking institution prepares meat-broth for outdoor poor relief (Vienna on the contrary has contractors and *Cantineure*) ; last but not least, there is a special brewery which brews the beer for the institutions at a cost price of from 10–11 pfennigs a litre.

The expenses for 1891–92 were :

In the cooking institution,	1,711	marks
" bakery,	53,859	"
" brewery,	27,095	"
" wayfarer's lodge,	14,510	"
Total, including the expenses in the drug-store,	138,061	"

This outlay is one of the most justifiable for the purposes of poor relief, and all other considerations are of minor importance in comparison with it.

How unfavorable a comparison would be for Vienna may be seen from the foregoing ; in the following chapters we will discuss the steps which Vienna has taken to lessen the danger of lack of employment.

* In Vienna the average cost is 18–22 kreuzer.
† Compare *Socialpolitisches Centralblatt* (Berlin), No. 26, 1893.

V.

Measures against Lack of Employment; Statistics and Insurance of the Unemployed; the Werkhaus; Labor Insurance and Poor Relief.

The preceding account of the Vienna poor relief system shows that in a certain sense the " Regulations " recognize the important difference between destitution proper and mere want, and make practical use of it; but the division lines are not marked with sufficient clearness, and no proper distinction is made between inability to work and lack of employment, nor between temporary and continued inability to work.   Hence also the frequent inadequacy of agencies intended to provide against lack of employment or of sufficient income, such as wayfarers' lodges and employment bureaus, to comply with the large demands made upon them at the present time.*

That lack of employment, and not merely aversion to work, is often the cause of poverty will probably not be denied; but—and here the value of correct social statistics becomes evident—as long as there is no record kept in accordance with the requirements of modern statistics, of the various factors which must be considered in the study of the economic phenomenon of lack of employment, we shall always be groping in the dark, and each one will feel inclined to attribute pauperism to lack of employment, or to aversion to work, according to his own political point of view.   While a social democrat stated the number of the unemployed at Vienna to be from 30,000 to 40,000, a university professor declared at the same time that it amounted at the most to one or two per cent. of the working population.   The few thorough statistics on the unemployed made in Germany, Switzerland and England—such an undertaking, as is well known, is not easy to carry out—show that last winter at Mannheim 6 per cent., at Schkeuditz 7 per cent. (of the population), at Leipzig 9 per cent., at Möckern, a suburb of Leipzig, 10 per cent. (of the population), and among the Berlin printers 17 per cent. were out of work.

It is not to be assumed that these figures would be much smaller at Vienna; reason enough, it seems to me, in the interest of a rational system of poor relief, to provide work in the first place, and then to revise thoroughly this chapter of our policy concerning the poor.   It

*Cf. *Die Humanität* (*VI Jahrgang, No.* 7), in which it is rightly said : " The first leading principle of every rational poor relief is *work instead of alms.*"

is true that we find lower figures, but this is explained by the fact that many workingmen did not receive or fill out a question blank. On the other hand, we see in Swiss cities, for instance, energetic measures for introducing insurance against failure of work ; for the above figures do not receive their real value until we find out how long every workingman has been out of work ; two or three months without work, which is the average period, are more than sufficient to conjure up the dread spectre of poverty.

It will be said that this subject is not within the limits of poor relief proper. Our answer to this is the fact that at Ludwigshofen the overseers themselves managed the statistical records on the unemployed, and that the president (*Regierungspräsident*) of the Prussian province of Silesia obliged the magistrates of cities of more than 10,000 inhabitants to organize official intelligence offices, and decreed that "in future he would recommend the dismissal of complaints of refusal of poor relief, only when the magistrate concerned should furnish proof that the plaintiff had been provided with a chance to work by the city authorities, but had not taken advantage of this chance."

This very rational idea, which, as is well known, forms an integral part of the Elberfeld system, ought to be adopted by the Vienna poor administration, for the existing regulations are not consistent with efficient poor relief.

Vienna, it is true, has a private association for securing work; the trades unions also find work, and the "Home for Apprentices" has developed a useful activity. Under the terms of the "Regulations," nothing can be done by the community. And the fact shown by statistics,* that the employment bureaus always have more candidates for places than places to be filled, is a sign of the prevailing lack of employment, and the poverty which goes hand-in-hand with it.

Employment bureaus (*Arbeitsnachweise*) alone are not enough; actual work must really be provided, if a large proportion of those

---

* From 8000 to 9000 persons annually try to find employment through the "Association for Providing Work" (*Verein für Arbeitsvermittlung*) ; of these, 18 to 20 per cent. are left over from the previous year, and only 30 to 40 per cent. obtain work; the same may be said of the "association for placing apprentices" (*Verein für Lehrlingsunterbringung*) ; in the city office for finding work for apprentices, 878 situations and 1380 apprentices were registered in 1889, and 608 apprentices were provided with situations ; some of the employment bureaus of the trades' associations show somewhat better results.

who seek work and have registered are not to be sent away without having had their wants satisfied. Moreover, the already existing associations which we have mentioned cannot possibly procure work without compensation.

Here, then, a reform would be necessary, by the establishment of wayfarers' lodges and an official employment bureau (cf. Berlin, Paris, London, with their Workingmen's Exchange, etc.), and by insurance against lack of employment. This branch of "working-men's insurance" is supposed to present the greatest difficulties, and so it does. But in this matter also, as mentioned above, we are able to point out examples worthy of imitation, such as Berne, the canton of Basel, and others. We have still to discuss the only existing way-farers' lodge, the city *Werkhaus*. And to its honor it should be said, emphatically at once, that it is not an imitation of the English "workhouse," where the expenses of living are kept at a lower rate than in the Vienna *Werkhaus*, where the inmates are compelled with greater strictness to do even the most disagreeable work, and yet do not get the proper training for future independent wage-earning, and where even children are confined, though lately sepa-rate schools and dwellings are being erected for the care of depen-dent children.

How then does an individual seeking work obtain admission to the *Werkhaus?* How far does his admission give him the right to claim work?—a privilege which should be granted to all, especi-ally to those who are still able and willing to work, but are out of work, that is, to all younger people who become destitute. On the other hand, these persons ought to be under an obligation to work, and the commune or the state ought to have the right to enforce this obligation in case of necessity. This compulsory labor, how-ever, ought not to be enforced, as has been done hitherto in most institutions of this kind, in such a manner as to frighten away all the better elements ; to individuals already hardened it makes the insti-tution like a prison, a half-despised, half-welcome place of refuge for a short time, to be left again as soon as possible. This is unfortu-nately very much the case with the Vienna *Werkhaus*. People are admitted after examination by a physician and a thorough clean-ing, either by voluntary registration—and by this method of admis-sion their claim to work seems practically to be acknowledged*—or

* But the *Werkhaus* can accommodate only 500 to 600 persons at one time.

by commitment in the police courts in case any one is found without means of support or legitimate income.

Those admitted, a very mixed crowd of workers, as may be seen, receive besides free lodging the *Werkhaus* fare, and in return for this have to do the work allotted them.   After finishing his task a man can leave the house ; if he has done more than the minimum task, he is paid for his extra work on leaving the institution finally.   The work goes on until the task is finished, with an hour off at noon. The privilege of staying out, which, after the work is done, regularly extends to 7 P. M. in winter and to 8.30 P. M. in summer, may be prolonged for the purpose of looking for work.

Unruly behavior is punished by the allotment of a heavier task, or by giving smaller rations for a time ; in case of continued insubordination, delinquents are handed over to the police.   Drinking, smoking and gambling are strictly prohibited.

This treatment, although it reminds one somewhat of school, may possibly do for men and women embittered by distress; for vagabonds and confirmed loafers it only serves as a subject to sneer at and is, besides, much too mild.   But if any one who is able-bodied refuses to go to the *Werkhaus* he forfeits every claim to other support and may be handed over to the police—to what end ?   To be held in confinement, and after his release to begin the dangerous game over again, until he becomes hopelessly demoralized, or a real criminal to be sentenced for a longer term in prison.

But let us return to the *Werkhaus* and study some of its statistics ; we shall find many interesting facts.

On the one hand, we find that the 1,008 persons who were at the *Werkhaus* in 1890 represented about 140 occupations, almost one-third being day-laborers.   Of these, only a small number remained in the institution over a week, viz. 114 from one to two weeks, 54 from two to three weeks, 36 from three to four weeks, 107 from one to two months, 89 from two to three months, etc.   And yet at least part of these could have obtained work there that would have been in the line of their occupation if the *Werkhaus* had been differently organized ; if it carried on various trades for the community under its own management, instead of giving monopolies to city contractors.*   And the number of punishments shows that most of the people are not averse to working.   Of the 1,008 inmates in 1890,

---

* Of course only such trades as would not injure the smaller tradespeople, manufacturers and artisans.

only 62 cases in which a penalty was inflicted are registered. But the whole outcome of their economic wisdom is the production of a few staple articles bought exclusively by manufacturers, such as bags, large and small envelopes, paper bags (in 1890, 60 millions), scolloped tags and labels, pasting, etc.*   Besides this a very small amount of tailoring is done for the use of the institution, and some of the bedding is made on the premises.   As a result of this condition of its productive activity, the proceeds of work done in 1890 amounted to 17,138 florins, while the total expenses came to more than 50,000 florins, and of this sum only 3.000 florins went to the workingmen as pay for extra work.

It is worthy of note also that the *per capita* cost per day in 1890 came to 42.03 kreuzers, of which 22 kreuzers were spent for food ; while in the six homes the average cost was 57.3 kreuzers, the maximum being 75.68 kreuzers, the minimum 45.99 kreuzers (in the younger institution at Liesing).   With this may be contrasted the fact that of the 4,072 inmates of the other institutions only 642 were under 50 years of age, and 1,165 under 60, while the *Werkhaus* sheltered only 109 persons over 50, and 773 between 20 and 40. In the former institutions there are then 84 persons in every 100 who are either entirely or almost entirely incapable of earning anything, who can no longer work, and who therefore do not require such strong food as the 90 persons out of every 100 in the *Werkhaus*, who are in full possession of their strength, and are compelled to do work which is so little in the line of their chosen occupation.

* Another example of interference on the part of the authorities with personal liberty is worthy of imitation. I refer to the latest report of the Marburg House of Correction for Men, in the *Allgemeine österreichische Gerichts-Zeitung*, of April 15, 1893 ; there they have workshops for carpenters, blacksmiths, locksmiths, weavers, tailors and shoemakers ; they also have agriculture.

The net income from work done amounted in 1890 to 7,384 florins, in 1892 to 25,678 florins. During the last year 730 convicts were supported 156,069 days, of which 94,198 were working days, 911 were days on which extra work was prescribed as a penalty, and 19,982 were holidays. The cost of living amounted (without bread) to 21,871 florins, or 14 kreuzer *per capita* per day. Such cheap living would not be possible in Vienna, and could not be recommended ; but we would recommend the excellent organization of the work ; and it is worthy of note that manufactured articles were provided almost exclusively for imperial offices and authorities (parts of uniforms, etc.), and that only turners and bookbinders furnished articles to private contractors.

This calculation may not contain exactly the same items on both sides, but one thing is shown clearly, namely, that not nearly so much is spent, either relatively or absolutely, for preventive poor relief as for the final provision for the aged. We can therefore only repeat: lack of employment, whether involuntary or through aversion to work, must be done away with when the individual is able-bodied, in the first case by an official supplying of work, or by institutions providing work, in the second by houses of correction (*Zwangs-arbeitshäuser*). For although by the law of 1885 the community of Vienna has the *right* to prescribe to such persons as are able to work, and have no legitimate trade or other means of support, some work corresponding to their capacity, in return for money or food, it does not follow that the community is under any *obligation* to practice this kind of poor relief; and as we have seen, this method is not sufficiently adopted.

If such a person refuses to accept the work assigned he is punished or detained in a house of correction (minors in a reformatory), for not longer than three years. Of these institutions also there are not enough, and their number must certainly be increased in order to accomplish the perfecting of the poor relief system. Our attempts to diminish pauperism, as far as it is a consequence of lack of work, would be greatly assisted by the rapid perfecting of the laws on workingmen's insurance, which are preventive in their very nature, as well as by a generally wise policy regarding the poor, and a wise poor police (*Armenpolizei*). As yet the Austrian workingman has no law on the insurance of the aged and infirm ; but there is no doubt that for the poor funds of Vienna, such laws would be of great economic value. Statistics on the decrease of poor relief in the kingdom of Saxony inform us that, as a visible result of working-men's insurance, there has been a reduction in the number

of those assisted because of accidents, from 2,463 in 1880 to 1,378 in 1890 (a decrease of 43 per cent.);

of those assisted because of sickness, from 25,070 in 1880 to 18,859 in 1890 (a decrease of 26.5 per cent.);

of those assisted for other reasons, from 66,185 in 1880 to 60,659 in 1890 (a decrease of 14 per cent.);

while the population in these years has increased 17 per cent. These statistics of course are open to the objection that the records of boards of poor relief and of private organizations cannot be depended on for ten or twelve years back, as to whether the reason for assistance was accident, sickness or some other cause.

To make a similar comparison for Vienna we must limit ourselves to the expenses for the care of the sick. The percentage of increase in these since 1888* is really a little less than that in the expenses for the care of pauper children ; but this difference is too infinitesimal to enable us to draw a definite conclusion as to the effect of the workingmen's insurance on the poor tax. Possibly there may be some significance in the reduction of expenditure for medicine from 22,787 florins in 1888 to 19,330 florins in 1889, and to 19,506 florins in 1890.

We have also spoken of the poor police. In this department of what one might call "repressive" poor relief, the regulations are very numerous and most actively enforced. That, together with the problem of lack of work, *Schubwesen*,† commitment and detention, prostitution, vagrancy and tramps, treatment of released criminals, intoxication, servants' homes, people's homes, etc., should be brought under reasonable regulations based on the principles of true social economy, is as inevitably necessary as that influence should be brought to bear on savings banks, saving and loan associations, all aid-funds, pawnbrokers' establishments, building and credit societies, and on all institutions generally which, though started by private individuals, touch the economic sphere of those who are weak from the economic point of view.

Thus our policy concerning the poor forms an integral, inseparable element in the general great social economy of the day.

VI.

Charity Budget; Consolidation of Revenues; Centralization (Private Societies).

An all-around reform of the poor relief system is of the greatest importance for the Vienna charity budget.

Here we must again say emphatically that even after the adoption of such a poor tax as we propose, the present regular revenues of this budget should remain the same; they would only change holders, *i. e.* instead of the community and numerous professionals, the state alone would assume control over all the money and other revenues.

---

*The law of workingmen's insurance against sickness has been in force since July, 1888. Since we have no data on poor relief given in case of accident, the accident insurance law cannot be considered here.

† The English poor law recognizes the so-called "irremovability," *i. e.* that nobody who has lived in a place longer than a year without having received some relief can be sent off to another community.

The largest fund (in point of expenditure, though not in amount) which has been used for charitable purposes so far is the general charity fund. Its balance sheets for the last few years show an income and expenditure of two and a half millions in round numbers. But for years this fund has been considerably in debt to the community, which every year has had to make up its deficit. Since 1882 this deficit has amounted to over a million florins a year, so that the debt of the fund to the community, which amounted to 2½ million florins in 1873, increased to 5 millions in 1881, to 6 millions in 1883, to over 7 millions in 1885, to 8½ millions in 1887 and to 9½ millions in 1890.

Since 1893 the expenditures of the fund have been included in the regular estimate of the community, and its deficit has vanished. Nevertheless, the revenues of the charity fund, although they have remained the same as before, will hardly make up to the community the expenses which now fall on it instead of on the fund. The expenditure not covered by the regular revenues for charitable purposes* would have to be provided for by the tax we have proposed and by the contributions of the states. By this arrangement Vienna would have to spend money on a far greater number of poor than now, but its expenses would be lessened through an increase in the number of overseers and a consequently more rational and economic poor relief.

The consolidation of the various funds and endowments would mean an important simplification of the poor finances; for their various purposes would no longer be absolutely necessary. This proposition would probably be violently opposed in collecting the large city fund for the aged (*Bürgerspitalfond*), and such an opposition would have some justification in tradition; but the difficulty might be solved by guaranteeing to citizens now living, in the event of their becoming poor, the same benefits as before, but not extending them to others in future.

It is clear that the adoption of a principle on which to base the reform of all philanthropic organizations is of great importance financially and presents much difficulty. It is possible that, while the revenues remain the same, one item or another might increase, or that new expenses would have to be provided for. The balance of income and expenditure must therefore be carefully considered

---

* Interest, income, legacies and donations, taxes on music permits, succession and auction taxes, poor lottery, fines, etc.

before one ventures to draw up the preliminaries of the future charity budget.

Since the time of residence of a pensioner is not recorded at Vienna, it is difficult to calculate by how much the number of persons to be aided would increase by the introduction of domicile relief.*

On the other hand we are able to state how many florins Vienna pays each year to people having settlement rights in Vienna but who are living in other places (in 1891, 247,377 florins), and to compare with this the sum refunded on the temporary outlay made by Vienna for the poor from other places ; the total expenditure for 1891 amounted to about 600,000 florins, of which about 300,000 florins were refunded. Both figures are subject to modification, though it is impossible to say exactly how much; the former, because the people having settlement rights at Vienna but living elsewhere may have acquired a claim to domicile relief at their places of residence, and because there the length of time for which such persons have been absent from their settlement commune would not be known unless they had been absent for more than ten years. Finally, balances between the national poor associations (*Landarmenverbände*) would have to be struck, a problem which cannot be solved with even approximate accuracy, and which, if solved, would in practice involve complicated operations.

Taking it all in all, the introduction of domicile relief, whether to be acquired by two or by five years' residence, would probably not result in that simplification of the poor administration which one might expect. Add to this the doubts raised in the German literature of the subject and in practice, and it would be difficult to remain an enthusiastic defender of this method of poor relief. And why should the time be fixed at two or at five years? Why not three, four or six years? Or why not from three to five years? We think that anybody should be entitled to aid from the state as a whole

---

*Inama Sternnegg, in his book *Die persönlichen Verhältnisse der Wiener Armen* (Vienna, 1892), states the time of residence at Vienna of about 10,000 persons with no settlement rights at Vienna, but aided by the Association for the Prevention of Pauperism and Begging (*Verein gegen Verarmung und Bettelei*) as follows :

Up to 1 year	1.6 per cent.
1 to 2 years	2.9 "
3 to 5 years	5.4 "
6 to 10 years	14.8 "
11 to 20 years	34.9 "
Over 20 years	40.4 "

simply on the ground of his being in need of aid, and not on the ground of his settlement or his residence. And so the nationalization of poor relief with the addition of a poor tax, as described in the beginning of this paper, would lead to a natural solution of the problem. And here we would point out the beneficial influence which the institution of the poor tax has exercised on the charitable morals of the countries where it has been introduced, acting as a wholesome restraint.

And so it would be at Vienna; an elastic poor tax, which might be called an infallible barometer indicating the status of poor relief at any time, awakens a livelier interest because not simply a moral one; for every citizen who has the means must bear his share of the expense; every variation for better or worse in municipal prosperity will be carefully noticed and anticipated, and every effort will be made to check as quickly as possible any lowering of economic conditions in its very beginning by every kind of private and social co-operation; preventive poor relief will be adopted to a greater extent, and our policy regarding the poor will become the common concern of all; every one in his own sphere will seek remedies and improvements.

So we have no fear for the success of the following principle: nationalization of poor relief as regards finances and claims for aid; if necessary, the levying of a poor tax.

When all the other reforms proposed by us in poor relief proper, and in preventive care of the poor, which might be simplified and made more economical in various ways, are carried out with wisdom and justice, the expense of relief will hardly be greater comparatively speaking than now, and if a "kreuzer rate for the poor" (*Armenzinskreuzer*) were to be imposed on the inhabitants of Vienna, the collection of the necessary amount would certainly not be felt.

There is one more reform needed, and we have already touched on it: public and private poor relief must be brought into touch with one another. Various attempts (the latest in 1883) have been made at Vienna to bring the two closer together, but so far without success. The two systems which are now separate might at least have a common financial administration, and they should be in constant touch with one another. In the various branches of philanthropic work, especially in the care of the sick and in personal intercourse with the poor, it would be impossible to do without the active assistance of willing individuals or associations; but the finances and administration might be centralized under the community, if only to attain by this concentration a reduction in the cost of administration, which is at present considerable. In other cities—smaller, to be sure, than Vienna—a more or less cordial co-operation between private and public charities has been attained, generally with gratifying results.

But this step, we think, must be preceded by a closer union of all charitable societies which have a similar object (as nursing, starting and supporting cheap eating-houses, intelligence offices, providing shelter). Only if the societies are thus organized can co-operation exist in a community. For there is no other result of our social energy which can and must be so uniform and at the same time so greatly diversified as charity; uniform to avoid duplication of work, diversified to obtain as quick and as thorough work as possible.

Several German and Austrian cities have succeeded in thus central-izing poor relief. We mention the Dresden central office of the Union of Charitable Associations, 1883; also the union of the com-mittee for poor and sick relief at Mayence with the charitable socie-ties of that city, made on June 17, 1884. It is the purpose of this union to " promote an equal distribution of alms, and to guard against fraud, to check begging and vagrancy of strangers, and to prevent the surreptitious acquisition of domicile relief." The organization and direction of business is managed about as in the Austrian city of Gablonz; the mayor calls meetings of representatives of the different societies for joint consultations; in Gablonz, the books, question blanks and registers of the union are kept together with the city books, blanks and registers.

Vienna's poor relief should be reformed, 1, by a common organiza-tion of the countless charitable societies and small societies,* together with constant individual effort for the poor—poor relief proper; 2, by an intimate connection between the societies so organized and public poor administration.

Most of the Austrians and Germans who write on the subject of the poor speak against bureaucratic, and for a more personal treatment of charity, and this treatment would be the natural result of a more individualized poor relief.† On the other hand, these writers repeat

---

* Their number increased from 216 in 1882 to 280 in 1886, with an expendi-ture of 1,128,167 florins; and to 375 in 1890, with an expenditure of 1,153.326 florins.

† Cf. Löning in Schönberg's *Handbuch*, 3rd ed., Part III, p. 966; Mischler, *Die Armenpflege in den österreichischen Städten*, Vienna, 1891, p. 88; Sedlaczek and others.

emphatically that under all circumstances the state (or country) must assume control of communal poor relief and the supervision of private poor relief.

It is not necessary to go so far as A. Wagner, who says that the obligation of the communes to aid is a kind of communism, because they have no influence whatsoever over the individuals who are a drain upon them ; and he demands for the communes a right of vetoing improvident marriages, and recommends the introduction of obligatory savings (*Zwangshilfscassen*) instead of poor relief. Our plans of reform aim in the first place at a revision of the settlement law; that is, we desire neither the principle of settlement nor of two or five years' residence, but unification of the poor administration and a general poor tax.

At the close of this critical review of the Vienna poor relief system may be placed two tables compiled from the Vienna statistical annuals; the figures, despite their not being exact, show beyond doubt, first, that in the course of the last decade the expenditure of Vienna for poor relief has increased much less rapidly, indeed often more slowly than the population; secondly, that the burden of this expenditure has even decreased somewhat in proportion; thirdly, that some symptoms point to the conclusion that Vienna has become, if not richer, at least not very much poorer.

Year.	Population.	Amount of mortgages.	Amount of interest.	Number of vacant dwellings. which rent for 400 or 500 florins.	Unpaid taxes.
		Florins.			Florins.
1882	725,935	237,257,000			5,617,651
1883	736.773	236,677,000	records	records	4,500,213
1884	747,772	245,399,000	wanting.	wanting.	4,131,946
1885	758,935	249.733,000			4,431,745
1886	770,265	256,900,000	26,900,000 fl.	1416	4,546,000
1887	781,764	267,900,000	30,860,000	2091	5,184,500
1888	793,434	280,000,000	31,000,000	2000	5,067,100
1889	805,278	291,000,000	30,400,000	2306	5,410,600
1890	817,299	299,000,000	32,800,000	2975	6,218,400

Year.	Number of inhabitants in the ten old wards.	Cases aided.*			Expenditure in florins.			Number of cases aided in 100 inhabitants.		Expenditure for poor relief *per capita* of population.	
		From public	From private	Total.	From public	From private	Total.	From public funds.	Total.	From public funds.	Total.
		Means.			Means.						
1863 to 1871	581,644	100,204	40,248	140,152	2,922,149	445,218	3,367,367	17.2	24.1	5.02	5.71
1872 to 1882	679,277	110,267	53,389	163,685	3,830,442	743,098	4,573,540	16.2	24.0	5 64	6.70
1883	736,773	148,027	107,480	255,507	5,317,620	961,577	6,279,197	20.0	34.6†	7.21	8.52
1884	747,772	149,413	108,191	257,604	5,331,817	970,952	6,302,769	20.0	34.6	7.16	8.47
1885	758,935	153,120	123,173	276,293	5,495,799	1,066,924	6,562,723	20.3	36.6	7.28	8.70
1886	770,265	153,600	128,973	282,573	5,567,251	1,128,167	6,695,418	19.9	36 6	7.22	8.69
1887	781,764	155,899	134,446	290,345	5,535,705	1,097,946	6,633,651	20.1	37.4	7.14	8.56
1888	793,434	181,719	137,152	318,871	5,416,381	1,180,136	6,596,517	25.7	40.6	0.89	8 40
1889	805,278	175,284	137,860	313,144	5,486,127	1,166,276	6,652,403	21.0	39.0	6.89	8.36
1890	817,299	177,184	153,326	330,510	5,363,608	1,153,326	6,516,934	21.6	40.4	6.56	7.97
Change 1883 to 1890	+ 10.9%	+ 19 6%	+ 42.6%	+ 30.3%	+ 0.8%	+ 19.9%	+ 3.3%	+ 1.6	+ 3.8	— 0.65	— 0.55

* We say cases aided, not persons aided, because we want to avoid counting one person several times.

† The great difference between 24 and 34 cases aided is explained by the apparently large increase of persons aided from private funds (from 53,389 to 107,480); the real reason is simply this, that the data of charitable associations before the appearance of the annual (in 1883) were very scant.

Note.—It is a significant fact that in 1883 there were 34.5 cases aided to every 100 inhabitants, of whom 20 received aid from public funds; in 1890, on the other hand, there were 40 1 and 21.6, *i. e.* an increase of 3.8 and of 1.6,—while the expenditure for poor relief *per capita* of population has fallen from 8.51 florins in 1883 to 7.97 florins in 1890 (a decrease of 0.55 florin.)   The average expenditure per case is 20 to 22 florins.

CHARITY IN TURKEY.

T. FLAKKY, IMPERIAL OTTOMAN COMMISSIONER-GENERAL TO COLUMBIAN EXPOSITION.

Invited to assist the sessions of the World's Auxiliary Congress of Charities, Correction and Philanthropy, and honored with membership in this assembly, composed of so many eminent persons from all parts of the civilized world, I beg your indulgence to say a few words on this important, I must say the most important, question of the day, from both the moral and social point of view.

I feel embarrassed by my lack of confidence, and shall not attempt to submit to this honored assemblage new and practical ideas or theories on a subject so familiar to you all. The charities and philanthropic institutions of the Ottoman Empire are not well known to our Western neighbors, hence my great desire to say a few words on the subject.

Let me first of all congratulate you upon this first attempt to bring together men from all nations to discuss subjects relating to humanity. The aim of humanity must be not only equal, but also relative easiness of life for everybody ; otherwise a great portion of mankind, deprived of the vital necessities of life, will either be lost in crime or will strive to procure through improper means what is refused to them by hard circumstances and by their fellow-citizens. Certainly many a criminal is born with a predisposition to crime, but in countries where the comforts of life are easily procurable, the number of criminals is always far less than where pauperism prevails. But even where economical laws are best observed, some unexpected circumstances, such as disasters, international wars, commercial and financial crises, bring all to naught. The intellectual inequality between members of the same community eventually reduces one portion of it to the depths of misery, and makes it the duty of the favored members to save the rest—to restore them, if not completely, at least as nearly as possible, to their former prosperity. Surely many a horrible crime might be prevented by this intervention of society, by relieving the miseries of the poor and keeping them in the bounds of human comforts, ideas and manners. So long as there are guarantees enough for the relief of disasters and misfortunes, society has nothing to do ; but the helpless are worthy of its care, and the barbarian device, *Væ victis*, must be forever forgotten.

A well-extended and well-combined system of charities does much to prevent crimes and the necessity for correction; but correction may also be considered as a charity. Correction means the separation of the actually degraded members of society from their more law-abiding neighbors, a means which relieves the latter from a bad neighborhood and the influences of vice. A good system of correction, besides doing its work as a means of punishment, succeeds in many cases in making good and honest citizens of bad men, by subjecting them to its rules based on civil law.

To prevent humanity from losing its moral virtues because of its material misfortunes, and to help those who have already lost these qualities to regain them, is what we call philanthropy. These considerations show why, in my mind, I see such an intimate relation between these two words, charity and correction, and how the two lead to this idea of philanthropy, which is the motto of this distinguished assemblage.

I must apologize for the length of these introductory remarks and proceed at once to explain briefly the state of charitable institutions now existing in my country. In Turkey charity has always been considered as a public and private duty. Two essential elements of Turkish life give to it a prominent position amongst human institutions. These two elements are, as you all know, the time-honored customs of the Turkish race and the principles of the Mohammedan religion. The Turkish tribes have always mixed charity with hospitality. The stranger, be he poor or rich, coming to a tent to seek shelter or refuge, is always welcomed and furnished with all means of subsistence and comfort. These habits still characterize the nomadic tribes and also the more stable population, amongst whom every village, besides caring for its own poor, possesses a special house where strangers are received, lodged and nourished without any cost.

As to the Mussulman religion, it is universally known that the relief of and the respect for the poor have been raised by it to the rank of a state institution.

Mohammed belonged to a tribe in Mecca governed by a class of wealthy merchants, who formed a real plutocracy amongst the Arab nation. Poverty was of course despised by these men, and it was certainly more difficult to press upon them respect for the poor than any other social or moral reform. Mohammed succeeded in changing the ideas of his people on this matter as on many others; and he devoted all his time to the welfare of the growing Mohammedan community, paying no attention to his personal fortune. His motto was, " Poverty is my glory," (*Al fakree fahry*). His great endeavor was to establish a perfect equality between the poor and the rich. He succeeded, and the result is that to-day Turkey, like every other Mohammedan community, is one of the most typical democratic countries, without any kind of nobility or social distinction except such as is conferred by the state for the needs of administration.

One of the five principles of Islam is the *Zekat*, which is a tax on the wealthy class for the maintenance of the poor. In times of conquest, the fifth part of the spoils was sent to the *Beit-ul-mal*, or public treasury, and devoted to the same purpose by the state officials. *Zekat*, a regular public tax in the first century of the Khalifate, has ever since been regarded by all Mussulmans as a religious duty. Every rich Mussulman who possesses articles of luxury gives a yearly amount, in proportion to his wealth, to the poor, and so fulfils his obligation for the relief of the poor, an offering which is said in the Koran to be the form of prayer most agreeable to the Almighty. Personal effects, money, goods used in commerce, and the ornamental articles used by ladies are of course excepted from the charge of *Zekat*, as they do not imply a luxury which may cause grievances to the poorer classes. My countrymen are all under the influence of these national habits and religious ideas, and hence a man who is indifferent to the misery of the poor is considered a monster devoid of any humane sentiments and subject to the hatred of his fellow-citizens.

There is no uniform law in Turkey giving to the state poor relief the features of a regular institution. The cause of this must be found in the fact that there poverty has a thoroughly different meaning from that of other countries. In Turkey the possession of land is quite evenly distributed, and nearly everybody has his share, small or large, in the national domain. In fact every man is a landowner, and it is very difficult to find one who has not a parcel of land somewhere. Even such men as are known to be poor have their own homes and need only the necessary means of subsistence. No one has to sleep in the open air when night comes. There are no homeless people in Turkey. Consequently there was no necessity of having a kind of poor law giving shelter to the needy, and only a very few destitute people are directly cared for by the national government in places specially assigned to that purpose.

The consequence is that there is no pauperism, no regular and permanent class of poor in Turkey. Therefore what is most needed is special means of alleviating temporary need or accidental suffering. The destitute are provided with the means of subsistence without putting them in regularly established poorhouses, thus prejudicing their standing among their friends and acquaintances. Governmental relief for the poor is carried on by different channels and with an efficiency truly remarkable. The imperial family, especially his Majesty the Sultan, expends a considerable part of his revenues for this purpose. When the sovereign or the members of the imperial family go out, money is always distributed to the poor assembled on the street. A portion of the special cash fund of his Majesty and that of the Ministry of the Civil List is expended for persons who apply to imperial magnanimity to alleviate their needs. A special fund is allowed in the palace to help such of the poor as present regularly attested petitions to the sovereign. The marshal of the palace is charged with the management of this sum. The first secretary of the palace also has lately been placed in charge of another regular fund instituted by his Imperial Majesty Abdul Hamid II. In case of special emergencies caused by accidents, such as fires, earthquakes, famines, and other public calamities, the Sultan always takes the initiative in the distribution of succor to the needy, and invariably he is the first to come forward and assist to heal the wounds of the injured and alleviate the misery of the helpless. At the recent earthquakes which destroyed a great part of the district of Malattiah, all the houses in villages and in cities were rebuilt by the government without any cost to the people, and thus this great public calamity left no trace behind. Even in districts far from Constantinople many needy people have regular allowances paid to them from the privy purse of the sovereign.

The government treasury also pays annually large amounts of money for the needy, and a special pension fund is destined for this purpose. Pension funds for the families of all the civil and military servants of the empire were first instituted during the reign of his Majesty. This has instituted a financial power in the country, leaving no poor people among the classes that were once dependent on the salary paid by the government to the members of families. The poor are allowed a certain sum monthly by the government treasury, on the presentation of official certificates duly attested and sworn to by some reputable citizens of the ward where the applicant resides.

In addition to all these institutions, his Imperial Majesty led in the establishment of a great home in Constantinople for destitute people of all religions and denominations. This home for the poor will contain workshops, places of worship, schools, etc., in one word, all that is required for the social and moral progress of the inmates. The erection of the required buildings for this purpose has been carried on with great energy and enthusiasm, and when completed and equipped, it will be a magnificent addition to the humanitarian establishments of the world, and a great credit to its originator, the present sovereign of the Ottoman Empire.

The *Vakoufs*, namely "pious institutions," also undertake a great part of the poor relief work. *Vakoufs* are real estates, the incomes from the rent of which are devoted, under certain prescribed rules, to different charities, such as the maintenance of places of worship, schools, public fountains, hospitals, etc. These foundations have been mostly established by Ottoman sovereigns, while some of them are the gifts of private men, but all are under the charge of the Imperial Ministry of Pious Foundations—*Evkof*. In some cases *Vakoufs* are under the control of the eldest son or the head of the family of the man who is the founder of the institution. *Vakoufs* provide for the needs of the poor in different ways: first, by giving life pensions or rations to them; second, by the *Tmaret* system, which is rather peculiar to Turkey. *Tmarets* are large places where, daily, cooking is done by the *Vakouf* and given without cost to the people who apply for it. Everybody can go there at the appointed times and receive his share of the day's fare without any formality. Constantinople contains more than two hundred of these places, and every important provincial city can boast of many places of this kind. The poor of a ward can have their daily meals in these *Tmarets*, and poor students, especially those who are studying in *Medresses* (theological schools), can pursue their studies without any appreciable cost for board, being lodged in the schools and nourished by the *Tmaret*.

As to actual private charity in Turkey, it is done on a grand scale. The people think it a moral duty to give alms, and this tendency, beside leaving no room for great miseries, has even the effect of inducing some idle men to beg favors from others. Every family gives the surplus of its daily food, with old clothes and other household and personal articles which are not needed, to the poor. Thus many poor families obtain all that is necessary by the generosity of their neighbors. Wealthy individuals often take upon themselves the marriage of a poor girl who is acquainted with their families. Cases are not rare in which a small house, with all the necessary household goods, is presented to the bride, and they even procure a situation for the bridegroom, thus enabling him to support his wife. Often the residents of a ward collect money to help to marry the poor girls of their neighborhood, and so no girl is left unmarried, when she is of age, on account of poverty.

The hospitality practised in Turkish cities is also very peculiar. Sometimes a whole family goes to another family's house and remains there as guests for days or even weeks. The poor are not despised, and a poor man acquainted with a rich family can bring there his own people and remain some time as guests. This is, of course, a great alleviation to the poor man's purse, and enables him to enjoy more easiness of life when he stays in the house of his rich relative or friend.

The above considerations show why pauperism, as understood in some other countries, is an unknown thing in Turkey. That is a good thing, for in the absence of pauperism the extreme hatred so natural between the rich and the poor is avoided, giving place to more geniality and true brotherhood between citizens of all situations, classes and positions. May these hatreds and distinctions, which are the principal sources of actual embarrassment in social questions, and which are the result of the supposed superiority of the moneyed class over the poor, never arise in the land of Turks, but may our old and time-honored customs flourish more and more, combined with the influence of occidental civilization which is invading our land and totally transforming it—to the better, we may hope.

PROCEEDINGS AND DISCUSSIONS.

FIRST SESSION, JUNE 12, 1893, 8 P. M.

The first session of the section on the Public Treatment of Pauperism, of the International Congress of Charities, Correction and Philanthropy, was a general session, and was called to order at 8 o'clock by Mr. F. H. WINES, vice-president of the Congress, who introduced as chairman of the section, Mr. ANSLEY WILCOX, of Buffalo, New York.

Mr. WILCOX, upon taking the chair, spoke briefly of the importance, in the United States, of the study of the public treatment of pauperism, and commented upon the lack of system in state and municipal relief; also upon the absence of reliable general statistics of pauperism, which is in part due to the variations in the methods of relief pursued by the local authorities. He expressed the hope that the presentation of European theories and their discussion by this Congress might lead to the development of an intelligent American system of poor law administration, which could be put in the form of a statute and generally adopted in this country.

The first paper of the evening was read by Mr. ROBERT TREAT PAINE, of Boston, on *Pauperism in Great Cities.*

The chairman called upon Mr. HENRY C. BURDETT, of London, England, to discuss the paper read by Mr. PAINE. He responded in the following words:

Mr. BURDETT.—What strikes us English about Mr. Paine and his methods is this, that he has gone to the root of the problem, and has furnished us the means of solving it, if we will only acquit ourselves like men and women, by giving "love and personal service." In one of the districts of London, a district of 20,000 people, there has been established an association known as the Friendly Workers' Association. It is managed by a committee consisting of representatives of all religious denominations, under the chairmanship of a layman. The object of forming this pan-denominational committee has been to utilize to the full the forces represented by the twin sisters of love and personal service. The method pursued has been to take a census of the people in the district, and then we have gone to work upon the facts, and I am glad to say we have successfully solved the difficulties, so far as that district is concerned.

But that is not all. Another attempt has been made, which is now being worked out under the heads of all religious bodies in the metropolis, to solve the social problem. Our idea is to get London divided into Friendly Workers of manageable proportions, and then, by the aid of pan-denominational committees and friendly workers, to stir up and awaken throughout the metropolis the feeling, that it is not so much the duty of the aggregate mass to solve this problem, as it is the privilege of individuals to give themselves to the work, and to bring by this personal service something far more valuable and beyond all price, the gift of oneself, if only for a limited period, that this problem may be solved once and for all.

It is said that London, with her six million people, is too large to handle. My answer is that any one who holds that opinion is unworthy of civilization as it should be in this nineteenth century. Surely, if our sires were able to deal with the problems which beset them in their day, we, their descendants, with our improved methods, would not acquit ourselves like men, or be worthy of our sires, if we were to allow any aggregate mass to make us hesitate or pause in the effort to solve this problem.

Professor C. R. HENDERSON, of the University of Chicago, read a paper on *Public Relief and Private Charity*.

SECOND SESSION, JUNE 13, 1893.

Mr. ANSLEY WILCOX, of Buffalo, presided. Mr. JOHN H. FINLEY, president of Knox College, Galesburg, Illinois, acted as secretary.

Mr. OSCAR CRAIG, president of State Board of Charities of New York, read a paper entitled, *American Administration of Charity in Public Institutions*.

The CHAIRMAN.—The next paper is by Baron von REITZENSTEIN, of Germany, on *The International Treatment of the Poor Question*. It will be read by the secretary. The secretary then read the paper.

The chairman invited Miss CATHERINE H. SPENCE, of Australia, to address the section.

Miss SPENCE.—In South Australia, where I went in 1839, there was a range of wooden buildings, called "Immigration Square," where immigrants received room and food for a fortnight, until employment could be found for them. The duty which the state owes to the poor has never since then been lost sight of in South Australia. The government takes the care of the poor upon itself, and in order to diminish the number of those wholly dependent upon institutional charity in almshouses and asylums, it has organized a system of outdoor relief which, I think, is unique and healthful, and which, so far as I know, has been wisely administered. If a widow is left with young children and without means, instead of taking her children from her and placing them in district schools, as would be done in England, the South Australian government aids her with rations. She is supposed to maintain herself and one child; for herself and two children she has one ration; with three, one and a half. The rations are not in money, but consist of food, bread, meat, tea, sugar, soap, salt and rice. Many respectable families are brought up in this way, the mother doing what she can to earn her children a living. By this means fewer children are thrown entirely upon state maintenance than in any other province in Australia.

In regard to the old people, we have a "Destitute Board," appointed by the government, which says to a son or daughter, "Keep your old father and mother and we will allow you one ration." Consequently we have fewer old men and women in the almshouses than any place in the world. But this system needs to be watched. It has the effect of reducing the number of those who become entirely pauperized so long as an old man and woman can keep a house above their head; but when they are past work they will get a ration and a half. We have no able-bodied men in the "destitute asylum" at all; they may have a night's lodging, that is all; we have only in our destitute asylums old people who are blind or infirm, whom I should like to see in a better place. I don't think it is a happy thing for old people to be always by themselves, without the patter of little feet or the stir of life. I do think there might be some way of boarding out old people, such as I read of in a little pamphlet I got here. There is a movement in South Australia to get a better home for the respectable poor than what is called our destitute asylum.

In regard to children, they are removed from institutions and placed in homes, generally country homes. The government pays for their keeping, and furnishes registers of inspection (voluntary inspection), thus giving to hundreds and thousands of ladies all over Australia an opportunity to visit these places.

I know there is a great prejudice against outdoor relief; the fashion in England is to give no outdoor relief; they say, "If people want to live, let them go into the workhouses." I do not know that it is right, if our brothers and sisters have fallen, to thrust them with others amongst whom they should not properly be. I have read in the reports of bureaus of beneficence that temporary help is given in time of trouble. I have known families in dire distress to apply for a night's lodging who would never ask for a cent; I have known a mother to pawn her wedding-ring who would not ask for a cent. But all official charges must be regulated; therefore it is well that private benevolence should aid in that way. But the objection to private benevolence is that the money all comes out of a few pockets; that thousands of women and men, who can afford to pay well for the support of the poor, escape. You have here your poor-rates, and you say the rates are not sufficient for the maintenance of the infirm and poor, but that they must be supplemented by the work of active men and women. This thought was especially borne upon my mind when I attended the Australia Charity Conference in Melbourne, where they have no poor-rate, but regard private benevolence as quite sufficient. There, naturally, a few people support all the hospitals. Why should not everybody help to support these hospitals? Therefore I approve of the rate system. I believe that it is the duty of the state to care for its poor and afflicted and infirm; but it should not exonerate the private people from giving their services. By and by there will be no use for so much charity, because there will be more justice. Baron von Reitzenstein, in his observations upon the difficulty of public poor relief on account of political methods, touched upon what seems to me the essential weakness of America, and I have come to America for the purpose of advocating a reform in your electoral methods, to inaugurate improvements in such methods.

Mr. ROBERT TREAT PAINE, president of Associated Charities, Boston.—I have listened with great interest to the remarks of Miss Spence, and I wish I could ask one question. What are the observed results upon these families of children, with their widowed mothers, where relief is given in this way? I should suppose that the fact must be known to all the neighbors, so that the children of the family are, as it were, marked as paupers.

Miss SPENCE.—Singularly enough, it is not considered a disgrace for a woman to take rations, or medical assistance; if the father of the family is ill. It is regarded as a right. I think that to help a woman to bring up her family in their own home is the best thing that can be done for her. But it is felt to be a disgrace to go to the asylums. They feel that it is not right to let an old father or mother go to an asylum or almshouse.

Mr. PAINE.—I agree that the family should be kept together, but I doubt whether any method is wise which proclaims to all the boys and girls in the neighborhood that any family is, by reason of the death of the father, brought down so low that they must be in daily receipt of public relief. Is there not a better method? I cannot but think there is just a little bit of that wicked element in boys that will lead them to taunt and jeer at their playmates under the circumstances mentioned. My question is whether, if public relief must be given, it ought not be given in a more private and secret way; more in the form of a pension, or a monthly allowance, with overseers employed, so that the neighbors may not know that the wagon of shame stops in front of certain homes. Why can it not be done quietly? I wish to seize this opportunity to find out how far we might go, and whether the cause of the widow and of the children cannot be taken care of in a better way, a more friendly way, with the neighbors absolutely ignorant of the fact, and perhaps with the children not knowing that they are aided; whether the relief might not be taken from some church, or by some individual, and given in a quiet, tender, considerate way, until the time comes when the children could be self-supporting.

Mr. P. W. AYRES, secretary of Associated Charities, Cincinnati.—I, too, would like to ask if there is not such a way, and I would like to tell Mr. Paine that in our city we have kept to the idea, which I supposed they had in Boston, of securing private pensions from private sources for certain cases of this kind, where there is a widow with several children who ought to be kept with the mother. We have now a certain amount of pension money in hand. We have adopted this system within the past few years to keep the mother and children together by means of private pensions. We do it in various ways; sometimes we go to a few wealthy gentlemen and say that we want $125 a year or $2 a week for three years until the boy, who is now 11 years old, shall be 14. Of course we find families in which the children are very small and it will be a long time before they are self-supporting. It is more discouraging when you find children from 10 to 12 years of age, but we have, in answer to the gentleman's question, a plan in Cincinnati which has been successful in some ten or twelve cases. We have private pensions for women and children; these pensions are so administered by friendly visitors that the family does not know it is an object of charity; but sometimes it is wise to tell the family so they may not have a feeling of fear lest they may not know where the next meal is to come from. There are instances where we have $125 laid up for a family and they know nothing about it.

Miss ZILPHA D. SMITH, general secretary of Associated Charities, Boston.—It is the proudest and happiest moment of my life that I am able to stand before you and say that in one district in Boston (the seventh ward) we have solved this problem, not only for widows and children, but for all the poor. We have provided private charity for every deserving poor person that may ask for it. We did not do it by looking about us to see how much was to be done, by taking a bird's-eye view and saying, "Here are so many people and it will take so much money"; but we saw the poor families becoming demoralized. They would say to us, "If my husband dies I can go up to the pensioners, and it is no matter whether I save anything or not"; so they do not save. Now, as we do not live under a socialistic system, people, in order to save their character, must provide for themselves. We should not take away from these widows and children the sense of independence, the feeling that they themselves are able to provide for themselves. So we established a society for home saving; but the difficulty was that they did not care to save. There are a great many people who could take care of themselves if they only thought they could, and we are making out a list of these people. It is really marvellous, when you come to work out the problem, how few people actually need help. A gentleman who had visited Switzerland once said that he inquired for almshouses there. They said there were none. He asked, " What do your poor people do?" "Oh, they have sons or daughters that take care of them." "Suppose they have no sons." "Well, they have an uncle or an aunt or a niece." "Suppose they have no one." "Well, everybody has some one." So it seems, when you come to study into it, in every family there is almost invariably a way for them to get along, either by the help of some relative or by their own individual efforts. I think if others would begin as we have and say, "Now we will take this or that family," taking the easy ones first, gradually we could take every single family and make them independent. Then your people would begin to do as ours have and join a Home Savings Society, and you would find that they will soon have their twenty or twenty-five dollars saved, and they will take a proud pleasure in it. I know that we have a number of families who own their own houses out of town and enjoy themselves in their homes, and when they come in to see me they look just like my visitors; I open my eyes when they walk into the office, and I think " It is a visitor," and I look up and find they are my old poor people.

Mr. J. R. BRACKETT, of Baltimore.—It seems to me, in listening to this very interesting discussion, that there is entirely another side to the question. I do not believe that to take money from the public treasury helps in any way to bring the two classes together, the prosperous and the poor. Where you get hold of a rich man and give him an opportunity to take his money from his pocket and help some poor struggling being, you do bring the classes together; and it looks like a great pity not to do this.

Dr. J. W. WALK, general secretary of the Society for Organizing Charity, Philadelphia.—I would be extremely sorry if in my city widows and orphans were ever made to feel that the poor director's wagon would come around and back up to their door and cause the blush of shame to arise to their cheek. We do not want to undermine that idea of independence which is the very best thing among our people, and which has turned this great wilderness into a garden in the last hundred years.

Now, Mr. Chairman, the keynote, or rather two keynotes have been struck, one by Miss Smith, when she said that by thorough investigation you will find immense unsuspected avenues to self-help, and the other was struck by Mr. Paine, when he said last night that people are determined to raise themselves. I can say, with an experience of fourteen years in Philadelphia, that we have in that city of over a million people very few families of widows or children who, if they had the poor relief, would not take it. We work under one or two specially favorable conditions. One is our building association system; almost every poor workingman has a share in a building association. Another is the wonderful development of co-operative insurance. Co-operative insurance societies have paid out $35,000,000 in the last twenty-two years; they extend all over the United States, and are extremely popular in Philadelphia. Still another is Girard College, which receives half-orphan boys. When a man dies in Philadelphia, very often one of his sons is put into Girard College, and there the boy will be given an education. Then we have the fund for coal which amounts to $18,000. We do not find it necessary to make permanent pensions.

THIRD SESSION, JUNE 15, 1893, 10.30 A. M.

Mr. ANSLEY WILCOX presiding; Mr. JOHN H. FINLEY acting as secretary.

The CHAIRMAN.—The first paper which will be presented is by Mrs. MAY MCCALLUM, of London, on the *English Poor Law System, its Intention and Results*, and will be read by Miss JULIA LEAVINS. The paper was read.

The CHAIRMAN.—The next paper is by Mr. WILLIAM VALLANCE, of London, clerk to the Whitechapel Board of Guardians, on *Poor Law Progress and Reform, exemplified in the Administration of an East London Union*, and will be read by Mr. T. GUILFORD SMITH, of Buffalo. This paper was also read.

Mr. PROSPER VAN GEERT, of Belgium, read a paper on *Charity in Belgium*.

The CHAIRMAN.—We thank Mr. van Geert sincerely for the clear account of the subject which he has given us. We thank him for coming here and presenting his paper to us in person, because it adds greatly to the interest to have it read by the author.

We have some time still remaining to us, and I think that the pleasantest course that could be taken now would be to dispense with the further reading of papers and to call for remarks on the papers already presented. I shall therefore call upon Judge Follett, of Marietta, Ohio.

Judge FOLLETT, of the State Board of Charities of Ohio.—Many persons say that we ought to have no outdoor relief: but why? It is demonstrable that in many states (my own, I know, is one) outdoor relief increases pauperism. But the people seem to desire it, and neither political party dares make an effort in the legislature to abolish it. It may in the end abolish itself. The trouble is that the relieving officers are personally benefited by the distribution of patronage, but the relief granted does not benefit the public. I visited a county in Ohio and talked with the county officials in regard to a certain form of relief, which I will not describe here, but which would reach from 100 to 150. I said: "Tell me, do you really think it benefits those who receive it?" "Well, I think that two out of 150 may be benefited." "And," I said, "the rest are injured?" "Yes, all the rest are injured." And yet that man would not dare to have me mention his name; he knows that I will not. Wherever outdoor public relief is given it has the effect of relaxing the energies of men struggling to take care of themselves, which is an injury to their manhood. That is the basis of the objection to it.

I am sorry, therefore, that some of our foreign friends, when asked to discuss outdoor relief, at once begin to describe some system of social charity, some individual process of family or personal visitation of the poor. Of course, in cases of distress we may go to the afflicted in a friendly way and, taking a man by the hand, say, "John, are you not in trouble?" "Yes, my wife is sick, my child is afflicted; I haven't been able to get work." And you can either send something to the house or slip a piece of money into his hand. But that is not public outdoor relief.

I endorse cordially what has been said in Mr. van Geert's paper; it shows that certain things may be done outside of institutions. I approve of the remarks of Mr. Paine in the same general direction. But caring for and helping boys can hardly be called outdoor relief. When we discuss the question of public or private outdoor relief we ought to confine ourselves to the point. What is done for the public should be for the public good, and what is done for individuals should not be a peril to them. We had in our county a man who was thrifty and lived independently, but he received aid at one time and he stopped work at once. His energies were paralyzed; he felt that the public owed him a living. There is a great difference between the poor and the pauperized. The pauperized control the relieving officers. They say to them, "Give me so much," or "Increase what you give me or I will work at the polls for your defeat." That is the road to destruction, to anarchy and ruin. There are so many phases of this question that I will not take any more time. We must not let the recipient of relief become dictator as to its form and amount.

The CHAIRMAN.—The remarks of Judge Follett suggest very forcibly one great evil which exists in some of our cities in connection with poor law administration. The public administrators of the funds of the poor should be appointed and not elected, so that they may at least be free to do the best that their powers and intelligence will permit them to do.

I will ask Miss ZILPHA D. SMITH, of Boston, to speak.

Miss SMITH.—I was glad to hear Mr. Vallance's paper, because it seems to me that the history of outdoor relief in London is more instructive and beneficial than in Berlin or Philadelphia. As to outdoor relief being bad in Berlin, that may have been simply because it was administered under bad conditions; but in England there was no such trouble. There they have been able to abolish outdoor relief, without hardship to the poor, and bring about a better condition of things. It seems, therefore, that the evils of outdoor relief are inherent in the system.

I had the pleasure, four years ago, to talk with Mr. Crowder, one of the guardians of the parish of St. George, which is even poorer than that of Whitechapel. He told me that he made it a point, in his board of guardians when they began to refuse outdoor relief, to visit in person every family whose application had been rejected. He was, I think, a rich man himself; at least he was in comfortable circumstances; but whether or no, he was determined to see the right thing done; and he found that there were many legitimate ways in which the poor could take care of themselves, without breaking up families or going to the workhouse. He said that it would have been more difficult in a district less poor, for the fact that poor people can successfully appeal for help to their neighbors renders it harder to convince them that they can do for themselves.

In Brooklyn, outdoor relief has been abolished by gradually leaving first one family and then another off the list as they become able to care for themselves. That process began long before they had an almshouse. When the list was reduced to something less than twenty, then they said, "These people must have an almshouse." They built an almshouse in a wealthy location, thinking they would have about seventeen inmates, but when it was ready only one of them went there.

Mr. A. O. WRIGHT, of Madison, Wisconsin.—My experience for a number of years as an inspector of the poor and of the charitable institutions in the State of Wisconsin, has led me to the deliberate conviction that the less that is done in the way of charity the better it will be for the state and for charity. It is impossible, perhaps, to abolish public poor relief, but it is possible to abolish public outdoor relief. That certainly can be done, except, perhaps, in agricultural communities. There are agricultural communities where it could not be done; but there every resident knows every other resident. I do not think that institutional relief can yet be dispensed with. It has the indispensable means of dealing with those who refuse outdoor relief. We say to them, "If you refuse outdoor relief you can go to the poorhouse." I am speaking about what has been done by the State Board of Charities of the State of Wisconsin. They found that a labor system was desirable in the poorhouses, and it has been introduced into nearly every one of the Wisconsin poorhouses. The result is that the inmates are happier than when they had nothing to do.

Public poor relief is in no sense charity. It is a form of socialism. The only true charity is that which is voluntarily and privately given. It is not charity to collect taxes from me and give the money thus obtained to such persons as may be selected by a public official. That is socialism. But it is charity for Miss Smith to take money freely given by individuals and with that help to lift up those who are cast down. Public poor relief cannot do that; it doles out its allowances in small amounts to the pauperized. Private charity is capable of giving adequate relief, and it aids not merely those who are pauperized, but the worthy destitute, whom it saves from becoming paupers.

Mr. PAINE, of Boston.—I desire in one word to express the great pleasure with which I listened to the paper of Mr. Vallance. His thought is of infinite value, in its application to the general condition of the very poor who belong to the working classes. What he said is, to my mind, the very hinge of the question. If we can teach the people, if we can convince the socialists, if we make the clergy of all denominations understand, that this lax relief is demoralizing and injurious, we shall accomplish marvels. On the other hand, I do not quite see why it is necessary that private relief should be administered under the same strict limitations. I have never understood the problem. When one sees in the report of a private relief society in Brooklyn that ten thousand dollars spent in a year gave relief to about ten thousand families (40,000 souls), at the rate of a dollar a family, that puzzles me. I do not perceive the use of this little dribbling, petty policy of doling out relief in small sums. Relief, where the demand for it is real, should be given generously and in adequate amount. We have families in Boston who receive two hundred or three hundred dollars a year in relief. Is it not the fact that where these great relief societies descend to doling out help at the rate of one dollar a family, they do as much harm as public outdoor relief could do?

The following papers were presented and read by title: *The Work of the London County Council in Relation to Public Health and the Housing of the Working Classes*, by Mr. JOHN LOWLES; *The Austrian Poor Law System*, by Miss EDITH SELLERS; *Poverty and its Relief in Austria*, by Dr. MENGER; *Sketch of the Organization of Public Poor Relief in Austria*, by Dr. FRIEDERICH PROBST; *Poor Relief in Vienna, and its Reform*, by Dr. RUDOLPH KOBATSCH; *Charity in Turkey*, by Mr. T. FLAKKY.

The section adjourned.

FOURTH SESSION, JUNE 16, 1893, 2 P. M.

In the absence of the chairman of the section, Mr. JOHN H. FINLEY presided.

Mr. A. O. WRIGHT, of Madison, Wisconsin, read a paper on the *Causes of Pauperism and the Relation of the State to it.*

Dr. L. L. ROWLAND, superintendent of the State Hospital for the Insane, Salem, Oregon.—I would like to inquire how we are to avoid running in a circle upon this question? A few meetings ago it was argued that outdoor relief should not be permitted; and at another meeting it was said that it would be far better to afford the mother help at home than to take her children away from her.

A VOICE.—From private sources, however.

Dr. ROWLAND.—I did not so understand it. But I do not want to discuss the question. I merely ask, how are we to help those who require but little help, and yet not encourage pauperism?

Mr. WRIGHT.—It seems to me that just such cases are those which most appeal to private benevolence. If there were no public relief for them, there would be found to be plenty of charity in the country. The one great evil of outdoor relief is that it destroys the motive to private benevolence, and by eliminating from relief the element of sympathy, converts it into a cold and mechanical arrangement on the part of the state.

Mr. P. W. AYRES, of Cincinnati.—We may congratulate ourselves that we have listened to such a paper. I wish that it might be laid before some of our state legislatures, in the hope of cutting off outdoor relief to a greater extent than has yet been done.

There has been a feeling on the part of the Board of State Charities in Ohio that it would not be advisable to abolish all outdoor relief, because it does not seem practicable everywhere to meet the need by private contributions. It is agreed that in large cities it can be abolished. As a practical worker, I am sure that there it is always harmful. The societies and churches in Cincinnati or any other large city are abundantly able to care for all cases of temporary distress.

My mind has been dwelling upon the possibility of substituting for the present outdoor relief in country districts, systematic co-operation by the benevolent and Christian people of five or six or more counties, through the employment of a private agent, who could investigate and report upon cases of distress, so that the want could be intelligently and completely and promptly met. In large cities we work to advantage, because the population is compact and we can reach a case quickly. With a paid agent for six counties to distribute money raised from private sources, all needed temporary relief could be given at a far less cost than the public now pays for it.

Mr. LUCIUS C. STORRS, secretary of the State Board of Charities of Michigan.—The plan suggested by Dr. Ayres is certainly ideal. I suppose that by the time that the next four-hundredth anniversary of the discovery of America is celebrated we may see it adopted. Mr. Wright knows as well as myself that at present it is not practical. But I am glad of the opportunity to say that I hope, when the committees of the National Conference of Charities are appointed at Nashville next year, the committee on charity organization will be so constituted that both the city and country will be represented on it. There is no antagonism between the two, and we want advice and instruction and experience from both sides. Our city friends describe methods of work admirably adapted to cities; but a large number of us come from smaller places, and what we want to know is the best way to relieve poverty in rural districts and in towns. One complements the other, and both should go together.

Mrs. LOUISA R. WARDNER, of Chicago.—I wish to ask Mr. Wright's opinion of indiscriminate private charity. I have been attending the Conference of Charities for many years and I have often heard the recommendation not to give alms to individuals. Now you say that the poor should be relieved by private charity. What do you recommend? Is house-to-house charity the proper method where there are no organized charities?

Mr. WRIGHT.—My paper does not cover that ground. It would make it too long if I had tried to cover everything; so I omitted the question of private charity. But I will say that, as between lavish public poor relief and lavish private poor relief, it is a far less evil to have it given by private charity.

Mrs. WARDNER.—You mean individually?

Mr. WRIGHT.—Or by societies either. The charity organization societies have covered that ground.

Mr. ROBERTS, of Wisconsin.—I want to ask Mr. Wright a question. Very little has been said in regard to poorhouse administration. I know a little about the poorhouses of the state of New York, and how difficult it has been to provide systematic, continuous work for the inmates. Have you any suggestions to make touching that point?

Mr. WRIGHT.—I read a paper before the National Conference of Charities at San Francisco on that subject. My experience has been in country poorhouses rather than in those of large cities. The least successful attempt in that line made in Wisconsin is in Milwaukee. Of course the problem is harder in the city than in the country. Yet most country poorhouses do not provide the occupations they might. There is a variety of industries on a farm, and some kind of work can be assigned to almost every inmate. One secret of success, in addition to the kind but firm determination of the superintendent and matron, is the making of certain individuals responsible for the discharge of certain daily duties, so that the organization of labor does not require to be renewed every morning. The benefit is not in the money value of the labor, but in the discipline.

The CHAIRMAN.—I have been very much interested in a scheme in vogue in England known as the Brabazon scheme. The inmates are taught to make fancy things, to sew and to carve; and one is surprised to see what these poor people can do with a very little training. Some ladies of the district give instruction to the inmates, visiting the workhouse once or twice a week, and in that way keep them constantly employed. An effort has been made on this side to carry out the plan in one or more of the poorhouses in the state of New York, and the result has been satisfactory. An account of the work of Lady Brabazon may be found in the State Charities Record, which may be had on application to the State Charities Aid Association of New York.

Mr. P. W. AYRES, of Cincinnati, Ohio, read a paper on *Free Public Employment Offices in Ohio.*

The next paper, on *Immigration of Aliens*, by Mr. ARNOLD WHITE, of London, was read by Rev. H. H. HART, of St. Paul, Minnesota.

Professor E. W. BEMIS, of the University of Chicago.—The immigration question has greatly interested me. Restrictions upon the freedom of immigration are demanded for the protection of the standard of living of our working classes. The depressing influence of a low standard of living on the part of immigrants is especially felt in our slum districts. Pauper immigration is responsible for the transfer of the sweating system to American soil. It complicates the troubles in our mining sections, and it is the cause of much violence in strikes. It unloads upon us a radical element very hard to control.

In discussing this question with workingmen, we discover the existence of a divided sentiment. Some of the labor leaders favor restriction. They take the ground that an educational test would be a good thing; that we should keep out, let us say, all immigrants over fifteen years of age who cannot read and write their own language. You know that came very near passing the last Congress. It is believed that a majority of both houses was in favor of the bill, but it came up in such a form as to require a two-thirds vote, and so was defeated.

I notice with interest the statistics in a late report of the New York Commissioners of Immigration as to the relative illiteracy of the various nationalities, as shown by the ability of all over fifteen years of age who had come to New York during about nine months of the year 1892, to read and write. From nearly all the Germanic peoples, English, Scotch, Norwegian, Swedish, Danish, Germans, etc., not more than 1 per cent. were illiterate. From Ireland less than 10 per cent. But from Eastern and Southern Europe the illiteracy of some nationalities went to more than 50 per cent. This shows that an educational test would keep out the very immigrants whom we would like to keep out. It would not keep out all the Jews, but it would affect the other nationalities quite sharply.

In talking with recent immigrants I find them disposed to favor immigration, for two reasons. One is the desire to have their relatives here; the other, that a large portion of the very poor in this country are becoming radically and extremely socialistic in their tendencies. They are glad, for instance, when a trades-union is in anyway hampered by a decision of the courts, as was the engineers' union by the Toledo decision. They are delighted at anything which tends to crush out effort on the part of workingmen, in order that they may be driven into socialism. They are glad to see wages temporarily reduced, thinking that it will produce a crisis dangerous to the present industrial system. Inasmuch as immigration will increase the slum population and hasten the coming crisis, they welcome it. That element is growing very rapidly, recruited by immigration. For that very reason, of course, we oppose it.

One of my students lately investigated the character of the foreign-born who send money to Europe through the postoffice to help their friends come to this country. He found that more than half of them are unable to sign their names.

I have also been impressed with statistics showing the average amount of money brought into this country by immigrants; it is, for the majority of nationalities, less than thirty-five dollars per capita.

A VOICE.—The immigrants probably conceal the amount of money they have with them.

Professor BEMIS.—That may be so. But I feel that we ought to restrict immigration, and I believe that the movement is spreading among the wage-earners themselves. Some people think it is contrary to the spirit of our fathers, but Thomas Jefferson, in his *Notes on Virginia*, opposed strenuously the encouragement of immigration from the continent of Europe, preferring to wait for the natural increase of our native population.

M. STANISLAS H. HAINE, of Antwerp, Belgium, addressed the section on the subject of the *Mont de Piété* in Antwerp. He said that the *Mont de Piété* is an institution established by the government for the purpose of loaning small sums of money on personal property. Such loans are made at seven per cent. For a period of two years, the largest sum loaned is $200 and the smallest forty cents. The original capital was contributed by the government. This institution has been in operation since 1830, and has earned enough to repay to the government nearly the whole of its original endowment. The profits have averaged about $4000 a year. It employs about thirty clerks, and there are several branches, in different parts of the city. The five directors are nominated by the city council for four years. Money is loaned without interest when the applicant brings a certificate from the public administrators of charity that he is unable to pay interest; but this seldom happens. The directors usually calculate to loan about four-fifths of the intrinsic value of the article deposited as security. They have sometimes taken stolen goods, especially from other cities. On proof of ownership, the owner is given back his property and the loss falls upon the institution. Articles in pawn are kept for thirteen months after the expiration of the loan and sold within the ensuing year.

A paper on *Tramps*, by Professor JOHN J. McCOOK, of Trinity College, Hartford, was read by Mr. ALEXANDER JOHNSON.

Mr. A. O. WRIGHT, of Wisconsin, read a paper on *Vagrancy*.

The CHAIRMAN.—General Brinkerhoff tells me that they have no vagrancy problem in Ohio. I should like to know why.

General ROELIFF W. BRINKERHOFF, president of the State Board of Charities of Ohio.—I simply meant to say that the vagrant question is not there so serious as to attract our attention as members of the State Board of Charities. Mr. Ayres knows more about the tramp question than I do, because he comes from the city of Cincinnati.

The CHAIRMAN.—Have you anything to say in regard to this question, Mr. Ayres?

Mr. P. W. AYRES.—No. The last paper read stated that a good many tramps are the product of the slums in large cities. I am inclined to think that the young man from the slums is too debauched to become a tramp; he hasn't the requisite energy. Their ranks are more largely recruited from the young men in small towns. While on the floor, I wish to ask if anybody knows of any employment for prisoners in small jails?

Mr. WRIGHT.—Go to Media and see for yourself. The beauty of the separate system, in the Eastern Pennsylvania Penitentiary and in several of the Pennsylvania county jails, is that labor can be carried on without the aid of machinery; the industries followed are such as carpet-weaving, basket-making, braiding mats, knitting and the like, which can be performed by individuals in single cells. It has been suggested that convicts should be employed to work on the roads, but a chain-gang is a demoralizing spectacle. The remedy is worse than the disease.

Mr. RICH.—I think that one great cause of vagrancy is the disproportion between production and consumption. While in London, England, eight months ago, I was told that there were 500,000 criminals made so by circumstances over which they had no control. I was told that others were working sixteen hours a day. There are 40,000 'bus-men alone in the city of London who work sixteen hours a day, for about five dollars a week in our money. I saw a band of workingmen who had been made tramps by circumstances, carrying a banner with this inscription, "We demand the right to work." There are tens of thousands in our country who demand the right to work, but cannot get it, who are first made tramps and then criminals because this demand is not met.

I am a German by birth. I occupied a pulpit for eighteen years in the German Reformed Church. I thank heaven that the first thing I had to learn when I returned from service in the army during the Civil War was to handle a saw, a chisel and a hatchet. I have tried to find the solution of the social question by taking a practical view of it, and so I applied in this town for work. I have gone where I could see the condition of labor with my own eyes. I applied at the Fair the other day for employment, and here is my badge, number 211. When I asked for employment that morning it was announced that 100 would be engaged. There were 500 there, and 300 of them were sent home in two hours. In three hours after that, 50 more were dismissed, and then 50 more. I happened to be one of the fortunate ones, and I saw the fierce struggle for work. God give us more men that will deny themselves, leave their pulpits, mingle with the lower classes, and there, in contact with their suffering, speak a word to those who are in authority, urging them to use their power and influence to help mankind to a higher level.

I glory in what General Booth has done in England. I had a card of admission from him to his House of Rescue, and I saw some of the grand work he is doing in the houses which he has erected for tramps and for the poor. But, my dear friends, do you not know that the work given by him to a tramp, in one of these homes, takes the bread out of the mouth of some poor family, and robs some father of work who has a wife and children dependent on him? This labor problem is the problem of our age. Until we are filled with true charity from above, with love and good will to man, until we are willing to sacrifice and to suffer, and deny ourselves some of our comforts for their sake, we shall never solve this problem. God give us mercy! God give us charity!

The CHAIRMAN.—The gentleman has certainly named the fundamental principle of the solution of all social problems.

The following papers were read by title: *Private Unofficial Visitation of Public Institutions*, by Miss LOUISA TWINING; *Relief by Work in France*, by M. GROSSETESTE-THIERRY, of Paris; *Pauperism and Crime*, by Mr. JOHN R. WEBER; *Municipal Provision for Shelter of Homeless Poor in Boston*, by Mr. THOMAS F. RING, of Boston; *The Problem of Inebriate Pauperism*, by Dr. T. D. CROTHERS, of Hartford.

The section then adjourned *sine die*.

INDEX.